PENGUIN BOOKS

SHADOW OF THE NOOSE

Richard Cooper is the author of several books, including *Codename Icarus*, which was made into a television series for the BBC, and *Knights of God*, also adapted for television and shown on TVS for a young adult audience. His first major book and television series was *Quest of Eagles*, for which he won the Pye Television Award for the best children's writer in 1980. He has a number of other distinguished credits for dramatic works for both stage and television and has recently created a television series for the BBC based on the early life of Sir Edward Marshall Hall.

D1362638

RICHARD COOPER

SHADOW
of the
NOOSE

PENGUIN BOOKS

For my wife

PENGUIN BOOKS

Published by the Penguin Group
27 Wrights Lane, London w8 5tz, England
Viking Penguin Inc., 40 West 23rd Street, New York, New York 10010, USA
Penguin Books Australia Ltd, Ringwood, Victoria, Australia
Penguin Books Canada Ltd, 2801 John Street, Markham, Ontario, Canada l3r 1b4
Penguin Books (NZ) Ltd, 182–190 Wairau Road, Auckland 10, New Zealand

Penguin Books Ltd, Registered Offices: Harmondsworth, Middlesex, England

First published 1989
Published simultaneously in hardback by Viking
1 3 5 7 9 10 8 6 4 2

Made and printed in Great Britain by
Richard Clay Ltd, Bungay, Suffolk
Filmset in Monophoto Garamond

CHAPTER
ONE

It was the spring of that year, and on this day, though the sun shone, clouds from France were blowing towards England on a cold wind that pulled at the man's coat-tails and rippled the sea pool at his feet. His gloved hand held the rim of his silk hat, and he was leaning forward a little, his eyes narrowed and watering.

One or two passers-by on the promenade, hurrying against the wind, gave him a glance, wondering what he was looking at, so still, so well dressed, alone in that wide emptiness. A white gull cried high above and behind him, and he swung, suddenly, to look at it. Shivering, he pulled the collar of his coat closer and walked on quickly, almost running, his feet crunching the stones like those of a man pursued. He came to the weed-greened steps from the beach and ran up them, stopping at the top, his hand on the iron rail, taking a deep breath.

A young girl, thought to be delicate, who was down here for her health and enduring a little gentle exercise on the promenade with her mama before luncheon, stopped at the sight of him. How could she not, when she was face to face with a man as handsome as he?

She had been taken to a museum once by her governess, who had hurried her on, averting her chaste eyes, past a statue of a naked Greek god. Surely this man was that god come again in frock coat, silk cravat and pin-striped trousers? He was tall, well over six foot, and broad-shouldered with it. And his head was noble: his eyes wide apart, his nose strong and perfectly shaped, his lips generously full and his jaw firm. His eyes held a questioning, wondering, frightened look, and his lips were parted, as if he would speak. Instinctively she lifted a hand and moved towards him, but Mama, noticing that she was no longer at her side, turned and called her name. The wind blew a strand of hair across her eyes, and she pulled it back, still looking at him. Then Mama called again, and she was not to be denied. With a frown of regret, the girl gave a hopeless shrug of her shoulders and walked after her mother.

She was stronger than they all thought and lived through two wars and great loss, but to the day she died she never forgot the spring morning in 1894 when she met Apollo on Brighton Promenade.

He watched her go, then turned away, gripping the railings, his shoulders bowed. He could see nothing now; his eyes were blinded by tears.

It had been she, he could have sworn it, come to him again: the impatient manner in which she had pulled the hair from her eyes, the way in which she looked at him, the sweet grace of her being. Only at the last, as she turned away, did she become this other person, this stranger, whom he would never see again. Never, never again. Nor would he see the woman, so like her, whom he had killed.

He groaned and pushed himself away from the railings. His head down, blind to the people on the promenade, he turned his back on the wide sea and walked into one of the narrow streets that wound through the old town.

Scudding clouds had blown over the face of the sun, and a few drops of rain spotted the pavements. A newspaper boy sheltered in a shop doorway, and his piping voice blew on the wind. ''Orrible murder!' he cried. 'Read all about it!' The man strode past him, his head still bowed. '*Terrible* murder!' the lad shouted after him, stepping hopefully out of his shelter. 'Latest!' The man stopped, turned and looked at him. The rain was coming on heavier now, and the scrawled letters on the boy's placard were beginning to run. 'MURDERESS FACES TRIAL FOR HER LIFE!'

'You should be ashamed,' he said, 'selling such lies.'

'Not me as prints 'em, guv,' the boy whined. 'I only

sells 'em. Here y'are.' And he held out a dripping paper.

The man gave the boy a penny, took the paper, glanced at the headline, then threw it into the fast-filling gutter and walked on towards his home.

As he came into the hallway of his father's house, he could hear their voices from the dining-room. The parlour maid came running along the passageway, tutting her annoyance at his dripping hat and coat. 'Should have taken your brolly, Master Eddie,' she said, helping him off with his coat and putting his hat on the table. 'And the Master and Miss Ada waited ages for their lunch. You know how he hates that.'

'Yes. I'm sorry.'

Hearing their voices, his sister came from the dining-room, a napkin in her hand. She and he were very alike, though he was the younger of the two. They shared the same good looks, but his masculine strength and purpose sat a little uneasily upon her. A handsome woman, it was said, not pretty, not fetching. Striking was the word. They also had the same sudden and violent temper; quick to rise and quick to fall, but frightening while it lasted to those who felt the force of it. Not that he or she knew this – so far as they were concerned, no damage was done, and the cause of their rage was forgotten a moment later. But those who had been lashed found it more difficult to forget or forgive. Unlike her brother, though, she had married well; her husband was a Labouchere. Her wedding ring had given her position, wealth and social cachet, and she never forgot it.

She looked at the parlour maid, who was brushing the rain off the top hat. 'Leave that for now,' she ordered, 'and fetch Master Edward a dry coat.'

The maid bobbed a curtsy and ran up the stairs.

'Wherever have you been?' she asked him.

'Walking. I needed some air.'

'And we needed our luncheon.'

'You should have started without me,' he said, trying

7

to smooth his curling hair in the hall-stand looking-glass.

'We did. If you want soup, I'll ask cook to warm it.'

The maid ran down with a grey frock-coat, which she stood on tiptoe to hold for him while he slipped his arms into the sleeves.

'No matter. I'll go straight on to the fish.'

She shook her head. 'That's eaten too.'

He gave a sigh. 'All right. A slice or two of meat. Don't make such a fuss '

She looked at him and nodded. 'We'd better go in.'

Old Dr Hall, their father, was at the head of the table. Wherever it was that brother and sister had got their looks from, it certainly wasn't from him. He was plump and comfortable; his nose was rather beaked; his fluffy white hair, which also grew down the sides of his face, met in a fringe under his chin. He radiated no force other than imperturbable calm and good cheer. He was the very picture of a Victorian family doctor, which was what he had been all his working life.

A vast coal fire roared at his back as he stood carving a joint of beef, and he was sweating in the heat of it. A maid was at his side, holding a silver serving plate. He lifted a slice of rare meat on the fork and held it for a moment, looking at his son.

'You know what time luncheon is in this house,' he said, placing the beef on the dish.

'Yes. I'm sorry, Papa. I didn't realize how long I'd been walking.'

Dr Hall sighed. 'Well, sit yourself down now.'

Hall sat, facing his sister.

'Why on earth you want to walk when Papa keeps a coachman and horses, all eating their heads off, I simply can't imagine,' she said.

'I needed some time to think,' he murmured.

'About this wretched case of yours, I suppose,' she said.

'That's right,' Hall said, turning to the maid and helping himself from the serving dish.

'You know what I think about *that*,' she said, grimly, as the maid moved towards her.

He was spooning vegetables on to his plate. 'Yes, I do,' he replied, tersely. 'You've told me often enough.'

'You should never have taken it on.'

He banged the spoon back into the dish.

His father sighed, noting the sign of mounting rage. A quiet luncheon and a quiet life, surely, he deserved that much. 'They tell me it's Eddie's great chance,' he murmured.

She brushed this aside. 'Great chance, fiddlesticks! Great ruin, more like!'

Her brother leant back in his chair, his right hand drumming on the cloth. 'Fact is,' he said, a tremble of anger in his voice, 'ruin or no ruin –'

Her head on one side, she looked across at him. 'What? What then?'

He took a breath, trying to keep control. 'She's not guilty.'

Dr Hall glanced under his brows from one of his children to the other, then slid the wine decanter nearer and poured himself another glass of claret, thinking that Ada would be too busy with Eddie to notice.

But this was to underestimate her. Keeping her eyes on her brother, she lifted her hands in a gesture of despair and let them fall. 'Edward, oh, *really*!' Then she flicked a glance at her father. 'And you'd never have been allowed *that*, Papa, not when Mama was alive. Wine at *luncheon*! Much less a second glass.' She took a sip of her water to prove her point.

Hall's head was lowered, but his eyes were blazing. 'No. Not guilty. Not of murder.'

Dr Hall sipped his wine. 'Fortifying,' he murmured, 'on a cold day.' He pushed the decanter towards Edward.

'Quite guilty enough in my book, that's all I can say!' Ada cried. 'Women such as that! *Well!*'

Hall poured himself a glass of wine and gave the decanter back to his father. She saw that his hands were trembling. 'Thank you, Papa,' he said. He turned towards his sister.

9

'Women such as what, Ada? What women have you in mind?'

'This is not a fit subject for the luncheon table,' she said, primly. 'And, apart from that, *pas devant les domestiques.*'

'Apart from your execrable French, *what women?*'

She looked away, her chin held high, and gave a nod of dismissal to the maid. 'I have said. It's not fit.'

'Truth's fit!' he cried. 'And justice is fit!'

Dr Hall tapped the rim of his glass with a spoon. 'Children! Please!' he begged. In vain.

'Justice?' Ada flung back at him. 'Oh, I'd give her justice all right! All the justice in the world! Enough to last those women for quite a long time, I'd say!'

Hall was white with rage. He covered his eyes with a hand. 'This is intolerable,' he whispered.

'Now then!' their father said. 'You've both gone quite far enough.'

'What you have to see,' she said, ignoring him, 'and look at me, Edward, when I'm speaking to you . . .'

'I don't want to know,' Hall said.

She shook her head. 'To lose a case at this stage in your career – and a case that's been trumpeted about in every ha'penny newspaper in the land –'

'It's not lost till it's fought!' he cried.

'Hopeless! It will break you – as it would break any other lawyer!'

'Then let it!'

'You may, but I will not!' Too late her anger at his sullen obstinacy faded. She leant across the table, putting a hand on his wrist, but he pulled away. 'All our hopes rest on you,' she said, trying to bring gentleness into her voice. 'You know that. They were dashed from you once . . .'

He looked at her. His eyes were wide, frightened, and his face was white.

She drew back. 'Of that we shall not speak. Your wife – and all that followed –'

Their father's voice was quiet, but this time there was no

mistaking its authority. 'No, indeed we shall not,' he said. 'That is a subject which we do not discuss in this house.'

Hall shook his head, closing his eyes. 'No, no,' he whispered.

'I'm sorry, so sorry,' she said. 'But all that's over, Eddie. Finished.'

Hall looked towards his father. 'Is there any more wine, Papa?' he asked.

Ada got up and carried the decanter to him, putting a hand on his shoulder as she filled his glass. 'I want the best for you always. Only that. You know that I do.' He looked up at her, took her hand and held it for a moment. 'Leave this case,' she whispered. 'Please!'

He rose to his feet, looked into her eyes, then shook his head. 'May I get down, Papa, please?'

'When you've eaten your luncheon.'

'I've no appetite for it. I'm sorry. And I've work to do. There's a life hanging on it.'

The woman who had caused the newspaper boy to stand in the rain, a brother and sister to quarrel – a quarrel that was echoed in every pub and club in the country – and journalists to churn out column upon column of conjecture, sat alone in a cold cell hard by the Old Bailey.

She was unworthy, one might think, of a nation's fascination. Never, at any time in her life, had she been pretty, and the years had not done well by her. She was thin-lipped and hard-faced, yet still clung to those tattered pretensions that, when she plied her trade as a whore in the Haymarket, had given her the joking title of 'the Duchess'. Marie Hermann, undoubted killer of an old man who was her client, was waiting trial for her life, and knew full well what the verdict would be.

A key turned in the lock. Hearing it, she straightened herself, folded her hands in her lap and prepared herself for elegant behaviour. A wardress came in carrying a tray of food, which she put down on the table. Marie didn't given her so much as a glance. That was how the aristocracy treated waiters, whatever fancy names they gave themselves.

'All right, dear?' the wardress asked, giving her a friendly smile.

Marie dignified her with a look. 'No, I am not all right. Bleeding freezing in here.' There was more than a trace of her native Austrian in her voice. She pulled her shawl tightly round her self. 'English weather.'

'Eat this, then. Warm you up.'

Marie rose, came to the table and touched the edge of the plate. 'Cold,' she said.

'Came as quick as I could. Them kitchens is miles off.'

Marie sat, dipped the spoon into the greasy stew and tasted a drop of the grey liquid in a ladylike manner. Not so ladylike, she spat it out on to the floor. 'Pig swill.'

The wardress sighed and sat on the other chair. 'Good as you're getting,' she said complacently. 'Eat it up.'

Marie put the spoon down and slowly turned to face her. 'Is this a zoo that I must be watched while I feed?'

The wardress pursed her lips and shook her head. 'You're special, you are, Mrs Hermann. And I'm specialling you.' Marie made no reply, but stared at the wall before her. 'When they've done with you,' the wardress went on, 'and your trial's over, and all that, there'll be two of us with you, night and day,' she nodded her satisfaction at the thought, 'keeping an eye on you.'

Marie shrugged, then picked up the bowl of food, sniffed it, wrinkled her nose in disgust and, without any change of expression, threw it at the woman's head. But the wardress had been too long in the business to be caught out by a trick like that. She ducked away from the plate and, with a look of mild curiosity, turned to watch the food slide slowly down the wall.

'Now, Mrs Hermann,' she said, 'that wasn't very nice. Not nice at all. Not *ladylike*.' She stood, chose a key from the bunch at her waist and unlocked the door. 'I'll get you a cloth. And a bucket.' She went, the door clanging shut behind her and the key turned in the lock.

*

It had been his room ever since his parents moved into this house, and all the flotsam of his life had washed up on this narrow shore: a favourite cricket bat from his school, Rugby, old books, toys, photographs – one of himself in his college cricket XI in pride of place over his cluttered desk – and, mounted on the wall, part of his collection of guns, the first of which had been given to him by his father as a seventh birthday present. All of his days were there, and he could stretch out a hand and touch the past.

There he sat in the gathering dusk, his lamp unlit, looking out on to the darkening garden, thinking of his life and of the chance that was now before him. It was there, no doubt at all of that, if he could but find a way to seize it. But could he? Could anyone? In his heart he acknowledged that his sister and all his colleagues were right. The Hermann case was hopeless, and he knew of half a dozen men – established men with their thousands a year rolling in – who'd taken one look at it, laughed and sent the briefing solicitor packing.

Every prejudice in the great British mind was against her. She was foreign. She was an ageing whore and mean-spirited with it. She'd killed the old man, beaten him to death – there was no getting away from that – and then she'd done her very damnedest to hide his battered body. Whatever jury was empanelled would be itching to see her hanged. Give them half a chance and they'd pull the lever themselves.

He looked down at the pile of newspapers on his desk, and every headline told the same story: 'MOST TERRIBLE MURDER OF THE AGE!', 'MURDERESS ARRESTED'. Oh, they didn't just tell the story. They shrieked it. There was simply nothing that could be done for her. But he, like a fool, had taken on the terrible task of trying, somehow, to make bricks out of a pile of stinking straw.

Wearily he swept the newspapers aside and sat, his head bowed in his hands, trying desperately, as he had done since he accepted the brief, to find a line somewhere, a way forward. Try as he might, there was none to be found. His eyes closed in tiredness, and his thoughts fell from the problem.

In the darkness of his mind he thought of the girl on the promenade, the pretty girl, so soft, so gentle, so ready to ease his pain. But she had not been allowed to. She had gone far away, and he was left, alone with the memories that destroy, as she, his love, had been destroyed. By his hand, as surely as if he had held the instruments of her death. The days to come must hold his battle to save the woman in the prison cell from her guilt. But what advocate could come forward to save him from his?

He groaned aloud and opened his eyes. As he did so, in the blink of an eyelid he saw the flash of a white dress running through the bare-branched and dripping trees at the end of the garden. He strained forward across his desk, searching for a sight of her. But she was gone, and only the reflection of his white face looked back at him in the window glass.

He pushed his chair away from the desk and, almost against his will, knelt by the leather trunk at the side of the wall. The discarded newspapers had fallen on top of it, and he swept them away. He took a small key from his watch chain and held it for a moment, knowing that once that key was used and memory unlocked, dark dreams and agonies of spirit would be let free in the dusk-shadowed room. But he could not help himself and, with trembling hands, turned the lock and lifted the trunk's lid.

The scent of her came to him at once. He closed his eyes, letting it become part of him. Then, opening them, he saw the folded silk, the posy of dead flowers, the lock of blonde hair curled on a ribbon, the packet of letters with the ink already fading and, on top of them all, a small and tasselled pencil tied to a programme of dances from a ball.

He opened it, lifting it into the dying light, and saw the initials by the dances. Who were these men, these strangers, who had held her in their arms through waltz and mazurka, polka and quadrille? Had they memories? Did they recall, if only in passing, that night when the air was so warm, so heavy, so music-filled?

The initials stopped, with only six dances remaining. They had all been his.

CHAPTER TWO

That waltz had been all the rage that year. The barrel organs
ground it out in the streets as children danced around them;
the uniformed brass bands thumped it through the parks; and
lovers, strolling on the sunlit grass and into the shadows of the
tall trees, walked to the insistence of its one-two-three, one-
two-three. And now as he stood, bronzed from his year abroad,
chatting with his friends, the orchestra in the ballroom was
swooping to its rise and fall. This was his first day home, and
the tune was new to him. He thought it vulgar but very catchy,
and as he talked he tapped a finger on the edge of his champagne glass to the beat of it.

Because he was bored with tales told too often, because he
wanted to stretch his legs, he drained his glass, slapped a back
or two, made promises for further meetings and strolled towards the music and the dancers.

And then he saw her.

She was dancing, looking up into her partner's face, smiling.
He could hear his heart pounding, louder than the music. He
turned away, closing his eyes. He would have to go, escape
from this place and from all the pain she had brought to him.
There were steps leading out and he ran up them, not daring
to look back. But at the top he paused. One glance, just one, a
memory that he could hold, and he would have done with her.
He turned slowly for that last look, and as he did she, on a
swing of the waltz, was facing him and their eyes met. He saw,
as if time stopped, her eyes widen in recognition. She bit her
lower lip and then she was turned away from him by the
music. He was rooted to the spot, drinking in every detail of

her – her golden hair piled high, her long, slender neck, her wide-skirted, flower-scattered white dress.

Unsmiling, his face set, he walked down the steps and through the dancers, towards her. He was at her side. He tapped her partner on his shoulders. 'This is my dance, I think,' he said, his voice trembling.

She frowned, shaking her head. 'No, no, I –'

Her partner recognized him. 'Sorry, Hall. You'll have to wait your turn.'

'This *is* my turn,' Hall said, his face as hard as stone.

She knew that look of his, and it took her breath away. They were standing, the three of them, in the centre of the floor. Her arms fell to her sides from her partner's hand and shoulder. 'Yes,' she whispered. 'It is his dance. I'm sorry. Some mistake on my programme.' She looked at Hall, her eyes wide. 'I'm sorry.'

Hall nodded to the man, saying nothing, and held out his arms to her. For a moment Hall and she stood, looking at each other. One might have thought that they were strangers from the emptiness of their expressions.

'We had better dance,' she said, coming into his arms. It felt easier there, almost safe, the danger fading, as they moved to the waltz, the music holding them, turning them like marionettes. 'I didn't know that you were back in England,' she murmured.

'No more than I knew that you would be here.'

'Would you have come had you known?' she asked.

'No.'

'Nor I. But I shall go – after this dance.'

'You can't do that,' he said.

'I must.'

'No!'

She was trembling, frightened. 'Please, Edward! *Please!*'

'I will not allow it,' he said, his voice low, hoarse.

Her head was turned away from him. 'We're no good, not together. I know it,' she said, tears in her voice.

'We can't be apart. I understand that now – seeing you again.'

'My aunt's here somewhere. Find her for me, I beg you! Let her take me home!'

He held her closer than ever, his voice one with the blood that roared in her ears. 'All that I want in life is to be near, to shelter, to be close. I need, *I need*!'

She felt as if she might faint: the room was hot, the music beating, the dancers circling close. 'I can't breathe! I can't see!' she gasped.

An arm round her, he led her quickly through the dancers, past the orchestra. The conductor smiled at them, bowing as they passed through the doors.

They were in a long corridor that led to the street. At the far end of it the old woman who looked after the hats and cloaks turned in her chair and stared at them.

The girl looked up at Hall and shook her head. Beneath his hand on her waist he could feel the tremors of her body.

'Cooler here,' he whispered.

She made no reply, but leant against the wall, her eyes closed.

He came near, his hands on the wall at either side of her shoulders. 'I ran away from you,' he said. 'But I won't do so again.'

She opened her eyes and looked at him. She felt very weary. 'Edward, I've told you –'

'It was no good. Paris, Australia – all this long year. They were only a time and a space away from you, waiting.'

She took a few steps down the corridor, nearer to the still and watching old woman. There was a door at her side. She touched the handle and turned to him, not looking into his eyes, then opened the door and went in. The old woman stood, about to speak, but Hall, frowning, silenced her with a glance and went into the room.

It was a place for storing chairs and tables, which were stacked on either side. The gas light of the street lamps shone in through a high, barred and dusty window. Cabs rattled past in the road, and the talk of passing walkers drifted into the room.

She stood, the window behind her, her white dress shimmering in the light, her face in shadow.

'I love you,' he whispered.

She nodded, slowly. 'I know.'

'And you . . .?'

For a long moment she made no reply but simply looked at him. She saw him for what he was: so strong, so tall, so handsome. And she thought of a life, long years ahead, spent with him. She thought of her fingers in the curls of his hair, his body pressed against hers, all his love and ardour flowing into her, making her his.

Beside him, this wonder of a man, what were all the others she had walked with, danced with, flirted with in her life? They were mere boys compared with him. There was no strength in them, no manliness. And yet with him there was danger. She knew it. She had to be strong; she had to save herself from that, break away from this man, live in safety. But she thought of the glory of his body, lying close, his arms around her. She wanted him.

'You asked me a question – before you went away,' she said.

'Yes.'

Hearing her own words as if listening to a stranger talking, she said, 'I might give you a different answer now.'

He too was afraid. He knew that she could be cruel, could wound him. She had done it once, and he had thought that it would kill him. Would she do it again now? Not daring to look at her, his voice shaking, he said, 'You will marry me?'

'Yes! Oh, yes!' she gasped.

His arms around her, he kissed her, over and over.

Her hand trembling, she pulled open the buttons of the bodice of her dress and pressed herself close to him, feeling the mystery of him stiffen against her stomach. She wanted to touch, to know about a man. Her hand slid down his side.

Gently, he pulled away. 'My life shall be your shield, your fortress,' he whispered.

A flood of shame and of guilt swept over her, and her hand covered her open bodice. 'Go, please. Go now,' she said, her eyes downcast.

'No! Please, please,' he murmured, trying to hold her again.

'It's time,' she said, pushing past him. As she opened the door, the harsh light of the corridor flooded into the room.

He seized her from behind and kissed her white shoulders, her neck.

Without looking back at him, she walked away.

He stood in the consulting room, while his father got ready to set off on his morning rounds, slipping into his battered old Gladstone bag bottles of medicines and round boxes of pills which he had dispensed himself in his laboratory the night before.

'I thought that all that business with the girl was over and done with,' his father said.

'It can't be.'

Dr Hall snapped the bag shut. 'Then you've wasted a whole year gadding about all over the world.' He looked at his son under his eyebrows. 'The money – well, it's money. But your life, boy! Your *life*!'

'Can only be with her! The year's taught me that much, Father.'

'Have you told your mother?'

'No.'

'She's not going to be well pleased.'

'And you?'

Dr Hall didn't answer him immediately, but walked over to the window and stood looking out, his hands thrust deep into his trouser pockets. 'I suppose,' he sighed, 'I want you to be happy.'

'I shall be.'

Dr Hall turned and looked at him, frowning. 'I don't think so. No, I really do not.'

They were silent for a moment.

'You've never liked her, have you, Father? Not since we were children.'

His father shrugged. 'Liking doesn't come into it. I speak, I suppose, as a doctor.'

'She's in perfect health. What's being a doctor to do with it?'

'Oh, physically I'm sure she's well enough.'

Hall frowned. 'Then I don't understand you.'

His father cleared his throat. 'How well do you know her family?'

'I'm not marrying her family.'

Dr Hall came nearer to his son. 'And thinking that, my boy, is the mistake that we all make. You will be taking on not just her but the whole tribe. Believe me.'

'Tribe?'

'The mother, for instance.'

'Oh, Father, for heaven's sake! The woman scarcely ventures out of her room.'

Dr Hall nodded. 'Precisely so.'

'What does that mean?'

He put a hand on his son's shoulder, holding him fast. 'It means that in her there's a streak of something strange. And I see the same quality in the daughter.'

Hall was fighting to control his temper. 'Strange? I see no sign of it. Not in either of them.'

'It's there none the less. *They are not as other women.*'

'How? How are they different?' Hall cried.

'They walk in a different world. Those are the only words I have for it. But I know it, and I've seen it in other patients.'

'You're wrong.'

'*No,*' his father shouted, 'in matters such as this I am not wrong!'

His son swung angrily away towards the door, but Dr Hall grabbed his shoulder and pulled him round. 'I would not, I would absolutely not, spend my life with such a woman!'

They looked at each other. Hall bit his lip and took a deep breath. 'Father, I swear this to you. I cannot live without her.'

Dr Hall shook his head slowly. 'Then God help you,' he said, his voice low. He straightened his shoulders. 'So be it, then.' He put his head on one side, an eyebrow raised. 'Of course, there is another matter. One that your sister will certainly raise.'

'What's that?'

'One of her relations is in trade, and Ada has views on such things.'

'Then she's a snob.'

His father nodded. 'Very probably. But, to pursue the matter of trade, how do you intend to support this wife – and, presumably, your children?'

'I hadn't thought of it.'

'I'm sure you hadn't. But tell me now: where's the money to come from?'

Hall looked away, frowning. 'I'll go back into the City. I'll make money there.'

Dr Hall gave a slight smile. 'Oh, Edward, really! You tried that once, and you hated it. When you left that counting house and went up to Cambridge you said, if you remember, that it was like being let out of prison. Well? What makes you think it would be any different now?'

'I'd have someone to strive for.'

'Oh, no. It makes no odds, believe me. It would break you – and your marriage.'

Hall was silent, his head lowered. He knew that in this, if in this only, his father was right. It all came back to him – the feeling of confinement, the long hours perched on that high stool, the numbing drudgery.

'You'd better start thinking, my boy. The girl's father was a colleague of mine. And I will not have you go to his widow, whatever I may think of the woman, and make a fool of yourself.'

Hall lifted his head. 'I could go into the Church. Mama would like that.'

Dr Hall sat on the edge of his desk. 'She'd be delighted. It's what she's always wanted for you, and you'd look very fine in your canonicals, I don't doubt. You'd set many a woman's mind on higher – or nether – things. But it's not for you. And there's not a penny piece to be made at it.' He looked at his son, quizzically. 'Well?'

'If –' Hall murmured, then said no more, unable to finish.

'Yes?'

'If I went back to Cambridge and finished my degree . . .'

His father nodded. 'To become a lawyer?'

'It's what I was reading.'

His father pushed himself up from the table and walked again to the window. 'I'm keeping the carriage waiting,' he said.

'And your patients. I'm sorry.'

'Oh, they're not going anywhere.' The doctor turned to his son. 'Did you enjoy reading law?'

'Not much, no.'

'And there's nothing else? Nothing you'd rather do? Schoolmastering? Something like that?'

'God forbid.'

'And it's no use at all my asking you to think of medicine?'

'You know it's not, Father. We've been through that before.'

'I suppose that the law's an occupation fit for a gentleman.'

'I suppose it is.'

Dr Hall nodded. 'Then you'd better do it.'

'The only thing is, Father –'

'What?'

'I don't think I can wait two years to be married.'

'And I don't think you've very much choice. I've funds for one, Edward, but not for two.'

'I can't! I can't do it!'

Dr Hall picked up his hat and his bag from the table. 'Then there's nothing I can say to you. Go to her mother and tell her that you want her daughter's hand in marriage. And that hand had better get used to very hard work because her husband will have neither fortune nor vocation.' He moved towards the door, then stopped, his fingers on the handle. 'And don't forget to tell me what the lady has to say in reply to your interesting proposal.'

Hall came over to him. He knew when he was beaten. 'I'll write to my old college.'

His father turned to him, smiling. 'Really? Is that what you've decided to do? Well, now, I think that you're probably very wise. Pleasant enough place, Cambridge. Pleasant enough. And two years will soon pass, believe me.'

But the two years at St John's College did not soon pass. They dragged, day after wearisome day. He had been given the rooms in New Court that he had last time he was up; this was meant, perhaps, to show him that his year away had been no more than a hiccup in the groves of Academe. But he soon found that sitting at the same desk, looking out on the same view, hearing the same shouts of the undergraduates as they passed by his windows, proved only the breadth of the ground that lay between the freshman of twelve months ago and his present self. He had been scarcely more than a schoolboy then, he thought; no wonder Ethel had turned him down. But now he was a man of the world – travelled, experienced, sophisticated.

What could they know of life, he brooded, these bawling boys, chucking a rugger ball about and yelping at the fun of it? They had not drunk with the artists of the Latin Quarter as he had done. They had not sat in life classes and learnt to paint as he had done. And none of them had, with pounding heart, tapped at midnight on the door of a pretty little *midinette* and attempted to surrender his virginity to her experienced caresses. (The attempt had been an abject, humiliating and fumbling failure, but he didn't brood about *that*.)

What they did know, however – or, at least, one or two of them did – was how to study. And he did not. He could, with effort, force himself to sit in a library, in his rooms, in the schools, and endeavour, with all his might, to drive this dull, necessary information into his head. But an hour or so of it was enough, and then he had to get up, get out and *move*.

The college cricket XI was some relief. He had let his name be put forward with a show of reluctance, remembering promises made to his father, but, once in, he knew the happiest hours of all his time at Cambridge. To stand, eyes narrowed against the sun, tapping his bat on the turf, muscles tense – there was release, certainty and joy.

Now, in his last term, with finals yawning like a grave at his feet, even his cricket had to be given up. And the books were as impenetrable as ever. So when his sister proposed that she and his fiancée should spend a day with him, his heart leapt and he jumped at the chance of stepping off the treadmill.

He crossed the days off his calendar and spent much time in careful preparation. Ada had tucked into her letter an order drawn upon her husband's bank for twenty pounds, and he spent it well. Plovers' eggs, smoked salmon, pâté de foie gras, the freshest of vegetables, the tenderest lamb and the rarest of hot-house fruit went to the buttery, with strictest orders as to how they were to be prepared and served.

When the last day was ticked and he woke to the dawn, he thanked God for a clear blue sky and summer sun. He dressed with care to fill in time, with his patient gyp went over once more the rituals of the luncheon to come and then, after a last glance at the flowers in their vases, the silver on the white cloth and the bottle of *fino* on the mantelshelf, he left for the railway station with only an hour and a half to go before their train was due. He chose the smartest four-wheeler on the cab rank, tipped the driver a half-crown not to accept any other

24

fares and waited, pacing the platform and peering down the line for the plume of steam.

At last it came and she was there, leaning out of a window, waving to him. He ran alongside the train, touching her finger tips, laughing with happiness at the sight of her.

The luncheon was a huge success: even Ada said so. The food had been much praised, the women surprised that a house full of men could manage so well, and the wines sipped and savoured in the golden light.

Now, as they tasted the Monbazillac and toyed with their fruit he leant back in his chair, enjoying their pleasure and the glory of his love. Truly, she had never looked more beautiful; the silver-grey silk of her dress and the lace fichu at her throat showed off to perfection the grace of her neck and the soft creaminess of her skin. He could almost have wept with joy.

She looked across the table, caught and read his eyes and, lowering her head, she smiled.

Ada saw the look between them and stirred uneasily. 'Have we all finished?' she asked.

Hall lifted the wine bottle. 'Perhaps . . .?' he said. But they demurely covered their glasses. He filled his own, not caring about Ada's frown.

'Are you sure that's wise, Edward?' she said. 'I thought that you had work to do.'

'Not today,' he smiled.

'No day should be wasted,' she said, as she pushed her chair from the table and stood up. 'At all events, I'll clear the table.'

'Oh, leave it,' he murmured, wanting the sun, the wine, the scent of flowers from the open window and the presence of his love to linger for ever. 'My gyp will see to it.'

Unwillingly, Ada sat down again. 'Gyp?' she asked.

'The fellow who waited at table. My servant.'

'I thought you'd hired him.'

'Oh, no. He's here all the time.'

'You do yourselves well,' she said.

He nodded. 'Well enough.'

Like him, she had energies that could not be repressed. She got up again and walked over to his desk, touching the piles of books that covered it. 'You have to read all these?'

''Fraid so.'

'I can't imagine anyone being so clever,' Ethel said, smiling at him.

'It's one thing to have the wretched things on the desk,' he said, laughing, 'but it's quite another to read 'em.'

'You can do anything – if you want to,' Ada said, primly.

He shook his head. 'Not that, I can't. And why should I? What does it possibly matter? Someone or other said this or that in 1600 and something. Then someone said something quite opposite. Then their Lordships gave their learned opinion, and we all traipse back to precisely where we started from. And I've forgotten where that was in the meantime.'

'Oh, dear,' Ada sighed.

'I simply do not understand it. And I'm not sure anyone else does either. Roman Law, Saxon Law – what's all that to a burglar?'

'Leave it,' Ethel said. 'Let's go for a walk down by the river. It will be cooler there.'

He sprang to his feet. 'Come on, then!'

Ada shook her head. 'We've taken up quite enough of your time. Miss Moon and I will walk, certainly. A luncheon such as that needs to be walked down. But you will stay here and work.'

He was about to protest but she was not to be gainsaid. 'You do want me to tell Papa how hard you're working, don't you?'

'But I am working! A donkey couldn't work harder!'

She was adjusting her hat in the looking-glass over the firegrate. 'And donkeys don't give luncheon parties. Or take strolls.'

'It would do me the world of good.'

She came over to him and kissed him on the forehead. 'Ladies must be given some time to themselves, Edward. You stay here and we'll be back within the hour. And you can tell that gyp of yours that we shall be wanting tea.'

'But –'

'No buts. Work.'

'I hate it.'

'I'm sure you do.' She turned to Ethel. 'Come along, my dear.' Remembering something, she looked at her brother. 'A man was hanged last week, and my husband said that a half-way to decent lawyer would have got him off. Think of that, Edward, as you're working.'

It *was* cooler along the backs but still too hot to do anything other than stroll slowly as laced parasols warded off the danger-ous sun and bustled skirts started the dust from the dry grass.

An undergraduate, red-faced and sweating in his straw boater and high starched collar, was punting on the river. He smiled and lifted his hat to the pretty women. Ethel smiled back at him; Ada gave him the privilege of a distant nod.

'Lovely day for the river!' he called. 'Like to come boating?'

'Make no reply, my dear,' Ada murmured.

Ethel gave him another smile and shook her head. They walked on in silence. Then she glanced at Ada from under the brim of her hat and said, 'Ada – I may call you that, mayn't I?'

'We are soon to be sisters, in law at least, so of course you may.'

'Thank you. And you must call me Ethel. If you want to, that is.'

Ada nodded. 'Were you about to ask me something?'

'Yes. I was. It's Eddie.'

'What about him?'

'He's not going to fail his examinations, is he?'

'No, of course he isn't,' Ada smiled. 'When you know him better, you won't be taken in by any of his performances. What he wants, he generally gets. As you should know.'

'Yes, I do know that.' She had stopped and was looking along the river at the young man in his boat, distant from them now. 'Ada . . .,' she said, the light from the water rippling across her shaded dress and face.

'Yes?'

'Why don't you like me?'

Ada wasn't sure that she'd heard aright. 'What did you say?' she asked.

'I said that you don't like me, and I don't know why.'

Ada looked away. 'I've nothing against you. Nothing at all.'

'But that's not quite the same thing as liking me, is it?'

'We scarcely know each other – not as grown women. Friendship must be given time to flower.'

'Yes, I suppose so,' Ethel said.

'Whatever put these thoughts into your mind?' Ada asked.

Ethel looked at her, then shook her head. 'What time's our train?' she said.

'Six. Are you feeling all right?'

Ethel walked on, twirling her parasol slightly. 'Yes, I am. Perfectly all right. Why do you ask?'

'Because you've said such odd things.'

'I say many things,' Ethel smiled.

'And do you mean them?'

'I think I do. After all, I've said that I'll marry your brother. It's what he wanted, and I am going to do it.'

Ada was beginning to be out of patience with the girl. 'You sound as if you were doing him a favour,' she said.

Ethel came closer to her, taking her arm. 'Listen,' she said, 'I know about marriage. Everything. I mean – a man . . . and . . .'

'Do you?' Ada said, pulling away a little.

'Yes, I do. And I want it – that state of being. Every night, in my bed, I think of it. And I think of him lying at my side. I think of how strong he is. He'll hold me tightly in his arms, and . . .'

Ada did not let her go any further. 'This is not something

we should discuss,' she said, taking her arm away from Ethel's.

Ethel looked at her, puzzled, as well she might be. Like every well-brought-up young lady of her class and her time, she knew no more of sex than she did of trigonometry. 'Why not?' she said. 'Isn't that how you are with your husband?'

'If I were, then I would not tell a soul about it. Not a living soul. Such things are – sacred.'

'Of course they are. I know that well enough. But who else can I talk to?'

'If need be, a girl may, in the privacy of the home, discuss these things with her mother and with no one else!'

Ethel shook her head. 'Since Papa died, Mama doesn't wish to talk about anything, much less marriage.'

Ada stopped and looked hard at her. 'There may be certain things that you should know, but this is scarcely the place or the time.'

'There may never be another. And I do want to do my very best by Edward.'

Ada walked on. 'Come and see me. And you may stay, for a while, if you wish.'

'Something – something now. I do need to know this, for I've been thinking about it such a lot. Please!'

'What? What is it?'

'Each month, when I am – unwell. What happens then? With my husband?'

'He will sleep in his dressing-room,' Ada said, her voice cold. Really, she had never been so embarrassed in all her life. 'Until you are quite recovered.'

'Oh,' Ethel said, her voice distant and dreamy. 'I wondered.'

A cloud had drifted across the sun. Ethel closed her parasol. 'I think it will rain before bedtime,' she said.

Ada looked up at the sky and shook her head. 'I think not,' she said. She glanced at her fob watch. 'Let us go and see if Edward has some tea for us.'

'Yes. Wine does make one thirsty. Don't you find that?'

'Tea is always welcome.'

Ethel slipped her hand through Ada's arm again. 'At least, Ada,' she said in her friendliest of voices, 'you now know why you dislike me. I have done that much for you.'

Ada sighed and shook her head. The girl was quite impossible.

'But I shall make a good wife to your brother.'

'I certainly hope so.'

Ada was right: he did get his degree. It wasn't a glittering result; there was no question of his walking away with a starred first, college prizes and a fellowship. Those things were for other men; he had enough for his purposes. So he stood, rather drunk, by the bank of the Cam and, one by one, dropped his law books into the star-scattered river.

'Won't you be wanting those, Hall?' an equally tipsy friend asked. 'From what I've seen of lawyers' rooms, they have rows of the damn things.'

'Oh, you buy 'em at so much a foot. Along with the rest of the furniture.'

And, with dignity, he slowly knelt down to be sick.

Ada hadn't wanted it, not so soon. Mrs Hall hadn't wanted it, not for years. And Dr Hall hadn't wanted it at all. But the day was here now.

The whole family was together in the family home. And, whatever doubts they all had about this marriage, Edward's joy went some way, whenever he was in the room, towards dispelling them.

His father, so far as he could, had kept out of the way during the weeks before, and now, left to himself, he would have slipped down to his club, until the last minute, to sip a brandy and seltzer water and keep his thoughts to himself. But the women seemed to think that, for some impenetrable reason, he should be here, so here he sat in a corner of the dining-room, which was already set for the wedding breakfast. He pushed aside a frond of a potted palm brought in from the conservatory, like the rest of the flowers and shrubs that crowded the space, and observed the passing scene. He frowned in irritation at the scurrying housemaids, the aproned gardeners and the wandering relatives. He had thought that he had finished with this turning of his house into an hotel when the last of his daughters had married. He had thought that he could rely upon the bride's family to take charge of all this damned nonsense. But there, as in so much else, this girl was a case apart.

He shook his head, thinking of her. She was a looker, there was no doubt about that, and he could well see what had ensnared Edward, but there was still, filling his mind, a nagging fear. Oh, she was always perfectly polite and charmingly pleasant whenever they met, flirtatious even, which was right and proper and how a girl ought to behave with the father of her intended. Yet, all else apart, he did not like the way she looked at his son when she did not know that anyone was watching her. It reminded him uncomfortably of a glutton reading a menu.

He heard his wife calling for him from the stairway and, wearily, he got up to answer her. But she immediately called for someone else, so he sat again in his corner, took a cigar from the case in his pocket, lit it and leant back.

Young people, he thought, have a great capacity for blundering blindly through difficulties and somehow, through God's fondness for fools, coming out more or less unscathed. The girl could change. His son might be able to handle her. It was possible.

CHAPTER
THREE

~⌒~

The organist was playing one of those hushed compositions that can wander for ever, carefully avoiding melody, suitable for any occasion whether it be commemorative, funereal or nuptial.

Hall sat in the front pew on the right-hand side of the aisle, his brother Frank, who was his best man, at his side. From behind him he could hear his mother's sniffs as she wept quietly.

He felt ill and repeatedly swallowed the bitter taste of bile that rose in his throat. When the carriage had come to the door, their coachman smiling down at him and touching his top hat with the butt of his flower-tied whip, Hall had had to run back into the house to be sick. It would always be with him, this weakness at moments of tension and danger. Frank was whispering gossip and jokes in his ear, but Hall wished his brother dead – or at least a long way from this hard pew in Hove Parish Church.

The organist struck up, fortissimo, a more determined tune, and Hall felt a tug on his sleeve from Frank who was now standing, smiling down at him. He was vaguely aware of a sussuration of silk as the ladies in the congregation rose. Standing uncertainly, he turned and looked down the aisle of the church.

She was there, waiting, her arm in an older man's, white flowers at her waist, an ivory lace veil covering her face, the pale lemon of her dress falling in sculpted waves around and behind her. The June sun flooded over her from the high windows, patterning her with rich, deep colours: she was mystic, magical, a picture of enchantment from an illuminated missal.

Tears sprang to his eyes as he looked at her, and all the romance of his nature was aroused by the vision. Words and thoughts tumbled in his mind, but all rushed to one end: this pure, this heavenly maiden would have, for all of his life, his adoration, his devotion and the service of his chivalry. At her feet, kneeling, he would lay his triumphs. He would shield her from all the world's harm and cruelty. He would rescue her from every danger. He would be her willing slave, her acolyte, her worshipper.

All of these things he promised as she slowly, unsmilingly, walked towards him. No priest at ordination ever dedicated himself more purely, more single-mindedly, to his God than did Edward Marshall Hall to his bride. And no priest ever paid more dearly for his vocation.

The wedding breakfast was a feast of joy for him. She was at his side, now and for ever. Their eyes constantly sought and found each other's; her hand was on his again and again, searching, pressing. He thought his heart would break with happiness. When she went to change into her travelling clothes it was as if the sun had gone from the room.

Frank came over to him, pouring more champagne into his glass. 'Got the steamer tickets?' he asked.

Hall, never taking his eyes off the door through which his love would come back to him, patted the pocket of his coat and nodded.

'Your hotel reservation's fine – all that's seen to. Hotel Domenice – for God's sake, don't forget that. It seems there's some sort of garden in a courtyard of the house. I've asked for rooms looking out over that. Be quieter than the street. Let you sleep late, eh?' He dug Hall in the ribs, laughing at his joke.

Hall nodded, not smiling.

Frank shrugged his shoulders and looked at his watch. 'Wish she'd hurry up,' he said.

'Woman's privilege,' Hall murmured.

'Tell that to the train driver.'

Ada came into the room, looking round over the heads of the guests until she saw her brother. She came quickly towards him.

'Is she ready?' Frank asked.

'Almost.' She turned to him, giving him a quick smile, laying her fingers on his arm. 'Frank – I wonder if I could have a quick word with Eddie?'

Frank nodded. 'Need some more wine anyway,' he said and wandered towards a waiter.

Ada gently pulled Hall into a corner of the room by a window. 'Are you all right for money?' she asked.

'Oh, yes.' He smiled. 'Papa's –'

She interrupted him. 'My husband's put an open draft at his bank at your disposal. Draw on it as freely as you like.' She slipped a piece of paper discreetly into his pocket. 'Here's the address of their Paris branch.'

He shook his head. 'It won't be necessary. Truly.'

'You never know.'

He took her hands in his and leant forward to kiss her. 'I've so much – in all my life – to thank you for.'

She held on to his hands, looking deeply into his eyes. When she spoke, unusually for her the words didn't come easily. 'Eddie . . . there's something I've wanted . . . very much wanted to say to you . . .'

'What?'

'This girl, your wife . . .'

He smiled at her. 'I never saw anything so pure, so lovely as when she came to me in church, in all that light.'

'She's very pretty.'

Hall shook his head. 'More. Oh, so much more than that!'

Ada looked away. He was surprised to see that her cheeks were reddening.

'These last weeks,' she said, 'all the fuss, preparations –

34

now, today, all the excitement and strain. And a long journey on top of all that. She will be very tired, Eddie.'

He shrugged. 'We both will be.'

'You don't understand what I'm saying.'

Hall held her hands again. 'Oh, yes, I do,' he murmured.

'I'm speaking to you – as a married man.'

'I know.'

For a long moment there was a silence between them. 'We have talked together, she and I,' Ada said.

'Yes?'

'And Eddie . . . there are some women who . . .' She could not go on but looked away from him.

'Say it. Go on.'

'Who are not as others. In their . . . needs.'

He frowned, not understanding her.

'You must protect her!' she said. 'You must protect her *from herself*!'

'I don't know what you mean. Protect her?'

'Yes!' She looked at him, searching his eyes, trying to find again that common ground, that almost telepathic sense, that had been between them when he was a child and she had taken the place of a mother who had been always too busy with her prayers and charities to get to know him. 'If you don't . . . if you can't,' she shook her head, trying to drive a terrible picture away, 'then she will be – destroyed. By *herself*!'

He smiled down at her. 'In church today there was a window. And God's light was on it. In the glass there was a picture of a knight, all in golden armour, kneeling before the Virgin.'

'And are you the knight?'

'I will be. I swore that oath at the altar.'

Tears came to her eyes. 'But she . . . *she* . . .' Unable to say any more, she threw her arms round him. 'Oh, Eddie, Eddie,' she sobbed.

He held her close, but his eyes were on Ethel as she came through the doorway. 'I shall have to go now, my dear,' he said.

Ethel was radiant, smiling at the guests, wedding bouquet in her hand. She tossed her head back, laughing, and threw the posy high in the air. Little Frances caught it, as she was meant to, and looked at Edward, blushing and biting her lower lip.

He made his way through the roomful of people, picked her up and kissed her. 'It won't be long,' he said. 'You'll find a good man – a really good man.'

'Someone like you?' she whispered, her arms tight around his neck.

'Oh, better than that, I hope!' He laughed and swung her around before putting her down.

'Just leave her alone,' Ethel said, putting her arm through his, 'or I'm going to be jealous!'

'Come on, my love,' he whispered in her ear.

The carriage was waiting, and the guests ran down to it, making between themselves a path through which the bride and groom could walk: but they didn't walk, they ran, heads bowed to avoid the showers of rice that their friends and relatives were throwing as they cheered and laughed.

The sun shone from a cloudless sky, dazzling as it reflected off the polished brass of the horse leathers and the gleaming panels of the coach. He handed her in, then turned, smiling.

Ada was on the top step of the house, their parents at her side. They waved: Dr Hall cheerily, his mother tearfully and Ada making only the slightest of gestures.

The vicar stood behind them. 'In all my years,' he said, 'I have never seen such manly grace matched with such divine womanly beauty.' He sighed, turning to Mrs Hall, who would, he felt, understand his meaning. 'So, my dear, must our aboriginal progenitors have seemed in that last dawn in Eden.'

The carriage rolled on its way. Ada, who had always thought the vicar a great fool, gave him a withering glance and went into the house.

The cheers and laughter died away from them and only the

sounds of the horses' hooves and the creak of the springs broke the silence of the carriage as they drove through the dusty, silent, rich streets. They sat holding hands, not knowing what to say.

He squeezed her hand, smiling at her.

'This sun, Eddie,' she said, frowning slightly, 'it's very bright – and it's in my eyes.'

'Oh, my darling, I'm so sorry,' he said, as if the gleam of the sun were his fault. He reached across her to pull the blind down.

She drew a quick breath and leant her head against the cushions as she felt the weight of him on her legs. He didn't notice the light touch of her fingers as she ran them over his thighs.

He sat back, in his corner. 'Is that better?' he asked.

'Doesn't Mrs Hall get a kiss from her husband?' she whispered.

He smiled and slid his hands up her arms. Holding her shoulders, he pulled her closer and kissed her, meaning it to be light, gentle, a token of his love.

She gave a slight moan of pleasure and opened her mouth to his kiss, flicking the tip of her tongue over his.

'My darling, oh, my darling,' he murmured.

She was kissing him, over and over, passionately, hungrily, trembling in his arms as if she would take the whole of his being into herself. A storm of desire burst over him too, and he held her with all his strength, answering her kisses with his own.

She pulled down the blind on his side of the carriage as they kissed, and she stroked his face, his shoulders, his arms, until her hand could rest on his leg, feeling the tight, held force of him. Her hand moved until she could press it between his legs. Under the thick material she could feel him, throbbing, hard.

'This is all, all, I've ever dreamt of,' she gasped.

The carriage stopped at a crossing. They could hear the coachman shout something to the sweeper. Hall lifted his head for a moment, then looked at her, seeing the wild desire in her eyes, feeling her hand gripping, moving over him.

Nothing in his life, not youth, not Paris, had prepared him for this urgent hunger. The picture came back to him of a golden knight at the feet of a blue-clad virgin, and with it came words – promises sworn, his sister's plea to protect Ethel from herself.

His love was no less, his desire no weaker, but he took her hand, held it to his lips and kissed it tenderly.

She came close to kiss him again on the mouth, but he, trembling, pulled away. 'It must be gentle, our love. So gentle,' he whispered.

'Gentle?'

'Yes.'

'Not like this?'

He shook his head. 'No.'

She drew away from him into her corner of the carriage, her hands tightly folded in her lap.

'It must be *love*,' he said.

'I've done something disgraceful, haven't I?' she said, her cheeks scarlet.

He tried to come close to her again, but she moved away from him.

'My dear, oh, my dear,' he said.

She looked at him, and her eyes were cold as they flicked over his face, noting his paleness, his clouded, troubled eyes, his set jaw.

'What am I to you? Now, here, what am I to you?' she said.

Suddenly he was frightened. His heart was pounding and he was finding it hard to breathe. He felt that she was going from him and knew, clearly, that what he said and did now would mark the rest of his life.

'You are my wife.'

She considered this, head on one side. 'Yes?' she said, her voice clear and emotionless. 'And what is that?'

A wave of love, of longing, such as an exile feels when the

land of his birth slips beyond the horizon, flowed over him. 'You are my heart's light. And my soul's need. You are my life.'

'*And?*' she cried.

He closed his eyes, shaking his head from side to side. There were no words to tell her how he felt.

'*And?*' she said again, her voice louder, hoarse, strident.

'You are my own darling, my vision of heaven,' he stammered.

She turned away from him, pulling the blind cord, letting the thing rattle up. Sunlight flooded in. Her body, forced into her corner, was tensed like a spring. 'I do not love you,' she said in a voice so detached that she might have been talking about the weather or the houses that they passed.

He stiffened as though he had been struck a mortal blow.

She turned to him, a slight smile at the sides of her mouth. 'I have never loved you. Not like that. And I never shall, that much I swear.'

'Dear God in heaven,' he whispered.

The tension went from her body, and she leant back against the cushions as though she had been thrown there. Her eyes were closed. 'Yes, that's it. Yes,' she murmured.

The carriage stopped. They heard the coachman clamber down. In a moment he opened the door and stood there, smiling.

Hall looked at him. 'In a moment, Dick,' he said.

The coachman, puzzled, stood back a pace.

Cool air flowed in through the open door. Hall turned to her again. 'Then what are we doing here?' he said.

'I really think that we ought to get out,' she said.

'*Please!*'

She looked at him, frowning. 'Well may you ask,' was her only reply to his question. Then briskly, businesslike, 'We shall have to hurry or we shall miss our train. And I'm not sure if there's another connection with the steam packet tonight.'

CHAPTER FOUR

They had caught the boat. The sea was calm, the last of the evening sun golden on the waters. Ethel had asked to be left alone and he, with a stiff bow, had walked from the frowsty saloon on to the deck, where he stood now, the wind blowing through his hair and giving an illusory colour to his ashen cheeks.

His mind was in turmoil. His thoughts would not come straight but were driven into a mechanical jigging to the time of the pounding of the engine and the splash and drive and turn of the paddle wheels.

She had to love him. She *had* to. A love as strong as his had to have an object. That made sense. And, the object found, secured by vows, by custom, by desire, must turn to that love, must be a part of it, must *be* it. If he loved her, then she loved him. All else was gibberish. It had to be.

He thrust himself away from the rail and stood, head bowed, hands behind his back. A shouting child, running away from someone, banged into his legs. He looked down at the laughing child, his eyes cold, full of hate. Why should anyone have happiness when he had none?

He turned on his heel and walked the deck, past the lounging passengers and the couples strolling arm in arm. He detested them all, their cheap clothes, their stupid braying voices, their being alive.

He could face them no longer and swung quickly down the stairs to the saloon, his feet clattering on the steel steps. Would to God that a storm from nowhere would sink the lot of them.

He paused at the foot of the stairs. One of the officers of the packet boat, on his way to the deck, stopped, his hand on the rail, and looked at him. 'Not feeling unwell, are we, sir?' the man said.

Hall turned to him. 'I would suggest that you mind your own bloody business,' he said through clenched teeth.

The officer was about to tell him what he thought of this remark, but the sight of Hall's eyes changed his mind. He nodded briskly and went on his way.

She was still there as he had left her. She looked up at him as he stood over her in the cabin. 'Did you want something?' she asked.

'I came to ask *you* that.'

'I have already told you what I want. To be left alone.'

He hesitated.

'You heard what I said, didn't you?'

He nodded. 'We shall be landing in twenty minutes.'

She sighed. 'Good.'

He went back on deck and leant once more against the rail, looking out over the sea. The line of land before them must be France, and his life, waiting.

He gripped the marked wood of the rail so tightly that his knuckles gleamed white. A movement from him now – a step up, a second's hold, a last look at the sun and then a turning fall into the dark coldness – and all would be ended. He took a breath, thinking of it, desiring it.

The child at whom he had glared before was at his side, tugging at his coat. He looked down at him. The child's face was tear-streaked now. 'I've lost my ball,' the boy said. 'Gone into the water.' And he let his head go back in a wail of despair.

'Then it's lost for ever,' Hall said. 'And there's nothing anyone can do about it.' He walked away, leaving the sobbing child. But after a step or two he turned and came back to him, taking a sovereign from his pocket. 'Buy another one in Boulogne,' he said, pushing the coin into a sticky hand. 'You get better ones there anyway.'

He was neither pleased nor displeased to see the abrupt end to the tears as the boy looked at his sudden and previously unimaginable wealth. That much money would buy him ball, bat, boat, shrimping net – all that he had ever longed for. He was too thunderstruck for words. God had come to him on a big boat.

It was late when they got to the hotel. This was Ethel's first journey abroad, and she had looked with some interest from the fiacre as they rattled along the newly built boulevards.

This interest was hope for Hall: it was almost as if she were coming back to life after an illness. 'There are so many places I want to take you, to show you,' he said.

She nodded, considering this. 'That will be nice.'

And at the hotel her mood lightened even further. No attention was spared them: bags were carried; backs were respectfully bowed in reverential greeting. Here was *milord*, of huge wealth, power and breeding, fetching – oh, what an honour – his bride for their wedding night to *this* hotel! Truly, nothing would be too much trouble. The slightest desire, the merest breath of a wish, would have instant fulfilment.

And such a couple! The man tall, of a handsomeness that defied description, from the god-like curls of his hair to the polished leather of his undoubtedly hand-made boots. It was as if, the smiling chambermaid thought, a statue of a Greek god had stepped from the Louvre and slipped into more fitting clothes. Truly, this was a lucky woman. Oh, the thought of the night in store for her! It was enough to make a girl faint.

And the attendant head porter looked at Ethel as she walked, with such dignity, up the deep-carpeted, brass-railed stairway. What a figure! The breasts so firm, so rounded, fruits ripe and ready for tasting. The bustle of her dress (which was, he allowed, more than a little provincial, but nothing that Paris would not swiftly put right during the coming days) swung fetchingly and delicately from side to side, echoing the silken movements of what were surely soft and yielding buttocks. A man would have something worth holding there, would he not? He raised his eyes and his thoughts reluctantly from this temptation and took in the pride of her long and elegant neck, the lustrous gleam of her high-piled, golden hair, the cool invitation in those wide blue eyes as she turned her head to smile at him. Tonight would be a true coupling of the gods, untrammelled by human weariness, on the shores of Elysium.

Lamps were already gleaming in their suite. They were shown the sitting-room, with its crackling fire in the grate against the chill of the dangerous night airs, its deep-buttoned chairs and lace-covered table, the warm and scented water already poured into wide basins. Then, as a fitting climax to these wonders, the manager threw open white-panelled doors to reveal the soft invitation of the bedroom, where a shaded lamp threw a low light on to the turned-back silken covers of the generous canopied bed.

Discreetly the manager lowered his eyes at the sight. 'A little food and wine before sleep,' he bowed. 'It is already on its way to you.'

'No, thank you,' Ethel said. 'I want only to retire.'

The head porter raised his eyebrows. Oh, without question, this would be a night to remember. Was such a man worthy of her? He glanced at the *milord* and decided, sadly, that he was.

Hall nodded to them. 'This is all very satisfactory,' he said. 'And now –'

'Of course,' the manager agreed, clapping his hands to shoo the servants from this hallowed place. 'May I wish you, *m'sieur-dame*, all joy and happiness for all your days. And nights.' He gave a slight smile and backed out, closing the door quietly behind him.

They were alone at last. Hall stood and looked at her. She returned his gaze expressionlessly, then turned away.

'It's been a very long day,' he said. 'You must be exhausted.'

'I am very tired,' she said.

Hope flickered in his breast. He knew almost nothing of

women: Rugby School and Cambridge had made sure of that. And hadn't his sister said that he must make allowances for tiredness? Maybe all marriages started like this. Perhaps this was what women were like – showing great passion and then modestly retreating behind pretended indifference.

'Then rest,' he said, trying to smile.

She nodded and went through the doors to their bedroom. He made to follow her, but she quickly turned on him. 'No,' she said, 'I want you to stay here.'

He turned away, slipped off his coat and flung himself into a chair. He heard the doors close and then silence. He put his finger tips to his aching eyes, lost in some vast mystery that was beyond his comprehension.

Tired as he was, he felt deeply restless. After a while he got up and went to the window, throwing the shutters back and opening the long window wide. As Frank had promised, their rooms did indeed look down upon a courtyard. In the light from a room on the ground floor opposite he could see a gravelled path circling some white-flowered shrub in the centre of the space.

From the lit room he heard a voice singing, and it was a song that he had heard before – three years before, when, hurt in love, rejected by the woman who was now his wife, he had fled to this city. It was light on the air, full of sadness and longing for home in Provence. It had moved him then, lonely as he had been, and now on this, the happiest night of his life, he bitterly reflected, it brought tears to his eyes. Through a mist of tears he could see the singer as she worked in what must be the hotel kitchen, her sleeves rolled up over her brown and rounded arms as she slowly scrubbed a great bowl. Shoulders bowed, he closed the shutters on the night and the song.

He heard, coming from the bedroom, the hiss and splash of his wife pissing into the chamber pot. And that, he thought, was as near as he was likely to get to the intimacies of married life.

After a moment she came through the doors. She was wearing a high-collared peignoir over her white silk nightdress.

'I need to wash,' she said.

He nodded in the direction of the still steaming bowls of water.

'With your back to me, please,' she insisted.

He shrugged and pulled his chair round so that it faced the shutters. The song had stopped now, he noticed, and the girl was laughing and squealing as some man, whose low voice could also be heard, made some proposal to her. He stirred in his seat, hearing Ethel pour cold water into the bowl from the ornate jug that stood at its side. He heard her dabbling her hands in the water, then a faint splash as she washed her face. She was silent now. She must be drying herself, he thought.

He cleared his throat and made to turn in his chair.

'No, please,' she said. 'I'm not quite finished.'

'You're quite safe,' he said bitterly. 'I merely wanted to say something.'

'In the morning. We must talk then.'

'I want to say it now.'

'Then say it.'

'Before we came away – my sister spoke to me.'

'About me?'

'Yes.'

'Then it can't have been to my advantage,' she said, her voice muffled by the towel.

'She said that you may be . . . in some way . . . different.'

She stopped towelling. 'From whom?'

He stood, turning to face her. She immediately clutched the towel, holding it in front of her.

'Oh, for God's sake!' he cried. 'Put that thing down! I'm not going to touch you! What do you think I am?'

Reluctantly she lowered the towel, then let it fall to the floor. 'Who am I supposed to be different from?' she asked.

'Other women. She thinks that.'

Ethel thought about this for a moment, then gave a slight shrug. 'How can I know?'

'I can't answer that. Obviously I can't.'

'In what way am I different? Did she tell you that?'

He shook his head.

She gave a slight laugh. 'No. She wouldn't. And you? Are you like other men? In the way that she meant?'

'I believe so.'

'I can't know that either. Can I?'

'Thank God.'

'That your wife is a virgin? A prayer taught at your mother's knee, Edward, and drummed home, no doubt, by your wretched sister.'

His face flushed with anger. 'Nothing against her. I won't have it!'

'How they have broken you, those women!' she cried.

'I am more in one piece than some!' he flung back at her.

'Yes,' she said, going towards the bedroom, 'you may well be.'

He thought that she had gone to bed but she came back into the sitting-room, unpinning her hair, shaking it free on to her shoulders. She had a hairbrush in her hand and, head on one side, she stood before the fire, vigorously brushing the long and glowing tresses. 'You must be hungry,' she said. 'You haven't eaten since breakfast. And you didn't eat much then.'

'Good God! You think I have an appetite? After –'

'They would get you something, I'm sure, if you asked.'

'No.'

She kept on brushing her hair, the strokes steady, rhythmical. 'I thought that a man who loved,' she said, 'loved with his mind and his body as one.'

This was too much for him. 'I do! I do love you, mind, soul, heart, body! *I love you with my whole being!*'

He had drawn nearer to her, but she moved quickly away from him. 'Don't dare come near me!' she cried.

He stopped, looking at her.

'In your mind!' she said. 'In your head!' She was tapping the back of the brush against her other hand. 'And I can't live there.' She turned away from him, putting the brush on to the mantelshelf, then leant against it, looking down into the fire. The flicker of the logs outlined her body for him. He moved closer, aching with desire. As if she sensed him, she went on talking in a low, rapid tone. 'What man does to woman, calling it love, is filthy, disgusting, *animal*! Forcing your way into her body, tearing, breaking, blood on you, on that pulsing veined thing! And you, your hands, sweating, sliding in sweat over her!'

He was still now, aghast, numbed by horror.

'I know, I know what you would do,' she gabbled on, 'and talking, talking all the time, your breath in my mouth, fine words, fine, oh, fine! And still that part of you pressing into me!' She threw her head back, hands clutching at her hair. 'I will not have this!' she screamed.

He came to her, seizing her shoulders, dragging her to face him, though she struggled in his grasp. '*I would not use you like that!*' he cried, his face close to hers.

'Use?' she spat at him. '*Use* me?'

'We are man and wife!'

She went limp in his hands and he let her go. They stood facing each other, panting. Then she turned away. 'If you ask them, they will find you a room of your own to sleep in.'

'How far would you shame me?' he gasped.

She turned to him again. 'As far as you would shame me.'

He nodded slowly, watching her as she moved restlessly about the room, picking up the towel, folding it, putting it back on the washstand.

'Is this our life? Is this what it's to be?' he asked, his voice quiet.

She looked at him thoughtfully, then went towards the bedroom. 'Make what you can of it,' she said, going in and closing the doors.

He stood, miserable, humiliated and helpless. He heard the key turn in the lock. And then a wild, blind anger took him. He ran at the door and kicked it, shattering the lock.

The door flew open, and he saw her standing by the bed.

She looked at him, her lips drawn back. Then, with a savage gesture, she took the front of her nightdress in both hands and tore it open. He saw her breasts, pink-circled, nipples erect. With a choking sob he ran towards her, his hands reaching out blindly.

But she immediately knelt on the bed, covering her breasts with the torn flaps of her nightdress. 'Don't touch me!' she hissed, 'don't dare touch me!'

He saw that there was hatred, burning, implacable, everlasting, in her eyes. He stopped, cold fear gripping his gut. This woman could kill him. Or he would kill her. There could be no other outcome if he took so much as one more step into that room.

Shaking like a man in a fever as he stared at her, the last shreds of control slipping from him, he backed out of the doors and closed them.

He stood, head bowed, then noticed that his hands were wet. He opened them and saw the blood flowing from the wounds where his nails had dug into his palms. He crossed the room to the wash bowl and dipped his hands into the water she had left. The blood circled and clouded. He shook the water impatiently from his hands, took a handkerchief from his pocket and pressed his hands into it until the blood stopped flowing.

What to do? What to do?

He looked round the room. He could not stay there for a moment longer. He had finally died in that place.

He ran towards his coat, pulled it on and, by force of habit, straightened his tie and smoothed his hair. Then he was out and in the corridor.

The head porter who was at the top of the stairs, pressed against the wall, listening and entertaining lubricious conjectures as to what the cries, shouts and bangs that the English were making could mean, caught a glimpse of him as he came through the door. Adjusting his waistcoat, whistling a tune he had learnt in the army at Sedan, he went back down the stairs with insouciance.

Hall, trying to appear composed, walked through the hallway of the hotel. The manager came from his cubby hole, bowing.

'*M'sieu* has changed his mind,' he asked, 'about some food?'

The head waiter came from the restaurant at the side of the hallway. 'A table is set,' he said with a smile, 'and there is good food. Soup, a little fish, a cutlet.'

'No,' Hall said, and the manner in which he said it, the evident strain and tension in his voice, caused the two men to exchange discreet glances.

'I think that *m'sieu* would like some wine,' the manager said.

'But certainly!' the head waiter agreed, holding open the glass-paned door to the restaurant.

Hall shrugged. It would be as good an answer as any and less exhausting than tramping the streets. He followed the waiter, who led him to a side table in the restaurant, clicking his fingers to the *sommelier*, who was already running forward, wine list in hand. A chair was slid back for him and Hall sank into it gratefully. Beyond all else now, he was deathly tired.

The *sommelier* proffered his list while the head waiter struck a match to light the candle on the table. Hall waved the list away. 'Cognac,' he said, 'and I don't care what the label says.'

'I will bring *m'sieu* of our very best.'

The waiter leant over him. Truly, he thought, this man is in a terrible state. The marriage night must have been one of much frenzy to so exhaust such strength. Pity the woman, he shrugged. But to Hall he merely said, 'If I may suggest, *m'sieu*, a morsel of bread would be wise. The morning will dawn brighter.'

Hall nodded wearily. 'Whatever you say.'

'At once, *m'sieu*.'

The *sommelier* was there, holding a bottle towards Hall as if it were the first ritual in a sacrament, but Hall merely pushed a glass towards him. 'You may leave the bottle,' he said, as the man poured the spirit. The *sommelier* nodded gravely and walked away.

Hall took a gulp of the brandy, not tasting the fineness of it, grateful only for the numbing fire in his throat and stomach.

The restaurant had seemed to be empty, but as he looked round in the darkness he saw that there was one other guest at this late hour: a plumpish, middle-aged man in a light suit who sat sipping wine and writing in a notebook. Aware that Hall was looking at him, the man looked up, gave a slight bow of his balding head and went back to his note taking.

Hall took another mouthful of brandy and then noticed that a basket of rolls was before him. The waiter placed a plate and knife on the table and said, 'If there should be anything more . . .'

'There will not be,' Hall said.

The waiter bowed and silently withdrew.

Trying to bring the day into sanity, Hall crumbled a roll and put some bread into his mouth. At the taste of it a great hunger came over him. Greedily he tore the roll and ate, washing it down with mouthfuls of cognac.

In the manager's cubby hole he and the waiter were conferring. 'The English I will never understand,' the manager was saying. He shrugged his shoulders. 'But they pay . . .'

'He will need help, that one,' the waiter said, 'to return to his bed.'

The manager smiled. 'It will be attended to. And if he needs any further help with his duties when he gets there, then I, for the honour of France and the Hotel Domenice, will do my utmost.'

'I too will run to the colours.' The waiter laughed.

'The English, the English, the English,' the manager murmured.

CHAPTER
FIVE

He woke blissfully happy: he had dreamt that he was standing in the church, looking back down the aisle and seeing her walking towards him, all the colours of heaven scattered around her.

Then, as his eyes opened against the harsh sunlight that streamed through the open window, he became aware of the pain in his neck, shoulders and back. He was half lying in one of the arm chairs and, as he looked round the room, all the fearful memories of the night came back to him.

Someone was tapping at the door. He threw the blanket that had been placed over his legs to the ground and tried to rise, but the young chambermaid was already coming into the room, carrying a tray of coffee and croissants.

'Oh, thank you,' he said, and sank back into his chair.

She smiled at him and nodded, clearing a place on the table at his side for the tray. He saw that there was only one cup and plate. 'And this for *madame*, please, also,' he said.

The chambermaid turned her head, looking at him, puzzled. 'But *madame* has gone out, *m'sieu*.'

'Out?' he blankly replied.

'Very early. It was she who asked me to carry this to you.'

'Yes, of course. I remember, now. She told me. But, alas, she forget to tell me where she was going. Did she speak of it to you?'

The girl was pouring his coffee. 'No, *m'sieu*.' She put the coffee pot down and went to the door.

'She knows no one, you see, in this city,' he said.

She paused, hand on the door and turned to him. 'In Paris, *m'sieu*, one soon makes friends.'

The girl left him. He took a mouthful of coffee, then, on a thought, went into the bedroom. He half expected to see all Ethel's clothes gone, anticipating that she might have left him for good and returned home. But her dresses were hung neatly in the great press that stood on one side of the room. That much, he supposed, he could be thankful for: she was still with him.

But where was she? She knew nothing of the dangers of this place, of any big city. Anything could happen to her. He would go out now and fetch her safely home.

He was almost at the door when he caught sight of himself in the glass. He looked terrible: unshaven, eyes dark-shadowed, the clothes he'd left his home in yesterday creased and crumpled. He paused for a moment, rubbing the bristles of his chin. She would think nothing of him if she saw him like this.

He quickly stripped and washed in the clean water that had been put in the bowls. He noticed that a brass jug of hot water had been set out for him to shave with. It was tepid now, so it must have been there for some time.

He flushed scarlet at the terrible thought that all sorts of servants in this hotel must have seen him lying in the chair – seen him and drawn their own conclusions. What should have been between him and his wife was now common gossip below stairs.

And he was right: talk ranged freely there, dividing along predictable lines. The men suggested, not too subtly, that he must be a monster of depravity to affect that charming young girl so. After all, they agreed, we all know of the English vice. But the women clucked and raised outraged voices: to have such a man and not know how to handle him was folly at best and selfish, old-maidish frigidity at worst.

'But if she does not love him?' the head porter mused.

His wife, the housekeeper-in-chief, rounded on him. 'What has that to do with it?' she cried. 'A bed can be made comfortable even with the most wretched of creatures!'

By her look he knew well whom she meant.

*

She had hung up his clothes too, and that, he supposed, was some sign of care and affection. He dressed quickly and, as always in his life, however black his despair, he experienced a glow of pleasure from the feel of fresh, clean linen next to his skin. He carefully tied a silk cravat, fixing it with his favourite pearl pin, enjoying the feeling of the high starched collar under his chin. He picked out a white waistcoat from the rack and then his lightest grey suit. On such a day as this remaining cool would matter.

He gave his tall grey hat a brush with his sleeve, slipped on his lemon-coloured gloves, picked up his stick and, with a final glance at himself in the mirror, went out of the room.

In the hallway the manager looked up from his desk and smiled. 'Good morning, *m'sieu.*'

Hall nodded and would have gone on his way into the bright sunlight of the street that could be seen through the open doors, but the manager came over to him, wiping his pince-nez with a silk handkerchief. 'A thousand regrets, *m'sieu,*' he said.

'For what?'

The manager, head on one side, let his eyebrows rise. 'The illness of *madame.*'

'Oh, yes, thank you.' So that was the line, he thought, keeping his face impassive.

'These maladies of the head,' the manager sympathized, 'are indeed terrible. One can become a martyr to them.'

'My wife suffers badly.'

'In truth,' the manager agreed. 'But I think, *m'sieu,* that you will find your room agreeable and comfortable.'

'It is.'

The manager shook his head. 'No, *m'sieu.* Your *new* room. You have not yet had the pleasure of viewing it.' He went to his desk and picked up a key. 'Number thirty-three. It is, alas, on the floor below your wife's suite. But it has the same view. *M'sieu* wishes to inspect it now?'

'Thank you, no,' Hall said, pocketing the key. 'I'm sure that it will be admirable.'

The manager bowed. 'I trust that *madame* will soon be fully recovered and that you will be able to resume your previous room. And your holiday.'

'I hope so.'

'I will arrange for your clothes and so on to be moved,' the manager added.

But Hall, not hearing him, his cheeks scarlet with mortification, was already passing through the doors and into the street.

Contrary to all fears, *madame* herself seemed to be in remarkably good health. She had walked a long way, slowly, loving the difference of this city, stopping often to peer into the shop windows, enjoying the sights and smells of new foods and, above all, new clothes, even though they made her feel dowdy and overdressed. There would be time to do something about that, she thought.

Oh, wouldn't she just give them all a surprise at home when she turned up looking so smart, so elegant. She couldn't wait to see the expression on the face of that sister of Edward's when she saw her. Now there was a woman who was *really* badly dressed. No idea of style, none at all. All that heavy golden jewellery: those great carriage-lamp pendants that swung and (she could swear) rattled from her ears. She'd have a shock, that was for sure. She smiled at the thought and saw her smile reflected in a window.

A man said something to her, but as she couldn't understand a word of what he was saying, it was easy to give him a dignified but cold stare and walk on her way.

She came to a large square and, with some reluctance, crossed the heat and light of it, making sure that her white parasol shaded her face from the sun. On the other side of the square, through a space between buildings, she saw trees. A garden, perhaps, that would be open to the public. It would be cool there, and it would be pleasant to sit for a while.

The gardens were public and, what was even better, open on one side to the river. She found a bench under a tree and sat looking round her. A large, palace-like building was on her left, and she looked up at it, wondering if that was where the President lived. She would have to ask Edward, she thought. Her brow clouded at the thought of him, and she turned away from the palace and enjoyed instead the sight of the children playing in the garden, of their nurses gossiping in the shade.

A man, well dressed, obviously a gentleman, was sitting on a bench at some distance from her. She saw that he was looking at her and turned her head from him – but not before she had seen him politely raise his hat.

She half rose from her seat, meaning to walk away from these unwelcome advances. But then she changed her mind. Why, she thought, should we always be the ones who have to move? I've as much right to sit in this park as he has. So she remained where she was, looking straight ahead. All the same, she wished she'd brought a book.

Her husband was tired. At first he'd walked purposefully, visiting the places where he thought she was likely to go: the Arc de Triomphe perhaps, for that, at least, she knew – she had guessed that it would be like Marble Arch, it was true, but it had been in her mind – the rue de Faubourg St Honoré, where, he thought, the dresses might have attracted her, the place de la Madeleine. He remembered that old churches bored her, which gave him an excuse not to cross the river to Notre Dame.

In none of these places was there a glimpse of her. Wearily he went into a pavement café and sipped an absinthe. His was a hopeless quest, he knew that, but he also knew that he had to carry on with it. Whatever she might feel about him, he could not bear the thought of her lost in this huge city, helplessly looking round for him.

The thought of her being lost made him realize that he had

pursued a false trail: he had assumed that she would have destinations in mind and would have set out to see them. But she could have had nothing particular in mind: she knew of none of the places he had trudged to. If she found them at all, it would be by accident only.

He tried to remember if she had ever said that she liked paintings. He couldn't for the life of him recall, but, if she did, she might just have known of the Louvre. He got to his feet, throwing a couple of coins on to the fluttering bill on the table, and walked on down the avenue de l'Opéra and along the narrow street of Pyramides.

He passed a jeweller's shop. Distressed though he was, he could not resist a glance in the window. Jewels had been an obsession with him ever since, as a boy, he used to sit by the hour in the back of just such a shop as this one in Brighton, watching the old jeweller set or re-set pieces, listening to him talking about these beautiful, mysterious stones and laying the foundations of a store of knowledge which was to last him a lifetime.

He gazed into the dark window, finding some comfort in the light of the jewels, the lustre of the gold. These, at least, were eternal. A jewel would not be one thing today and another tomorrow. Such things could be worn as badges against disaster and the uncertainties of time. Perhaps they had always been that to him: perhaps they always would be. Why, even at Rugby, where he had been both prouder and poorer than most of the others, he had managed to augment scant pocket money by carefully planned buying and selling expeditions to London. Faced with a precious stone, he knew what he was at.

His eye lit upon a brooch. It had a simple setting, but the gold had been carefully worked some time around the 1740s by the look of things, and the small emeralds were decent enough. If he bought it for her, brought it back in triumph, would she soften towards him? She should; it was a beautiful piece.

He imagined the scene – she sitting before her dressing-table glass, he casually putting the brooch against her dress. She would see it in the glass, her eyes would light up, she would turn to him, smiling . . .

He went into the shop. The bell on its spring clanged in the darkness. The shopkeeper shuffled in, looking at him suspiciously and asked what he wanted.

Hall, with a practised air of indifference, asked about a necklace in the window. The jeweller, long in the business, knew that this handsome Englishman with the good French accent was probing, an informed customer. He pulled aside the curtains at the back of the window, wondering which piece really interested the man but for now, as an opening gambit, fetching out the over-priced necklace.

As they talked and haggled, a carriage clattered past. The noise of it caused Hall to repeat a question, and he frowned in exasperation, then waited until the racket died away. He didn't take his eyes off his bargaining antagonist: if he had looked out of the window, he would have seen his young bride in a smart landau, laughing at some remark made by a middle-aged, immaculately dressed man who sat facing her, one hand lightly on her knee.

His purchase of the brooch made at last – at some thirty francs cheaper than its starting price – Hall came out of the shop. He looked up and down the street, then remembered that he was on his way to the Louvre. He thought about it for a moment, then decided against it. If she had gone in, he would never find her in that warren of corridors and galleries. What, then, to do?

The vision of him surprising her with the brooch came back to him. He turned on his heel and walked back quickly towards the place de l'Opéra. He would get a fiacre there and go back to the hotel. By this time, he thought, she would be tired enough to have made her way home. She would be there in their room, he was sure of it, and by every means at his disposal he would make things right between them. It could be done. It *must* be done.

They had been tired last night; she had been overwrought; but today all things could be made new. He felt the power to do it in his heart, in his body. He would start again as if this were the first day he had ever met her, wooing her gently, carefully, leading her lightly to love.

Once back at the hotel, he almost ran up the stairs to their room. He turned the handle of the locked door, calling her name.

There was no reply, only the afternoon silence of a slumbering hotel.

He felt the shape of the large key in his pocket, took it out, tried to force it into the keyhole. It didn't fit. Cursing under his breath, he tried again, and then he remembered. This was a key to another room. His room.

As he stood, irresolute, a chambermaid poked her head out of the linen room at the end of the corridor.

'*M'sieu* wished to go into *madame*'s room?' she asked.

'If you please.'

She came towards him, searching for the key from the ring at her belt. '*Madame* has forgotten something?' she asked.

'Yes.' He shook his head. 'No . . . I needed to get something. For myself.'

'But we have moved *m'sieu*'s things. This morning I –' She was swinging the door open.

'Never mind,' he said, seeing in the room Ethel's coat thrown over the back of a chair. 'I had to go out on some business. Where is *madame* now?'

The chambermaid was already walking away, back to her linen closet. 'In the courtyard, *m'sieu*,' she called, over her shoulder.

'The courtyard?'

'But yes.' She stopped, turning to him. 'It was some inconvenience, but the gentleman insisted.'

He went quickly into the room, throwing open the shutters

that had been closed against the heat of the sun. Before he saw her, he heard her laugh. She had never laughed like that for him, he thought, freely, openly, delighting in something. Not even when they were children, playing a game. That laugh pierced him to the heart.

A table had been placed in the courtyard, on the shaded side, directly opposite their room, and there she sat, leaning back in her chair, one leg crossed over the other, lazily swinging her foot. One elbow rested on the table and her finger tips were at the side of her head. She was beautiful.

The man, a stranger, was leaning forward in his chair, smiling, speaking to her. An old man, Hall thought, forty at least. But well preserved, his grey hair well cut, as was his suit. Where, in God's name, had she met him? And how was it that they were now so friendly?

His first thought was to go out again, avoiding this new problem. But that wouldn't answer. He would have to join them, face this man, wondering, as they went through the usual courtesies, if she had told him anything of their life together.

He closed the shutters, made sure, in the glass, that he had something of the elegance of the older man and went downstairs.

Ethel gave a low laugh, then looked at her companion.

'What's amused you now?' he asked, smiling.

'A thought.'

'Share it. Please.'

'It's simply that this is the first time I've ever stayed in an hotel.'

'I don't believe you,' he said.

'Oh, it's perfectly true. If we went up to London, we stayed with my father's aunt. She was a funny old stick.'

'And are you enjoying hotel life?'

'Oh, yes. One can have anything.'

'Like a child let loose in a sweet shop.'

'I suppose I am.'

He leant closer to her. 'There are many tempting confections on the shelves,' he murmured.

'I know,' she nodded. 'And I intend to taste them.'

He nodded, gravely.

'Do you live in an hotel in Paris?'

He laughed. 'No, my dear. I have an *appartement* here.' He was silent for a moment, enjoying the sight of her, so young, so innocent, so happy. 'Perhaps,' he went on, 'while you are in Paris, you and your husband would do me the honour of dining with me.'

'Oh, that would be splendid!' she cried, clapping her hands.

'Another sweet from the jar?'

'The topmost jar, on the most special shelf,' she smiled.

Nor did her smile fade when she saw Hall in the doorway. 'Eddie!' she cried. 'I've been wondering where you'd got to.'

The man rose, holding out his hand in greeting.

'This is Mr Temple-Smith,' Ethel said, as if it were the most natural thing in the world.

'Mr Hall,' Temple-Smith said, shaking his hand.

'Marshall Hall,' Hall corrected him, coolly.

'Hyphenated?'

'No. But Marshall Hall all the same.'

Ethel raised an eyebrow. This was new, but if that was what he wanted . . . And she supposed it did sound rather better. She would quite like being called by that name. 'I'm so sorry, Mr Temple-Smith,' she said. 'We became such good friends so quickly that I forgot to tell you.'

'Not at all,' Temple-Smith said. 'Now look: let me go and get another chair.'

'I will do that,' Hall said.

'Oh, no! Do let him, Eddie,' Ethel said. 'They made the silliest fuss about our coming out here, and Mr Temple-Smith had to be very forceful with them.'

'And about their serving us tea,' he said.

'That was even worse,' she agreed. 'Honestly, you would have thought we'd asked for opium.'

Temple-Smith went towards the door. 'I'll get the chair.'

Hall sat at the table. 'Where did you meet him?' he asked, a tremble of anger in his voice.

'Now don't go into one of your sulks,' she said. 'I got very lost in some gardens or other, and he came across, knowing – though I don't know how – that I was English. He works at our Embassy, and he said that it was his job to rescue poor travellers.'

'Indeed?'

'Oh, yes. And in no time at all he'd found such a smart carriage, and he took me all over, through a sort of wood with great big houses in it –'

'The Bois de Boulogne.'

'That was what he said. Only he just called it "the Bois". I remembered from school what *that* meant.'

'You can't just – *go* with someone like that!' he said, the anger very clear now in his voice.

She leant back, suddenly less animated. 'What business is it of yours?' she asked.

'You are my wife, and it's my duty to be concerned about you,' he said. 'I've been worried out of my wits.'

'You'll have to get over that,' she warned. 'Truly you will.'

Before he could say any more, Temple-Smith was back, a chair-carrying porter following him.

'I've asked them to fetch us more tea. Had to repeat the instructions for making it, of course. Lovable people in some ways, but so dense in others,' he said, pointing to the precise spot where he wanted the porter to place the chair. 'Don't you find that?' he asked Hall.

'No. But I do find that many of them speak English.' He turned to the porter. 'Thank you. And I'm sorry to have put you to so much trouble.'

'Thank you, *m'sieu.* For you, it is no trouble at all,' the porter smiled, as he bowed to Hall and left them.

'You've made a friend for life there.' Temple-Smith grinned as he sat in the chair. 'You should think of joining us at the Embassy. I can see that there'd never be a war with you around.'

'My wife was telling me that you're on the Embassy staff.'

'Oh, he's something *very* grand, Eddie!'

Temple-Smith shook his head, laughing. 'Not grand at all: a humble Second Secretary.'

'Quite grand enough,' Hall said.

Temple-Smith shrugged this aside. Looking first at Ethel, then at Hall, he said, 'Your dear wife seemed to have got herself somewhat lost.'

'She told me.'

'But, as you see, I have returned her to you. No harm done.'

'I am grateful to you, sir,' Hall said, stiffly.

'But I'm afraid that I did give her an awful wigging about wandering around on her own.' Hall was silent. Temple-Smith looked over his shoulder at the door to the courtyard. 'What the devil are they doing with this tea?' He turned again to Hall. 'She should be accompanied,' he said, a hint of reproof in his voice.

'I shall make sure that she is from now on,' Hall replied, grimly.

'Oh, such a lot of fuss!' Ethel laughed.

'What shall we do with her?' Temple-Smith smiled at Hall.

'Whatever one can,' Hall said, his voice soft as silk.

'Let's not talk about it any more,' Ethel said firmly, then, turning to Hall: 'Mr Temple-Smith has very kindly asked us to dine with him. Isn't that lovely?'

'Indeed it is, and most kind, but I'm afraid we –'

'Which night shall we come?' Ethel interrupted.

'I was about to say . . .' Hall went on.

Temple-Smith put a hand on Hall's arm. He felt the muscle flinch at his touch, but it was what he expected, so he wasn't deterred. 'My dear fellow, the ladies must never be disappointed.' He turned to Ethel. 'If your husband permits, would tomorrow at eight be convenient?' He turned to Hall. 'Do you permit? I would like so much to see you both at my table.'

A waiter had brought their tea and was setting it out.

'The French, as you know,' Temple-Smith went on, ignoring the man, 'simply loathe inviting any one into their homes, so asking any of them to dine is out of the question. And as for my esteemed colleagues at the Embassy – well, now, I think them pretty dull old dogs. So make my life happy. Do come.'

'We shall be there,' Ethel said, as she poured their tea.

'Splendid,' Temple-Smith murmured, as he raised the cup to his lips, 'which is more than I can say about this hell-brew.'

Temple-Smith had a fund of anecdotes about the oddities of foreigners: the Viennese, the Hungarians, the Russians (who were pretty scruffy on the whole), even the Chinese. He had served in many places: Ethel was entranced. Only the Prussians seemed to merit his approval. They were pretty decent types, by and large. He told them to mark his words, that the future lay with them. Nordic peoples together. Once with 'em – and they always kept their word, that had to be said – why, there was simply no limit to what could be achieved. A world waited.

As Hall did, for him to finish this drivel and go.

And go he did at last. But there was a silence at his departure. Ethel had yawned and said that she was going to rest before dinner. Hall accompanied her into the hotel, which was beginning to shake itself into life for the evening ahead, and followed her up the stairs.

'Have you seen your room yet?' she asked, as they came to that floor.

'No.'

'Don't you think you'd better?'

'In a while.'

She stopped and turned to him, one hand on the banister rail. 'Eddie, I need to rest.'

'There is something I must say.'

'Won't it wait until dinner?'

'It's not dinner-table gossip.'

'Oh, dear,' she sighed. 'Very well, then, let's get it done with.'

They went up the next flight of stairs in silence and, still not speaking, went into her room.

'I made sure that they hung your clothes properly,' she said, as he closed the door.

'Thank you.'

She sat in an arm chair, hands quietly folded in her lap. 'What is it you wanted to say?' He remembered his resolution of the afternoon and smiled at her. She didn't smile back at him as he sat facing her. 'Well?'

'That I love you.'

She looked down. 'I've told you how I feel about you.'

'That was last night.'

She raised her eyes to him, and there was pity in them. 'No, it was for ever.' She shook her head. 'I'm sorry. I wish – oh, you don't know how much I wish – that things were different between us. But they're not. And they will never be.'

'Do you know why you've changed so much?' he asked, his voice low as he tried to keep the pain out of it.

She thought about this for a moment as her foot tapped restlessly on the carpet. 'I don't think I have changed, not really. I always knew that we were – different. I told you that before you went away. And I told you again when you came back. But I thought that something in you had changed and that everything would be possible. But it hadn't. And it isn't.'

'I will change in any way that you want me to,' he said urgently.

She smiled at him, shaking her head. 'The change that is needed would make you into a completely different man, Eddie. And you can't be. Any more than you could turn yourself into a pygmy to suit my mood.'

'Just tell me what it is you want.'

She nodded. 'Very well, then. I want you not to have been born of the parents you were. I want you to deny every value they ever gave you. I want you never to have gone to the school you did, never to have played one single solitary game of stupid cricket, never to have gone to the university and never to have decided to be a lawyer. And if you had to be cursed with a sister such as you have, I would want you to strangle her with your bare hands and make the body into a rug for me to dance on. Is that enough to be going on with?'

He laughed, his head back, and she marvelled at his grace and beauty, his neck strong but still slender, his jaw firm and his teeth white against generous lips and bronzed flesh. She noticed that he had cut himself slightly while shaving, and she had a great need to touch that wound and feel those muscles under her finger tips.

But she sat, hands still folded.

He was smiling still. He took a small blue box from his pocket and held it out to her. 'This, at least, is a start,' he whispered.

She took it, turning it in her hands. 'What is it?'

'Open it and see.'

She was grave as she looked from the box to him. 'No, you must tell me.'

'A bauble – not fit for you but pretty enough.'

She opened it and lifted the brooch out. 'It is pretty,' she said, not smiling. 'Did it cost a lot of money?'

'Less than its worth.'

She rose, putting the brooch back into its box and laying it on the dressing-table. 'Thank you, Eddie,' she said. She turned to him. 'Now, my dear, I really must sleep for a while.'

He nodded. 'Yes. Sleep.'

She went into her bedroom and closed the door. She undressed slowly, folding her clothes neatly. When she was naked, she stood for a while before the looking-glass, accepting, without any conceit, the beauty of her body.

She slid between the sheets and lay on her back, waiting for him to come to her, ready at last to take him. He must know that that was what she truly wanted.

She heard the door to the sitting-room close quietly and his footsteps as he walked down the corridor. She turned on to her side and wept silently for shame and for loss.

CHAPTER
SIX

On the day of Temple-Smith's dinner party the weather had changed. The brilliant sun of yesterday merely glowed today behind shapeless cloud, and the air in the streets was motionless, heavy and humid.

Hall had taken her for a drive to the Latin Quarter so that he might show her his old haunts, but she was hot and bored, unable to share with him the excitement of finding that, in this city of perpetual demolition and building, nothing here at least had changed. Restaurants where he had spent his last sous on a meal (and, oh, what meals) meant nothing to her. They looked frowsty and fly-blown and she would have choked on a crumb from such places.

Now, as darkness fell, thunder rumbled round the city and the roofs and chimneypots shone blue in flashes of lightning.

Ethel had taken a long time in her dressing, going back to her room not once but several times to alter some detail or find a different piece of jewellery. At her first appearance she was wearing the brooch that he had bought her, but now it was discarded in favour of some other piece. He frowned, noticing the change, minding less the rejection of his gift than that the replacement was paltry, the diamonds badly cut and clumsily set. But he made no comment.

As a result of all this they were late.

Temple-Smith's *appartement* was in a street of tall buildings off the Etoile. 'Doesn't look very much,' Ethel said, as he handed her down from the fiacre.

'Appearances can be very deceptive in Paris,' he told her.

'I hope so,' she said, looking for the bell at the door.

'No.' He smiled. 'One just goes in.' He opened the door.

The concierge, an old woman, her grey hair scraped back in a tight bun on the top of her head, leant from her narrow doorway and looked at them suspiciously.

'We are guests of Monsieur Temple-Smith,' Hall assured her.

'The *m'sieu*'s guest has arrived,' she said, not to be disarmed.

But Temple-Smith was already running down the stairs towards them. 'I'm so glad you've come,' he cried. 'I was afraid that the storm had put you off.'

'An Englishman cannot be deterred by the threat of rain,' Hall said, 'or we should never set foot outside the door.'

'Oh, how very true.' Temple-Smith laughed as, with a courtly bow, he leant over Ethel's hand, lifting her fingertips to his lips. 'You are very welcome,' he murmured. He took Hall's hand, shaking it firmly and patting him on the shoulder with his other hand. 'Splendid, my dear fellow, splendid!' He led them up the stairs.

'I do apologize for our lateness,' Hall said.

Temple-Smith turned to them. 'Late? Are you late?' he said.

'I fear so,' Hall replied, as they went onwards.

'Then it is of no consequence whatsoever,' their host assured them, throwing open the doors to his salon.

Ethel's breath was taken away by the magnificence of the room. The walls seemed to be covered in the palest of blue silk and there were lights everywhere; a crystal chandelier in the centre of the room and candles on each wall. A white marble statue stood in a corner; paintings in elaborate gilt frames crowded the walls; and there was not a surface that didn't carry a triumph of flowers. The rosewood desk, the side-tables and the chairs were all of the period of the Directoire and gleamed in the light.

'This is beautiful,' she gasped.

'One tries to preserve a modicum of comfort,' he smiled.

A maid was at Ethel's side, slipping off her cloak. At the

same time a manservant relieved Hall of his coat, hat and stick. With a bow, they disappeared.

So taken had they been by the appearance of the room that they had not noticed the young man who stood by the fireplace. Temple-Smith brought him forward, saying, 'Now this is the most confounded nuisance. I'd so hoped that we would be dining *à trois*, but we've got this young wretch, I'm afraid.' He turned to Ethel. 'Do you mind?'

'Not at all.' She smiled.

'Then that's all right. I can let you meet the creature.' He put an arm on the young man's shoulder. 'Mrs Marshall Hall, Mr Marshall Hall, may I present Lieutenant Raoul de Ponthieu of Her Majesty's Indian Army.'

The young man was smiling easily at Temple Smith. He was certainly good-looking, although not in Hall's heroic, statu-esque way. Where Hall was broad-shouldered, this man was slight; where Hall was fair, he had hair black as a raven's wing; where Hall had a clear, direct gaze, the other had dark, heavy-lidded eyes; and Hall's bronzed complexion was in sharp contrast to the ivory lustre of Ponthieu's features. His hands were long and thin, almost feminine, but all the same, as he briefly held Ethel's gloved hand, she was struck by the strength of his grasp.

'He's just passing through Paris,' Temple-Smith was saying. 'He's always passing through somewhere or other – and it's usually my house, wherever it may be. God knows who's looking after the Indian Empire.'

'You're very hard on him,' Ethel said, as their host led her to a chair.

'Hard? On that one? Oh, my dear lady, one cannot be. He's a friend of the Earl of Northesk, who happens to be a kinsman of mine, otherwise I'd boot him out.'

'Take no notice of him,' Ponthieu said, as he sat near to Ethel. 'He's been like this since I was at Harrow. An ever-present refuge.'

'Harrow?' Ethel said. 'I thought that you must be French.'

He laughed, showing his small, white, and even teeth. 'Generations back. I don't speak a word of the language, but the name opens all sorts of doors in Paris.'

'Most of which would be much better kept locked,' Temple-Smith said. His manservant had come into the room again, bearing a tray of glasses. 'Now, my friends, would any of you care for a cocktail before dinner?'

'I don't think I've ever had one,' Ethel said.

'What are they?' Hall asked.

'A very bad habit that I acquired in Washington. But quite delicious.'

'Then we shall try one. Won't we, Eddie?'

Hall nodded and the servant offered them their drinks.

'Oh, it's nice!' Ethel said as she sipped. 'Lovely.'

Hall would have given all the cocktails in the world at that moment for a mug of foaming ale, but he nodded appreciatively. 'Gin,' he said.

'And all sorts of nice things,' Temple-Smith agreed. He turned to Ethel. 'Yet one more jar on the shelf?'

'One more,' she smiled. 'If I'm not careful, the shop will be empty.'

'The stock is constantly changing, I do assure you. You never come to the end of it.'

The dinner was long. Dish followed dish, each with its own rich sauce and a different wine. The storm had now fully broken, and Hall's head was throbbing from the rumble of the thunder, the oppressiveness of the sumptuous dining-room, the heaviness of the food and the liberality of the wines. The conversation would have been as weighty as the food had it not been for the adroitness of the host and the enthusiasm of Ethel. Hall did not say much; neither did Ponthieu, who seemed content to be an observer of the scene, his dark eyes taking everything in.

At last they had consumed the final course, and Temple-

Smith led them back into the salon, Ethel's arm held closely in his.

'At least,' he said to her, 'you have been spared the barbarism of having to gossip with the old ladies while we men swilled our port.'

'It always seems to me to be a silly thing to do,' she said.

'A convention designed entirely for the purpose of enabling gentlemen to tell improper stories. And since they're usually too drunk to remember how the jokes end, it should lapse forthwith.'

They sat in the chairs they had occupied before dinner. 'What do you say, Marshall Hall?' he asked, as the servant offered them brandies and liqueurs.

'The custom has some uses,' Hall said.

'Such as what?'

'It allows us to smoke.'

'Please! If you want to, any of you –' Ethel said. 'I quite like the smell of cigars.'

'Are you sure?' Temple-Smith asked.

'Oh, yes.'

Temple-Smith gave a glance to the manservant, but he was already opening the lid of a humidor.

Ponthieu shook his head lazily and took a gold cigarette case from his pocket. 'If you can tolerate cigars,' he said to Ethel, 'I hope that you won't be offended by these.'

'Not at all.' She looked around, smiling, her eyes dancing with pleasure as the tobacco smoke rose. 'This feels terribly bohemian,' she giggled.

'Of course it does. And so it should – in Paris,' Temple-Smith said. 'In Dover there is a large shed. Did you see it? Over the doors it says "Her Majesty's Customs". Well, I always abandon mine there: whatever customs Her Majesty keeps at Windsor, we have very different ones here. Thank God.'

'It is, indeed, another country,' Hall said.

'You like it?'

'Yes. Very much.'

Temple-Smith looked at him speculatively for a while before he spoke. 'Have you ever considered the diplomatic service as a career?'

Hall shook his head.

'Why not? You have, I am sure, ample gifts.' He turned to Ethel. 'And think how splendid he would look in the uniform. Yes?'

'Uniform's a great bore,' Ponthieu drawled. 'Have to keep a fellow just to polish buttons.'

'He looks splendid in anything,' Ethel said. 'I think so anyway.'

'And I am sure that you're right.' He faced Hall again. 'No, but seriously. Why not?'

'I haven't the advantage of your connections.'

'Oh, those days are fast going, my dear chap. Talent! That's what's called for now.'

'I'll stick to the law.'

'Isn't that overwhelmingly dull?'

'Yes,' Hall admitted. 'Dreary.'

'Well, then!' Temple-Smith cried.

Hall drew deeply on his cigar and then let the smoke out slowly. A thought had come to him, and he held it for a moment before speaking. 'But it's my aim to take the dullness out of it. That's what I want to do.'

'Impossible!'

'Very probably. But I intend to try.'

In the fiacre on their way back to their hotel Ethel was animated and excited. 'I wonder if we'll get to meet him,' she said.

Hall tried to stifle a yawn. 'Who?'

'That relation of his. The Earl of . . .'

'Northesk. That's what he said.'

'It would be wonderful! Oh, it's a whole new world, Eddie! And he could help you, I'm sure he could, in getting customers.'

'Clients.' He looked at her. 'But I don't imagine that our world and that of the Earl of Northesk will overlap much.'

'Then we must make them,' she said determinedly. She put an arm through his and snuggled up to him. 'Oh, Eddie,' she breathed, 'this is better than Brighton.'

He put an arm around her, holding her close, and she seemed to be happy to rest on his shoulder. 'For a time,' he murmured. 'For a little time. But I will give you better, far better, than the company of people such as that.'

'Will you?' she smiled.

'I've sworn it. And every drop of my life's blood will go into it. *I shall work.* Oh, how I shall work!'

'And me?' she whispered, keeping very still. 'What shall I do?'

'Be at my side, of course.

She sat up. 'We're almost there,' she said, looking out of the fiacre. 'At your side. I suppose that is where a wife has to be,' she sighed. The excitement of the evening fell from her like a cloak she had borrowed and had to give back.

The fiacre stopped and he handed her out. 'All is still the same between us?' he asked, in a low voice.

She looked at him coldly. 'Just the same,' she said, withdrawing her hand and going into the hotel. 'I will see you at breakfast.'

They got through the rest of their honeymoon somehow. To the perpetual puzzlement of the hotel servants, they had kept to their separate rooms each night, spending only their days together.

During those long and golden days he showed her the sights of Paris. Sometimes she seemed to be enjoying herself, and he would hope against hope that she was beginning to feel more fondly towards him, but then, for no reason that he could discover, her mood would change and she would withdraw completely from him into some dark world of her own.

Perhaps if Temple-Smith had got in touch with them again, introduced them to more of his friends, she might have stayed in the light. But the letter of thanks which Hall sent to him after the dinner party produced no response other than a brief note in which he hoped that they would enjoy the rest of their time in Paris.

Hall, at his wits' end as how to please her, bought her presents — more pieces of jewellery, whatever clothes she fancied — and for a time these gifts might lighten her mood. But later she was quite likely to reprove him for his extravagance and to remind him that the £500 bequeathed to her in her father's will as a marriage settlement was not to be squandered by him.

By the end of their stay it seemed as if she was coming to believe in the polite fiction of her illness. She complained of headaches and lassitude and, certainly, she was eating less and less. She picked at meals wherever they ate and sent most of the food back untasted.

He wanted to fetch a doctor to see her, but she rejected this angrily, asking only to be left alone.

So it was no sorrow to either of them when their bags were packed and they were on their way to the railway station and home.

CHAPTER
SEVEN

Home they came, to a suite of rooms which he had taken in Seymour Street. When they had looked over them before they had married, she had run from room to room, laughing with delight, clapping her hands with joy. They were perfect, she had cried, a real home of their own. He had stood by, laughing with her, ecstatic in her happiness. And together they had traipsed from shop to shop, choosing, with great care, such pieces of furniture as they could afford.

On the train back to Brighton they would sit, head to head, making notes on scraps of paper, adding up the costs and feeling virtuous about the fact that they were getting so much for so little. Then they would solemnly visit each other's houses, selecting judiciously what they wanted from what his parents and her mother had said they could have.

Ada, predictably, offered them money enough not to bother with any of this, but a warning look from Ethel was enough to prompt Hall, with a quick kiss, to decline the assistance.

Then there had been the great day when the painters and paperhangers had called, bearing pots and sample books. They had sent the men away and happily wandered through the rooms alone, leaving the female relative who had been pressed into service as chaperone drearily drinking tea in the tiny kitchen while they held up scraps of paper and material, trying to match paint to paper to carpets to curtains. And they would forget what they had chosen, then get themselves into a terrible muddle, but they laughed themselves out of it.

At last everything had been decided by Ethel: it was to be as she wanted it, and clear instructions had been given to the workmen that the place had to be decorated, swept and dusted against their return.

But when that day came and their cab rattled up to the door, Ethel was feeling unwell. She had reason for sickness, goodness knows: the Channel had been rough, tossing the packet steamer about like a cork in a millrace. Hall had survived the journey well enough; he had always been a good sailor and found the storm invigorating, but poor Ethel had suffered dreadfully.

Before the train left Dover for Victoria, Hall paid the guard to ensure that they had a carriage to themselves. Ethel sat shivering in a corner, white-faced, eyes closed, the blind on her side of the carriage pulled down.

Their cab rattled to a halt beside their home. Ethel merely nodded her thanks that they were there and got out, Hall supporting her up the steps to the house.

He had wanted to carry her across the threshold triumphantly, but while he fumbled for the key, she leant against the wall, her breathing shallow and fast. He got the door open and she walked inside. 'What a terrible smell,' she said, her voice weak.

'It's the paint. It will go.'

She shook her head. 'It's awful.'

He helped her to a chair. 'Come, sit down. You'll soon feel better.'

She sat for a moment, her eyes closed, a hand holding her side to ease a pain. 'These rooms,' she said, 'are too expensive for us.'

'You wanted a good address.'

'We can't afford them.'

'We'll see.'

'No. We can't.' She pushed herself up. 'I'm going to bed.'

'Let me help you,' he said, coming quickly to her side.

She pushed his arm away. 'I can manage, thank you.' She went out of the sitting-room and into what was to have been their bedroom, closing the door behind her.

'Do you like it? Are you pleased with the decorations?' he called.

She didn't reply.

*

The spare room was not comfortable. When they had taken that bed from Ethel's house, she had joked about the peculiar agonies of it, but, they laughed, it would certainly speed the staying guest on his way. As Hall tossed and turned on it, he groaned at the joke. He had not been able to find the spare sheets and blankets and had had to wrap himself in a couple of top coats.

So it wasn't surprising that he woke early to begin his life as a lawyer. As he bathed and shaved (in cold water, since he didn't know how to light the kitchen range), he listened for the sounds of Ethel rising and, perhaps, going into the kitchen to cook some breakfast. It didn't occur to him that no food had been bought. How could it have been? Food was something that servants fetched into the house, then cooked and served. The operation was mysterious, removed and as reliable as dawn following night. He dressed, taking his time. But there was still no sound of Ethel.

He went into the sitting-room, pulled back the curtains and let the blinds up. It was still only eight o'clock, and his appointment with Mr Tindal Atkinson, QC, wasn't until half-past ten. He sat for a while, wondering what to do, then tiptoed to Ethel's door and lightly tapped upon it. There was no reply, so he opened it carefully and looked in.

She was awake, the sheets pulled up under her chin, looking at him watchfully. 'Did you want something?' she asked.

'I was wondering about breakfast.'

'Is there any?'

'I don't think so.'

She turned on to her side, closing her eyes. 'Then that answers your question,' she said.

He stood, biting his lower lip. 'Are you feeling better?' he asked.

'Not very much, no,' she said.

'Should I –'

'No, nothing! Just let me be.'

He went out, closing the door.

There being no point in staying there, he left the house. He could walk to the Inns of Court. It would save a cab or omnibus fare and, besides, he needed the exercise. He struck out at a brisk pace, cutting down Portman Street and on to Oxford Street. The shopkeepers' lads were taking the shutters down, whistling cheerfully and calling to each other. Only the black-coated men walking firmly towards the City seemed to be unhappy. What had it all been for, he wondered? Those long years at school and at university? Were they only for this, that he should go from the fresh, sweet morning air, to some dingy room in a lawyer's office stinking of musty books? Would he ever whistle at his work?

Certainly, there seemed to be no opportunity for whistling or even smiling in the cramped outer office of Atkinson's chambers in Dr Johnson's buildings. So dark, so old, so dismal they seemed that it would have been no surprise if the good Doctor himself had walked in. No one had taken a scrap of notice of Hall. A harassed old man, who had introduced himself as Mr Atkinson's clerk (Hall supposed that he wrote the letters), had taken his card, put it in his pocket, waved him to a chair and forgotten all about him.

Other men who may or may not have been barristers came and went, one or two of them arguing with the clerk in language that may as well have been Hottentot, but all of them letting Hall understand that he was merely in the way. At last they departed, some to other rooms in the warren, others, carrying what seemed to be blue laundry bags and armfuls of papers, to the outside world. The clerk gave him a final look of pity tinged with contempt and went into a side room, slamming the door loudly.

He was alone with his thoughts, his only companion an antique long-case clock which ticked the seconds arthritically. As one might have expected, the face declared that the time was half-past three and chimed dolefully. Dust motes slowly settled in a thin beam of sunlight. An hour later the door burst open and a fat, sweating, red-faced man thrust his head round the door. 'Ellis?' he said.

'No, I'm –'

'Where is he?' the fat man cried.

'How should I know?'

He came into the room, producing a bundle of papers tied up in pink ribbon from a pocket in the tails of this coat and dropped them on the desk. 'Tell him from me, will you,' he said, pushing his face near to Hall's, 'that he's a bloody thief.' And, with a nod to emphasize the words, he left as quickly as he had come.

After a moment two doors opened simultaneously. Through one came the clerk. 'Who was that?' he asked Hall.

'I don't know. He didn't say. He left these papers.'

Through the other door an even older man dashed into the room and gathered the papers up. He read them, spectacles on the end of his nose, at a furious pace, occasionally licking the tip of an ink-stained forefinger to speed the process even further.

'Was there any message?' the clerk said, looking at Hall.

'Only that Ellis is a bloody thief.'

The older, shabbier man let out a barking laugh.

'Is this Ellis a client? Some criminal to be defended?' Hall asked. The other man lifted his eyes from the papers and looked at Hall. The clerk seized his moment and the papers and withdrew to his room, once more banging the door.

'That's Ellis,' he said, nodding at the door. 'And the description's fairly accurate. And you – what do you want?'

'To see Mr Tindal Atkinson.'

'What for?'

Hall's temperament had never been serene, and today it was being strained to breaking point. He had had no sleep, no food and a long walk. And now to be cast up in the company of these lunatics, then ignored and insulted, was too much.

'To get my bloody money back.'

The old man looked at him suspiciously. 'Money? What money's that, sir?'

'The money my father was foolish enough to pay for me to enter this madhouse!' Hall shouted.

'Name?' the old man said.

'Marshall Hall!' he cried.

The old man smiled (if the thin elongation of his lips could be so described) and held out his hand.

'Tindal Atkinson. I've been expecting you. Whatever kept you? You'll have to be a sight more punctual than this, my boy, if you're to make any sort of name at the Bar.'

'I've been –'

'No time for excuses,' Atkinson interrupted, ushering him into his room. 'Come in, come in.'

In contrast to the dinginess of the outer office, his room was extremely pleasant. A coal fire burned brightly in the grate; there was a big, old-fashioned desk, portraits on the walls and leather-bound books stretching from floor to ceiling.

Atkinson waved him to a chair before his desk and produced a bottle of wine from a cupboard. 'I usually have a glass of Madeira at about this hour,' he said. 'I find it sustaining.'

Hall nodded. A glass of wine would certainly not come amiss. Then he noticed that the old man had only put out one glass, which he proceeded to fill. The bottle was firmly corked and put back in its cupboard.

'So,' Atkinson said, smacking his lips, 'you seek an apprenticeship to the law.'

'Yes.'

'With me as your master in the mysteries of our craft?'

'My father had your name from our solicitor.'

'Did he? Did he now?' Atkinson smiled and took a sip more wine. 'Our whole fortunes are based upon the strength of our name with such people.' He nodded at Hall. 'There, you see, you've learnt something already! Madhouse or not, money well spent, eh?'

'I sincerely hope so,' Hall said.

Atkinson gave an airy wave of a hand. 'Not that I concern myself about money. And because your father's given a certain sum to my clerk does not mean that you will get a pupillage here, sir! Not so! Not so at all! I turn down far more men than

I take, let that be quite clear between us! *You* must bring something to *us*. Something of value greater than filthy lucre. Money can be given back. My clerk sees to all such things. The law is above pecuniary considerations.' He suddenly dived at his blue laundry bag and took from it a tattered black gown. He held it towards Hall. 'What do ye think that's for, eh?'

Hall shook his head.

'The hood, man. Look at the hood.'

He could see no hood, only some gatherings in the cloth. 'I haven't the vaguest idea.' He hazarded a guess. 'In case it gets cold in court?'

'Nonsense, boy! That's a relic of a hood, of times past when we didn't take any money at all. Not a penny piece. Do I hear you cry, oh-ho, so how did we live? Well, I'll tell you. A grateful client, saved from the rack or from being hanged, drawn and quartered, used to slip a coin or two in the hood when the lawyer's back was turned.' He thought about this for a moment. 'Come to think of it, unless the man had the gown on back to front, which would have seriously impeded movement and gesture, there was no other way to do it.' He brightened. 'So, there you are. The clerk in a barrister's chambers argues with solicitors, agrees a brief fee and out of that come our emoluments.' He leant across the desk. 'Are you taking all this in?'

'I hope so.'

'So do I. Or your poor papa's wasting his pelf, isn't he?'

'Speaking of money,' Hall said.

Atkinson drew back into his chair like a tortoise into its shell. 'Yes?'

'If I may say so, sir, I'm a poor man and I shall need –'

Atkinson came out of his shell abruptly, interrupting him. 'What *I* shall need is the significant fact before us. Wouldn't you say so?'

Hall ploughed on. 'I'm sure you do. But, you see, I've only recently married and –'

Atkinson shook his head, cutting in again. 'Foolish, if I may say so without prejudice. Very.' He leant back. 'Now, then, what do you bring to me, young man?'

'I sent you confirmation of my degree. Cambridge.'

'So you did,' Atkinson nodded. 'And a very indifferent degree it was too, if I may be forgiven for saying so. What else do you fetch to these chambers?'

'I work hard.'

'So does a cab horse, but I would scarcely embark upon the course of teaching such a beast the rudiments of advocacy.' He looked at Hall, his eyes glinting like steel through his spectacles. 'Well, sir? What else?'

'I know about –' Hall was floundering. What *did* he know about?

'What? What do you know about?'

'Medicine! My father is a doctor.'

'Then perhaps you should have followed in his footsteps.'

'Poisons!' Hall cried. 'Surely that would be of some use in a case of – murder?'

Atkinson shrugged, looking away. 'Such ripe and stinking meat as murder seldom comes within our compass here. All-round sort of practice, this.'

He looked at Hall again and smiled conspiratorially, rubbing thumb and forefinger together. 'Where the money is, though, eh?' He laughed delightedly, then cut his mirth short. 'And what else do you enter in mitigation?'

Hall was desperate. Had his life been so empty of value? 'Guns!' he exclaimed. 'I'm a crack shot!'

Atkinson gave another crowing laugh, clapping his hands together in delight. 'Oh, useful! *Most useful!* You could always ward off the relatives of your unfortunate clients. Come now, let us be sensible, young man. Have you any relatives of wealth and influence?'

'None.'

'All told, not a very enticing catalogue of virtues, I'm afraid. You're sure there's nothing else? No relatives who are bustling little Sussex solicitors, bulging with briefs?'

'Only one of my wife's. Her brother-in-law.'

Atkinson brightened. 'Now! Why didn't you mention him before?'

Hall shook his head. 'I don't like to trade upon them.'

'Good God!' Atkinson said, incredulously.

'And his firm only deals in probate. Things of that sort.'

'Money to be made there, boy.'

'Not by me.' He remembered something. 'And, of course – *yes*!'

'What?'

'I play cricket!'

'Cricket?'

Hall smiled. 'Oh, yes. Steady bowler, nothing flashy. But rather a decent bat.'

Atkinson looked at him in silence. Then he got the Madeira out again and poured himself another glass. Looking at Hall over the rim, he suddenly said, 'Stand up.'

Hall did so, and Atkinson examined him, head to toe. Then he slapped the pile of documents on his desk. 'Look at this lot,' he cried. 'Pieces of paper, what?'

Hall nodded, mystified.

'And so they are. But how much would you say all this paper's worth, eh?' He had taken on his crafty manner again.

'I've really no idea.'

'This paper's a grouse moor in Yorkshire, it's a house in Bryanston Square, it's a little place in Kent.' He banged the papers again, so hard that the dust rose from them. 'It's *money*!' He laughed, triumphantly. 'Twenty-three thousand pounds there! What do you think of that, then? Eh?'

'Incredible, sir.'

Atkinson thought for a moment, taking a gulp of wine. He banged the glass down. 'I'll take ye on!' he cried. 'I will! You said you can work – and I'll test that claim to breaking point.' He leant back. 'You're a good-looker. You carry yourself well. Such things matter to juries, mind. Yes, I'll take you on.'

'Thank you.'

'Who do you play cricket for, then? Village team?'

'No, sir. The Gentlemen of Sussex.'

'Do you? Do you, by Jove? Well, now, that puts a different complexion on things, I must say.' He looked at Hall approvingly. 'Gentlemen of Sussex, eh?' He waved him back into his seat. 'Sit down, man, sit down! I feel as if I'm addressing the dome of St Paul's. Now: your lessons begin. Are you ready?'

'Should I take notes?'

'What use would that be? A lawyer who can't remember simple facts has no right to be at the Bar. No, sir. *Listen.* I will explain to you my system, which has served me well these many years. My system is to master thoroughly the facts in the case. Then I write down my opinion as to the law of it without so much as a glance at the books.'

Hall was mightily relieved. 'Oh, that would be my system too, sir! Decisions of long-dead judges don't seem to be of the slightest –'

Atkinson held up a hand, his eyes almost bulging in their sockets. 'Do not complete that unfortunate sentence, sir! *Do not dare*,' he said, in a voice of thunder.

'I was agreeing with you!'

'No, sir, you were not!' Atkinson shouted. 'I was about to say that I then go on to compare my opinion in the case with that of the learned judges. In the books!' He hammered on the desk so hard that the papers rose and fell. 'The *books*!'

'Oh,' Hall murmured, crestfallen.

Atkinson rose to his feet. 'Ever heard of devilling?'

'I don't think so.'

'Well, now, devilling means that you feed on a mass of papers – commonly known as a brief – like a maggot on cheese. This brief will have been prepared by some illiterate villain of a solicitor. You will study this brief, searching out the law of the matter – in the *books*.' He waved his hand at the hundreds of volumes that lined the room.

Hall looked at them in despair.

'Then you will give your most unworthy opinion as to the best course of action for your master to take, noting it down carefully – and legibly. Then you will present it, with all good grace, to your betters. Hard work. *Devilish* hard work, what?' He gave a yelp of laughter. 'And not a penny piece will you get for it. Come along: you must make a beginning.'

He led the way into the outer office, where the clerk seemed to be continuing his interminable argument with the barrister.

'What do you think of all that, young man, eh?'

'It's very well, Mr Atkinson, and I will do it as best I can, but, sir, I need to earn money.'

At the mention of money the clerk and barrister turned to him, their mouths agape. Atkinson drew a deep breath and pulled himself to his full height, squinting at Hall down the length of his nose.

No one spoke.

Atkinson cleared his throat. 'As to that, well, we shall see. We shall most certainly see. But patience, my dear fellow, patience. Let that be your watchword.' He nodded to his clerk. 'Some work, here, Ellis, for this new member of our chambers. Plenty of work: he has an appetite for it.'

'Devilling?' Ellis asked.

'Devilling,' Atkinson replied with relish and turned to go back into his room. But in the doorway he swung round again to face Hall. 'One piece of advice I should have given you, for I proffer it to all the starters in the great race –'

'Yes, sir?' Hall asked, eagerly.

'Get yourself an air cushion. Finest invention of the century, sir! Benches in court are damnably hard, and you'll be spending year after year on 'em, watching your Master and learning. And never attempt to speak until I give you leave, for at present the orifice in your backside will be wiser than the one in your head.'

He looked around for appreciation of his joke, but Hall didn't understand it and the others had heard it before. Often.

'Year after year, year after year,' Atkinson murmured, as his door closed behind him.

Ellis took Hall's card from his pocket and looked at it. 'Mr Hall?'

'Marshall Hall. Both names together, please.'

'Has a ring to it – if ever it's rung,' Ellis grudgingly admitted. He waved a hand in the direction of the barrister. 'This is Mr Franklyn. Barrister-at-law, member of these chambers.'

'How do you do?' Hall smiled.

Franklyn nodded at him distantly.

'Can't find you a place in a room just yet,' Ellis went on, 'so, for the time being you'll just have to make do with a corner of the table here.' He went to a cupboard and fished out a pile of papers. He blew the dust off them. '*Rotledge* v. *Rotledge*,' he said, dumping the documents on the table. 'This should keep you going for a bit.' And then, agile as a monkey, he ran up a ladder on wheels that stood by a high bookshelf and ran his finger over the spine of the books until he found the ones he wanted, which he began to hurl down at Hall. 'Adolphus and Ellis, you'll be needing that. Carrington and Payne's *Reports*, *Nisi Prius*, Volume Eight, might well come in handy and *Choyce Cases in Chancery*, though that may be a bit antique for our purposes. Let me know when you've read it.'

He descended and from another cupboard produced an inkwell and a quiver of quills, which he put on the table. He saw Hall's look of utter despair. 'Don't look so worried, sir!' he said. 'Work steadily through. Take your time. That suit's been trickling on very nicely these last twenty years, so there's no hurry, none at all. *But do it right!* I'll not have Mr Atkinson made a fool of in court because you've been slipshod.'

Franklyn shook his head in sympathy. 'I spent two years on those papers,' he sighed, 'and the ones before 'em.'

'Now, Mr Franklyn,' Ellis cried, 'don't you go putting our new gentleman off his stroke!' He turned to Hall. 'First few months, I'll take the liberty of looking over what you've done. Between us we'll make it good. Just make sure you keep your quills sharp: I can't abide a splattering pen.'

He came closer to Hall, keeping his voice low. 'And, listen, a time will come when, if I like your work for us, I may just be able to sweep one or two crumbs from the master's table on to your lap.' He nodded, then whispered, 'I know about money – and the need of it.' He straightened and smiled. 'Now, I won't be disturbing you, Mr Marshall Hall.' He looked across at Franklyn. 'A word with you, if you please, sir. In my room. I might well have a little brief that would interest you.'

Franklyn was transformed by the news. His shoulders went back and his head came up. 'What sort of little brief?'

'Come along, sir,' Ellis said, firmly, leading him through the door, 'we're stopping Mr Marshall Hall's work.'

Hall looked at the books, papers and quills, and he groaned. Then he wondered about Ellis. He does much more than write letters and do the sums, he thought. In this dusty little world he has power. In fact, he'd be better off keeping in his good books than in those of old Atkinson himself. Far better.

He lifted the first paper from the pile and began to read.

At one o'clock (half-past five by the long-case clock) Franklyn swept him off for lunch in a chop house hard by Fleet Street. The meat was tough, the potatoes almost raw, and the whole swam in a greasy-grey liquid, but Hall was ravenously hungry and Franklyn didn't seem to notice what he ate. Indeed, much of his time was spent in exchanging legal gossip with various gentlemen wearing white bands at their collars, who, seeing him, hovered over them or poked their heads above the high wooden partitions that separated table from table in this dark establishment. The beer, however, was good. And when it came to paying their bill Franklyn explained that he simply had to change a sovereign, so that it wasn't worth their while to pay separately and Hall would be doing him a favour if he let Franklyn pay for them both. This came as a great relief to Hall: he had spent the meal surreptitiously counting the pennies in his pocket and wondering if there were enough there to settle with.

CHAPTER
EIGHT

They came out, blinking in the strong sun. The din of the traffic on Fleet Street rang in their ears. Franklyn stood on the pavement and let out a gratifying belch, tapping his chest. 'Fortified, I think, is the word to describe us, young Marshall.'

It was the first time that anyone had used that name and Hall's first thought was that Franklyn was talking about someone else. 'Oh, yes, indeed. Much better.'

Franklyn looked up at the clear sky. 'Far too good a day to waste on *Rotledge* v. *Rotledge*, wouldn't you say?'

'I have to get it finished.'

'Not today, you haven't,' Franklyn smiled, taking his arm. 'Nor tomorrow either. Come: we'll take a walk.' And he led the way towards Fleet Street, then the great bulk of St Paul's. 'Between ourselves, old Atkinson will be quite relieved you're not there. Saves him the task of teaching you something.'

Fleet Street was a solid pack of vehicles: horse-drawn open-topped omnibuses, their sides plastered with advertisements for Fry's Cocoa, patent medicines and the latest attractions at the Lyceum, the Alhambra and Her Majesty's, hansom cabs, growlers, broughams, dog carts and every other variety of wheeled object that one might imagine. The ammoniac smell of horse dung filled the nostrils but, like the crowded and jingling traffic, it was so much a fixed and eternal part of life that one scarcely noticed it. And then, mingling with this odorous brew, a steam engine puffed importantly over the cast-iron railway bridge that spanned the road, oily black smoke blowing down into the street from its brass funnel.

The pavements were as packed and noisy as the roadway: newspaper men streaming from their lunches to their offices, lawyers hurrying from the Inns of Court and back again, lady shoppers, their long skirts kept from the dust by a hook and chain arrangement; all was noise and movement.

'Ever been to the Old Bailey?' Franklyn shouted above the racket.

Hall shook his head.

'Ever seen a trial at all?'

Hall, feeling ashamed, again shook his head.

'Well, you're a strange cove to be wanting to be a lawyer, and that's a fact.'

'I saw a police court hearing when I was a boy. Christina Edmonds, the Brighton poisoner.'

'Very impressive.' He took his watch from his waistcoat pocket. 'Let's see what's happening at the Bailey. You'll learn more there than from *Choyce Cases in Chancery*.'

Hall's heart leapt. Now at last he would penetrate to the heart of the mystery, entering the high temple of his faith, the greatest criminal court in the Empire.

As they turned the corner to it, his immediate reaction was one of heavy disappointment. The building was old, grimy and deeply depressing.

Franklyn saw his face fall. 'What's the matter? Not impressed?'

'It's a slum!'

'It's Newgate Gaol,' Franklyn said, looking up at its stone squatness. 'The courts are only an afterthought. Take heart, friend. Wait till you get inside.'

The entrance was as forbidding as the exterior. A dark and narrow corridor ran the length of the building, with entrances to the courts off it. It was as crowded as Fleet Street and almost as noisy. White-wigged and gowned barristers were conferring with their clients and with the relatives, friends and benefactors of those clients. There were so many of them pressed into the small space that the most intimate revelations

89

had to be bawled and shouted to the low and echoing stone ceiling. Officials of the court hurried to and fro, hopelessly shouting names at the top of their lungs. One large family completely blocked Hall's and Franklyn's way, loudly weeping and lamenting and clinging to each other for support.

Franklyn pushed them aside without so much as a glance, let alone an expression of sympathy.

'Poor people,' Hall said, as they emerged on the other side of them.

'Biggest villains unhung!' Franklyn cried, not caring if they heard him or not. 'They're the Kelly's of Rotherhithe, and they've kept folk like you and me in hot dinners for a lifetime. Let's hope that they're passing on the family traditions unto the next generation.' He stopped at a door. 'Here we are. Court Number One. A decent little murder's on. I fancy it's what we need.'

He pushed open the heavy door and they went in. The terrible din of the passage could still be heard as the door closed, but it was at least somewhat diminished. It was the truly appalling stench that hit Hall first, and it was enough to turn the stomach of a slaughterman, a nauseous mixture of stale sweat, excrement and gas from the spluttering jets that had to burn, day and night, in the gloom. He wrinkled his nose in disgust.

Franklyn, seeing his expression, leant towards him. 'The stink of Newgate Gaol,' he explained. 'That's why the judge has a posy in front of him.' He nodded towards the small bouquet of flowers on the judge's desk.

'God in heaven!' Hall exclaimed, holding a handkerchief to his nose. 'He needs it.' He looked around the small, packed room, and saw what many had seen before him: that the busiest court in the land was a disgrace to justice. Such daylight as crept furtively into the place filtered through three high, dirt-streaked, square-paned windows. Before them the jury was packed along two rows of a high-backed cattle pen.

At right angles to them, high in a wood-panelled box, the

prisoner, a mild-looking little man, was doing his best to stay awake.

In the centre of the room, around a table piled high with papers, white-wigged lawyers kept up a low buzz of conversation among themselves. Another lawyer stood at a bench behind his colleagues. He was addressing the court, but his voice was scarcely louder than those of his gossiping learned friends and seemed to be having about as much effect on the proceedings. The red-robed judge, under a high canopy, was writing in a large ledger and seldom lifted his eyes from it. He could have been writing his memoirs, a sonnet, his will . . .

Franklyn found a space on a bench by the dock and unceremoniously shoved the occupants along so that there was room for him and Hall to sit. Hall could make no sense of the court, but Franklyn leant forward, chin on hand, eagerly listening to the advocate and occasionally nodding at some telling point. 'This man's good,' he said to Hall, in a penetrating whisper, 'isn't he?'

'Can't hear a word he's saying,' Hall complained.

'Really?' said Franklyn, surprised. 'Well, I suppose you get used to it.'

'I hope so.'

'Of course, the outcome's certain.'

'Is it?'

'Oh, yes. The fellow will hang.'

There having been a temporary lull in legal chatter at the table, his phrase rang out over the whole court. The prisoner turned lugubrious eyes upon them, unsurprised, and the judge cleared his throat. Franklyn half rose, dropping a sort of bob of his head in the judge's direction, which seemed to be an adequate apology. The judge went back to his book, and the counsel for the defence, not one whit abashed, resumed his droning address to the somnolent jury.

While her husband had been having his first bitter taste of the law, Ethel had risen, still feeling unwell. Her period had started, to make matters worse, and that always put her through extreme pain. She sat for a while in her peignoir, feeling more miserable than ever before in her entire life.

A cup of tea would have been pleasant, and she walked through to the kitchen to see if she could discover how to make one. But there was no guidance there, nor any form of heat.

She sat by the big table and cried for pain and for loneliness. She stayed there for a long time until, shivering with the cold, she went to her room to fetch a shawl. While she was putting it on, the bell of their door rang. Looking quickly in the mirror, she pinched her cheeks to get some colour back, pulled the paisley shawl tighter about her and almost ran to open it, desperate for company. Who knows who this visitor could be? A friend, even perhaps her mother, although that was almost too unlikely to think about.

She wrestled with the unfamiliar catch and threw the door open, smiling. But the smile faded when she saw who the caller was.

'Welcome home, my dear.' Ada smiled and leant forward, her cheek ready to be kissed.

Ethel pecked at it but still stood, door in hand.

'Aren't you going to ask me in?' Ada asked.

'Yes, of course. Do, please, come in.'

Ethel saw that a coachman was standing behind her sister-in-law, a great basket, covered in gingham cloth, in his hand.

'Bring that in,' Ada ordered, and the two of them swept past Ethel and into the sitting-room. Ada nodded to a place on the carpet. 'Put it down there, then you may wait on the carriage. I'm sure that Mrs Hall and I have much to talk about.'

The coachman did as he was asked and left them alone.

'Mrs *Marshall* Hall,' Ethel corrected, in a small voice.

Ada was pulling off her gloves. 'What?'

'It's what Eddie wants to call himself.'

'Does he now?'

'He thinks it sounds better.'

'He is at his work, I take it?'

'Since very early this morning.'

Ada looked round the room. 'This is all very nice,' she nodded. 'Tasteful.'

'Thank you.'

Ada shivered. 'Do you like a room as cool as this?' she asked.

'No. I'm freezing to death.'

'Then don't be such a little goose! Tell the parlourmaid to light the fire!'

'We haven't got one.'

Ada threw up her hands in horror. 'Why ever not?' she exclaimed.

'Because we can't afford one.'

'You can't afford *not* to have one, that's for certain,' Ada said, pursing her lips. 'And a cook?'

'No. We've not got one of those either.'

Ada shook her head. 'Thank goodness for my prophetic soul,' she said, kneeling and pulling the gingham cover off the basket. 'I worried in case your cook wasn't used to Edward's fads and fancies, so I brought one or two things I know he likes.'

She began taking dishes from the basket and placing them on the table. 'A jug of mutton broth, a salmon, game pie, a brace of pheasants, one of my special plum cakes – and one or two other little bits and pieces.'

'That's very kind of you.'

'It looks as though it was very necessary. Otherwise the pair of you would have sat here, hand in loving hand, slowly starving to death like the babes in the wood.'

'I'd have found out how to cook something.'

'Would you now? Have you ever cooked anything before?'

'No.'

'There we are, then.' She looked at Ethel reflectively. 'Would you not feel warmer if you dressed?' she asked.

'I've been – unwell.'

Ada understood. 'Forgive me.' She gave a regretful smile. 'Well, my dear, I must say I'm rather sorry.'

'What for?'

'That you're not – how shall we say? – bringing us good news.'

'What sort of good news?' Ethel asked, puzzled by the drift of the conversation.

'That you're preparing to be a little mother,' Ada smiled, patting Ethel's hand – though she was wondering, in view of her brother's passionate nature and what she feared of Ethel's character, how that happy outcome had been avoided. This girl was far too ignorant to have taken any means of preventing it, that was for sure.

'But how can you possibly tell?' Ethel cried, fearing for a moment that Eddie must have written to his sister, telling her of the state of their marriage.

Ada shook her head unbelievingly. This girl was as backward as a savage. 'If you had been . . . *enceinte*, then you would not have had your monthly sickness.'

'Is that true?'

'Perfectly.'

Ethel thought about it for a moment. 'Oh, goodness,' she said. 'It would almost make it worth while.' She thought again. 'Does it stop for good?' she asked.

'No, only until you have finished feeding baby. Unless, of course, you get a wet-nurse, which is to be highly recommended.' Ada got to her feet, smoothing down her skirt. 'Now,' she said, firmly, 'with your permission, I shall make us both a nice cup of tea.'

Ethel shook her head. 'You can't,' she said.

'Why ever not? Has Edward placed some embargo upon tea drinking?'

'No. But there doesn't seem to be any means of getting a kettle hot.'

Ada sighed. 'I want you to lead me to the kitchen and coal hole. Tea must be drunk, so, I suppose, a range must be lit.'

'You know how to do it?'

'No, thank God. It is a skill I have never had to acquire. But all things are possible if one puts one's mind to them. Even lighting a range.'

And at last, by dint of much effort in blowing the recalcitrant coals and pulling and pushing shelves and levers, light it she did, blackening herself considerably in the process. They sat before the glowing range, drinking their tea and warming their toes.

'You can't go on like this,' Ada said.

'No, I know we can't.'

'A woman can always . . . manage. But a man coming home from his work needs food. He needs comfort. He needs *ease*.'

'Yes?'

'To provide these things is our duty.'

'Is it?'

'Of course it is. It is why we marry.'

'Then I don't know what we shall do.'

'I do,' Ada said, putting her cup down. 'I know perfectly well, and I will brook no objection. I am going round to the Servants' Registry right now. I am going to engage for you a general cook and a skivvy for the heavy work. Parlourmaids can wait; footmen one can do without at a pinch. But the first two are essential to any home.'

'I've told you, we can't afford them!' Ethel cried.

Ada turned to her in the doorway. 'I want no argument about this. I can get a decent plain cook for £14 a year and a skivvy for half that – some young girl who'll be glad of the work. And I can think of no better way of spending my money.'

'I don't want your money!' Ethel flung at her. 'I've married your brother, not you.'

'It's my brother I'm thinking about,' Ada said, her face red with anger, 'make no mistake about that! I will not see him suffer!'

'*Suffer?*' Ethel shouted. 'Is that what you think marrying me has brought him? *Suffering?*'

'If he is to be given no food and no warmth – then yes!'

'These things *I* will give him. Now, please go, Ada, before either of us says something which we may later regret.'

'I came to help.'

Ethel looked at her coldly. 'I am quite sure you did, and you have done. But you're doing no good now. Please go.'

Ada fastened her bonnet strings and pulled on her gloves.

'See that Edward gets a meal from what I have brought,' she said. And, as an expression of charity in the light of this detestable girl's condition, she gave a peck of a kiss to her cold cheek and left.

Ethel waited until she heard the front door shut, then went into the sitting-room, gathered the foodstuffs into their basket, marched back into the kitchen and scraped the lot into the fire. She threw herself into a chair and felt better.

But she was hungry. And, she supposed, Eddie would be too when he came home. She thought about this for a moment, then went quickly into the bedroom and dressed.

Hall was beginning to notice the smells and squalor of the Old Bailey less, though his handkerchief was still in his hand. By listening very hard he could make out most of what counsel for the defence was saying. Franklyn, certainly, was completely engrossed, as were some of the barristers around the table. In fact, one or two were so captivated that they had given up their private deliberations and had turned round to face the speaker. The judge continued to write, but he seemed to have reached an amusing part of his great work and was smiling very slightly.

Hall looked at the jurymen. He was sure that, whatever impression this latter-day Demosthenes was making on his peers, he was leaving the jury as cold as Sunday's mutton. They were visibly struggling, in this foetid and stuffy room, to stay awake. And yet, he thought, the fate of the prisoner rested in their hands. Wasn't that the cornerstone of the whole edifice of the law? What matter if a lawyer was well regarded in the Inns of Court, what matter if chop-house gossip admired his juggling of legal precedent, if these men remained untouched? He jogged Franklyn's elbow and pointed to them. 'They don't understand a word!' he whispered.

Franklyn shook his head impatiently, unwilling to miss a word of the speech. 'Oh, take no notice of them,' he said. 'The judge'll tell them how to find when he comes to his summing-up.'

'But this is a disgrace,' Hall murmured. 'It's a mockery.'

Franklyn wasn't listening: he was translating a Latin joke that counsel had cracked to the mirth of all in court – apart from the prisoner and the jury, that is.

Hall didn't see the point of it either. He sat back, looking round. Was he to spend his life in this place? Was he to be like the ass at present on his feet? If the answer to those questions was yes, then he'd might just as well walk down to the Embankment on his way home and jump in the river.

And yet something was happening in this room. There was a structure here, however it might be being misused or ignored this afternoon. If a man could avail himself of that – the form, the opportunity – then all things could change.

Law, with its tomes, its clanking history, its Latin tags, its circumlocutions, was deeply dispiriting and tedious to Hall, a lead weight on his spirit. Ergo, he smiled to himself, since he was, whatever else, a most typical Englishman, it must be as wearisome to every other layman, including the men of the jury. They wanted what he had wanted when he came into this court: they wanted life, they wanted drama, they wanted to find a line that would stretch from their lives to that of the man in the dock. From these thoughts a certain warmth flooded his heart as excitement gripped his mind. He stirred restlessly on his bench. 'I have to go,' he whispered to Franklyn, who nodded absently, still listening to the argument.

*

Ethel, bearing bravely the great basket which Ada had left, walked through the streets around her home. One or two curtains twitched, and a few passing matrons turned at the sight of such a young, well-dressed woman, obviously of their station in life, descending to the duties of an errand boy. But Ethel ignored them. If she couldn't share a bed with her husband (and that thought was more abhorrent than ever to her), then she could certainly share a table. She would learn, and he would be proud of her.

She found a butcher's shop and bought some chops. The butcher promised to send his lad round every morning for orders, which would be delivered within the hour. The grocer made the same bargain, as did the fishmonger and the greengrocer. They all smiled; they all rubbed their hands and bowed her out of their shops. And they all knew a green 'un when they met one. Her sugar would be carefully mixed with white sand. Her bacon would be ever so slightly rancid. Her vegetables would be the indifferent produce kept at the back of the shop. Her meat would need teeth of steel and a digestion of iron. She would be rooked left, right and centre.

Her last port of call was a bookseller's where she bought a copy of *Mrs Beeton's Household Management*.

Once home, with this propped on the kitchen table, she fried the chops and boiled the potatoes and cabbage. For speed, she thought that they could be put in the same pot. That, surely, was a discovery that Mrs Beeton had been too slow to make.

By the time Hall came home the table was set, their new silver and china looking very well on the starched white cloth. (She would have to learn to master the mysteries of the copper in the kitchen corner, she thought. For now, she would get the address of a reliable laundry.)

Hall was full of admiration for all that she had done and ate the meal with every appearance of enjoyment – though he agreed with her that perhaps potatoes and cabbage would fare better in different pans. Now, the meal done, he pushed his plate aside and held out his hand to her across the table.

She took it, smiling at him. 'I will be a good wife to you, Eddie,' she said. 'I know there's some things that I just can't . . . can't do. But they're not the important things, are they?'

He shook his head, squeezing her hand.

'All the rest,' she went on, 'I'll do better than anyone's ever done them.'

He kissed her hand, then put it down. 'I've a surprise for you,' he said.

'What's that?'

'I called at our bank at lunchtime.'

'What for?'

'To see how our accounts stood.'

'And how do they stand? Almost collapsing, I would have thought.'

He shook his head, still smiling. 'No. That's just it, you see. I'd done my sums badly. Papa's allowance is £30 a year more than I thought it would be.'

She clapped her hands. 'Eddie! That's wonderful!'

'Yes, it is. And it's going to be for *you*.'

'Me? How? I don't want anything. Truly!'

'Just listen,' he insisted. 'Someone in chambers gave me an address of a Servants' Registry. So I went round there, straight from the Old Bailey – we lawyers just call it the Bailey, by the way – and I've hired a cook and a skivvy for you!' He sat back, beaming. 'There! I told you it was a surprise!'

Her eyes were on her hands in her lap. 'Yes,' she whispered, 'it is.'

'Aren't you pleased?'

'Of course I am,' she said, as she rose. 'Very pleased.' She wasn't smiling. 'I'll take these dishes now.' She piled the dishes on to a tray and went to the kitchen.

'Fine!' he called after her. 'I needed the table anyway. I've work to do.'

When she came back in, rolling her sleeves down, he didn't look up. He had taken the lamp from the side table and, in its light, was poring over a mass of yellowing papers and books.

She sat for a while, watching him work. But this was limited entertainment, and as the clock struck ten she rose, wished him good night and went to her bed.

He scarcely noticed her going. If the path to where he wanted to be lay through the thickets of *Rotledge* v. *Rotledge*, then he would hack them out of his way.

And he never, ever told her that the someone in Chambers who had directed him to the Servants' Registry had been Ada or that the windfall in their bank account had dropped from her well-stocked tree. He had to take a burden off his wife's shoulders, so Ada had insisted. The argument was irresistible and the secrecy inevitable. It never gave him a troubled thought.

The cook whom Ada had selected for them was good enough. She had a limited repertoire, and the days of the week could be accurately identified by what came to their table, but at least the shopkeepers, finding their goods returned *en bloc*, began to deliver edible foodstuffs – and at half the price they had been charging Ethel. As for the skivvy, she was a strong, good-hearted country girl, quite willing to work from six in the morning until ten at night, with a Sunday afternoon off each week and a half-day once a fortnight. Master and madam were pleasant folk, always ready with a smile, so what more could a body ask?

Mrs Beeton was put away, never to be looked at again, and Ethel passed the time by staying in bed until eleven, dressing slowly and then spending her afternoons, if they were fine, strolling past the shops and choosing what she would buy if she had the money. After that she would usually sit in the park for an hour or two, watching the carriages of the great folk go by as they took their afternoon drives. Sometimes she would think of Temple-Smith and wonder if she would ever see him again: he had to come home some time, she thought, and these, surely, would be the folk he would know. One day he would be there. His carriage would stop; he would open one of those shiny doors with the coat of arms on them and hand her up. She would be looking down on the dreary housewives sitting under the trees, waiting for life to happen, as the carriage, her carriage, bowled along to Park Lane. But, however hard she looked for him, he never came.

Wet days were a torment. They could be spent only on the sofa in the sitting-room, watching the light slowly fade on the white ceiling, the hours marked by Mary, the skivvy, rattling coals on to the fire.

Sometimes a friend from Brighton would be up in town for a shopping day, and she would enjoy herself then, showing the way around, being very metropolitan and a little bit patronizing about the manners and ways of the provinces. Once her mother came to stay for a couple of days, but she was taken ill while she was with them and a doctor had to be summoned, which caused more expense. Ada came very rarely and only when she was sure that Eddie would be at home.

Ethel would have liked to make some friends, but where could they be found? Not among Edward's set, that was certain. The occasional dinner party to which they were invited was ineffably dreary; no one at the table was under fifty, and the conversation resembled a tour of the Newgate Calendar.

So their days passed. Hall worked harder than he had ever done in his life, and she drifted slowly into an ocean of mindless boredom.

The autumn was upon them now, and day after day the house was shuttered by the grey, everlasting fogs of the city. London Particulars, Edward said they were called. Well, she wasn't very particular about them: they were silent gaolers to her hours. She ordered Mary to pull the sofa next to the fire, and there she lay. That, at least, was a change.

One day, when the grey light had faded imperceptibly into blackness, she must have slept well: when she woke in the firelight Hall was sitting in the armchair opposite.

'How long have you been there?' she asked, stretching.

'About half an hour.'

She struggled to get up, throwing the shawl that covered her over the back of the sofa.

He gently pushed her back. 'No, stay there,' he said.

She did as she was bid, looking at him watchfully.

'Not much of a life for you, this,' he said, after a time.

She said nothing.

'I think we need a change of air. Both of us. We should get away from town for a bit.'

She sat up now, leaning closer to the fire. 'Does that mean a visit to your parents? Brighton?' she said.

'No,' he laughed, 'it most certainly does not. What change would that be?'

'Where then?'

He kicked a smoking coal back into the grate, and the spurt of flames lit the corners of the room. 'I used to do quite a lot of shooting,' he said, 'and I enjoyed it.'

'I know you did. Well?'

'A fellow I knew at Cambridge, name of Ashburnham, has a father . . .'

'What of him?'

'Lord Ashburnham.' He looked at her. 'He's invited us down for the weekend.'

'Oh, Eddie!' she cried. 'When?'

'This Friday,' he laughed, enjoying her pleasure. 'His place is in Norfolk. Good sport to be had, I'm told.'

'Oh, never mind that!'

'It matters to me.'

'Oh, yes, but – what shall I wear?'

'Who cares?'

'I'll go and look through my things now!' She ran to her bedroom, and the time before dinner was happily spent as she tripped in and out, holding different dresses against herself for him to judge.

Now there was to be some life! Now, at last, there would be some *people*!

CHAPTER NINE

A wagon was waiting for them when they got off the train at the village halt. A number of other people, men and women, came from separate first-class carriages and converged on the same vehicle. They knew each other well enough, and talked at the same time in loud, self-confident voices, but they were strangers to Edward and Ethel. Their conversation seemed to concern itself entirely with the activities of other people, equally unknown to the Halls, so they sat in silence as the wagon trundled through dripping country lanes in the October dusk.

At last they came to a pair of cottages, recently built by the look of them, in the style of Swiss chalets, at either side of huge iron gates.

'Oh, they're nice,' Ethel whispered to Hall, 'picturesque.'

A woman emerged from one of them and swung open the gates. With a nod from the coachman, they drove on to the crunching gravel of Lord Ashburnham's drive, which curled for another half mile past banks of rhododendron bushes shiny in the drizzle. Then the house came into view – a massive Georgian structure with a colonnaded portico and spreading wings. Ethel gasped in wonder.

'Hope to God we don't get dumped in Little Ease,' a woman next to her was saying to her husband.

Ethel thought the woman was speaking to her. 'Is that a village?' she asked politely.

The woman laughed, showing her teeth like a startled mare. 'It's a bedroom,' she said, 'though I'd defy any human being to sleep in it. Cold as charity, damp as a dungeon and every plumbing fixture in the house runs through it.' She turned to stare indiscreetly at Ethel. 'Your first visit?' she asked.

'Yes,' Ethel said, blushing under her gaze.

'Well, if mine hostess offers you the Venetian room, plead advanced arthritis and galloping consumption, that's my advice, because if you haven't got them now, you will have by the time you leave.'

The wagon came to a halt under the portico, and the passengers clambered out, still loudly chattering. The coachman and his lad piled gun-cases, bags and portmanteaux on the steps; footmen gathered them up and carried them into the house.

A grey-haired old man and his plump wife were at the doors of the house, greeting their guests, but the names they called were of no help to Ethel, as they all seemed to have nicknames or truncated Christian names, such as 'Boodle', 'Stuffy' or 'Minnie'. They could have been the Earl of this, the Duchess of that or just some plain mister from the City. She couldn't tell. When she and Edward clambered up the steps, however, they were received more formally, though the smiles and handshakes seemed to be sincere enough.

As they were the last of the wagon party, their host and hostess shepherded them through the marble-floored and high-pillared hall towards an open door, through which could be seen a massive log fire burning in a highly ornamented grate, where their fellow guests were gathered.

'I do think that introductions are a bore,' Lady Ashburnham was saying, 'and one never remembers the names. Some of the people you probably know anyway, and the rest you'll soon find out about.' Ethel smiled rather nervously and nodded. She didn't know a soul there, and everyone was so busy chattering among themselves that she didn't think she ever would. Lord Ashburnham was at Hall's side, apologizing for the absence of his son. Seeing to the beaters, he explained.

Their hostess resumed her seat at the tea table by the side of the fire and, aided by a trio of housemaids, passed cups of tea to the new arrivals, enjoining them to forage for themselves for food. The old hands needed no invitation; they were already piling their plates high with muffins, sandwiches, scones and cakes, still talking loudly. Hall made his way through them, emerging after a few moments with food for himself and his wife. 'Always reminds me of the first day at a new school,' he said to her, 'but it settles down after a bit.'

'I hope so,' she said and bit into a muffin, inwardly cursing as the butter ran down her chin.

Lady Ashburnham came over to them. 'Oh, good,' she was saying, 'you've managed to get some food. I always think that tea-time is like nothing so much as feeding hounds, don't you? Everyone barking and baying at once.'

'We're doing very well,' Ethel smiled.

'I'm so glad.' Lady Ashburnham examined her. 'You've some butter on your chin. Don't mind me telling you, do you?'

'Not at all,' Ethel said, dabbing at her chin with a handkerchief.

'That's it. All gone.' Lady Ashburnham nodded. 'I've told them to take your things up to the Venetian Room. You'll be wanting to tell your maid and your husband's man to unpack.'

'No, I –'

'I'm sure you'll be happy there. I always think it's the nicest room in the house.' And, with a smile and a nod, she was gone.

The Venetian Room lived up to its reputation: as Hall remarked, the all-pervading smell of damp led one to suppose that the Grand Canal ran past the window. And the coal fire burning in the grate did little to dispel the chill that caused their breath to cloud on the air.

'Only for three nights,' he reassured her.

'Which we'll be lucky to survive.' She shivered.

He shrugged his shoulders. 'I'm going to find a bath. It'll give you a chance to get on with your dressing.'

Eventually the bathroom was found with the help of a passing footman. It was, apparently, the custom of the house to provide hip baths in their rooms for guests during the hunting season, but mere pheasant shooting could claim no such coddling.

An elderly couple were before him, so he had to wait in the corridor for his turn to face the terrors of the rumbling gas geyser that heated the spluttering trickle of water.

By the time that he returned to their room, Ethel was dressed and huddled over the fire, a blanket from the bed around her shoulders.

'You took your time,' she grumbled, her teeth chattering as she spoke.

'There's only the one bath.'

'You'd better hurry all the same. We're going to be late.' She pulled the blanket around her more tightly.

'Are you going down to dinner in that?' he asked as he brushed his hair.

'It would be the sensible idea.' She nodded towards the bed. 'In the absence of your valet, I've laid your clothes out.'

He saw them in the glass: his evening suit and starched shirt. He turned to her. 'What are you wearing?' he said, dreading the answer.

'My blue silk.' She saw his expression. 'Do you think it's too low-cut or something?'

'No. It's not that.'

'What then?'

'My dear, they don't dress. Not on Friday. Dress is for tomorrow and Sunday.'

'You might have told me.'

'I'm sorry. I thought you knew.'

She got up, the blanket falling to the ground. 'No. I didn't know. But then, I'm not so accustomed to gracious living as you.'

'It's I who should be sorry. I should have said.'

'Yes, you should!' she flung at him. 'Well, what *am* I to wear?'

'What you had on this afternoon?' he ventured.

She gave him a withering look and flung open the doors of the vast wardrobe. 'Oh, God, I'm hating this!' she said, as she threw dress after dress on the bed.

By the time they came down there was no sign of any of the company. They poked their heads into the room where they had had tea, but that was in darkness, only the flicker of the dying fire casting a faint glow into the room.

They stood in the hallway, wondering what to do. Then she heard voices from behind another door. Opening it, they saw that all the guests were assembled, standing in a semi-circle round the fire. All heads turned to them as they came in, and the conversation stopped.

'We were beginning to think that you were lost – or that you'd changed your minds and gone home,' Lady Ashburnham said, the hint of a reproof in her voice.

'Entirely my fault, I'm afraid,' Hall said. 'I lingered too long in my bath.'

'Good God, you deserve a medal – or a place on the next polar expedition.' A young man came towards them with a smile.

'Stephen!' Hall cried. He turned to Ethel. 'My dear, may I introduce Stephen Ashburnham? I told you, we were together at Cambridge.'

Stephen took her hand and held it, smiling into her eyes. 'Mrs Hall,' he said, 'your wretch of a husband underestimated your beauty quite grossly. I don't care what arrangements Ma's made, but I'm taking you in.'

'What's this about my dinner arrangements?' his mother said.

'I've just messed them up. You don't mind, do you?'

'Oh, it's all informality and pot-luck tonight,' she said, 'so I don't suppose it will matter.' And she began shepherding her guests into pairs.

Hall gave his arm to a woman who was introduced to him simply as 'Duchess'. Whether that was a nickname or her title, he had no way of telling, but he should have known that she was the reigning society beauty of last season. Maybe she would be supplanted by next June, but for now she ruled London absolutely.

Lady Ashburnham, for all her faults, had a certain aesthetic sensibility, and the pairing of his looks and her grace was irresistible. Besides, it would be too blatant to send her in with the Marsh boy, who was, of course, the reason for the Duchess's sudden interest in field sports. Not that Lady Ashburnham cared about any of that in the slightest: it was a great catch getting the Duchess to the party, and naturally all concerned in the affair could be relied upon to behave with perfect discretion and *savoir faire*.

In fact, had Lady Ashburnham but known it, the charms of the young baronet were beginning to pall upon the Duchess. He was such a demanding young man that his place at the very centre of her heart was in some danger. So the Duchess was relieved to find that the house party included among its men this wonderful specimen, so tall, such a perfect head, held with divine pride, and his eyes, searching, with a hint of deep feeling. Might he, she wondered, be the one who would – ? But that was to gallop ahead of the field. Certainly, she would give him the favour of her attention during dinner and learn if the promise he held could be fulfilled. She was a great believer in fate. Ah, kismet, she would sigh as her maid roped her pearls around her white throat.

As they walked in their stately procession towards the dining-room, she tripped slightly, which was unusual for her, since she prided herself on her perfect carriage and deportment. Hall's strong hand was immediately at her elbow, supporting her.

'Tell me,' he was saying, 'are you really a duchess?'

'The *Peerage* tells me so,' she smiled.

He was silent for a moment. 'And the Duke . . .?'

'Is your conversation made up entirely of questions? You are a walking penny catechism.'

He laughed. 'Forgive me. It's probably because I'm a lawyer.'

Oh, so that was what he was, she thought. Bad, but not completely beyond the pale. But she said, 'I always thought lawyers to be grey, dusty little men.'

They were at the table now. A footman pulled out her chair and she sat, with Hall at her side. 'That,' he was saying, 'is because you only ever see us in grey wigs.'

'Surely,' she said, 'if one can help it, one never sees lawyers at all.' She tried to steer the conversation into livelier channels, though the task wasn't easy. He had seen none of the plays or musical comedies that everyone was talking about; Covent Garden might as well have been in Mongolia; he did not seem to have read any of the latest books. But still, ignorant as he undoubtedly was, he had a curious, thrilling magnetism. He was very, very attractive. She wondered if he knew it.

He was telling her of his hopes and ambitions, and she allowed her mind and her eyes to wander towards the girl he had come down with; obviously his wife. Pretty enough, the Duchess conceded, but she doubted if there was any real depth to her. That she would doubtless discover when the men went off to their bird slaughter tomorrow and the women were left to their own devices.

If Hall had found a radiant and stirring beauty at his side, Ethel was less fortunate. Stephen was attentive and kept up a rattle of conversation, but his talk was all about her husband and his splendour. She was taken yet again through a college cricket match when Edward had saved the day, then over an assortment of grouse moors where he had bagged more birds than all the other guns together.

Lady Ashburnham rose and the ladies rose with her. Ethel thought wistfully of her last dinner party, when she had been able to sit listening to man talk, drinking her liqueur with the scent of the young officer's Turkish cigarette wreathing her hair. But tonight she must sip her coffee in a chilly drawing-room and listen to chatter about people she had never met.

The men, flushed now with their port, joined them. But

they had no sooner come than their hostess decided that, given the rigours of their travel that day, they must all be longing for their beds. Really, Ethel thought, the woman is a tyrant. *She* wasn't at all tired. An hour and a half in a first-class railway carriage was scarcely an expedition to the Khyber Pass. There was, however, no choice. Wives found their husbands and made their way to the Great Hall, where a brilliance of candles, each in its gleaming brass holder, was placed on a table at the foot of the sweeping staircase. As each couple passed, a servant handed the gentleman a candle, and the lights bobbed their way up the stairs to the bedrooms.

By the end of dinner Hall had been thinking of a dilemma: he had never shared a bed with his wife, but tonight there seemed to be little choice in the matter. She could scarcely expect him to ask his hostess for a separate room or to sleep in one of the hard chairs. He wondered how she would deal with the problem. Please God, he thought, let there be no recurrence of the wedding-night hysteria.

As things turned out, he needn't have concerned himself. The fire in their grate had burned low, and the temperature had dropped even further: the very water that had been set out on the washstand had become so cold that a film of ice had formed on its surface. Ethel was chilled to the very bone; her discomfort extinguished all other thoughts. A decanter of brandy, glasses and a biscuit barrel had been placed on a side table near the bed. Hall poured a glass each for them. Her teeth rattling on the rim, she gulped the fiery liquid, coughing at the bite of it, but it was very necessary. It would have been physically impossible to sip and dally. She asked him to turn his back while she undressed and shivered into her nightdress, but she was in such a hurry that she didn't look to see if he had complied.

When she had clambered into the high bed, she found that a stone hot-water bottle had been placed between the sheets.

Pulling her nightdress down over her toes, she held it gratefully between her feet.

Lying on her side, her back to him, she heard him undressing: first the winding of his watch, then the clatter as it and its chain were put on the dressing-table, then the loose change from his pockets rattling beside it. After that a silence as he, presumably, was taking off his clothes and putting on his nightshirt.

The bed creaked as he got in. He blew out the candle, and the room was in darkness, only the dying glow of the fire lighting the ceiling.

He had his back to her. 'Good night,' he said.

She pretended to be asleep and didn't answer.

They lay, both awake, listening to the sounds of the great house. The floorboards in the corridor creaked. Someone was passing, as silently as possible. A door was heard to open and then softly close. After a moment the sequence was repeated, but by someone going in the opposite direction.

Curiosity got the better of her. 'There seem to be a lot of people about,' she whispered.

'Yes,' he said, knowing full well the meaning of these footsteps in the night.

'What can they be doing?'

'Paying calls on their friends,' he said, the gurgle of a laugh in his throat.

'At this time of night?'

'When better – for some friendships?'

She realized what he meant. 'Oh,' she said.

In a room beneath theirs, the muscular rump of Sir Harry Marsh, Bart, rose and fell rhythmically over the placid body of the Duchess of Wintrincham. Eyes open, staring at the shadows on the ceiling, her hands relaxed on the pillow above her head, she wondered, not for the first time, if he considered this to be a form of physical exercise.

'If you're still awake in an hour's time,' Hall was saying, 'you'll hear the whole thing again – but going the other way.'

'Does it always happen?' she whispered.

'It's the way they live.'

'Disgusting.' She was silent for a time. 'Eddie?'

'What?' he said, his voice muffled by the blankets that he'd pulled up to his eyes.

'You've stayed in houses like this before.'

'What of it?'

'Have you done that sort of thing?'

'No, course not.'

'Is that true?'

'Yes. Now, go to sleep.'

The hot-water bottle had cooled. She pushed it to one side. 'How can anyone sleep in this ice-house?'

He was silent and still for a moment. Then he turned towards her and put a hand on her shoulder. 'You're shivering,' he said. He put his arm round her, pulling her close, his knees behind hers so that she was cradled in his lap. She stiffened, but the warmth of his body was so comforting that she slowly relaxed with him. She felt his penis harden against her and tried to pull away from it, shivering again, but he held her tightly.

'I've waited so long,' he whispered.

'Don't, oh, please, please don't,' she sobbed, fearing the strength of it, the force of it, this hard, throbbing thing that pressed into her.

His hands were lifting her nightdress and moving over her body. 'I will be gentle,' he was murmuring.

She turned on to her back and looked up into his face. He kissed her; she opened her mouth to him. He rose above her, kneeling astride her body, pulled his shirt over his head and threw it on to the floor. She touched him gently, feeling the hair of his body. Then, almost against her will, she let her fingers circle his penis and marvelled at the silken softness of its skin.

He groaned in ecstasy. Urgently, still holding him, she drew him on to her and held him, feeling him moving like some blind animal under her hand. With a gasp he thrust hard into her, and fierce, shooting agony flamed through her. She cried out, but he thrust again and the pain mounted. She pushed him away, crying, moaning, but he wouldn't let her be. It was as if he were tearing her apart. At last, fighting, hitting him with all her strength, she broke away, but he came back to her, holding her, pressing so tightly that she thought she would suffocate. Then she felt a warm wetness against her legs and he was still.

She put a hand on the wetness. Not daring to look at it, she sat up and scrubbed frantically at it with the hem of her nightdress.

'Oh, God! Oh, God! How could you?' she sobbed. 'To spew *that* over me!'

He tried to put a hand on her, but she threw him off. 'It happens!' he said. 'That is what happens. It's how a baby is –'

'Not with me!' she cried. 'It must never happen with me again!'

He sat up and tried once more to hold her, but she rounded on him, shaking with hate. 'If you ever touch me again,' she hissed, 'I swear before God Almighty that I will kill you!'

He fell back against the pillows.

She got out of bed and pulled the heavy curtains open. The frosted light of the moon lay in the room. She slipped into her peignoir. 'Fetch me some light,' she ordered.

He got out of bed, found matches and lit the candle. He walked towards her, the warm glow of the flame between them. She looked away quickly from his nakedness.

'I am sorry,' he said, as he gave her the candle.

She took it and went towards the door.

'Where are you going?' he asked.

'To the bathroom. I am unclean.'

Sir Harry Marsh, seeing the light coming towards him down the corridor, huddled in the shadow of a doorway. Ethel passed by without seeing him, although he recognized her.

'Well, I'll be damned!' he said to himself, under his breath. 'The attorney's wife. Who ever would have thought it?'

As he went back to his room, he wondered which of his fellow male guests could be the lucky fellow. The only name that fitted the bill was that of young Ashburnham – and he's supposed to be the lawyer's friend, Sir Harry mused. He shook his head. There were limits to behaviour, and if Ashburnham were the girl's lover, then he was in danger of transgressing them. He made a mental note to tell Phyllis all about this. She liked titbits of gossip. The next day, after breakfast, he mentioned the sighting and was mildly surprised by the depth of her interest, but then, he thought to himself, one could never fathom women.

Hall stood in his butt, cradling his gun, the taciturn man who was to be his loader behind him.

It was a beautiful day, the stubble still rimed with frost in the hard sunlight and a distant, skeletal line of trees throwing fierce shadows on the hard ground. Far away he could hear the sounds of the beaters moving towards him. He swung his gun to his other arm and thrust his cold hands deep into his pockets as, eyes narrowed, he looked up into the almost white sky.

Stephen called out to him from the next butt. 'All right?'

Hall nodded, still looking at the sky.

'Sleep well?' Stephen shouted, smiling.

Hall glanced at him, then looked away quickly. 'Not particularly,' he said. And that, he thought grimly, was more than true.

'It's really too bad of Ma,' Stephen was laughing. 'Putting you in that hell hole. ''Fraid new guests always get it. Sort of initiation ceremony.'

'The room's well enough,' Hall grunted.

'Next time you come –' Stephen was saying, but, before he could complete the sentence there was a whirring of wings as the birds rose. Hall's gun was already pressed comfortingly into his shoulder and, swinging with perfect rhythm, he fired one barrel, not needing to look at the flap and break of the dying pheasant as it fell, then the second, and passed the gun back to the loader, all in one smooth, free flow. His other gun was already up and firing, the smell of cartridges mingling with the sweet, frost-sharp air.

Dogs were barking excitedly, and the line of guns was an almost uninterrupted roar of fire.

'This,' he thought to himself, 'is truly to *live*.'

For the first time since his marriage he might have called himself happy.

Immediately after breakfast Ethel had pleaded a headache and gone back to her room. It had served her mother well enough, for all those years, she thought, so there was no reason why the same excuse shouldn't be pressed into service on her behalf.

A maid had already cleared and lit the fire. Ethel huddled up to it, the eiderdown from their bed wrapped around her shoulders. The top of her legs and her stomach still hurt, and she massaged them. She had once heard the word 'rape', spoken in a scandalized whisper, pass between her mother and some crony of hers over their teacups. When she had asked them what it meant, they had looked uncomfortable, and her mother had told her to leave the room, but the friend had muttered that it was what happened to a poor woman when a beast of a man 'forced his attentions upon her – *down there*'. That was what he had done to her. She had been raped; that man, whom everyone liked, whom everyone thought was so good, so handsome, had raped her. He was worse than the lowest of criminals in his sordid courts, and she only wished that there was some way in which she could tell the whole world just what sort of a man he was and see him brought to justice.

It was all too horrible to think about for long, and she determined not to, but then a truly fearful thought flashed into her mind as she wondered if he had been telling her the truth when he'd said that the wetness that had stained her body made babies. If he was, then she must be pregnant. Today she wouldn't think of it. She wouldn't think of anything nasty at all. She made herself think of sitting in a warm garden in a faraway country, where she could live alone and without fear.

She must have slept for some time, but she was awoken by a tapping on her door. Lady Ashburnham came into the room, carrying a glass of milky liquid on a silver salver. 'Are you feeling better, my dear?' she asked, putting a cool hand on her forehead.

'A little,' Ethel whispered.

Lady Ashburnham handed her the glass. 'Then drink this, and it will complete the cure.'

Ethel took a sip of the medicine and looked up at her. She wondered, briefly, if she could pour out her troubles, but she knew she couldn't. The nightmare must never be spoken of, not to anybody.

'It's a recipe my old nurse used to make up for me. Thank God she had the wit to write it down before she died.'

'What's in it?'

'Oh, I haven't the vaguest idea: I leave Cook to see to it. But I wouldn't be at all surprised to find that good French brandy played its part.'

'It's very nice,' Ethel said, sipping some more.

In fact, it was a choice mixture of laudanum, cinnamon, brandy and milk, a sovereign specific against most ailments, guaranteed to bring ease of labour and a good night's sleep to any nanny, as her charge snored into silence.

'Now,' Lady Ashburnham said, taking the empty glass, 'what you need, my dear, is some good fresh Norfolk air. Come: let's go and see what our brave hunters have done with their day. You'll need to wrap up: it's always dangerous to go from a hot and stuffy room such as this into the chill of outdoors.'

The rest of the women were already assembled, but Ethel was

pleased to see the beautiful Duchess smile at her and move up to make a space for her to sit.

'Mary Ashburnham tells me that you've been feeling unwell,' she said, laying a solicitous hand on Ethel's.

'A headache. That's all.'

'But such things are terrible. Are you better now?'

'Much, thank you.'

The wagon was rolling down the drive, the women chattering like starlings. The Duchess glanced at the depressing view, then turned back to Ethel. 'And your visit here – are you enjoying it?' Her practised eye watched eagerly for the response. Nor was she disappointed, as Ethel blushed.

'Quite well, thank you.'

'I'm so glad.' She slipped a hand into the crook of Ethel's arm. 'Now, let's while away the tedium of this absurd winter picnic with a really good gossip. Tell me, do you know Edie Farquhar?'

'I don't think so.'

'Well, all that I can say is, you've been lucky. She is rapidly turning into a complete dragon. At the very end of last season she decided, quite out of the blue, that she would give some sort of ball. My dear, I ask you! The house is a mausoleum, pure and simple, and the poor dear orchestra was hard put to not to break into the funeral march. Naturally, hardly anyone turned up. I mean to say, who would, willingly? One had to be there, of course, but a more ghastly evening I have never spent in all my life. I tell you all this because now that we all know you, and like what we know, an invitation card from her may well fall on to your mat. When it does, take my advice and get your cutlery boy to take it straight back with "Not known at this address" written very large all over it.' She leant back, enjoying Ethel's pleasure in her chatter. 'You and that handsome husband of yours are bound to be made much of,' she smiled. 'And so is that good-looking Ashburnham boy.' Again she watched for Ethel's response and, as she expected, her companion's eyes opened a little wider.

In fact, Ethel was trying to remember who the Ashburnham boy was. Ah, yes, she thought, he was that hero-worshipping bore at dinner. She frowned at the memory of his praise of Edward.

Even better, the Duchess thought. She's attempting a pretence, but she's not fooling *me*. 'Stephen, isn't it?' she said, sweetly.

'I believe it is,' Ethel said coldly, still thinking of her husband.

Little minx, the Duchess thought. Oh, what devious people the middle classes were, to be sure.

With more such pleasantries and chatter, the journey to the coverts passed very agreeably for them both.

Tables loaded with food – game pies, cold chickens, legs of ham and sandwiches – had been set out in the scant shelter of a hedge, and a large pan of soup bubbled on a spirit stove. Dogs ran around barking, looking for scraps, and the full household of servants attended to the guests.

Most of the gentlefolk had shooting sticks, and with these rammed into the cold ground they perched and ate as though famished but managed, somehow, to keep up a continuous flow of loud conversation throughout.

Ethel wished that her husband hadn't been so selfish as to neglect to bring such devices for them, and she stood self-consciously trying to manage a napkin flapping in the wind, a full plate of tough chicken, her knife and fork and a glass of wine.

She was disappointed that the amusing Duchess had wandered away from her to chat with other people – people who seemed to be able to make her laugh too.

Edward, of course, was at the centre of a circle of stick-sitters, all leaning forward, congratulating him on his shooting. One of these acolytes was Stephen Ashburnham. While laughing at a joke of her husband's, his eye had lit upon her standing alone. He immediately pulled his stick from the ground and came over to her.

'This is awfully bad,' he said. 'The most beautiful woman in the whole party left like this to fend for herself.'

'I'm perfectly happy, thank you,' she said.

'Happier still if you had somewhere to sit,' he smiled, plunging his stick into the ground for her.

She sat on it, giving him a grateful smile, but managing to keep her balance on the wretched thing wasn't quite so easy as it looked. She teetered dangerously backwards and forwards. He took her plate and glass. 'That chicken looks fearfully chewy to me,' he said. 'Let me get you something else.'

The Duchess, taking the place in Hall's circle that Stephen had vacated, observed these gallantries with a happy smile and turned her attention on the handsome husband.

As the servants were piling the dirty plates into hampers after luncheon, Lady Ashburnham rounded up the women for the journey back to the house – except for the Duchess, who was not to be dragooned by anyone and who insisted, to Harry Marsh's surprise, on staying to view the sport.

Lord Ashburnham, a man of liberal spirit when it came to the social niceties, accepted this revolutionary proposal with alacrity and shepherded her to Hall's butt. The Duchess made a moue of disappointment at her lover, and took her appointed place. 'This young fellow,' the old man cried, 'is far and away the best shot among us, so if it's sport you're after, dear lady, stick by him.'

Hall gave her a nod, then took a gun from his loader. She had sense enough to let him concentrate on his shooting, though after the first couple of drives all the beaters' efforts couldn't put up the sort of game that they'd had in the morning. So by mid-afternoon Hall and the Duchess had plenty of time for conversation, and the loader, trained to discretion, withdrew slightly so that they could talk undisturbed. Frozen to the marrow as she was, she learned a great deal about him: how his father had bought him his first pistol when he was seven (what an extraordinary thing to do, she thought to herself), and how he nearly killed an old man on Brighton beach with it as he fired at the 'O' in some lettering on a hoarding behind which the poor gentleman was enjoying the sea breeze; how his legal career had really begun with his being dragged along to the police station by the irate old man who was, by the grace of God, unpunctured; how he scared off the notorious burglar and murderer Charlie Peace (of whom she'd never heard) by a timely display of his firearm when the villain was reconnoitring their grounds.

But then, when he had told her about his year's stay in Paris and she had asked him the reason for this interruption in his university career, he grew uncommunicative and looked away. Suddenly he faced her again, and it seemed as if he were about to blurt out something of significance, but at the last moment he changed his mind and stood, head bowed, his hands thrust deep into his pockets.

There's something there, she thought, that might well repay delicate inquiry. There would be time enough.

As the winter dusk was beginning to draw on, he showed her how to aim the gun, standing behind her, his arms round her shoulders, steadying the gun in her hands. By good chance a lone bird flew above them, and he lifted the gun for her. He told her when to pull the trigger, and the creature fell earthwards.

'You've a natural eye,' he said.

'Do you think so?'

A dog was already retrieving the bird, and when it came back to them, Hall took it from the dog's jaws and handed it to her.

'A souvenir of the day,' he said.

Hiding her shudder of revulsion, she took the trophy. 'I shall insist that I eat this for my dinner,' she said. 'Or do you think I should have it stuffed and mounted?'

He laughed. 'It won't be ready to eat for a few days yet. It has to be hung first.'

Before they could say more, old Ashburnham was leading them back to the carriages and wagons. 'Pretty good bag, I'd say. Not a bad day's sport.'

No, not bad, the Duchess thought. Not bad at all.

As soon as the other ladies had returned home, they had been given beef tea to revive them after the privations of their day. Then, when life had returned to their chilled limbs, they had gone to their rooms, some saying that they had letters to write, but all, in fact, seeking the comfort of bed, the better to prepare themselves for the delights of the evening and the night to come.

All, that is, except Ethel. Apart from its freezing temperature, the Venetian room was a place where memory, kept at bay so far, might come flooding back. So she stayed by the fire alone, flicking through the pages of the society magazines. She was interested to see that some of her fellow guests were written about or portrayed in the pages, and she was now able to put names to a few faces. Oh, how she could drop these glittering names into conversation, she thought, when they got back to London, if only she had someone to converse with.

The light in the room began to fade, but she sat on, dreaming by the fire. Maids came in to tend to the coals and to clear away the deep bowls from which the guests had drunk their beef tea. They looked at her curiously, hoping that she would move before they had to set for tea. Ethel took the hint and rose. She wandered over to the long windows looking out over the parkland. It would soon be night. She shivered and, under the gaze of a cheeky-looking young girl who was already putting away the magazine she had been reading, went out of the room and into the wide passage that led to the Great Hall.

She didn't know where to go in the silence of the house, and she felt a fool standing there. When a footman came down the stairs she pretended an interest in one of the antique statues but, to her embarrassment, found that she was peering, with some concentration, at the Dying Gladiator's private parts. To simulate purpose, she strode back into the passage and through the first door she came to. This was evidently the library, as books covered its walls from floor to lofty ceiling, and a sombre desk in the middle of the room was piled high with more volumes. Had there been light or warmth in the room, she might have settled there, though the chances of finding some nice book seemed a bit remote, but it was too dark and too cold, and she went out again.

At least, she thought, as she tried the next door, she was getting a tour of the place. It would have been silly if she'd gone back to their tiny rooms in Seymour Street without having seen it all. So she inspected the music room, with its grand piano and racks of sheet music, the ballroom, the great state room, in all its unused and forbidding grandeur and then, at the very end of the corridor, a pretty little room with flower-painted walls whose windows opened out on to a pillared terrace and small garden.

It was the only room in the house where she had felt happy and at ease. She sat by the window, not minding the cold, and thought of the lucky people who could live in a house that held a room such as this. To be able to come here, day after day, watching the hours go by and the seasons change – that, surely, would be to know contentment.

She heard voices in the distance as the women came down from their rooms and then the loud masculine voices of the shooting party as they stamped into the hall, but she sat on, indolently, as if she were enjoying a warm bath.

The light went, but she remained in the darkness, looking up to the star-filled sky, and, in that peace and quietness, she let memory in. And she could face it. What Edward had done to her was savage and cruel, but, surely, all men were not as he? And he would not do it to her again; she wouldn't permit him to. Together they could make a life. She would find some friends; he would occupy himself with his work. They could really be quite cosy.

Determined now, and at peace, almost willing to forgive her husband (though never, ever to forget), she rose, stood for one last minute looking out over the silvered garden, then quietly went out.

When she entered their room he was at the mirror, energetically brushing his wet hair, a brush in each hand. The sight irritated her; she had told him, over and over, that with hair as curly as his, it would resist any attempt at taming.

He stopped for a moment, looking at her in the glass. 'Wherever have you been?' he asked. 'We were all worried about you.'

'There was no need. I just wanted to be on my own for a while. Nothing wrong in that, surely?'

'You're all right, though, aren't you?'

She gave him a cool look and opened the doors of the wardrobe, picking out her blue silk frock. How could he be so insensitive?

'If you've finished dressing,' she said, 'then perhaps you wouldn't mind going downstairs.'

He pulled on his evening coat. 'No, I don't mind in the slightest. Don't be long, though, will you?'

She sat on the edge of the bed, fingering the silk. What she would really have liked to do was to warm herself thoroughly by the fire, wrap herself in every shawl and blanket she could find and then huddle into the bed and sleep. But she knew that that would create the most awful fuss, so she stood by the fire and began to take off her clothes.

Dinner was a much more formal affair than it had been on the previous night, and the guests were marshalled in strict order of precedence as they went into the dining-room. Ethel took the arm of a nondescript, middle-aged man who was introduced to her as Jacko someone-or-other and was something in th

Foreign Office. She had a spark of hope and, as they walked, asked him if he knew Mr Temple-Smith. He didn't, other than recalling vaguely that he was in the Embassy in Paris.

His interest was in growing tropical flowers in his hothouse, and he was sure that she would be as fascinated as he was by their cross-pollination and care. In a brief lull, as he tried to recall the name of particularly rare species, she turned her attention to the dinner companion on her other side. This was Harry Marsh, who was deep in a muttered dispute with the Duchess, so there was no help to be found there.

Edward, she saw, was being made much of by all those around him and obviously thoroughly enjoying himself. She sighed. If only they knew, she thought, the sort of man he was. But in this house you could do no wrong if you could shoot lots of little birds.

Her neighbour remembered the name of the flower and soon launched again into his discourse.

The candles flickered into a blur before her; tuberoses gave off their overpowering scent from high silver vases; and smilax trailed everywhere. She would have given anything to close her eyes and sleep, but she had to nod and smile, to ask questions and be impressed by the answers and, all in all, to behave like a lady. She picked at her food, sipped her wine and did her best.

After dinner the men drank their port quickly – not so that they could enjoy the drawing-room company of the ladies but rather so that they could go to the gun room, drink whisky, tell stories and leaf through the game books with Ashburnham.

Hall, glass in hand, was looking at the guns in their cabinets. He took a fine piece out, balanced it in his hand and gave a nod of appreciation. 'Purdey,' he said.

'Fine pair of guns,' his host agreed. 'My pride and joy, those.'

Hall looked up at him. 'One day,' he said, 'I shall have a pair of guns like these.'

His host laughed. 'God help the little brown birds of Norfolk when you do,' he said. 'There'll be no sport for the rest of us!'

'Oh, I'll leave you one or two,' Hall said, as he regretfully put the gun back.

Ashburnham put a hand on his shoulder. 'Just like to let you know, Marshall,' he said, 'that my doors are open to you at any time. You'll always be welcome at my shoots.'

'Thank you. I'll take you up on that, I warn you.'

'Splendid!' Ashburnham came a little closer to him. 'M'wife and I are a little bit concerned about that pretty little wife of yours though. You sure she's enjoying herself? I mean to say, is this quite her sort of thing?'

Hall looked away. 'She's . . . very delicate,' he said.

'Oh, the poor soul! Air a bit bracing for her down here, is it?'

'I think so.'

'Then maybe she'd be happier staying up with her chums in town.'

Hall frowned and took a gulp of whisky.

'Mind you,' Ashburnham went on, 'that bloody Venetian room would freeze the balls off a brass monkey. I'll make damn sure you get something better next time.'

When the men came back to the drawing-room, Hall found that his wife had excused herself and gone up to bed.

The Duchess sympathized and came across to him, carrying a glass of brandy. 'I do know how she feels,' she said. 'I was telling my dinner companion,' and she glanced across the room at him, 'young Harry Marsh there, that I've an awful fear that I'm starting with a headache too.' She sat beside Hall. 'On the other hand,' she said, in a low voice, 'I may not be.'

'I do hope not,' Hall said, receiving the message clearly, as her knee brushed against his.

'So do I,' she sighed. And then, as she flicked a piece of stray cotton from the hem of her dress: 'My room is directly underneath yours. Such a pretty view.' She paused for a moment, looking up at him. 'In daylight.'

'Or at any time, really,' he murmured.

'Quite.'

She put her coffee cup to her lips and he took a sip of brandy, leaning back in his chair. 'I asked you a question last night.'

'Did you?'

'On our way into dinner. About the Duke, your husband.' He leant towards her. 'Isn't it a pity that he couldn't be here?'

'Oh,' she said, smiling, 'he has many interests. The estates keep him very busy. He's up at the Scottish house now. Spends a fearful amount of time there.'

'What a shame.'

'Isn't it just?'

When Hall came to their room Ethel was asleep, curled into the far side of the bed. He saw that she had taken the long bolster and put it at her back, running as a barrier down the length of the bed.

He leant over the fire, and all the business of the day, which had kept memory at bay, fell away from him. He was back again in the long and dark tunnel that had no ending or light. How was he to travel down it?

His marriage was a farce, a travesty, but whom could he tell? His family had warned him about her often enough, though, he thought bitterly, they didn't know the half of it. He couldn't face his parents, his sister, and say to them, 'You were right. I've failed – again.' And yet if he did that, what then? Separation? Divorce? He shook his head at the thought. He could not leave her.

He went over to the bed and looked down at her. Her face was calm, peaceful and lovely. He could not leave her because he loved her. No diversion, no release such as waited him in the room below, could alter that. It was for ever.

He groaned aloud in his misery, undressed quickly and got into bed. Even in her sleep, she moved away from him. He lay on his side, his back to her and her blasted bolster, and, wide-eyed, he saw the night through.

And the Duchess, before she slept, crossed him off her list. There were some horses that, however promising they looked in the paddock, didn't come up to snuff in the point-to-point, hesitating at the first fence. The young attorney was clearly one such, and there was nothing to be done about it.

The world was a big place, with lots of handsome men in it. Men, she thought, ruefully, of her own class. Breeding, in the end, will out.

She snuffed her candle and slept the sleep of the just.

CHAPTER
TEN

They left by the milk train on Monday morning. It stopped at every gate post, but it did get into London by half past nine. Hall saw Ethel into a cab and caught an omnibus to his Chambers.

Atkinson was there before him, though, standing in the outer office and rubbing his dry hands. 'Been mixing with high society, I hear, Marshall,' he cried, giving his barking laugh.

'And low,' Hall muttered.

'Well, now, I can see that you're a man of parts! Oh, yes, indeed! No need for us to worry about fat brief fees for *you*!'

'Mr Atkinson, there's every need,' Hall said.

'So you tell me. Such a day may well dawn,' he smiled. 'But not yet awhile. You've not been called yet, young fellow, nor even taken these stupid examinations, have you now?' He paused, looking Hall up and down as he took his hat and coat off and hung them on his peg. 'You're a hard worker, though, I'll grant you that.'

'Thank you,' Hall said, sitting at his desk and pulling a pile of papers towards him.

'So I think we ought to get this new-fangled damn thing out of the way and get you called.'

'The Bar examinations?' Hall said, appalled at the thought.

'Don't look so petrified.' And, like a conjuror, he whipped a sheet of paper from his inner pocket and slammed it on the desk. 'Part One you're excused for some reason to do with that appalling degree of yours. That is what they tell me. And here,' he said, tapping the paper, 'is the full range of questions for the part you must take.' He turned towards his door, saying, over his shoulder, 'They say the examination's on Thursday morning. I'd be there if I were you, stupid waste of time though the thing undoubtedly is.'

Hall looked at the questions. 'Isn't this a strange examination if I see the questions before I sit it?' he asked.

Atkinson turned back. 'Strange isn't the word for it,' he said. 'But I don't want you to do anything at all for the rest of the week but write your answers out. As you do each one, bring it to me, and I'll put right what's wrong.'

'Thank you very much.'

'Then all you've got to do is to try to remember what we've agreed when you get into the examination room and write it all out again. Think you can do that?'

'I'll have a damn good try.'

Tom Ellis had come in during the latter part of this conversation and he leant over Hall's shoulder, running his stubby forefinger down the questions. 'I'll be getting you the books for question one,' he said, and climbed up his ladder.

For the next three nights Ethel saw little of him. He came home late, bolted his food and then, before the skivvy had had a chance to clear the table, he thrust the plates aside, dumped evil-smelling books on to the table and started writing without a word to her.

She had tried asking him about the examination, but beyond telling her that he simply had to pass it he said nothing. She would, as the rules she had set herself dictated, go to bed on the stroke of ten, leaving him at work. She was always asleep before he finished.

On the Thursday morning he was still there, pacing the room, learning lines, apparently, from a sheet of paper with his own handwriting on it. It was all very strange. She rang the bell for the skivvy to tell her that she could bring up the coffee, but nothing happened. She went to the kitchen to investigate, found that the coffee had boiled over and, knowing that he wouldn't want to be late, poured a cup there and took it into the dining-room.

But he was gone, leaving the room a mess of paper. She put the coffee down and started to clear the stuff away. She would have wished him good luck, she thought. She had reminded herself, as soon as she woke, that she would have to do that. Well, he could probably manage without her good wishes.

Manage he did. Like his degree, the result was not sparkling; he never could remember lines or regurgitate arguments, but he had sweated through the paper. He had satisfied the benchers of his Inn sufficiently for them to award him a pass.

If Ethel had thought that the pressure of work would slacken once the Bar examination was out of the way, she was mistaken. All through the winter, spring and early summer of 1883 he worked relentlessly. Atkinson was a hard task master, and as fast as Hall had worked through one brief for him, another would fall on his desk. Then with a moment's notice he would be hauled from his desk to accompany the old man to this court or that, where he would sit by the hour, listening to him conduct his cases. Worse than the boredom was Atkinson's habit of suddenly leaning towards him and, in a voice that penetrated the farthest reaches of the building, asking him to outline the next steps forward, the next question in an examination-in-chief or, even more startling, his opinion of the conduct of the learned judge.

It didn't do to let attention wander.

Then, on a stifling evening in June, he came home wreathed in smiles. When Ethel asked him what had pleased him so much, he disappeared into his room, only to reappear in a new barrister's wig and black gown.

'What do you think of that, then?' he cried, arms held out.

'You look very fine,' she said. 'But why are you dressing up now?'

'Dressing up? *Dressing up?* I'll have you know, my girl, that you are now speaking to a barrister-at-law!'

'But you've been that for months.'

'No!' he cried. 'I had to pass my examination, then I had to be called.'

'Called by whom?'

'The benchers of my Inn. Honestly, I've told you all this, time and again. You don't listen.'

'I do.' She shook her head. 'But it's all very puzzling.'

He sat down by her side. 'No, it isn't really. Listen: if a man wants to be a barrister, he has to belong to one of the Inns of Court. Now, I belong to the Inner Temple.'

'Oh, I know that.' She smiled, relieved to be on familiar ground. 'And you have to eat dinners there or something.'

'That's right. That's to prove that you really are there and learning something.'

'I see,' she said, frowning.

'And the Inns are run by the benchers – they're judges, Queen's Counsel, all the big toffs. And today they called me.'

'You still haven't told me what to, though.'

'The Bar, ninny!' He leant closer to her. 'It really just means a bar that separates, in court, ordinary folk and people like me.' He smiled with pride. 'I'm a barrister. I can now plead in any court in the land! *Anywhere!*' He sat back with a laugh of joy. 'I've done it!' He threw his arms up to heaven in triumph. 'I'm a *barrister*!'

She nodded. 'That's good. Well done, Eddie.'

'I should jolly well think it is.'

'And does that mean we'll have more money now?'

He got up and took his wig off, throwing it on the table. 'It will, one day.'

She was appalled. 'Not now?'

'No, not just now. I have to get known. I have to be briefed. It takes time.'

'Oh, heavens,' she said. 'How much more time?'

'How should I know? Months, maybe years. I don't know.'

She got up and went towards the kitchen. 'I'll go and see what's happening to our dinner.'

'I thought you'd be pleased,' he said, his triumph draining away.

'Oh, I am. But I'll be even more pleased when we no longer have to sponge off our families.'

He took off his gown. In his bedroom he stuffed it and his wig into his very own blue bag.

Work went on much as before, his nights spent in devilling for Atkinson, his days in trudging from court to court and sitting, as an unwilling spectator, while other men fought the cases – and collected the brief fees.

When he was free, which was seldom enough, he'd play tennis in the Temple gardens. He had only recently taken up the game, but, because it was his nature to be, he was passably good at it.

He tried to teach Ethel, but she, encumbered by a long and heavy skirt, a high-necked blouse, a stiff collar and a hat, found the game hot, tiring and tedious. And she could never manage to hit the ball.

Then, when London was at its most stifling in the summer heat, the Long Vacation came, with promise of escape. But he, mad for his new sport, had accepted a round of country-house tennis parties on their behalf, and that really was too much for her. To be thrust together with people who either ignored or patronized her, forced into the hateful closeness of a bed with a man she was beginning to loathe *and* expected to make a daily fool of herself at a children's game was beyond endurance. Downcast, he said that he would release them from all invitations, but this she would not allow him to do. It would be a relief to be shot of him for a time. So she insisted that he went to his tennis parties.

'But what will you do?' he asked.

Her lip twisted in a humourless smile. 'Why concern yourself about that now? It hasn't bothered you all year.'

'I shan't go if you don't come with me,' he muttered.

'Oh, for God's sake!' she cried, 'Go, please!'

'But you . . . I mean –'

'I shall stay with Mama for a while. The sea air will do me good.'

'Are you sure?'

'Oh, how many more times?' she sighed.

And there it was: they were to spend the summer apart.

As her hatred for him intensified, his love for her grew. He was not tempted to join the midnight promenades in the country houses in which he stayed, and the guests concluded that he was handsome but really a dull old stick and a typical lawyer, though pleasant enough to have around and a good partner at lawn tennis. They might have reflected on the fact that a man with such a cannon shot of a serve and such energy on the court could not be quite as dull as all that, but it never occurred to them.

As for his wife, she soon fell into the way of being a single daughter again, listening to her mother's complaints, reading quietly to her when she lay in her darkened bedroom, helping with her at home and accompanying her on return calls.

She quite enjoyed these decorous parties; none of the middle-aged or elderly ladies said anything to ruffle or disturb her – once, that is, that they had delivered the inevitable, delicately phrased questions about whether she was anticipating a happy event. Her mother became as adept as she at dodging the question. 'Poor dear Ethel,' she would whisper, 'is, like her unfortunate mama, *delicate*.' And the old biddies would cluck their tongues and nod sympathetically.

But one night, inadvertently, Ethel let slip to her mother that she was indeed delicate. *Down there*. When Ethel saw how her mother's interest flared up at this, she could have bitten off her tongue for mentioning it. But her mother was not to be gainsaid and pursued the topic vigorously. Ethel managed to give the impression that marital relations between her and

Edward were perfectly ordinary but that she suffered some pain both during and after she had, as her mother put it, 'fulfilled her wifely duties'. The upshot of this was that her mother took her to consult the family physician. She had wanted to be present while he saw her, but Ethel put her foot down at this: there were some things too private even for a mother's presence.

Indeed there were, the doctor thought to himself, as he conducted his examination. The girl, though married a year, was still a virgin.

He told her to dress again, then sat beside her. 'Is there anything you want to tell me?' he asked, gently.

She shook her head, not looking at him.

'Is the present state of affairs any fault of your husband's?'

She was tempted to say that it was, that it was entirely his fault, but when it came to the point she couldn't do that.

'It just hurts me so much,' she whispered.

'I can only ask you to have more courage. Let the ... marital act be completed.' He stood, looking down on her. 'And then, my dear, you must always remember that pain is a cross which *respectable* women have to bear.'

'Pain? Even after –?'

'Oh, yes. Only very debased women indeed have any joy in such things.'

'I don't think that I have enough courage. Not for that,' she said.

He put a fatherly hand on her shoulder. 'Don't think of it,' he advised. 'Think only of the happy outcome, when you are blessed with a son of your husband.'

She could cheerfully have slapped his smug face: no thought could be more appalling than that. But she whispered, 'I would be grateful if you would tell none of this to Mama.'

'Of course not.' He smiled. 'It is a secret between us.' He helped her to her feet. 'Now you run along and be a good and brave little wife, of whom we can all be proud.'

To her mother, as they drove home in the hansom cab, she

said that the doctor had found nothing physically wrong with her.

Her mother leant back, her eyes closed. 'That's a relief,' she sighed. But she was worried; her daughter was still pale and uneasy.

The very next morning an event occurred that went a long way towards setting Mrs Moon's mind at ease. They were having their breakfast silently, as usual, both reading their newspapers, when there was a loud ringing of the front-door bell. Startled, Ethel's mother got to her feet. 'Whoever can that be at this hour?' she cried, running towards the window and pulling the lace curtain back. She was reassured. 'Why! It's Edward!' It was fortunate that she had her back to the table and didn't see the colour drain from her daughter's face.

Within a moment he was in the room, bringing with him the man smells of tobacco and shaving soap. Under her mother's smiling eye, Ethel was the complete and dutiful wife, kissing him and allowing herself to be kissed as her mother bustled off to get him coffee and bacon.

Ethel waited until the door closed, then faced him. 'What on earth do you think you are doing here?' she asked.

He took her hands. She let them lie coldly in his. 'I had to see you.'

'Why? I'm not ill.'

'Because I was missing you most dreadfully.'

She took her hands away and walked to the window. 'It is all arranged. I will come back to you, to our rooms, when your work starts again.'

'I couldn't wait so long.'

She sat in the chair by the window and looked at him. 'What do you propose to do now? You can scarcely stay here. My mother's not well enough to have you in the house.'

'We're not going to stay here.'

'*We?*'

'Yes, *we*!' He crossed the room quickly and knelt by her side, pulling an envelope from his pocket.

'What have you got there?' she asked.

He dropped the envelope into her lap. 'Open it.'

She pulled open the flap and shook pieces of pasteboard on to her skirt. 'What are these?'

'What do they look like?' he cried, his head back, smiling.

She looked at one more closely. 'Railway tickets. And steamer tickets.'

'They are! My darling, I'm going to make up for everything to you. I neglected you all last year, leaving you on your own in those poky rooms. And I'm sorry for it, so sorry –'

He buried his head in her lap, trying to kiss her hands, but she quickly pulled them away.

It was at that moment that her mother came back into the room. She stopped as she saw them, smiling at the romantic spectacle. Dr Moon had never gone on his knees to *her*, not even when he had proposed.

'I've brought some hot coffee,' she said, putting the tray on the table.

Edward got up, smiling back at her. He really was a most dashing man, Mrs Moon thought. Ethel's a very lucky girl. 'It's so nice to see you, Edward,' she said. 'I do hope that you'll be staying with us for some time.'

'I'm afraid not,' he said. 'As a matter of fact, I've come to sweep Ethel away.'

'Oh?'

'Yes, we're going on a holiday of a lifetime – to the south of France, Italy, Switzerland, Germany. It will be wonderful!'

'We can't afford it,' Ethel said, looking away.

'Too late for that now! It's all paid for, everything!'

'Then get the money back. We're not going.'

Mrs Moon was scandalized. 'Ethel! Don't be such an ungrateful girl!'

Hall turned to her. 'Tell her, Mother dear, tell her how much good it will do her.'

'Yes, of course it will,' her mother said, her lips pursed. 'There's no question, Ethel! If Edward's gone to all this trouble just for you, then you've got to go. My goodness me, I wish I'd had the chance!'

Ethel looked from one to the other. 'You're both determined, then?'

'I'm afraid we are, my love,' Edward said, smiling.

Ethel sighed, leaning her head against the back of the chair. 'When do we begin this extravagance?'

'We sail on the midnight packet tonight!' He gave a roar of laughter, clapping his hands as if this were a great joke.

Mrs Moon gave a squawk of alarm and cried out that there was a great deal to do in a little time. But Ethel, unsmiling, got to her feet and went to the door. 'I'll begin my packing,' she said.

They travelled cheaply for English people of that time and kept away from hotels like the Domenice, where they had endured their honeymoon. Auberges, pensions and village inns were their resting places now.

He was gentle, courteous, considerate; he made no demands other than to be near her. When she wished to be silent, he walked quietly at her side; when she felt the clouds of sadness descending, he would delicately and subtly lead her back into the light. If she craved company and excitement, he would find a café or restaurant where there would be music and a crowded, noisy room, and there they would sit as he invented silly stories to make her laugh. And all of these changes of mood he would anticipate before she knew of them.

They walked a great deal along mountain paths that led to a fine view, then down into alpine meadows with the gentle tinkling of cow bells and the sweet smell of the wild flowers all around them, through town streets and into dark-shadowed, cool churches where they could seek out this or that masterpiece of art, Baedeker in hand.

Gradually, without even noticing it, she began to feel stronger and more at ease in his company. The sight of him coming towards her no longer filled her with fear; imperceptibly, she stopped hating him and came near to accepting him as a friend.

Lake Como was her favourite of all the places they visited and he, seeing her love of the place, counted their money and booked them into an hotel on the lakeside. It was a hotel that had begun with palatial hopes at some time in the 1850s but had quickly realized its proper station in life and settled for dusty elegance. Her room may have been small, but from its small cast-iron balcony it had a fine view of the width of the lake and, on the distant opposite shore, the town of Bellagio. It was his custom, early in the morning, to swim in the clear waters of the lake. She would sit on her balcony, brushing her long hair, still in her nightdress and peignoir and watch him. Always, before he dived from the wooden jetty before the hotel, he would turn and look for her and, having found her, wave and smile.

She watched him and wondered why she couldn't love him. He should be so easy to love – god-like in looks and stature, charming in manner and living only for her. Why then? It was no longer the terrors of a shared bed that lay between them; throughout the holiday he had, as a matter of course, booked separate rooms and never hinted in look, gesture or word at the possibility of making love. When he kissed her it was as a courtier, on her wrist or forehead. Passion seemed as remote to him as it was abhorrent to her. But there was something in his eyes when she caught him looking at her, something that wasn't lustful or even friendly, some quality that she couldn't define but that made her infinitely uneasy and held her growing feelings for him in check. So far she could go – but no further.

He was swimming in the gold-dappled lake, the wet curls of his hair gleaming in the sun. When he was so far from the shore that it was difficult to see him any more, he lay on his back, floating, without effort, enjoying the warmth on his body. Then he turned and dived down into the depths. She hoped that he was all right and wondered how, if some terrible accident befell him, she would manage all the difficulties of getting home alone. But he came to the surface, blowing water from his mouth and swimming for the jetty, his strokes strong and sure. She got up and went into the room to dress. He was always hungry after his swim, but he wouldn't begin breakfast on the hotel's terrace until she came down. She would have to hurry.

In the late afternoon, when the heat of the day was beginning to die, they took a boat for Bellagio and sat amidships while the boatman stood on his platform, sculling them across. How she loved this place, she thought: the mountains around them, purple in the light, their white-painted hotel and the straggle of narrow streets beyond it. To live here would be like finding again the peace of the garden room of the Ashburnhams' house in Norfolk. A secluded place, where she was not threatened. But could she live here with her husband? If he stayed as he was now, then it might be possible. But could he?

The boatman brought them to a flight of marble steps that led to a small promenade. Edward gave the man money and asked him to wait for them. He handed Ethel solicitously out of the boat, up the steps and into the town.

There was a great noise of banging and rattling as the shop-keepers took down their shutters for the evening's business, and the streets were already filling with the people, all dressed in their best, beginning the calm, leisurely but serious business of the evening stroll, the *passegiata*, in families or in amorous pairs (watched over, at a discreet distance, by a black-clad duenna). The young men walked alone, proudly, glancing at their reflections in the shop windows with assured approval and trying to catch the eyes of the girls with their families. The Englishman and his wife walked among them at their pace, her hand lightly upon his arm, parasol negligently held on her shoulder.

'No churches – not this evening,' she said.

He put a hand on hers. 'No. Today is for people.'

A young Italian man caught her eye and, for a moment, she

held his gaze boldly. But when she smiled it was at her husband. In this company of handsome, conceited young men he had no rivals, she thought. All the same, she took another look at the young Italian. 'And such people,' she sighed.

Hall saw what had happened and smiled with her, proud that her light-coloured beauty was attracting such attention. He held her a little closer and whispered in her ear, 'When we are old and very rich, all the fuss and bustle of life over and done with, we shall come back here.'

Her smile faded and she looked up at him, frowning. 'I can't think that far ahead.'

'Oh, I can. We shall buy a little house looking out over the lake. It will have a terrace and flowers in big pots, and we can sit and be easy.'

She stopped by a shop window and looked in it. Then she turned to him. 'You will still want to be with me – through all the years between now and then?'

'Yes. I can't think of a life without you. There isn't one, not for me.'

She thought about this for a moment, biting her lower lip. He felt her grip his arm tightly. 'Buy that house now, Edward. Then all could change between us, I know it could.'

He looked at her in the window, and there was in his eyes that mysterious expression that so confused her. 'The battle's not yet fought and won,' he said, his voice low and grave.

'Battle?'

'Oh, yes.'

'It was a silly thought anyway.' She shrugged. 'We haven't the money.'

'But we shall have,' he said, praying fervently that some chance hadn't just been lost. He looked along the street and saw tables set out before a small *albergo*. 'Let's sit for a while,' he said, 'and drink some wine.'

They sat contentedly enough, watching the passing show, until it was time to go back through the narrow streets to the waiting boatman.

That night there was a perfect moon over the mountains, which made a silver road across the dark waters. There had been a papist celebration in the city of Como at the other end of the lake, and now flotillas of small boats were coming home, each one with a lamp burning in the prow. People in the boats called to each other, their voices full of laughter.

Ethel stood on her balcony, unable to sleep, watching them. London and Seymour Street seemed far away; she wished them even further. If only one could hold a happy moment in time and stretch it to eternity, she thought.

She looked at the balcony to her left on the floor below. She knew that that was Edward's room, and she saw that he too was looking out over the lake. She was about to call to him to share her joy, but the words died in her throat. She went into her room, closing the sun-cracked green shutters behind her.

CHAPTER
ELEVEN

The bank manager opened the cardboard folder on his desk, shot his starched cuffs until they covered his wrists and, frowning, ran his finger down a column of figures. The sounds of the London traffic were hushed and distant. Hall, on the edge of his chair, cleared his throat. The manager's moving finger stopped and he looked over his pince-nez at him, thinking that he was about to speak. But Hall smiled nervously and shook his head.

The manager, having got to the end of the figures, pulled a piece of paper from his drawer, dipped a pen in the inkpot, shook off the superfluous blood-red ink and, in a flowing copperplate, wrote. He looked at what he had written and shook his head, more in sorrow than in anger. 'I fear that we have a total sum in overdraft of fifty-three pounds, eight shillings and fourpence,' he said.

'My wife has been unwell. A holiday was vital for her health's sake,' Hall said, his voice sounding unnaturally loud in the small room.

'Illness is a misfortune,' the manager said, 'but improvidence is a calamity of our own making.'

Hall was not to be sermonized at – certainly not by this man. He sat upright in his chair. 'I don't consider that I've been improvident,' he said.

The manager gave a grim smile and tapped the sheet of paper. 'The bank is not a charitable society designed to provide for your wife's health,' he said.

'Damn it all, man!' Hall cried. 'You'll get your money back. The overdraft is only temporary.'

'Indeed we shall, Mr Hall. But what I must ask you now is – when?'

Hall thought for a moment, his hands clenched in his lap. 'Obviously, I can't say that. You know what a barrister's life is like.'

The manager sat back in his chair, his legs crossed, one hand judiciously supporting his chin. 'I'm afraid I do,' he said, 'but that doesn't answer my question.'

Hall didn't respond. His mind was racing. He couldn't approach Ada again; she had already done more than she should for them. His allowance from his father wasn't due for another fortnight, and it wouldn't go anywhere near settling the overdraft. Where to turn?

'In the meantime,' the manager was saying, 'I'm afraid that the bank will not be able to honour any further cheques presented against this account.'

Hall looked up at him. 'We have a choice,' he said.

'Have we?' the manager murmured, doubting it.

'Yes. I want you to lend me a further fifty pounds –'

'Mr Hall!' the manager said, as if an improper suggestion had been made.

'Only for the afternoon.'

'I'm sorry, but –'

Hall pulled his watch and chain from his pocket, the tie pin from his cravat and the wedding ring from his finger. He piled them on the desk. 'And here's your security,' Hall said, already getting up.

The manager's eyes boggled at the sight. 'We are not a pawnbroking establishment, sir.'

'No matter!' Hall cried, going towards the door. 'Tell your cashier to give me the money.'

Time was of the essence, so he took a cab to Hatton Gardens. There, in jewellers' shops whose existence was unadvertised and unguessed at by the public at large, Hall went from back room to back room, examining stones, both cut and uncut, as they were poured from chamois-leather bags on to squares of velvet. Money was offered, laughed at, adjusted a little, shrugged at, adjusted again. At last hands were shaken and a stone or two would be slipped into boxes as sovereigns rattled on to the tables.

When all of the fifty pounds were spent, he took another cab to Tiffany's, in Regent Street. Sweeping past the bowing doorman, pushing aside an indecisive dowager, he demanded to see the manager. There was much whispering among scandalized assistants, but Hall was not to be denied; and a sight of the choicest jewel of his collection, a glittering and perfect emerald, was enough to persuade them that the manager indeed should be summoned.

The manager greeted him with cautious respect: he knew Hall of old, knew his knowledge and his skill. The two of them spent an hour going through Hall's collection, stone by stone, a price, after much delicate haggling, being agreed for each one. At the end of the hour a cheque for £131 10s. 3d. was written in favour of Hall's account. He had twenty minutes left before his bank closed. He could breathe again.

As he waited for his cheque to be sanctioned, he looked at the trays of jewels under the glass top of the counter. A pretty ring caught his attention. He tapped the counter, smiling, and the manager pulled the tray out for him. Glass to his eye, Hall examined it. 'Twelve pounds, you say,' he murmured, turning the ring around.

'Cabochon-cut ruby. Very attractive, I'm sure you will agree, at the price,' the manager whispered deferentially.

'It would be, but –'

'But what, sir?'

Hall held the ring towards him, proffering his eye-glass, which the manager declined, pulling out his own from his waistcoat pocket. 'It is, as you say, cabochon-cut,' Hall continued. 'It was probably, therefore, taken from some Indian setting. But the rounding, the rounding on top of the stone, my dear sir – see.' He tapped the ring with the tip of a pair of tweezers. 'Most clumsily done. I would estimate its worth at, at best, £9 10s.'

The manager put the ring down between them and leant towards Hall, both hands on the counter. 'Is that an offer, Mr Marshall Hall?'

'To take the bauble off your hands.'

The manager gave a slight bow of his head. 'I will tell them to adjust your cheque.'

'Please do.' Hall smiled.

The manager put the ring into a velvet lined box. As he was doing so, he gave Hall a careful look. 'Mr Marshall Hall, I would like to make *you* an offer. And please don't think me presumptuous.' The manager looked round to make sure that none of his staff could overhear him. 'I am being transferred to New York. A great honour, of course.'

'Congratulations.'

'I've dealt with you over many years. Very happily, on both our parts, I'm sure.'

'Indeed.'

'And my offer is – that you take over this branch in my place.'

Hall shook his head. 'You're not serious.'

'Perfectly. I know that you're a barrister, and that profession has great social cachet. But the firm would pay you very well. And, of course, there would be your commission. With your eye, you could be a rich man.'

Hall looked round the opulently furnished shop. 'You tempt me,' he said.

'Sufficiently for you to accept?'

Hall sighed. 'Would that I could, but, alas . . .'

'No?'

Hall laughed, 'I would ruin myself by buying the stock. But thank you for asking me.'

'Think about it.'

'Oh, I always will. Now, sir – my bank manager waits.'

With bows on every hand from the staff, Marshall Hall walked out of Tiffany's.

They spent a pleasant evening by the fire. Ethel sat at his knee, admiring the glowing ruby he had given her in the firelight, and Hall read to her from *Moths*, which they both thought to be one of Ouida's finest novels. He had a thrilling voice, of great range; really, she thought, he could be in the theatre, the way he made each character so very different.

As their little clock chimed ten, Hall closed the book. 'Bed time, my dear,' he said.

She rose and stood in the firelight, looking down at him.

'Sleep well.'

'And you.' She went towards the door. 'Don't stay up too long.'

'No danger of that. Work in the morning.'

She nodded and went out.

He took his accustomed place at his table, looking with apprehension at the pile of briefs that Tom Ellis put before him. He might never have been away. Then Tom pulled out one brief and looked at it thoughtfully, scratching his chin with a quill. 'This one might interest you, sir,' he said.

Hall very much doubted it but glanced at it. 'Why so?'

'It's come in from that relative of your wife's. A Chancery case.'

There was a faint flicker of hope in Hall's breast, but he quickly suppressed it.

'Think you can handle it?' Ellis asked.

'You don't mean –?'

Ellis was smiling broadly now, tapping the brief with his quill. 'Marked at five guineas. I take my shilling in the guinea, of course, plus my commission. The rest's yours.'

'Oh, my good Lord,' Hall gasped, sinking back in his chair.

'Comes on tomorrow, half past ten,' Tom said, going to his room.

'What shall I say? Tom, tell me!'

Tom turned in the doorway, grinning at him. 'I don't think it will be too much of a problem, sir,' he said.

Nor was it: Hall's role in the affair was to listen carefully for his cue and, when it came, to nod his head as a signal of his consent to a motion for an injunction against his client. He was terrified of nodding at the wrong time, so he nodded every time there seemed to be a pause in the proceedings. But at last Tom, sitting behind him, tapped his shoulder.

'That was the one, sir,' he whispered. 'Well done.'

'Was it? Was it really, Tom?'

'Never saw a better nod in all my life.'

Hall gave a sigh of relief. 'What do I do now?' he asked.

Tom was standing. 'Bribe the clerk to chambers with a pint of old and mild,' he said. 'There's a hostelry hard by.'

That was Marshall Hall's debut on the stage of justice.

It seemed as if it would have no successor, for the next day, and the day after that and in the weeks that followed, it was back to the old grind for him, devilling for old Atkinson, lugging a case full of papers home every night and, with barely time for a word with his wife, working his way through them, as Atkinson had promised him, like a maggot through cheese. The cases that he had to sit through in court seemed to grow drearier by the day.

One November morning he had made his way through the fog-shrouded Temple Gardens, where the trees stood like mournful scarecrows, dripping from every limb, and into the bustle of Fleet Street, where the fog seemed denser than ever. Cabs and carts suddenly appeared and vanished again, their sidelights useless in the murk. With a nod to the court attendants he went into the dismal fastness of the Old Bailey. 'Abandon hope all ye who enter here,' he murmured to himself.

Court Number Two had the appearance of an abandoned ship. The gas lamps shed a cold light on the mist that drifted around the room, and all was stillness. The judge sat like a statue; the jury had the air of men hopelessly awaiting a train that would never come; and the prisoner in the dock might have sat for an allegorical painting of dumb despair. Only the counsel for the defence showed a sign of life, and the slump of his shoulders indicated that that hung by a thread.

Hall took a seat on the hard wooden bench behind him. He had long since done what Atkinson had advised and now proceeded, very slowly, to inflate his air-cushion. The effect that this had on the court was electric: the judge turned to him, the jurymen stirred and all watched him like thirst-stricken travellers in the desert who spy an oasis.

The counsel for the defence, thinking that his advocacy had produced this sensation, stirred himself and wondered what he had said. But, following the eyes of the court, he saw that it was that confounded nuisance Hall again, who was always sighing and groaning through his finest effects.

He raised his voice to arrest the attention of the court. 'Gentlemen of the jury!' he cried. They, as men tortured, dragged their eyes back to him. 'I beg you to pay close attention to the matter in hand.' Hall had finished blowing up his cushion and sat on it. There would be no further entertainment in Court Number Two that day. 'Let nothing shield your eyes from the facts of this matter; my client's liberty hangs on your watchfulness.' He nodded to reinforce the point, then gave a grim smile and ploughed on. 'I do not, I am sure, need to remind you that all statutory offences require two elements: actus rea and mens rea.' He smiled hopefully at the jurymen, who gave him a look of weary loathing and confusion.

'The words of the Latin maxim will spring readily enough to your minds, that is beyond a peradventure: *actus non facit reum nisi mens sit rea.*' One of the jurymen shook his head dolefully. 'Is this matter,' the advocate asked the fogged ceiling, 'to be satisfied with negligence instead of mens rea?' He paused as if expecting an answer, but none came. 'A weighty question, indeed, which you must wrestle with. And I have no doubt whatsoever as to what your answer will be.'

Hall looked at the lawyer sitting next to him. 'How long's this damned torture been going on?' he asked in a whisper that carried to every corner of the room.

His companion seemed almost to have lost the power of speech, so petrified with boredom had be become. He held up three fingers. 'Three hours,' he croaked.

'Dear God in heaven,' Hall sighed, as the leaden-tongued advocate droned on. 'He's boring everyone to extinction. Look at the jury!' His companion did, and nodded tragically.

The judge, glad of the diversion, had listened to this carefully and agreed with every word. None the less, a certain decorum had to be maintained even in the teeth of adversity. He cleared his throat and gave Hall a warning glance.

Hall threw himself back against the bench. 'Damnable!' he said.

The judge tapped on his bench, silencing the eloquence of the advocate. 'One moment, Mr – er –' He looked at Hall. 'Might I ask members of the Bar present to make such observations as they feel called upon to offer in decent privacy outside my court?' Hall gave a bob of apology. The judge turned again to the advocate. 'Pray, proceed,' he groaned.

Counsel for the defence gave Hall a meaningful look, pulled up his gown and bore on manfully. 'I am grateful to your lordship.' He gave a glance at the mass of papers before him. 'The question hinges essentially upon the chattels real as distinct from the chattels personal of my client. I will, therefore, my lord, now address myself to the furniture.'

The judge gave a heavy sigh. 'So far as I am concerned, Mr – er, that is what you have been doing for the last three hours.'

So heavy was the mood of the court that Hall was the only

one to see the joke. He gave a guffaw of laughter but, noting all eyes on him, bowed to the judge, let down his air cushion with the sound of a lingering fart and made his escape. Unusually, the corridor was deserted, and Hall stood, uncertain as to what to do with himself for the rest of the day. To go back through the fog to chambers, and there to grind through another pile of papers, seemed to be a monstrously unappealing prospect, yet to listen to any further pleadings and limping oratory would be unendurable.

Hands in his pockets, shoulders bowed and head down, he wandered towards the barristers' robing room. At least it was warm in there, he thought. Why in God's name hadn't he taken the job at Tiffany's? He could have been looking forward to a cheerful evening – dinner in a restaurant and a pair of stalls at the theatre afterwards. Instead of which . . . He jangled the coins in his pocket.

So dismal was his mood that he didn't hear Tom Ellis call his name as he walked quickly behind him. It was only when the clerk tapped his shoulders that he turned towards him.

'Loafing about, Mr Marshall Hall?' Tom said. 'That'll never do, not for Mr Atkinson it won't.'

'Can you think of anything better?' Hall asked bitterly.

'Indeed I can, sir! I can think of mastering this brief,' he said, shoving a pile of papers into Hall's hands, 'and defending the poor client.'

Hall hugged the papers to his chest. 'Tom! You've come in the very nick of time.' He looked through the papers. 'Is it more than nodding this time?'

'Much more. Marked at a guinea and it comes on straight after lunch.'

'Where?'

'Here, sir. The Bailey.'

Hall let out a whistle and leant against the wall. 'What's the charge?'

'Breaking and entering.'

'What's the plea?'

Before Ellis could answer another barrister came running along the corridor from the robing room, calling Hall's name. 'Thank God I've found you,' he gasped, as he joined them.

'Whatever is it?' Hall asked.

'Case coming on at Marylebone. About three o'clock this afternoon.' He took a breath, banging his chest.

'What's the problem?'

'Problem is, my dear chap, that defending counsel collapsed this morning.' He held out a stack of papers in his hands, offering them to Hall. 'Can you take it on?'

Hall looked at Ellis. 'Can I, Tom?'

Ellis shrugged. 'Chambers hate to turn work away, sir.' He turned to the barrister. 'I accept the brief, on Mr Marshall Hall's behalf.'

The barrister let out a sigh of relief as the papers were handed over. 'Leave it with us, sir,' Ellis said.

The barrister nodded and disappeared into Court Number One.

'How the devil am I to be in two places at the same time?' Hall asked.

'You should know the answer to that one, sir, better than anyone,' Ellis grinned. 'Best trick in the lawyer's book. A devil, sir! A devil! And I'm going off to find you one. He'll be at Marylebone in time, never you fear. And you'd better be consulting with your client here. Never rains but what it pours, eh, sir?'

Hall, face to face with the grizzled old man in the cell, was outraged. Here was his first great chance, and this dense old con was going to take it away from him. 'But you can't!' he shouted. '*You can't!*'

The prisoner looked in a detached way at the green young lawyer they'd found him. New wig, new gown. Wet behind the ears, he was. 'Course I can,' he said.

'But listen, man!' Hall pleaded. 'You'll go down for two years at least.'

The prisoner leant back in his chair, eyes on the ceiling, as he did a quick sum. He shook his head. 'Eighteen months,' he said.

'Even so – at your age. I mean, think of it!'

'I have done,' the old man said, philosophically.

'Make a fight for it! Please!'

The prisoner gave a hollow laugh. 'With this judge? I know the old bastard. Should do – he's sent me down often enough in his time. We've grown old together, him and me. He knows the score, young man! Like I do! If I trips in there and offers him a "not bloody guilty", he'll take a fit, that's what he'll do, wasting his time, mine and yours, and the upshot won't be a two stretch. Oh, no. More like bloody four.'

Hall threw the papers on the table. 'I thought this was my chance,' he muttered.

The old man got up. 'Don't worry, son. Plenty more where I come from. If it's chances you're after, you'll get 'em.' He looked at Hall, still sitting dejectedly at the table. 'Come on!' he said. 'Let's get it done with. Guilty, mind – and no monkeying.'

Hall, rising, made a last effort. 'I could say that you –'

'Guilty,' the con insisted.

Hall sat, sunk in gloom, as the judge passed sentence.

'You are a hardened, inveterate and reprehensible criminal,' his lordship was intoning. 'Therefore I have not the slightest hesitation in sentencing you to a term of eighteen months' imprisonment.'

The old man bowed his head as if in shame but, as he did so, gave Hall a wink.

'In view of your advancing years, I will not condemn you to hard labour.'

'God bless your lordship,' the con cried fervently, raising his thieving hands to heaven.

'Be that as it may,' his Lordship said, 'I must tell you that if you had not thrown yourself upon the mercy of this court by entering a guilty plea, I would have taken a far harsher view of the penalty I have imposed.'

The con nodded humbly.

The judge gave a wintry smile at Hall. 'You are fortunate, Tompkinson, in your advocate: his advice to you was sound and true, and it has saved you from another two years' imprisonment.'

His lordship rose as the prisoner, with a grin at Hall, was taken below.

'All be upstanding,' the usher cried.

But Hall was already on his way out of court, hoping that the fog would have lifted sufficiently for him to make a quick dash to Marylebone. Maybe there'd be a fight for him there.

Ethel had not had a good day: the fog had kept her indoors and she had lain, as she had the year before, on the sofa near the fire. When she heard the door slam and the sound of Edward running up the stairs she groaned. Rough masculine energy would be the final affront to her low spirits.

He flung the door open and stood there, grinning.

'There's an awful draught, Edward. Please shut the door.'

He kicked it shut behind him. 'I think I've a surprise for you.'

She turned away. 'Not more extravagance.'

He came over to her and knelt at her side. 'Close your eyes.'

'I'm in no mood for childishness.'

'All right! Just open your hand!'

Frowning at him, she held out her hand. One by one, he dropped eight sovereigns into it.

'Where did you get these from?' she asked.

He thrust himself to his feet and, as if his energies could not be contained, walked to and fro in the small room. 'I got it, where I'm going to get lots more! From the law! The blessed, blessed law! That's where I got it!' He came back to her, grasping her hands. 'Two briefs! *Two!* In the one day! I tell you I didn't know whether I was coming or going! First the Bailey – and the judge was very decent there, I'll tell you all about it later, then slam, bang, rattling through the fog to Marylebone. And didn't I just make a fight of it! Oh, I tell you!'

'Eight pounds,' she said, putting the pile of sovereigns on to a side table. 'After a year's work. We pay the skivvy more.'

'It's more than most men get!'

She sat up, pulling her shawl round her shoulders. 'Then God help them, that's all I can say.'

Nothing could break his mood. He shook his head, smiling. 'My poor darling – you don't understand. And why should you? It's not a woman's business. But I tell you this; I know, I really do know, that my foot's on the ladder now! And nothing and no one will ever shake it off!' He was back at her side, pulling her to her feet. 'So! Tonight we celebrate! In style!'

The fog brought at least one blessing in its train: they were able to get a box for the play at the Lyceum Theatre. When Ethel had been in the schoolroom she had thought Shakespeare fearfully dull, but tonight's performance of *The Merchant of Venice* had changed her mind. She could not remember when she had been so enraptured. This may have had something to do with the fact that there had been rather more of Henry Irving in the play and rather less of William Shakespeare than scholars would approve.

She had sat, craning forward on the edge of her seat, loving every moment. Now, at the end, she was standing, clapping with her whole heart, along with the rest of the house. The cheers and applause reached a crescendo (discreetly augmented by the drummer in the orchestra pit), and a hand parted the curtains as Irving and Ellen Terry came on for their final bow. He was weary; a broken man, still in his Shylock wig and costume, exhausted by his art.

He lifted a hand to still the applause, and there was immediate silence. He was master of them all. 'Ladies – and gentlemen,' he whispered, as if that great voice had been broken for ever by its efforts, 'for receiving so kindly, so *nobly*, our play – we thank you. And, for permitting us – your players – to come in, though so briefly, to a small corner of your hearts . . .' He shook his head, tears on his cheeks, unable to continue.

Miss Terry looked at him, her sympathy shining out in the tiny gesture of compassion which she gave him as, hand in hand, they swept to their final bows.

Ethel, hands together in rapture, stood, staring at the curtain, as if willing the players back. Hall was in the darkness of a corner of their box, but the effect of the performance on him had, if anything, been even greater than upon Ethel. 'The power of the man,' he murmured. The *power*! He could do anything with these people.'

Ethel turned to smile at him, then, holding out a hand, pulled him towards her and kissed him. 'Eddie, oh, Eddie! That was *wonderful*!' She looked back, longingly, at the curtain. 'Will they come on again?'

Hall, who had sensed the mystery of a great art that night, shook his head. 'No. Not tonight.'

'I must see them. I must, just once more!'

He smiled. 'I'll try and get tickets for another performance.'

'No! Tonight! I want to see them tonight. Let's go backstage! Let's ask if we can see them!'

He shook his head. 'We can't,' he laughed.

'Of course we can!' She was leading him towards the door of the box. 'We can try, anyway!'

*

Irving's privacy was legendary; his dressing room was his castle and his life out of the limelight his own. The stage doorkeeper knew this, and they would never have got past him had they asked for the Chief himself; but Ethel, with a flash of intuition, asked to see a minor member of the cast and the doorkeeper looked them up and down, decided by their appearance that they were actors, and let them through.

As they walked along the narrow corridors, Ethel was entranced; the smell of sweat, scent and make-up was a whiff from another world, a world of light, of colour, of high romance, where all things were possible and loneliness and boredom had been banished.

Hall stopped a passing actor, who was still in his make-up and costume, and asked him which was Irving's dressing room. The actor gave them a curious glance, nodded towards a door at the end of the corridor and went on his way.

Hall made a last effort to restrain Ethel's enthusiasm. 'He won't see us,' he said.

'Of course he will! He'll be pleased!'

Hall shook his head, but gave a quiet tap on the door. It was immediately opened by a man in his shirt-sleeves. He looked at them, suspiciously. 'Yes?' he said, unsmiling.

Hall took a deep breath. 'We know that we're presuming on Mr Irving's time, but –'

'Who let you in?' the man asked.

'The man at the stage door. We just want to say how much we enjoyed the . . .'

The voice, the thrilling, magic voice of the great actor, came from the dressing room and rang down the corridor.

'Piss off!'

The man gave a nod of confirmation of the sentiment and slammed the door in Hall's face.

Ethel was crestfallen. 'How very rude!' she said, her face scarlet with shame.

The next door to Irving's had opened, and Ellen Terry was there in the doorway, looking at them. 'Yes,' she said, 'he can be. And he's also very tired and not really to be disturbed after a performance.'

'We didn't mean to disturb him,' Ethel said. 'Or you, Miss Terry.'

Ellen received this with a nod, but she was looking at Hall. My goodness me, she thought, he's a looker. Isn't he just.

Hall was smiling at her. 'Miss Terry,' he said, 'my opinion is nothing – nothing at all – but the way you gave the quality of mercy speech – it was just wonderful. I never thought of the real meaning of those words, until you spoke them. Thank you for that, and for all that you gave us tonight.'

'Are you in the profession yourself?' she asked him.

'I'm sorry –' he replied, not understanding which profession she was talking about.

'An actor, my dear man.'

He laughed. 'No, no. Nothing so exciting. I'm a lawyer, a barrister.'

'Ah. So that's why you liked the quality of mercy.'

'No, I liked it because it was great, great art. I would have been at your feet for it had I been a dustman.'

She opened the door wider. 'I think you ought to come in, both of you. Our corridor chatter will be disturbing Henry.'

That they should be entertaining Ellen Terry and an actor from the Lyceum company was something so amazing that, during the day of the dinner party when she was bustling through their rooms, making sure that everything was perfect for the evening, she would stop from time to time, wondering if she were dreaming.

Edward came home late, of course, and that was a worry, but he was dressed in the nick of time, practically as the door-bell was ringing, and, from then on, everything went famously. Miss Terry immediately, practically before she had taken her cloak off, told them that they must call her Ellen, and Fred Terriss, the handsome young actor who came with her, set out to dazzle and charm, telling her such stories of his life, how he'd been shipwrecked in the Falkland Islands (wherever they were, but he made them sound so romantic and dangerous), how he became an actor and such amusing gossip about other actors.

While he rattled on, Ellen had gone into a dreamy state, leaning back in her chair, looking at Hall. She touched his hand with her finger tips. 'Your courtrooms,' she murmured, 'are something like theatres, I think. Am I wrong?'

'Very poor theatres indeed, if they are.'

'But great and thrilling dramas take place there.'

He thought of the glories of the Lyceum and, in contrast, the smells and squalor of the Old Bailey. He shrugged. 'It's mostly very sordid and dull.'

She frowned. 'A man – or a woman's freedom, or liberty.'

'Oh, yes,' he nodded. 'Even, sometimes, life or death.'

'Well, then! You play in a drama – on a great stage.'

He thought about this for a moment, twirling the stem of his wine glass. 'I had never thought of myself as an actor. How could I? You have scenery, you have lights, and you have a play. I . . .' and he paused again, 'have nothing but myself.'

She smiled at him. 'I could be Portia without scenery or lights. I could be Portia here and now. And I would make you see a courtroom in Venice, or a house in Belmont. It's in me to do it.'

'And will you? Please?'

She laughed at his eagerness. 'No, I will not. But I could.'

He thought about this; Ethel and Fred Terriss were chattering on at the other end of the table, but he felt as if he were quite alone with this attentive, brilliant woman. He leant closer to her. 'If I could do that, if I could stand, in all that confusion and hold attention – as you can – and if then . . .' Words failed him as, wide-eyed, he pictured the scene.

'Yes, then . . .' she quietly insisted.

'If I could make a jury see a place, a house, a room, a street, I don't know . . .'

She nodded. 'If they are your audience, they have to see it. Or you lose them.'

He was gripped by the excitement of the thought. 'How? How do I do this?'

She gave a quiet laugh. 'It has taken me a lifetime to know. But you begin by seeing it yourself.'

Ethel had heard some of this. 'You want to make an actor of him, Ellen?' she laughed. 'Would he be any good?'

Ellen wasn't laughing, but looking at Hall. 'I think he could be.'

'Oh, do it! For heaven's sake, Eddie! It would be a sight better than what you're drudging away at now. It's so *dreary*!' And she laughed.

Ellen saw a flicker of pain in his eyes, before he looked down at the cloth. How long, she wondered, before this young man withdrew from his wife's scorn?

She looked at Ethel and smiled. 'It's been a lovely, lovely evening, but Fred and I rehearse in the morning. And Henry is so annoyed if we're late.'

'And you always are, Nell! You know very well you are!' Fred laughed.

Ellen was rising like a queen from a throne. 'Tomorrow, I promise, I shall be there on time.'

'I'll believe it when I see it.'

In the tiny lobby of their rooms, as Hall was helping Ellen on with her cloak, she turned to him. 'If ever you felt that you wanted to talk to me,' she murmured, 'it would give me great pleasure.'

'I was frightened to ask.'

'Never be that. You mustn't be.' She smiled at him. 'I've a cottage, at Smallhythe. I'll let you know when I'm going to be there. Perhaps you and your wife could come down.'

'I, that is, we, would love it.'

The cottage at Smallhythe was idyllic: half-timbered, with crazily sloping floors and a great fireplace in the low-ceilinged living-room. There, after dinner, Eddie and Ellen would sit, quietly talking, their heads close together. Not that Ethel minded; she knew that Ellen's affections were engaged elsewhere, and there were always others in the house-party to entertain her with their songs and gossip. Besides, from what she heard, Eddie and Ellen were only talking about boring law business.

Sometimes in the moonlit garden she would see the pair of them walking and she could faintly hear Ellen reciting a line of poetry, then Eddie saying the same line, but not half so nicely. She supposed that they must have got fed up with law talk.

They had stopped by the side of the small lake. He was about to speak, but Ellen put a finger to his lips. She murmured,

> 'How sweet the moonlight sleeps upon this bank,
> Here will we sit, and let the sounds of music
> Creep in our ears: soft stillness and the night
> Become the touches of sweet harmony.'

He took her hand and held it gently in his. 'I could fall in love with you, Ellen Terry,' he said, quietly.

'I know you could. But you won't.'

'No?'

'Oh, no.'

'Why not? Every other man in London has.'

She took her hand from him and touched his cheek lightly. 'Ah, yes. But other men do not nurse such a great love as yours.'

He turned from her and stood at the edge of the lake, his head bowed. 'A hopeless love,' he said.

She came to him and put a hand on his shoulder. 'Quite hopeless. I am so sorry for you.'

'You see it?'

'I do see it.' She was silent for a moment. 'And there is no escape.'

'I know that.' He turned to her. She was all silver in the moonlight. 'Sometimes I think that my heart will break,' he said, simply. 'And that's the truth of it.'

She shook her head. 'Hearts are really quite strong. They live – somehow. And they mend.' She came close to him. 'She must let you go. And you must let her let you go.'

'I can't do that.'

She moved away from him, walking slowly up the grass slope that led to her house. 'Then there is no hope for you,' she said, sadly. 'None, in all the world.'

They came often to her cottage at Smallhythe and occasionally, Ellen came to their rooms. Hall gained much from these visits: he was learning to control and project his voice and to extend its range; he was learning to use gesture simply and effectively and, above all, he was learning to put himself in another person's place.

He would thank her profusely, knowing the priceless gift she was giving him, and that one day it would be of far greater use to him than all the law books ever written, all the precedents and all the case histories. One day. It would come. She would laugh his thanks away. 'I only bring out what's already there,' she said.

And one hot August afternoon as they sat in her garden, she trying to learn lines for the next season's opening play at the Lyceum (never an easy task for her) and he reading the latest sensational novel, she looked up from her text and saw, anew, the negligent beauty of him. 'Marshall, my dear – maybe you should have been an actor. You're a natural,' she said. 'If you weren't so damned good looking, Henry would snap you up for the company.' She sighed, putting her book on the grass. 'But, then again, there would be a terrible danger that folk would look at you rather than him, and he'd never risk that.'

'He has handsome men around him. Look at Fred Terriss –'

'Ah, yes. But actors like poor Fred know their place, out of the limelight. You would never know yours. You'd be fighting him for centre stage.'

'Not true!'

'Perfectly true. So you just stick to the law.'

'I intend to.'

'That's all right, then.' She threw her book across to him. 'Cue me through Act One, there's a darling. I think it's almost there.'

It wasn't, not by a long chalk, but Ellen's variations on Shakespeare had charms of their own, and, listening to her, he thought he was the luckiest man alive.

As for Ethel, she too got much pleasure from the connection. She had friends enough now; amusing friends, flattering friends, eager to entertain her, make her welcome at their supper parties. And if Edward was too busy with his stuffy reading to come with her, then he seemed to be satisfied enough that she was enjoying herself.

Often when he came home he would find a note from her on his plate at table, saying that she would be home late and that he mustn't wait up for her. He knew flashes of jealousy, but he also knew what he thought of as her invincible purity. However compromising the situation, he knew, better than he knew anything, that she would be unscathed.

And, in this, of course, he was right. Some of the young men at those intimate supper parties had laid bets as to who should bed her first; but, though one young man in particular got quite a way, and she responded ardently enough to his kisses, once his hand was under her skirts and had got as far as her knee, she pulled away from him, and not all his well practised arts could take him any further. None of this detracted from her charms; the unattainable was infinitely desirable, and the invitations kept on coming. She kept on accepting them. They became her palliative, her drug. When she was at home of an evening she would sit by the fire, looking at Edward bent over his work at the lamplit table and she would remember the thrusting tongue of a man's kisses and his hot breath and trembling hands on her body. She would stir on her seat with desire, breathing fast, shutting her eyes the better to re-live the memory.

Then the shame, the deep, bitter self-hatred would flow over her and she would be tormented by the thoughts of her own baseness and the squalid, grasping evil of men. She would never, she would swear, accept another invitation from them, never. They wanted one thing and one thing only and she knew that it would be death to surrender that last citadel.

But in the morning, as the sunlight coloured the blind and she stirred sleepily in her bed, she would remember the excitement of being alone with a man, the heat of his eyes on her, the hoarseness of his voice when he spoke his love and she would smile, dress and take up the letters on the breakfast table with renewed pleasure.

Her husband never once came into her thoughts of sensuality, only into the darkness and guilt. Was he not, by everyone's admission, the most complete of men? Very well, then; he must typify the faults of them all.

None of this did he guess at. He thought that he knew her well enough.

CHAPTER
TWELVE

The days were coming to an end when the Queen's Justices rolled majestically on circuit in their great carriages, escorted into County Towns by outriders, pikemen and trumpeters, with a horde of barristers, solicitors and assorted hangers-on following hard on their heels in broughams, victorias and, for the impecunious, hackney cabs, there to fight for rooms in the inns and lodging houses. The advent of the railway train had meant that lawyers could, on a circuit like the South-Eastern, easily get to chambers and hearthside after court had risen and be back again for business the following day. Bar-mess nights, when the barristers gathered for drink, songs, silly fines and jokes in some well-stocked inn still happened, of course, the law being, of all professions, the most tenacious in clinging to custom, but the high days were gone for ever.

For Hall, who had joined this South-Eastern circuit as soon as he could after being called to the Bar, a stay in some sleepy country town was a respite from the drudgery of chambers, and a chance of actually getting on his feet and addressing a jury. It didn't happen, though; morsels were few and there were many who had waited even longer than he. So the days would pass, in one town or another, sitting in court, waiting, always waiting for the golden moment.

Then, one dreary day at the Lewes Assizes, it happened. He was on the barrister's bench when a man, a petty pickpocket, came up for trial. He said that he hadn't enough money to pay for a solicitor and so, without a solicitor's services a barrister couldn't be briefed and, without a barrister, he would have no defence. The judge looked down at him, tapping his pencil in irritation. 'Have you, Mr White, the sum of £1 3s. 6d. about your person?'

The prisoner looked puzzled. 'What for, sir?' he asked.

'Come, man! You know perfectly well! One guinea for a barrister and a half crown for his clerk. Have you this money?'

'I might have,' White said, guardedly.

'Very well, then. You may choose a barrister present in this court to defend you.'

White looked round: but he couldn't see any of the lawyers' faces, since they all had their backs to him, and most of them sank lower in their bench, hoping against hope to avoid the ill-paid chore.

One man, however, stayed upright and, in any case, towered over his colleagues. White pointed at the broad back. 'I'll have him,' he said.

Hall turned to see whom the man had picked in this dock brief, and saw the pointed finger and the hopeless expression in the man's eyes. He smiled and, not for the last time, a client felt reassurance in the confidence of that smile.

'Very well, then,' the judge sighed. He looked at Hall. 'Your name, please?'

Hall was on his feet. 'Marshall Hall, my Lord,' he said, his voice ringing out in the ill-lit and cramped room.

'Very well, Mr Hall, you may interview your client.'

Hall was on his way to the dock, but turned again to the judge. 'I think your Lordship misheard me. My name is Marshall Hall.'

'As you wish. Now do, please, make haste in this business. The list is long and the day is short.'

'I shall be as speedy as my client's case demands,' Hall said sententiously, and went to the dock.

'Now, let's make a good fight of this,' he said, gripping the rail.

'Never mind that,' White whispered. 'I haven't got the money, not to pay you I haven't.'

'How much have you got?'

White emptied his pockets and put the small pile of coins into Hall's hand. 'Fifteen shilling,' he said. 'And not a brass farthing more in the wide world.'

'This is the truth?'

'So help me God.'

Hall leant closer to him. 'Now, listen,' he said. 'I could get into trouble, serious trouble, if anyone found out that I'd broken the rules and spoken for you without the full fee.' He put the money back into White's hand and clasped his own around it. 'So keep your money – and keep your mouth shut. Now, let's get on with the job. You don't seem to be a successful thief, if this is all you've got between you and the workhouse.'

'Oh, I've given all that up years ago, honest.'

Hall nodded. 'I believe you,' he said. 'And this fifteen shillings was all that you had in your pockets when you were arrested?'

'That's right.'

Hall smiled. 'Very well, then. Let's see what we can do with that.'

The police constable was sturdy when giving his evidence in the solidly structured examination by the Crown prosecutor, a stockily built man with a slight Irish accent. The policeman went through the events without excitement; the matter was too routine for fireworks, and a conviction was certain. The constable had observed the man White for some time, seen him acting suspiciously, furtively even, as he mingled with the crowd at the fair, jostling first one, then another. When one of the people who had been in close proximity to the prisoner complained that his pocket had been picked, the constable had interviewed the said White and he had, in the course of that interview, concluded that he had sufficient information to caution the prisoner and effect an arrest.

Counsel for the Crown sat, making an inadequate attempt to stifle a yawn. This was a tedious case, unworthy of his high skills as a prosecutor. The creature had a record as long as time (which would be brought out before sentencing), and the sooner the business was done with, the better.

Hall rose for cross-examination of the policeman. He had, as yet, no clear line of defence. He looked round the courtroom in silence, head back, as Ellen had taught him to stand, consciously using his height, willing everyone in the room to look at him. As he waited, a thought, a dangerous thought, came to him. If he used it and failed, then the consequences would be dire: this penniless man had entrusted him with his freedom, and he could not betray that trust. He cleared his throat and concentrated all his force on the policeman.

'When you first saw my client in this crowd at the fair, Constable,' he began, spacing his words slowly, 'did you recognize him?'

The judge raised his eyebrows. Really, he thought, the calibre of these new young fellows at the Bar was lamentable. He tried to give Hall a warning look: this line of questioning would lead to certain disaster, but Hall wasn't taking his eyes off his witness.

The constable couldn't believe his good fortune. He smiled, seeing the prisoner already safely behind bars, which was where he belonged. 'Oh, yes, sir,' he said. 'I recognized him all right.'

'You are an acquaintance of his?'

The policeman was still smiling. 'Professionally, sir, yes.'

'Professionally?'

'That's right.'

'And what is the nature of this professional acquaintanceship?'

The policeman's moment had come, and he relished it. He produced his notebook and flicked through the pages, licking his thumb to speed the process until he found the page he wanted. 'I arrested the prisoner for the offence with which he is now charged on 13 June 1876. He was tried and found guilty and sentenced to a three-year term of imprisonment.' He looked at the judge. 'This, my Lord, was his third conviction on thefts.'

The judge nodded. Things would soon come to an end here, that was one consolation.

'On his release I had cause to apprehend him, on 5 April 1879, for a similar offence,' the policeman continued, smooth as cream. 'Once more the prisoner was found guilty and sentenced to a term of imprisonment. I understand that he has only recently been released from custody.'

White was holding his head in his hands, the picture of despair. Crown counsel was staring at Hall as if he couldn't believe his eyes, and the judge was rehearsing the sermon he would preach before sending the scoundrel down for the rest of his villainous days.

Hall seemed as pleased as the policeman at this information. He smiled and nodded agreeably. 'And tell me, Constable,' he went on, 'how many people would you estimate were in this throng at the fair?'

The policeman shrugged his shoulders. 'Difficult to say, sir.'

Hall seemed to be mildly surprised. 'Oh? Why is that?'

The policeman smothered a laugh. 'Because I wasn't looking at them. I was keeping my eyes on him.'

One of the jurymen sniggered, but Hall ignored him. 'Him?' he asked, his voice quiet now.

'Prisoner at the bar, sir.'

'You watched him, and only him, for the whole time you were observing this affair?'

'That's right.'

'So that, in fact, some other person could have been committing these thefts unseen by you?'

The policeman shifted his weight from one foot to the other. 'Not likely, sir.'

'Why?' Hall flung at him, his voice harsh and penetrating. 'Why isn't it likely?'

'Because he's known to the police as a pickpocket!'

'Oh I see! The dog has a bad name, so no other dog may bark or bite? Is that how you conduct your affairs? Is it, Constable?'

'I had reason to –'

'You had no reason at all! *None!*' Hall shouted. 'No reason to suspect my client other than what I would suggest to you is your native idleness and indolence!'

'Mr Hall,' the judge growled in warning.

Hall wasn't to be stopped, nor did he release the policeman from the cold fury in his eyes. 'Whatever was going to happen in that crowd, you were determined, before it even occurred, that you would hold this man responsible. It was the easy way, wasn't it? The idle way. He has paid his debt for whatever offences he may have committed in the past, but you, Constable, were set on demanding compound interest. *Is that not so?*'

'No, sir!' the policeman shouted back. 'I knew him of old, and I saw what he was at!'

'Did you now? And what, precisely, was he at?'

'Jostling. Shoving his way through.'

Hall leant against the back of the bench, as if astonished. 'Jostling? You actually saw him *jostling*? Well now,' he turned to the judge, 'I must seek enlightenment, my Lord. Has this new crime been added to the Statute Book? Common jostling?'

The judge came to the sweating policeman's defence. 'Perhaps you would be kind enough to tell the court what else in the prisoner's conduct excited your suspicions, officer.'

'By all means. Please do, Constable,' Hall added, helpfully.

'It's an old trick of the trade,' the policeman said. 'The thief distracts his victim and then takes his watch, valuables, anything.'

Hall nodded. 'We are all grateful for this enlightenment.' He thrust his hands into his trouser pockets and looked down, as if deep in thought. 'And how many watches did my client have in his possession at the time of his arrest?'

'None, sir.'

'None. What other valuables did he have about him?'

'Well, he wouldn't have. Would he? He'd have got shot of 'em.'

'Do not dare fence with me, sir!' Hall thundered. 'Answer straight! What other valuables did he have in his possession?'

'None.'

'And money? How much of that?'

The policeman cleared his throat. 'Fifteen shillings.'

'And how much was reported to you as having been stolen?'

'I later learned that some £20 in coin and three gold watches had been purloined. Plus a lady's reticule containing a valuable item of jewellery.'

Hall threw up his hands in despair. 'I wonder at this charge being brought, my Lord. Whilst this assiduous officer is, presumably, from what he has told us, hard on the heels of my client – or how else could he have seen, in that crowd, what he alleges to have occurred? – wholesale robbery is going on around him, unseen and undetected.' He turned again to the policeman. 'What, precisely, do you suppose, happened to these valuables?'

'Previous experience leads me to think that they were disposed of by the prisoner.'

'When? When did he dispose of them?'

'When he realized that he was under observation.'

'Oh, really? So, my client went through the crowd, scattering riches left and right. Did you see anyone pick these things up?'

'No, sir. Like I say, I didn't take my eyes off the prisoner.'

'And, in this close observation, did you witness him getting rid of money, watches and a lady's reticule?'

'He made certain suspicious gestures. Yes.'

'What sort of gestures?'

'He was a-twitching of his shoulder. Like this –' And the policeman raised and lowered his right shoulder.

'That gesture is likely to make you suspicious?'

'Very.'

'So now, we have another offence to run alongside jostling in a crowd: twitching in a multitude! The Statute Book is being rewritten before our very eyes. But, leaving these grave misdemeanours to one side, the sum total of your evidence is that at no point did you see my client steal so much as a brass farthing from anyone, nor did you see him dispose of anything, and when he was under arrest he had none of the stolen articles in his possession. Is that not the case?'

'I had cause for —'

'Answer "yes or "no", man!' Hall shouted.

The constable looked round; but there was no help to be had from anyone. He nodded: 'Yes.'

'Yes! And is it not the case that my client was arrested by you for no other reason than that he had, in the past, committed such offences?'

'He was the obvious suspect!'

'Was he now? And so, on those dubious grounds, every time he sets foot in the street, or ventures on the Queen's highway, he is liable to arrest for no other reason than that he is abroad?'

'If thefts against the person are suspected —'

'You immediately arrest the man White?' Hall interrupted.

'I would have reason to suspect him.'

Hall threw down the bundle of papers in his hand (a brief which he had been devilling, and nothing whatsoever to do with the present case) and turned to the judge. 'My Lord, this evidence is a farrago of indolent surmise and prejudiced conjecture. I most strongly submit that, on such shaky grounds as these, it would be manifestly unsafe to proceed with this prosecution.'

The judge stirred, tapping his pencil. He turned to counsel for the Crown. 'Mr Gill: do you wish to re-examine this witness?'

Counsel wearily shook his head. 'No, my Lord.'

'Have you any further witnesses?'

'No, my Lord.'

The judge nodded to the policeman. 'You may stand down, Constable.'

With a sigh of relief, the policeman left the box.

The judge looked at the jury. 'Gentlemen, I would wish you to withdraw for some time to the room reserved for you. And it may be that your duty will have been discharged in this case.' He waited while the jury shuffled out, and then turned to Counsel for the Crown. He cleared his throat. 'Mr Gill, it does seem to me to be quite extraordinary that this prosecution has been brought.'

Gill was on his feet. 'The police seemed sure enough of the case, my Lord.'

'Did they now? Did they really?' He shook his head. 'Then I most profoundly wish that they had presented the grounds for their certainties.' He gave a heavy sigh; he was as sure as the police that they had got their man and that the rogue was in the dock. 'But I have to say, given the facts before us, that I agree with Counsel for the defence. It would be unsafe, manifestly unsafe, to proceed.'

With a shrug of his shoulders, Gill sat down.

The judge looked over his spectacles at the prisoner in the dock. 'Mr White, I am ordering your immediate release. But this I must say to you: do not, I beg you, in future place yourself in circumstances, nor perform actions, which may render you liable to fall under the proper suspicion of the constabulary.'

'No, my Lord, I won't; I'll never do that again, not never,' White babbled, eager to be off before anyone changed his mind.

'And you may count yourself fortunate in your choice of defending counsel.'

'Oh I do, I do.' And didn't he just; and he'd more than that to be thankful for: if that daft copper had noticed that he'd got a new stallman in Ruby Evans, and that he'd been passing the stuff to her as soon as he'd dipped it, things might have been different; but, all the same, this big young lad in his new white wig had done well by him. He'd use him again, he would, given half a chance.

The judge turned to Hall as White scuttled away. 'Mr Marshall Hall, I must most strongly reprimand you.'

Hall was on his feet. He'd done it, he'd got his man off! Whatever this old man said was nothing to that. 'For what, my Lord?' he asked, unable to keep the triumph out of his voice.

'It appears that, when arrested, prisoner had only fifteen shillings in his possession. I assume that he has had no means of acquiring further wealth since then, and that, therefore, he had insufficient funds to brief you. And yet you accepted this brief, in clear contravention of all the usages of the Bar.'

'I am sure that he will pay me, my Lord,' Hall faltered.

'That is not the same thing at all, sir! You are not a money-lender, nor a charitable institution! Never do such a disgraceful thing again in my court, Mr Marshall Hall, or I may have reason to report you to the Benchers of your Inn.'

Gill was on his feet. 'I understand, my Lord, that a friend of the man White's, a woman by the name of Miss Ruby Evans, has placed certain small sums of money at his disposal. There-fore, my learned friend will be fee'd in full.'

Friend White's an artful, mean old bugger, Hall thought, as he gave a glance of thanks to Gill.

'Then why didn't you say so?' the judge asked Hall.

'I would have done, my Lord – given a chance.'

The judge grudgingly accepted this. 'I have to say, though, that you fought his case quite well. Keep on like that, and we might just hear more of you one day.' He got to his feet.

'All be upstanding!' the usher cried.

The court rose.

Hall walked on air out of the court; the day was his, un-doubtedly his, and the only cloud in the sky was that the business hadn't been resolved by the jury; that would have made his triumph absolute. He wished now that the judge had refused his plea for a dismissal and let the case continue. The steep and narrow streets of the old town, with the ruins of the castle looming over it all, were as a road in Paradise. Never, ever again would he know this sweet joy. No matter that he hadn't made a penny, and that his client had cheated him out of even the paltry dock-brief fee; he could always do more business with the jewellers to keep himself and his wife going. He had power! It was his, that mystical power of command he'd seen in actors. And with it, he could do anything.

He swung into his hotel, his silver-headed cane on his shoulder, his hat jauntily perched over one eye. He was looking forward to getting home again and telling Ethel about his triumph. Now she would have to listen to him and believe him when he painted his glowing picture of their future. She would have her carriage and pair and she would drive through the park with the best of them.

He was about to run up the stairs to collect his bag from his room, when he heard his name called. He stopped and turned, seeing the Crown prosecutor at the foot of the stairs.

'I've brought you a slight tribute,' Gill said, his long upper lip creased into a grin.

Hall smiled back. 'Kind of you,' he said.

Gill produced a bottle of claret from his coat tails. 'Now? Or at Bar mess, later?' he asked, waving the bottle.

'I wasn't going to go to mess. I was going home. I don't think there'll be anything else for me here.'

Gill sighed. 'Ah, the intemperate folly of youth. We'd better settle this bottle now. Come on down with you, will you, for God's sake! Aren't you tall enough without a fellow breaking his neck to talk to you!'

So they sat in the sunbeamed room and sipped their wine. Gill put his glass down and leant over the table. 'One thing I'll tell you, young shaver. When we cross swords next time, I won't be making the same mistakes again. I'm the best prosecutor on the circuit –'

'Are you now?' Hall smiled, taking a gulp of wine.

'Oh yes. But I thought that today was open and shut and that you were too wet behind the wig to do anything but stutter. I've the measure of you, though, and I tell you – next time you've a fight on your hands.' He looked at Hall reflectively. 'You take risks. All right; today you got away with it. But I'll break you next time you dare to devil with me.'

The power was still flowing through Hall's veins. He nodded, accepting the challenge. 'And you're methodical,' he said. 'I know that of you. So I'll always surprise you.'

Gill laughed. 'I'll beat the hide off you!'

'A dozen of these that you don't!' Hall said, tapping the bottle.

'You're on,' Gill laughed, 'and I'll claim the prize, don't you worry.' He lifted his glass. 'So! Here's to next time and my claret!'

Hall raised his glass to him. 'Next time,' he said. Then he sank back in his chair. 'If there is a next time. Here or anywhere.'

Gill considered this. 'Something of a dearth of briefs?'

Hall shrugged. 'You know what it's like, starting off.'

'Oh yes, don't I just,' Gill frowned. 'By the finish of my second year I was down to one pair of boots, and only the brown paper keeping the rain out of them. Oh, it's desperate all right, and don't I know it.'

'Things must change. Sometime.'

'They will,' Gill said. 'Don't you worry. In the meantime – whose chambers are you in?'

'Tyndal Atkinson's. Mean old wretch.'

Gill nodded. 'Oh, he's that, but he's a good Master. You could have done worse. Don't stay with him too long, mind. I'll be having words with you about that.'

'Change chambers?'

'Yes, and that right soon. I suppose old Atkinson has you devilling for him night and day?'

'Doesn't he just.'

'And never a penny piece to take home?'

'No.'

'Well, there's something we can do about that, at least.' From the same hidden pocket that had held the claret he produced a bundle of papers. 'Here's a brief I want devilling. Comes on tomorrow, and there's fifteen guineas in it for you. What do you say?'

'I say thank you,' Hall smiled.

'And I say that we have a nice bite of dinner, an hour in the Bar mess, then you burn a drop of the midnight oil on that little brief.'

Hall got up. 'I'll send a telegram to my wife. She'll be worried if I don't come home.'

'You do that.'

He began to feel that he'd made a friend for life. He was right.

He stayed more than an hour in the Bar mess; the wine flowed, conversation was easy and in Gill, whom he was soon calling Charlie, he found an attentive listener. He even began to tell him a little of the pain of his marriage, a thing he had never done with anyone, but Gill had stopped him with a shake of his head.

'That's for another day, Marshall.' He leant close to him. 'If you want to talk, then I want to listen. But the talk mustn't come from a bottle. All right?'

Hall bowed his head. 'Yes, all right.' He looked up. 'I'm sorry. I should never have mentioned it.'

'No, no, you were right to do that.' He rose. 'But now, you've work to do. I don't pay good money for nothing.'

Hall went back to his hotel and got the night porter to fetch him up a pot of black coffee. He settled down to the grind of his devilling, ordering the facts, suggesting a line of defence, bringing all that he could to what looked like a very black case for Gill's clients.

Dawn was beginning to break when, with aching back and swimming head, he put out his lamp and collapsed into bed.

But he was young and strong, and by the time he had eaten an enormous breakfast he was ready to face anything and strode along to the court as fresh as a daisy, the brief and his opinions on it neatly packed in his bag.

No sooner had he come through the doors than Gill came rushing towards him, a fat and worried man at his heels. 'There you are, Hall!' he cried. 'Whatever's kept you?'

'It's only half-past nine!'

Gill turned away. 'No matter, no matter!' He brought the fat man forward. 'Mr Marshall Hall, may I introduce the instructing solicitor in this case of ours, Mr Evett.'

Hall nodded his greeting, but he was surprised to see the horrified expression on the solicitor's face.

'But he's –' Evett said.

'New?' Gill asked. 'Of course he's new. A coming man. You'll be safe enough with him. He knows all about the case. Don't you, Marshall?'

Hall turned to Gill, pulling him to one side. 'Charlie, what the hell's going on?'

Gill grinned. 'You're going on, my boy. I've another case in Court Number Two, and it's come on this morning instead of this afternoon.' He nodded cheerfully. 'So I hope you worked well on that brief last night.' He was already walking quickly away down the corridor. 'Good luck. See you at lunch.'

Hall turned back to the solicitor, whose look of fear and desperation hadn't altered. 'I'm sorry, Mr Evett, for the short introduction.' He gave what he hoped was a reassuring smile, though his mouth was as dry as dust and his lips tight.

Evett shook his head. 'And I'm sorry, too, Mr –'

'Marshall Hall.'

'Yes Well . . .' He spread his hands in an expression of regret. 'I really must instruct a more – forgive me for this – but a more experienced barrister. We can ask for an adjournment.'

Hall's smile faded. Was this the way it would be, then? Turned down because he was inexperienced? How the devil would he get experience if no one would take him on?

'I'd make a fight for you,' he said.

'Yes. I'm sure you would, but . . .' He saw the hurt in Hall's eyes. 'My clients are very respectable tradesmen. This case means a great deal to them.'

'I know it does. I worked on the brief all night.'

Evett took a deep breath. 'All right,' he said. But Hall hadn't taken in what he said and still stood, head bowed. He slapped him on the back. 'Come on, Mr Marshall Hall. We'll get them off.'

Hall's head came up. 'You mean I –'

'We'd better be getting into court. Wouldn't do to be late.'

'Oh, right! Yes! Certainly!' Hall was already moving towards the robing room.

'Is there anything you'd like to ask me?' Evett said, running after him.

Hall stopped and turned to him. Evett saw that all the colour had drained from the young man's face. 'Where's the lavatory?' Hall whispered.

And the gigantic breakfast was returned to the citizens of Lewes.

Little of the brightness of the day penetrated the gloom of the ancient courtroom; it might as well have been the darkest day of December were it not for the breathless stuffiness of the atmosphere. The prosecuting counsel was on his feet and, whether or not word of the skills of his young adversary had reached him, he was taking no chances with the case. As Hall listened to him, his heart sank; this man was deadly in examination.

The worthy tradesmen, accused of receiving goods knowing them to have been stolen, sat woebegone in the dock, and on the witness stand was the man who had stolen a barrow-load of varnish before selling it to the defendants. His testimony was cast-iron and, despite all his work of the night before, Hall could see no way of breaking it. The line of defence which he had put up for Gill to follow would, he could see, break in the hands of his opponent. Rack his brains as he may, he could see no way forward.

The prosecution was bringing his witness to the point when he met the defendants.

'Now, tell me, Mr Palmer, where this meeting took place.'

'Back o' the Star and Garter,' Palmer told him.

'That is an inn, or hostelry?'

Palmer nodded. 'In a manner of speaking, yes.'

'Is it or is it not an inn?'

'Oh, right – yes.'

'Yes?'

'Yes.'

The prosecutor referred to his notes: he had a well set out plan of campaign and he was going to follow it to conviction. 'And who,' he asked, 'was present at this meeting at the rear of the Star and Garter Inn?'

Palmer nodded at the defendants. 'Them.'

The prosecutor was leaving nothing to chance. 'Would you point them out to us, please.'

Palmer obliged. 'Mr Foster and Mr Clegge,' he said, pointing.

'Thank you. And could you tell us what transpired at this meeting?'

Palmer settled to his tale. 'I said to 'em, in a way o' business, that I'd a barrowload of varnish what was going cheap.'

'And did either Foster or Clegge make any reply to that?'

'Yes, sir. Foster comes up close and says, "Is the stuff dead swag?"'

The judge lifted his head. 'What was that last remark?'

The prosecutor gave a wintry smile to his lordship. 'I will ask for a translation, my Lord.'

'Do so, please.'

The prosecutor turned to his witness. 'Dead swag? What do you suppose he meant by that?'

Palmer shrugged. 'Nicked.'

The prosecutor gave a sigh of exasperation. 'Please try to confine your remarks to plain English, Mr Palmer.'

'Stolen, then.'

'And how did you answer his question?'

'I gives a laugh. He knew what I meant.'

'Quite possibly he did. But, for our sakes, he took your laughter to be an affirmative answer?'

'Well, of course he did! Both of 'em did.'

'On your oath now, Palmer: do you tell this court that both of the defendants knew, at that point, that the varnish was stolen?'

Mr Evett gave Hall a nudge in his back, but he was already getting to his feet. 'My Lord, my learned friend is quite shamelessly leading the witness.'

The judge pursed his lips. 'I think that he is merely consolidating the drift of the witness's earlier answers. Do proceed, Mr Crawford.'

Crawford nodded and looked at Palmer, who was standing, one hand raised, as sanctimonious as a preacher. 'On my life, they knew the stuff was nicked.'

The prosecutor let this sink in with the jury for a moment. 'Was any money paid by the defendants for this barrow-load of varnish?'

'Two pound five shilling.'

'And who gave you this money?'

'Clegge. Two sovs and five shilling. In me hand.'

Crawford sat, murmuring, 'No further questions, my Lord.'

Hall was almost unaware of this; all his concentration was on the jury. Undoubtedly, they had been impressed by this evidence. Palmer had nothing to gain, and everything to lose; he must be telling the truth. That thought was, quite clearly, in every juryman's mind. How could they be moved? Was there a way? The judge was looking at him, but Hall still stared at the jury. He had to shift them.

'Mr Marshal Hall, do you wish to cross-examine or not?' the judge asked, testily.

'Oh yes, my Lord, I do indeed,' Hall murmured, but still he sat.

'Do get on with it!' Evett hissed in his ear.

Hall nodded – and then one of the faces in the jury box came into focus. The man was avoiding his gaze, and he realised why. He knew him – he'd played cricket against him, his first summer at Cambridge. It all came back to him. The man was a good sportsman; he'd been given out in what was a very odd leg-before-wicket umpiring decision, and he'd not argued but held his bat and gone on the long walk back to the pavilion – and this when his side wanted only three runs to win.

'Put yourself in a character's shoes and walk round for a bit,' Ellen had told him. More than shoes, Hall thought: today it would be gloves, pads, cap and box.

He was on his feet and, slowly, turned his gaze from the jury to the man Palmer, who was self-confidently leaning against the rail of the witness box. Hall looked at him steadily, holding his eyes until the man dropped his. 'How did you come to the knowledge that these goods were stolen, Mr Palmer?' he asked, in a very quiet voice.

'Because I knew who'd nicked 'em.'

Hall gave a slight nod. 'I see. And would you say that you were a friend of this thief?'

'Like I say . . . I know him.'

'For a long time? You've known him for a considerable time?'

'Oh, yes,' Palmer smiled.

'And you were friendly with him?'

Palmer pursed his lips, judiciously. 'Manner of speaking, yes.'

Hall gave him an agreeable smile. 'Thank you. This man, then, is a friend of yours of some long standing. And now, perhaps, you could tell us what has become of this . . . friend?'

Palmer stirred, uneasily. 'He got pinched.'

'Arrested?'

'That's what I said.'

Hall gave another smile. 'Almost. And how did this man, this thief, your friend, come to be arrested?'

Crawford got wearily to his feet. 'My Lord, with all respect to my young and learned friend – the matter of the conviction of the thief of these goods has already been dealt with in your Lordship's court. I really do not see –'

Hall shook his head. 'My Lord!' he interrupted.

The judge lifted a hand. 'I think that the line of questioning may conceivably have some relevance. We shall see. In the meantime, pray proceed, Mr Marshall Hall.'

'Thank you, my Lord.' He turned again to Palmer. 'I repeat my question. Your friend has been arrested; he has been convicted of the theft of these articles and sentenced to an exemplary term of imprisonment. Now, once more, how did this arrest come about?'

Palmer licked his lips and looked at Crawford, who gave him a quick nod. 'I did my duty by the law.'

'Indeed? How did you do this?'

Palmer cleared his throat. 'I informed the police against him.'

Hall looked down at his notes. 'And this altruistic act of yours occurred on 23 July last, did it not?'

'It could have been, I'm not a blooming calendar.'

'Oh, I do assure you, Mr Palmer,' Hall said, pulling himself up to his full height, 'that was indeed the date when you went to the police to inform against your friend. And that date was the very day after you had sold these goods to my clients, was it not?'

'I couldn't sleep!' Palmer said. 'It was on my conscience!'

Hall leant forward, as if he hadn't heard aright. 'Your *what*?'

'Conscience.'

Hall frowned, in sympathy. 'How very uncomfortable.' He looked at the witness coldly. 'And was your *conscience* eased by the very considerable reward the police gave you for informing against this man and then laying evidence against my clients?'

Palmer turned away. 'I'm not putting up with this,' he murmured.

Hall was on to him like a weasel after a rabbit. 'Oh, but you are!' he cried. 'You will put up with this and a great deal more before I've done with you!'

'Mr Marshall Hall,' the judge warned.

But Hall was in full flood now, and not to be stopped. 'You

will put up with standing in this court in the face of the contempt of the jury, you will endure the despite that sticks like a burr to the hide of the false friend, you will put up with looking into the eyes of these honest men, these true men, this jury – and you will read there the feelings that decency shows when it is face to face with *Judas*!' His fists were on the bench before him and he was leaning in to Palmer, his body a tense spring. 'How much were you paid?' he hissed.

Crawford, rattled, was on his feet again. 'This is unforgiveable bullying, my Lord!

Hall's voice rose above him, his words a whiplash. '*How much were you paid?*'

Palmer was sweating. 'It wasn't anything much,' he whispered.

'*Wasn't it?* Only a petty sum of money?' On an impulse, he took the coins from his pocket, clasped them high in the air, then threw them at Palmer's feet. 'Here! Grovel for more! Scrape the dust in your greed! For I put it to you, Palmer, that your lust for money, however ill-gotten, led you to the betrayal of a friend, then led you on to deceit, to lies, to a whole tissue of lies against these, my clients! Money was in your purse. You had handed over your friend to the police. And been paid. But there could be more gains, could there not? A little more, for a little lie. And you took it.' He raised an arm, pointing at Palmer. 'Did you not take more money for laying evidence against these two men?' he cried.

'No!' Palmer shouted, his voice hoarse.

Hall whipped an official-looking piece of paper from his notes and held it aloft. 'Will you persist in that against what is written here?'

'It weren't much' Palmer mumbled.

'How much?' Hall shouted.

'Thirty shilling.'

Hall dropped the papers on to the desk and slowly shook his head. He turned from Palmer, wearily, and looked at the jury. All their eyes were on him now. 'Gentlemen,' he said, 'you may think the sum appropriate enough.' He sat and leant back in his seat, eyes closed, his face a mask of disgust and loathing. 'My Lord,' he murmured, 'I have no further question of this *witness*.'

The court was silent as Palmer was dismissed from the box. But Evett was beside himself in agitation. He leant over Hall's shoulder, whispering in his ear. 'Mr Marshall Hall, I do protest! Such questioning is entirely unprofessional! In all my experience I have never known the like! This is not a bullring, sir!'

Crawford, in his final speech to jury, did a masterly job of demolishing the house that Hall had built. Whatever the motives, he said, that had led Palmer to inform the police, it was undoubtedly factually true that the varnish had been stolen and that the defendants had paid for it. It beggared credulity, he pointed out reasonably, that they had not known it to be stolen: how else could they obtain goods worth ten times the amount paid? He sat, well content with the obvious effect he had produced on the jurymen.

When Hall rose to make his speech, he knew that it was all to do again. He looked at the jurymen's faces and saw no hope. Straightening his shoulders, he concentrated all his attention on that one known man amongst them. The sportsman. The man of decent feeling.

'There is one thing sure in life,' he began, speaking slowly, his voice so low that they had to strain to hear him, 'and without that one thing, we are lost.' He paused, taking their eyes. 'It is the word of a man. His solemn word, given in the certain trust that, knowing him, knowing of a thousand other instances of his steadfastness, we can rely upon it. Without this, how could we conduct our lives in the common intercourse of society, in the sacred temple of hearth and home, in the very citadel of business and, gentlemen, perhaps above all, in these great courts of law? A man's word. His bond. Upon this, all rests. Take that away – and all falls.'

He stood, shoulders hunched, looking down; silent, deep in thought. He slowly raised his head to look back again at the jury. 'But what if that man be such that his word cannot be taken? What if our knowledge of that man tells us that he is a cheat? What if our apprehensions of his conduct show us that, in matters most sacred, he is, as the sturdy schoolboy would say – with more wisdom than his years would seem to allow – a *sneak*?' He lifted his hands, then let them fall to his side. 'Reflect upon that word from our playgrounds and school-rooms, gentlemen. Was there ever a lower form of life, a more contemptible fellow than the *sneak*? Every code broken; all honour, all reputation, lost. A *sneak*. Snivelling, twisting and, if we but knew it, time and again, *lying*? Did you ever condemn one of your playmates on such a word as his?' He shook his head. 'No. Never. For then our honour would have been as his. In the dust.' Once again he paused, searching their faces.

'Such is the case here,' he went on. 'My clients – respectable men, worthy men, standing high in the esteem of their society – are brought to this place and this predicament on one man's word. You have seen him. You now know him. And, knowing, *do you take his word?*'

'That is the crux of the whole matter before you. Can you trust the man Palmer? Can you? *Dare you?* I look in your faces and I see there a deep and sure love of the rock of certitude and the cleansing springs of truth. Hold to that rock, gentlemen! Drink of those waters!' He clutched the desk before him, exhausted by the effort he had put into his words. Then, his voice a dry and searching whisper, he said: 'And set my clients free!'

There was a profound silence as he almost collapsed into his seat. Then, from the back of the public gallery a man cheered. The sound had not died away before it was taken up by all the spectators and rolled, like a great wave, to the very feet of the judge.

The judge's summing up was cautious to the point of obscurity, but at least, Hall thought, he wasn't directing a conviction. As soon as he had finished and the jury had retired, Hall made his way out of court. As he passed, lawyers and laymen turned to look at him. Whatever he had done that day, for good or ill, it had not passed unnoticed. But now he had to get a breath of air; the atmosphere of the courtroom was intolerably heavy.

He stood by the doors to the street. People were passing; some on foot, some in carriages, some on horseback, but all were oblivious to what was happening in the court. And this seemed to him to be strange, that there should be an unheeding world out there.

A policeman was tugging at the sleeve of his gown. He turned to face him. 'I think they're coming back, sir,' the policeman said.

'They've not taken long,' Hall frowned. He read this as a bad sign; he'd hoped that he'd managed to sow enough seeds of doubt in a few of their minds for them to protract the business to the point when the rest of them would give up.

'No, they haven't,' the policeman said, walking back to the court.

Hall followed him and, as he came in, the first person he looked for was his acquaintance on the jury. The man was meeting his eyes now, all right; more than that, he was nodding a greeting and smiling.

The foreman was on his feet and the question was put to him. Without a moment of hesitation, in a clear voice, he gave their verdict: 'Not guilty, my Lord.'

It was, he averred, the verdict of them all.

Once again, the court burst into a storm of cheering, but Hall walked through it quickly. His work was done, and he was set on catching the 5.23 home. He was missing his wife desperately. What a story he'd have to tell her tonight!

The train was pulling out of the station when Hall saw Charlie Gill running alongside, porter puffing at his heels with his bags. He threw the carriage door open and pulled him in, catching the bags the porter threw. Gill fell into a corner seat facing Hall, struggling to get his breath.

'You didn't hang about, young Hall,' he gasped.

'Neither did you,' Hall smiled.

'Oh, well.' Gill patted his chest, blowing air out. 'Business tomorrow, at the Bailey. I'm an indecent assault.'

'Lucky you.'

'I never let luck come into my plans. Nor should you.'

Hall shook his head, smiling slightly still. 'Oh, I always leave space for the dove.'

'What was that?' Gill asked, pushing his head forward.

'Nothing. Nothing at all.'

Gill was silent for a time, watching the scenery fly past. Then he turned to Hall. 'You did well with that case. Very well indeed. Your final speech – not my style, you understand, not my style at all – but it was good. Didn't know you had such a way with words.'

'You heard it?'

'Course I heard it! Didn't you see me?'

Hall shook his head. 'I didn't dare take my eyes off the jury.'

'Well, there you are. Well done . . . and you got a verdict. Which is a damn sight more than I'd have done, I reckon.'

'Oh, come now, Charlie! I was only the understudy. You'd have got them off in half the time!'

'I don't think so.' He leant towards Hall and tapped his knee. 'Thought any more of what I said? About shifting chambers?'

'Hm,' Hall said, enigmatically.

'What does that mean?'

'Nothing. What should it mean?'

'Come on with you! There's something up that sleeve.'

'What a cross-examiner you are, to be sure,' Hall said, mimicking his brogue. 'All right, then, if you insist – it means that while I was in the robing room – after the verdict – Forrest Fulton came over. Said he wanted a word.'

Gill gave a low whistle. 'Playing with the big boys there, Marshall. He's got about the best criminal practice at the Bar. What did he want?'

Hall smiled, enjoying the moment. 'He said, old Charlie, that he was offering me a place in his chambers.'

'You don't say so!'

'I do,' Hall nodded. 'He said that a lot of the young men were pretty well duffers, but he thought there was an opening for me. If I wanted it.'

'You said "yes", didn't you?'

'I said "yes".'

Gill threw his hands up. 'Oh, don't I wish I'd had the foresight to bring a bottle of bubbly on to this damned train! Never mind – we'll see what we can do when we get to town, eh?'

'Another celebration?'

'It's called for, isn't it just!'

'Maybe one glass.'

'I should say so! Marshall, my boy, you're on your way! What a tale you've got for that wife of yours!'

The tale had to remain untold: when he got home the house was in darkness. He lit a lamp and rang the bell for the skivvy. When she came, she told him that the mistress had been out all day, that she'd only come home to change and gone straight out again. And, no, she hadn't said where she was going or how late she would be.

The girl must have noticed Hall's crestfallen expression. 'I'm sure she'll soon be home, sir,' she said.

Hall turned away, kicking the fire into life. 'Yes. I'm sure she will.'

She was about to go, but hesitated in the doorway. 'Would you like something to eat, sir?' she asked.

'Is there anything?'

'Cook said that she could always cut you a cold slice or two off the joint. Mutton it was, sir.'

His stomach heaved at the thought of it. 'No. No thank you. Tell cook she can send up some bread, and a bit of cheese, if there is any.'

'Very good, sir.'

'And fetch me the whisky decanter and a glass.'

He fell asleep in the chair by the dying fire and only woke, stiff and dry-throated, when he heard a cab in the street and the front door opening. He got up, meaning to go to her, but there was the sound of low voices in the hall, and he was too tired for meetings and greetings. Thank God someone's had the decency to fetch her safe home, he thought.

He stood, the excitement of the day beginning to return, whilst the front door slammed, the cab jingled off and Ethel came into the room. She was dabbing her lips with her handkerchief.

'I didn't know that you'd be back tonight or I'd have stayed at home,' she said, ignoring his outstretched hands.

'I told you – in my telegram.'

'Oh, did you? I didn't notice,' she said, slipping her cloak off and throwing it over the back of a chair.

'I've missed you so much,' he said.

She raised an eyebrow. 'Yes?'

'Yes.'

She sat, at some distance from him, in a chair by the table. 'How was Sussex? More drudgery for you?'

'Not this time.'

'Oh?'

He could keep his surprise for her no longer. 'I fought a case, an important case. And I won it!'

'Did you get paid?'

'Oh I will be. I met this man, this marvellous man – Charlie Gill – we must have him over to dinner, you'll like him, you really will –'

'Another lawyer?'

'Yes, but –'

'God help us,' she yawned, not bothering to cover her mouth.

Tiredness, whisky and a feeling of neglect worked together, and a dull anger gripped his gut. 'That was rather a rude thing to do,' he said, unable to keep his voice steady.

'What did you say?' she asked, as if mildly surprised.

'Yawning in my face –'

'I'm tired, Edward! Haven't I a right to be?'

He turned away from her. 'For God's sake! I've been away for days! Can't you even show a glimmer of interest in what I do?'

She sighed. 'I'm sorry. All right then: tell me about this case of yours. The one that you won.'

'It was nothing. It wouldn't interest you.'

'Please, Edward. I'm longing for my bed. But tell me, do, and then we can rest.'

'Matter of two tradesmen,' he said, his back still to her and his voice low, 'accused of receiving a barrow-load of varnish.'

She laughed. 'That's it?'

'Yes.'

'Oh, really! You lawyers, you are so *funny*!'

'Are we?' he said, his voice dry as dust.

'Well! What can such a piddling affair possibly matter? Now a murder, something like that – a really good murder – and I could understand all the fuss. But two *tradesmen*, stealing a pot of paint!' She shook her head. 'Was there anything else thrilling that you want to tell me about? Some other triumph?'

'Fulton Forrest's asked me to join his chambers.'

'Who's he?'

'Another dreary lawyer.'

She picked up her cloak. 'I hope he finds you a nice room. I'm going to bed now.'

'Shall we always go on like this?' he asked.

She paused, her fingers on the door handle. 'Yes, we shall. I warned you, long since, of that.'

He was looking at her, his eyes dark in his pale face. 'It's insupportable.'

She held his gaze. 'Then don't support it. Let me go.'

'No.'

'Then you have only yourself to blame.'

CHAPTER
THIRTEEN

Their lives went on in the same way. She had her circle of friends, he had his. Occasionally they overlapped, as when they gave their supper parties for theatre folk, or went down to stay with Ellen Terry. But for the most part they were separate. Charlie Gill had put Hall up for a couple of London clubs; and he was, of course, easily elected – for who would black-ball such an agreeable and easy fellow? On most nights for want of food or company at home he would dine and sleep in one or the other of them – preferably the Garrick, that was always his favourite.

They were much envied: the coming young lawyer, so handsome, so gifted and so charming, and his beautiful, vivacious and popular wife. It was, alas, true that occasionally, in that small village of London society, more prudish tongues would wag about the company she kept, but, somehow, word had got around of her incorrigible fidelity, and the breath of scandal died on the chill air of her undoubted chastity. She was, it was agreed, merely a high-spirited girl who would, when the nursery at last started to fill, settle down nicely and be a credit to everyone.

In the summer he played cricket and tennis; they were a sort of passion, and often in Chambers when some conference was boring him, he would throw down his papers, pick up his racket and go down to the Temple Gardens for a set or two. Others might have been censured for it, but not he. It was just one of Marshall's little peculiarities. As the days shortened he would sit at his ease in Chambers, chatting whilst he cleaned his guns, ready for the shooting season when the game flew sweet and he was the ever-welcome guest at the country houses.

The Prince of Wales was a nodding acquaintance and might have come closer, but Hall was a better shot than he and this *lèse-majesté* kept them distant.

At law he was doing reasonably well, slowly pulling himself up the greasy pole of his profession, changing chambers four times in as many years and beginning to make a bit of money. Nothing spectacular yet, for the big fees, the huge fortunes that some of his learned friends pulled down came with the fame of appearing in the well reported, gossiped-over, spectacular cases; the *causes célèbres*. But these rich pickings were jealously guarded by the big men and few others ever got a sniff at them.

That was the public life. When chance threw them together without company she was cool and distant, whilst he was attentive, careful of her wants, fetching presents to her as a worshipper might deck an idol. And this was as irksome as ever to her. Time and time again, she begged him for a separation, but his devotion was rock-like, and he would not and could not let her go.

When she was alone she would consider the prospect of walking from his house and breaking the bars of her prison. But how would she live? To go back to her mother was impossible; she would never accept the thought of husband and wife living apart, and would do her utmost to send her back to him on the very next train. As for supporting herself, making her own life, she had neither qualifications nor aptitude for it. It could not be, as her husband never failed to point out to her.

If their life together was a hell on earth to him, at least he had means of pushing it aside in the demands of his work; but she had no such release. Her looks were beginning to fade; her cheeks were hollow and her eyes, when she was with her friends, had a feverish sparkle.

Hall noticed it, of course, and was as solicitous as ever, begging her to see a doctor. But she knew the cause of her illness and contemptuously refused. Health would return, she told him, on the day when he went out of the door for the last time. At last, however, he had his way.

Dr Phillips was called and, in the manner of his profession, seeing that they were childless, ascribed her malady to the need of pregnancy. He examined her and, like his predecessor, was appalled to find that the hymen of this respectably married woman was still intact. He said nothing to Ethel, but left her to dress whilst he had a glass of whisky and a few words with the husband, who told him little of the state of their marriage other than that intimacy was abhorrent to his wife, and that he accepted this. There were, he said, other things in marriage than procreation.

The doctor frowned; this was not at all the way he saw the case, and he was determined to put things to rights, once and for all. He went back to his patient and told her that a minor operation was absolutely essential for her health and happiness. She closed her eyes and turned her head away. She knew well enough what he meant, and she wanted none of it.

But the good doctor was quietly insistent, patiently explaining to her that, in the female, most illnesses, especially mental illnesses, sprang from disorders of their child-bearing organs. That, he smiled, is why we use the word 'hysteria'.

'Such things, my dear, are common and can so easily be cured.'

Her tight-lipped silence was taken as assent and the next day his carriage was sent round to convey her to his surgery. Hall got someone to devil his cases for the rest of the week and stayed with her.

There were some difficulties when the coachman rang the doorbell: she was sobbing and crying that she would not go, and clung on to the door when Hall tried to lead her. But he knew his duty, for the doctor had told him of the imperative necessity of the operation, and he pulled her fingers loose and carried her out of the house.

Once at the doctor's, he and Hall held her while the chloroform was administered and she gave up the struggle.

Hall paced the waiting room, on edge, praying that all at last would come right. Within minutes it was over and Phillips came in to him, rolling his shirt sleeves down and smiling. 'Relax, man!' the doctor smiled. 'She'll be as right as rain in an hour or two.'

'Thank God.'

The doctor motioned Hall to a seat. 'You should have called for medical advice long since,' he said.

'It would have made a difference?'

'Oh, my goodness me, yes.' He looked at Hall for a moment. 'In some women, you see, the hymen is particularly strong. Rupture can be an agony. Most permit this – in the sacred cause of marital duty – but there are a few, more delicate souls, who cannot.'

'My wife is one such?'

'She was,' the doctor smiled. 'But all is right now. Take her away for a few days – somewhere in the country.' He leant forward, a fatherly hand on Hall's knee. 'And I think you'll find, my boy, that she will welcome your embraces.'

'This is certain?' Hall asked, frowning.

'As night follows day.'

It was out of season, so the hotel at Eastborne was only half full, and that with old folk and invalids. Out of caution and custom, he took two rooms for them, explaining, as a matter of habit now, that his wife was unwell and needed perfect peace and quiet. The clerk nodded his tactful assent and gave them rooms on an empty corridor.

They ate their dinner in silence; Ethel picked at her food, but drank well of the burgundy. The doctor had virtually prescribed it; she should have at least half a bottle every evening, he said, immediately before retiring.

She sipped her final glass whilst Hall had his brandy and coffee. (She couldn't join him in this: all stimulants were to be forsworn for ever.) 'Wine's not pleasant when you're ordered to drink it,' she said.

'You're doing very well. Finish it up.'

She took another mouthful, grimacing as she swallowed it. 'Horrid.'

He leant back, lighting a cigar. 'I think you're looking better already,' he said, taking care to blow the smoke away from her.

'I don't feel it.'

'You will.'

'When?'

He shrugged. 'I'm no doctor.'

She put the empty wine glass down, but held on to the stem of it, twisting it round. Some wine had spilled, leaving a stain on the white cloth. 'When I've let you sleep with me and I'm happily pregnant? Is that when?'

'I didn't say that, or think it.'

'It's what it's all for, though, all this. Isn't it?'

'The doctor believes that it would make you well.' He put a hand on hers. 'I don't ask it.'

She pulled her hand away. 'No.'

'I only want to –'

She got up. 'Oh, I know well enough what you want. You've told me often enough, God knows.'

He had risen, facing her. She took a step from the table towards the doors, but swayed, clutching a chair for support. He was immediately at her side, holding her.

'I think I need some help,' she said. 'I feel rather faint.'

The fire in her bedroom was smoking into the room, and he pulled the curtains back and slid the upper window down a little. 'I'll close it before I go,' he said, 'then you won't be sleeping in a draught.'

She stood, her legs supported by the bed behind her, nodded and began to unbutton her bodice. 'Don't look at me,' she said. 'See to the fire. See if you can make it burn up.'

He turned away from her and knelt by the fire, coaxing it into a blaze. 'I'll wait till you're settled,' he said.

'What did you say?' she asked, her voice muffled by her slip as she pulled it over her head.

'In bed. Wrapped up, snug.'

'Suit yourself,' she said, sitting heavily on the bed to kick off her shoes and slip off her silk stockings. She gave a hiccup.

He asked, 'Would you like a glass of water?'

Still obeying the rules of the game, not looking at her, he went over to the washstand and filled a tumbler.

She hiccuped again. 'Come on, hurry up,' she ordered.

He came towards her. Her clothes lay in a heap on the floor and she was under the coverlet. He held out the glass and, carefully, holding the sheet to her breasts, she sat up and drank it, her eyes never leaving his.

'Is that better?' he asked.

'We'll see. In about half an hour,' she replied.

'We?'

She nodded and, in an unhurried movement, threw the bed-clothes back and kicked them away. She was naked.

'Don't you want to find out if the doctor was right?' she asked.

He stood for a moment, looking at her, then began to tear off his clothes.

'No!' she cried. 'In the dark. I don't want to see you.'

He stumbled over to the lamp and she could see the obscene bulge in his trousers. She turned away, biting her lip.

She could hear his breathing, like a man who has run a long race, and then he slid into bed beside her. She put a hand on his shoulder. 'You're shivering,' she murmured.

'Yes.'

'Come here. Lie close.' His arm was around her and he pulled her to him, feeling the warm softness of her breasts against his chest. He found her lips and held her in a long kiss. Her hand was in his hair, feeling the spring and curl of it.

'I love you, love you,' he gasped, his firm hand following the sweet curves of her body. She shuddered with pleasure at the strength, the power of him, his huge hardness pressing into her belly.

'Do you?' she asked, 'After this long time, waiting?'

'Always, oh, *always*! I swore that I would –'

She stopped his mouth with an open kiss, then rained kisses on his neck, his cheeks. 'No more talking, no, please, no more,' she whispered and pulled away from him, lying on her back. 'Do it!' she begged. '*Now!*'

He knelt, looking down at her in the firelight and then, with a moan, lay on top of her, thrusting into her body. She gasped and then, as she felt him beginning to enter her, a flood of bitter wine and food rose in her throat. She turned her head, retching, choking. Still he was pushing, thrusting, her body dry and closed against him.

She managed to twist away from him and leant over the edge of the bed, vomiting.

Naked still, he cleaned up the mess with a towel, threw it into a corner and stood, looking down on her.

She was silently weeping. 'Now will you let me go?' she asked, in a small voice.

'Perhaps next time it would be better,' he said.

She shook her head. 'I cannot love you. I cannot,' she said. 'Tonight I swore that I would try. You saw what happened.'

'Live apart? For ever?'

'Please, Eddie. It will kill me to be in the same house with you for another day. If you love me . . . let me be, let me live.'

He turned away, wearily pulling on his clothes. 'I'll go first thing in the morning. I'll stay at my club for a while.'

'Oh, thank God,' she sighed.

'But avoid me, keep away. Don't torture me with a sight of you.'

'I swear it,' she promised.

Exhausted, her eyes were closing. She didn't hear or see him leave.

CHAPTER
FOURTEEN

It was Hall's habit to call in on Charlie Gill in his chambers from time to time. In their small world, he knew when his friend would have time for a chat. So on this snow-blown February day, Charlie wasn't surprised to hear the familiar footsteps on the stair, nor to see his friend in the doorway.

'Do shut the door, man,' Gill said. 'I'm getting blown off my chair.'

Hall kicked the door shut behind him and went to the fire, warming his hands at the blaze. Gill saw that his face was white and drawn.

'You all right?' he asked, as he took the sherry decanter from its cabinet.

'Perfectly.'

'Not caught a chill or anything?'

'Oh, for God's sake! Don't be such an old woman and pour the drink.'

'Yours to command,' Gill murmured as he filled the glasses. 'And are you taking your coat off? This isn't a pub, you know.'

Hall removed his coat and threw it over the back of a chair, where melting snow dripped from it on to Gill's prized Indian carpet.

He sat, legs crossed, trying to look at ease, and took a sip of the sherry. He pulled a face. 'If you don't mind my saying so, this is a damned poor fino you keep. Meant to tell you that for years.'

Gill chuckled. 'Oh, isn't it just! I've laid it down for im-pecunious barristers, heart-broken clients and greedy little solicitors. Never does to give any of 'em aspirations beyond their means.'

'Not so much of your "impecunious". This year's not been so bad.'

'I've noticed.' He took a sip of sherry. 'But the word is —' He left the sentence in the air, knowing Hall's confounded touchiness and temper.

'What word?'

Gill shook his head. This certainly wasn't the moment to say what he had been going to, and he was profoundly wishing that he'd never started on it.

'Come on, man spit it out! You were going to say something.'

Gill put his glass down. 'All right, then. Word is that you've either been turning briefs down or getting someone to devil them for you.'

'I wish people would mind their own bloody business!'

Gill considered this, his head on one side. 'Don't you go forgetting, Marshall, that minding other people's business is what lawyers get paid for. Now, come on with you, what are you at? You can't afford to turn work away, not at your stage.'

Hall got up and went to the fireplace where he stood, shoulders hunched, looking down into the flames. 'I've had . . . other things on my mind,' he growled.

'Do you want to talk about these . . . other things?' Gill asked, gently.

'It's why I'm here.'

'Ah.' Gill poured them both another sherry.

Hall was silent for some time, still gazing into the fire. Gill, to his surprise, saw that his friend's shoulders were shaking with sobs. He half-rose from his chair, then he changed his mind and sat again, waiting.

Hall blew his nose, straightened up and turned to him. 'I want you to draw up a deed of separation . . . between a husband and his wife.'

'This is solicitor's work, Marshall.'

'No, it's friend's work.'

'Do I take it that you're talking about yourself here?' Gill asked. He knew damn well he was, but in this matter, as he knew of old, dealing with Marshall was like walking on eggs.

'Yes.'

'Are you quite sure it's come to this?'

'Of course I'm bloody well sure!'

'All right!' He held up a placatory hand.

'Do you think I do this lightly?'

'Well, now,' Gill murmured, 'I know fine well that you don't, but you mustn't shout at me, Marshall. That's no way.'

'I'm sorry.'

'Not half so sorry as I am. Believe me in that.' He pushed Hall's drink across to him, then fiddled with a pencil on his desk. 'As a friend . . .'

'Yes?'

'I have to point out to you that a divorce would be harmful to you in your career. More than harmful. It would ruin you.'

Hall shook his head. 'There's no question of such a thing. Never.'

Gill shrugged his shoulders. 'Then –'

'No,' Hall interrupted. 'Never.' He sat, leaning forward, head bowed, his hands clasped in his lap. 'I will never marry again. And my wife –' He cleared his throat. 'My wife can have no desire to contract another marriage.'

'These are very absolute words,' Gill murmured.

Hall looked up at him, bleak desperation in his eyes. 'I say this to no one but you, Charlie, and it must never be spoken of again –' He couldn't finish the sentence, but looked away, swallowing.

'Trust me. *Trust me*.'

'My wife cannot . . . she cannot give herself to any man. It is impossible for her.'

'You have never . . .?'

'No.'

'Dear God, Marshall.'

'I thought you knew . . . from what I've said . . . in the past.'

'Something, yes. I knew that things were't easy between you, but not that.' He was silent for a moment, thinking of the hidden lives of men. 'Is it you that's wanting this separation, or your wife?'

Tears were streaming down Hall's cheeks. 'I love her, you see. More than life itself. She haunts my every moment, and she always will.'

In that room, God knows, Gill had seen some tragic things, heard some terrible stories. But nothing had so moved him as the sight of this proud man, his heart breaking.

'I'll see that things are put in hand for you,' he murmured, going to the door. 'Just you rest there. I'll have a message sent round to the clerk of your chambers, telling him you're unwell.'

As quietly as he could, he went out of the room. Once in the outer office he stood for a moment, deep in thought. The woman was a heartless bitch, that was for sure, to do this to a man. Then he sat at the big table, pulled a sheet of paper from the rack and began to write.

At first, the rooms seemed curiously quiet and empty, and Ethel could not fully realize that the silence would not be broken by his clatter on the stairs, the space not filled by his great height and bulk nor the air clouded by his cigar smoke. Even as she ate her dinner, she half-expected him to burst in on her.

But the sweet and blessed solitude was unbroken. She felt like a soldier in a war after peace has been declared. At some time, of course, she would have to say something to the servants about Eddie's absence, but not just yet. Like so many things now, it could wait; it needn't be faced. The evening stretched before her and she smiled at the idea of it. She had a good book from the circulating library and she would settle down with it by the fire, and stay up as long as she liked. She sipped her burgundy and enjoyed the prospect ahead.

From the kitchen she could hear the skivvy singing a song from the latest musical comedy. That too was a possibility; she knew where her friends would be after the show had finished. There would be light there, company and attention. She laughed aloud at the thought, pushed her plate away and went into her bedroom to change.

Hall came from the dining-room of his club. The porter, seeing him come towards him, knew his question before he asked it. He shook his head. 'Sorry, sir. No messages at all.' He was already turning his attention to another, more distinguished, member of the club coming in, rather unsteadily, from the street.

'Good evening, Mr Irving,' he said, giving an inclination of his head that might almost have been a bow to royalty.

'And no one has called – asking for me?' Hall said.

The porter was already walking towards Irving. 'Not a soul, sir,' he replied. 'Shall you be having supper?' he asked the actor.

Irving stood, swaying slightly, considering the question deeply. 'I think not, Frank.' He went on his stately way towards the staircase. Clutching the newel post, he saw Hall and turned his attention to him. 'Are you a member of this club, sir?' he asked, head back, squinting through his pince-nez.

'Of course.'

'New, though. Not seen ye around.'

'Couple of years since. My name's Marshall Hall.'

'Is it . . .? Is it now? Extraordinary,' Irving murmured, and began to ascend, watched anxiously by the porter. After a step or two he stopped, a hand on the bannister, and turned again to Hall. 'Ever thought of becoming an actor?'

'No.'

'Thank God for that.' He climbed another few steps and stopped to get his breath.

'Your leading lady – Miss Terry – is a friend of mine. And of my wife's.'

Irving nodded and gave him a sardonic smile. 'Nell gives her friendship very – readily. It is the most blessed quality of womankind.' He looked at the stairs before him, straightened his shoulders to the task and ran up them.

'Is it?' Hall murmured.

The supper party was all that Ethel had hoped it would be; the room was crowded, as she liked it to be, smoke-filled and noisy with talk and laughter. The young man next to her, a moustache barely sprouting on his top lip, was nervously pressing his leg against hers under the table. She smiled at him and gave a slight shake of her head, at the same time pulling her leg away. There were some things now that she would have to be careful of; she could never be compromised before – the presence of a devoted husband, albeit in the background, protected her from that. But as a single woman . . .

She leant back in her chair, looking round the room, seeing if any famous people were there. Disappointingly there weren't, but there was one face that she did recognize and she frowned, trying to place him. Almost as if he were aware that she was looking at him, he glanced across at her and their eyes met. For a moment a waiter came between them, but when he had gone she saw that the slight and sunburnt young man was raising his glass to her and smiling. She frowned, looking away. Then she remembered: he had been there at the dinner party that that man – what was his name – had given for her and Eddie on their honeymoon. She vaguely remembered that the young man had something to do with the army – and that he'd been very quiet. Raoul something or other, that was it. Under cover of making a remark to a fattish but jolly actress at the other side of the table, she took another look at the army man. He was still staring in her direction and his eyes held a questioning intensity. From somewhere within her she felt a slight shiver of fear.

*

As usual there was a pile of letters for Eddie on the breakfast table, set out on his side plate. She collected them up and put them on the sideboard; later, if she remembered, she would re-direct them to his club. Then, as she sat at her own place, to her surprise she saw that there was an official-looking letter to her, addressed in flowing copperplate. Frowning, she tore it open and read it, unable, at first, to make out what it meant. But after another slow reading, she saw that she was required, as a matter of urgency, to present herself at some lawyer's office in one of the Inns of Court.

She put the letter down, wondering what it could all mean. What had this lawyer to do with her? It couldn't be anything to do with the lease of their rooms: Eddie saw to all that sort of thing. She shook her head and put the letter aside. There was only one way to find out, she thought, as she chopped the top off her soft-boiled egg.

As she walked through Temple Gardens in the wintry sunshine, she wondered if she would bump into Eddie. There were lots of lawyers about, some of them wearing their silly little wigs, their black gowns billowing behind them. She remembered Eddie when he first put his lawyer's clothes on, thinking to surprise her. Well, at least he looked better than any of this motley crew, with their flapping papers under their arms, trying to look as if they were busy with matters of life and death, brows furrowed in deep thought. She looked for the finest man amongst them, but there was no sight of him.

In fact, she needn't have worried: Charlie Gill had made quite sure that Marshall would be well away in Maidstone before he called her to his Chambers.

And what a disappointment those chambers were! She had thought that lawyers worked in grand, imposing places; but this dusty, over-heated room was the sort of place that her father wouldn't even have let his patients wait in to see him. Really, when one thought of the airs these lawyers gave themselves. Chambers, indeed! More like slums, with their grimy windows, papers all over the place and that terrible smell of musty books.

With difficulty she turned her attention to this man Gill, whom she knew to be a friend of Eddie's, though she'd taken great care never to meet him. He was reading from the dreary document on the desk before him, and that was enough in itself to make her angry. What could Eddie be thinking of, bringing their affairs to the knowledge of every piffling little barrister in London? And why on earth did he think it necessary to have someone write a paper like this? They were living apart. So did lots of people; there was no need for all this legal flim-flam.

'Now we come to Clause Four,' Gill droned.

Ethel stirred restlessly. 'Quite frankly, Mr Gill, I don't see what all this is about,' she said.

He put the paper down and looked at her coldly. 'I have told you, Mrs Marshall Hall, several times,' he said. 'This is a document of legal separation.'

'Has my husband written it?'

'No. I am acting for him.'

'But he's asked you to do it?'

Gill frowned. 'Such a document had to be written.'

'I don't see why!'

He took his spectacles off, folded them and laid them carefully on top of the papers. 'I understand,' he said, 'that the separation *a mensa et thoro* is at your request, rather than your husband's.'

'It was felt best by both of us. And it was he who said he was going!'

'Did he now?' Gill asked, dryly. If he'd called her 'liar' to her face, his meaning couldn't have been clearer.

'If you want proof of that, I'm still living in our rooms. It's he who is missing.'

Gill put his hands together under his chin and pursed his lips. 'We shall come to the question of lease and disposal of chattels in one moment.'

'What does that mean?'

'It means,' he said, leaning towards her, across the cluttered desk, 'that the vacation of the rooms in Seymour Street and the disposal of the household effects therein will have to be put in hand.'

'Would he throw me out into the street?' she cried.

He shook his head. 'If you will be patient, Mrs Marshall Hall, you will discover that he is being more than generous to you.'

'Generous? Is that what you call it!'

He put his spectacles back on, cleared his throat and repeated: 'Clause Four. Mrs Ethel Marshall Hall as forementioned above in the Preamble being the wife of the signatory of this Deed shall hereby be paid on the first day of each and every quarter a sum equal to one quarter of all professional fees and emoluments which have been received in the preceding quarter by the aforementioned signatory Edward Marshall Hall Barrister-at-Law.'

'A quarter? Of everything he earns?' she asked.

Gill nodded. 'I told you that he had been generous. And he later stipulates that, if his income should diminish to a point where you would not be well provided for, he guarantees you the sum of £130 per annum.' He paused to let this sink in. 'I warned him against this, but he was insistent. It could beggar him.'

'Eddie's a good man. He always was.' She looked away. 'That's been his trouble.'

Gill shrugged his shoulders and went back to the document. 'Such moneys are to be paid by the undermentioned trustees without hindrance for as long as Mrs Ethel Marshall Hall as forementioned above in the Preamble shall be leading a chaste and virtuous life.'

'Did Eddie think of putting that in, too?' she asked, feeling her cheeks turning scarlet.

'As a matter of form, merely. He gave me to understand that you, Mrs Marshall Hall, are like Caesar's wife, above suspicion.'

'I think it's a terrible, wicked thing to put down. How could he?'

Gill put his head on one side and considered her. 'I think it's very bad law. And I told him so. But then, with respect, your husband is not a very good lawyer.'

She laughed, but there was no humour in it. 'You seem to think badly of the pair of us, Mr Gill.'

'Of you, Madam, I think nothing, since I know nothing. Of your husband . . . I know him to be one of the finest men I have ever met, whom I am proud to call my friend. I know him to have the capabilities to be a fine advocate,' he looked at her searchingly, 'if these sad events haven't altogether destroyed him.'

For the first time she noticed his Irish accent. 'Oh come, Mr Gill,' she smiled. 'Destroyed him? *Edward?*'

'It's conceivable.'

She held his gaze. 'You blame me for this?'

He sighed. 'I've appeared too many times in cases of divorce to apportion blame easily. Between a man and a woman – in their minds, in their hearts – who can safely enter that hidden world?'

'Who indeed? But you still think me a bad wife?'

He looked down at his desk, turning a pencil round in his fingers. 'A man aspiring to rise to the heights in our profession needs all the support he can get, from any and every quarter. Most of all from his partner on the great journey.'

She sighed. 'No one, ever, will speak in *my* cause. But it is there.'

He picked the papers up again. 'I must complete this reading to you.'

She tore off her glove. 'Save your breath. I will sign it, if that's what you want.'

'I cannot permit that. It must be read to you.'

'It's now or never, Mr Gill. A pen, please.'

'If you insist,' he said, dipping a pen in the ink-well and handing it to her. 'I have marked with a pencil the places where –'

'I see them well enough,' she said, signing her name with a

flourish. 'And tell Eddie not to worry about the rooms. I hate the wretched place. It reminds me of him.'

When she came out of the lawyer's room and stepped out into Temple Gardens, the sun had clouded over and a cold wind was blowing. She drew her cape closer round her shoulders and pulled up its little fur collar. But the mantle was made for style rather than warmth and she shivered.

Rather than walk up to Fleet Street and the Courts, where she might see Edward, she went down to the new Embankment, hoping to find a cab, wanting home, a warm fire and a cup of tea. But cabs seemed to have disappeared from the face of the earth. She stood, looking at the wide, fast-flowing grey river, and her thoughts were as desolate as the scene before her.

She hadn't thought that it would come to this: to lawyers, documents and having to give up their cosy rooms and servants. Somehow she had thought that he would be there, neither seen nor heard, not making any demands, but looking after her, as he always had done. It was selfish of her, she knew that, but it had always been so. There had always been someone to take care of her: her father until he died, then her mother as best she could and then Edward. Women were meant to be looked after; it was the natural order of being.

She could always, of course, go back to her mother. Or to her husband. With a shake of her head she dismissed both thoughts. She tightened her lips and lifted her head. She was strong. She was free. She had her whole life before her, and if she were to be happy or miserable in that life, it would be her choice, and hers only. As for her having to live, what was it that lawyer said? 'A chaste and virtuous life', and she knew well what a man meant by that – they need have no worries on that score. Her body was inviolate and no man would ever force an entry into that temple. And anyway, even if it weren't so, Edward could scarcely have some policeman watching her day and night. It was all stupid and insulting nonsense.

A weak ray of sunshine broke through the clouds and turned

the leaden Thames into silver. Happiness is our own choice, she thought triumphantly, and walked briskly alongside the river wall. She would show him, show all of them, just what she could do.

She stopped to look at a red-sailed barge ploughing through the waters, its sails shivering in the wind. A man on deck waved to her and shouted something. She hesitated for a moment and then waved back, laughing. It wasn't the sort of thing a respectable lawyer's wife would do, but then, she thought, she was done with all that pretence. Eddie's ghastly sister and the whole crew of sniffy women could jump in the river for all she cared. She was done with them at last. Thank God! *Done with them!* She could have shouted the words at the top of her lungs, letting all London know.

And, as for those poky rooms in Seymour Street – what did he think they were? Buckingham Palace? She'd give those up, no trouble. She wanted to leave them, she decided. She needed to, if her life was really to be new. Goodness knows, she had enough friends to suggest somewhere else to live. And, knowing those friends as she did, where they found would be much nicer. She thought of somewhere fresh and full of light, with the furniture chosen by herself, for herself. Oh, it would be so *good*!

Thinking these pleasant thoughts, walking briskly through the streets, she was home in no time at all – and she had saved the cab fare! Start as you mean to go on, my girl, she thought, prudently, as she rang the bell for tea and hot muffins.

Charlie Gill looked through his window and watched her as she walked away. She was a damned attractive woman, there was no doubting that. Good figure on her, nice little bum, pert head and well turned-out too, by God. And Marshall was such a man as to turn women's heads in the street; he'd been with him, many a time, when just such a thing had happened. So what the hell had gone wrong with the pair of them? Idiots, he sighed. Damned idiots.

He went back to his desk and slipped the document of separation into a cardboard folder. There were a couple of briefs on the desk needing his urgent attention, coming on as they were in the next week, and both of them tricky and complicated. It was his method to write out, in careful copperplate, every question that he would ask in examination and cross-examination and then, beneath each question, write every conceivable answer that witnesses could give. But such painstaking strategies took time, and these cases would need at least twelve hours each. He sat down, put on his spectacles, picked up his pen and prepared to begin. But he saw to his annoyance that Marshall's wife had pressed so hard on the nib that she had crossed it. He opened a drawer and began a search amongst the India-rubbers, pink ribbons and other detritus for a new nib. Whilst he rooted about, the thought of her came back to him. Did she have a case? Was there something on her side that hadn't been said, he wondered? Well, he would never know, he supposed. As ever, he would just have to rely on the facts as given. He found a nib at the very back of the drawer and fitted it to the holder. But getting the old nib out had left his fingers ink-stained and, irritated, he wiped them on his handkerchief.

With a sigh he pulled the papers towards him and started to read. But his mind kept wandering from the case. The scent of the woman was still in the room; maybe that was it. He threw his pen down. Damn it all, the afternoon had unsettled him, he might as well admit it. And that didn't happen often.

He took his watch out: maybe Marshall's case at Maidstone would have finished early; if it had, he might just have got the 3.23 and be back in chambers any time now.

Well, he needed some exercise and a breath of fresh air. He shoved the papers away and picked up the folder.

If Ethel had seen Edward's chambers, at number three Temple Gardens, rather than Gill's, she might have been more impressed. Newly built, spacious and with fine views of the gardens or the river, they were generally reckoned to be the finest going.

Marshall's a damned lucky fellow, Gill thought, and not for the first time either, as he ran up the stairs.

'Mr Marshall Hall back yet?' he ased the clerk as he swung into the outer room. The old man looked surprised.

'Well?' Gill insisted.

The clerk shook his head. 'He's not been, sir,' he said. 'He got young Mr Simpson to take it for him.'

'Did he, by George,' Gill muttered. 'He's in his room, then?'

'Yes, sir. Been there all day. Not been out for lunch or anything.'

Gill nodded, curtly and, without knocking, went into Hall's room.

He stood in the doorway, astonished by what he saw. Hall hadn't so much as looked up when he came in, but stayed crouching over the desk, where a filthy-looking old clock lay in pieces.

'Marshall! What the hell do you think you're doing?' Gill cried, slamming the door behind him.

Hall still kept all his attention on the works of the clock. 'Keep time, keep time, keep *order*,' he murmured.

Gill threw the folder down. 'Maidstone,' he said.

'What about it?' Hall asked in a low voice, still fiddling with the clock.

'You were supposed to be there. It was an important case.'

Hall leant back and looked at him reflectively. 'So they tell me.'

'Well?'

'Some young fellow or other in chambers went.' He bent over the clock again. 'Got to encourage the *jeunesse dorée*. Wouldn't you say so?'

Gill swung a chair round so that he could sit near him. 'Listen, my friend,' he said, 'if you're set on committing professional suicide –'

Hall looked up at him, his eyes wide. 'Suicide, you say?'

Gill took a breath. 'Then you're going the right way about it.'

Hall shrugged and looked away. 'Early eighteenth century, this timepiece. Fine bit of workmanship there, don't you agree?'

'Clocks are not my business. I'm a lawyer.'

'Well, so you are, Charlie. So you are, indeed.'

'And, as a lawyer – *your* lawyer, God help me –'

'Yes?'

'Your wife came to see me, at my request, this afternoon.'

Hall smiled at him, a look of pure happiness on his face. 'I've so wanted you two to meet. Isn't she lovely? Isn't she?'

'Very.' Gill held the cardboard folder towards him. 'Here's the deed of separation. She signed.'

Hall thrust the folder away. 'I don't want to see that.'

'Marshall, you'll have to –'

'No. Take it away, please.'

'It must be signed!'

Hall sighed and shook his head. 'Some other time. I'm very busy just now. Can't you see that?'

Gill put the folder on his knee and sat in silence whilst Hall went back to his clock-mending. Under the desk he saw a couple of fat briefs, still tied in their pink ribbons. Carefully, he edged them out with his foot. He saw that the first one was marked for Hall, with a fee of 300 guineas. The second one was less well-feed, but it was still worth 130.

'Too busy for these briefs?' Gill asked quietly.

Hall looked up, as if surprised by the question. 'What?'

Gill picked the briefs up and dropped them on the desk.

'Careful!' Hall cried. 'This machinery's very delicate!'

'Bugger the machinery, Marshall! I'm talking about your livelihood!'

Hall fastidiously pushed the briefs to one side. 'Charlie, I was once given a piece of advice, by a most distinguished actor. May I proffer it now to you?' He had got up from his chair and stood towering over Gill in the darkening room. He leant down, his hands on the arms of his chair. 'Piss off.'

Gill didn't move, nor did his expression change.

Hall pushed himself away and grabbed his coat from the rack in the corner of the room. 'I need a walk. And I'm going to take it.'

'Marshall – I –'

But Hall was already in the doorway. 'Don't you go touching that clock, mind. It's valuable.'

The door slammed behind him and Gill heard his quick steps passing through the outer office and down the stairs. For a moment he was still and then, with a sigh, he picked up the briefs and skimmed through them. Someone would have to devil these for Marshall, or his ruin was certain. Once word got out amongst the solicitors that briefing him was a waste of time and money, then the supply would dry up overnight. And bad news travelled amongst those gentry faster than a fire in a forest.

The young army man was there again, in the restaurant. For the life of her, she couldn't remember his name, but wherever she went these days she seemed to see him. It may well have been coincidence, and she sincerely hoped that it was, for his continuous presence disturbed her. There was nothing in his behaviour that was ungentlemanly and he never made any attempt to come over and speak to her, but she was aware that, whenever she glanced in his direction, his eyes would meet hers; so he must be watching her, waiting for her to turn his way. She thought of asking one of her friends to have a word with him, but if she did that she might well finish up looking very silly. The man had the right to sup where he wished, after all.

She thought that, perhaps, if she were to pass near him, he might stand up, introduce himself again and explain the mystery away, so she excused herself to her dinner partner. But, as she came by him, he was leaning forward, laughing at some joke of his companion's.

She stood by the mirror in the ladies' room, frowning. It was all most unsettling. In the mirror, she saw Florrie Green, her plump actress friend, coming in, and she smiled brightly at her.

'Who's the good-looker?' Florrie asked, as she went into a lavatory cubicle.

'Who do you mean?'

'Young feller-me-lad that's got his eye on you,' Florrie called.

Something warned Ethel to tell Florrie that she didn't know whom she was talking about, but, with a shrug, she said, 'You noticed him, too?'

'I should think I have!'

The chain was pulled and the lavatory flushed and Florrie came out, pulling her dress straight. 'Who is he, then?' she asked as she washed her hands.

'I only wish I knew.'

'Mystery man,' Florrie chuckled.

'My husband and I met him – I think – at a dinner party. But that was years ago.'

'Oh well. Some girls have all the luck. Wish he'd cast an eye over my little treasures, I don't mind telling you.'

'I just wish he'd leave me alone.'

Florrie looked at her in the glass. 'Don't worry, love. Sooner or later he'll make his play – and you can tell him where to get off. Or not.'

'I'll tell him, all right. Tell him to keep away.'

'Oh, yes?' Florrie lifted an eyebrow.

'I certainly will,' Ethel said, going towards the door.

'Oh, by the way,' Florrie called after her, 'are you still looking for digs?'

'I'm sorry?'

'Somewhere to rest the old weary head.'

'Yes. Yes, I am.'

'What sort of place have you in mind, love?'

Ethel stood for a moment, thinking about this. 'Somewhere

not too big. Nice address, if it's not too dear. And, oh, Florrie, more than anything else, somewhere I can be *free*!'

Florrie nodded. 'Free?'

'That's right.'

'I think I've got just the place for you. It's a Mrs Grandt runs the house. Nice old thing – I did a tour with her once, years ago. I think she'd suit you.'

'Yes?'

Florrie looked at her and nodded. 'If it's being free you're after –'

Florrie – kindness itself, Ethel thought – had sent a note round to Mrs Grandt, telling her that Ethel would be calling. She also told her old friend a number of other things about her prospective tenant, but Ethel wasn't to know that.

Now, as Mrs Grandt showed her the rooms, pulling back the heavy curtains with a swishing flourish, pointing out the various ornaments and precious pieces of furniture that she'd installed for her friends' comfort and delectation, Ethel was thinking that Florrie had done well by her. It was true that Eddie's sister, and people of that sort, might look down their noses at her landlady; she was running to fat, her dress was what they would call 'flashy', she wore rather a lot of jewellery, her high-piled hair was, perhaps, too black for one of her years, and it looked very much as if she had been applying *papier poudré* and rouge to her cheeks; but she smiled a lot and good-heartedness simply shone from her.

Ethel smiled back at her. 'Thank you very much, Mrs Grandt –'

'Hermione, my dear, just call me Hermione. All my friends do.'

'Thank you very much. It's a very nice name.'

Mrs Grandt gave a gracious nod, her many-ringed hands folded complacently over her stomach.

'And these are very nice rooms.'

'So pleased you like them, dear.'

'Oh, yes – they'll suit me *very* well.'

To Ethel's surprise, Mrs Grandt's smile faded. 'Ah, my dear,' she said, 'but what I've got to know is – will you suit them? Or me?'

'I'm sure I'll take care of everything.'

Mrs Grandt sat on a highly carved *chaise-longue* by the fireplace. She looked up at Ethel and patted a cushion beside her. Ethel, sat, puzzled. Mrs Grandt put a hand on her knee and leant close to her. 'Respectability, dear,' she said. Her breath smelt of something, some spirit or other; could it possibly be gin, so early in the day? 'Once that flies out of the window, who knows what walks in at the door. And whatever becomes of us ladies then?'

Ethel blushed. 'Mrs Grandt, I do assure you –'

'Hermione.'

'Hermione. I'm a thoroughly respectable woman. My parents are –'

Mrs Grandt smiled again. 'Of course you are. Anyone can see that, but I do have to be so careful.' She got to her feet again, not without effort, and tripped round the room, lovingly adjusting the ornaments. 'For myself, I'm a teacher. Music, that's my thing. Highest of all the arts, don't you think so, dear? It is my life, and I must share my joy.' She stopped, a china cupid in her hands, and looked at Ethel. 'You will be bound to see my pupils coming and going. Gentlemen, mostly. They're such good pupils.'

'I'm fond of music myself.'

'Are you? That's nice.'

'I only play a little. The piano, you know.'

Mrs Grandt carefully replaced the cupid on its shelf on the crowded what-not. Once again, her manner changed and became businesslike, not to say hard. 'It's usual for me to ask my guests for references. Oh, quite usual.'

'References?'

'That's right, dear. Would that be a worry to you?'

'Well – I must say, it makes me feel a little bit like a housemaid. Though I dare say someone would speak for me, if you really needed it.'

Mrs Grandt's lips were a tight line as she considered this, and her small dark eyes were hard as jet. 'Not your husband, though. You wouldn't get much of a reference from him, now, would you?'

Ethel looked down. 'I'm quite sure that he would support me in any way that –'

'Lawyer, isn't he?' Mrs Grandt interrupted. 'And quite the coming man, too. Oh, I keep very *au fait* in all such matters, I do assure you! I know who's who and what's what. Quite the rising star, that one, in such circles, I hear.'

'He's doing well, I believe.'

Mrs Grandt moved closer to her, though she didn't sit down. 'So what's the trouble, dearie? Between you and him? Been dipping his quill in a new inkpot has he?'

Ethel shook her head. 'He's moved chambers, it's true.'

Mrs Grandt gave a laugh. 'Oh, bless the girl!' she cried. She took Ethel's hand impulsively and kissed it. 'I'll take you on! We poor forlorn sisters have to stick together, when all's said and done. Wouldn't you say so?'

'Yes, indeed.'

'Isn't that what you'd say?'

'Yes.'

Mrs Grandt nodded and let her hand go. 'That's right. Rent's two guineas a week, payable a month in advance.'

Ethel swallowed. 'I'm afraid that's rather –'

'Very reasonable, I think, for such a respectable address.'

Ethel sat, biting her lip, wondering where she could find such a large sum of money, and be sure of it coming in. Well, then, she would just have to depend on Eddie going on doing well. But it seemed a dreadful amount.

Mrs Grandt sat beside her again, her stays creaking as she leant close. 'I know the world a little bit, you know. And I can tell you this for nothing. A lady, however respectable, once apart from her husband, finds it very difficult to get decent accommodation anywhere. Unless, of course, money's no object. Things are very different for *them*, I do assure you.' She paused, letting the thought go home. 'Two guineas. All found. Breakfast and supper. Reasonable enough for respectability, I'd have thought.'

Ethel came to a decision and nodded. 'I shall have to go to my husband's – that is – *my* bank.'

Mrs Grandt got up. 'Of course you will! You can fix up to move all your traps and things in. Then you might join me in a bite and a sip. Cosy, like, for your first night.'

'That would be very pleasant. Thank you.'

'Oh, that's all right! Now, don't let that bank of yours go closing, now. Keep an eye on the clock ... and I'll see you later.' She went out, all smiles, but no sooner had the door closed on her than it opened again. She poked her head round.

'Oh – I should have mentioned. But you know me, head like a sieve! I've no objection to visitors. Not a bit of it! So long as you just mind out to keep them *respectable*, if you take my meaning.'

Ethel didn't, and was completely at a loss as to what the woman was talking about. Of course her visitors would be respectable! Who did she think she was? Obviously Mrs Grandt was some sort of an eccentric. Theatre folk could be, she knew.

Now that she was alone, she took another look round her rooms. Oh, most of the objects were ghastly, really horrid, but, bit by bit, not giving any offence, she could replace them with more tasteful things of her own. Nothing from the rooms she had shared with Eddie, of course: she was done with all that lot, and glad to be shot of them, but things of her own. Chosen by her, for herself.

She laughed aloud. This was freedom! This was to be her own woman!

She raised her arms, exulting in the thought of it.

And that was how Mrs Ethel Marshall Hall, wife of Edward

Marshall Hall, Barrister-at-Law, grand-daughter of William Moon, Ll.D, famous as the inventor of type for the blind, and daughter of a well thought of Brighton physician, came to take up residence in a whore-house, managed by a bawd and procuress to middle-class, middle-aged gentlemen.

Little by little, and by dint of using every ounce of tact and quiet persuasion he possessed, Charlie Gill got Hall back to work. Briefs, of course, he would not look at, and Gill, cursing, gave up all his social life to devil them for him. He would patiently talk Hall through the cases in railway carriages, in the robing room at the Old Bailey, anywhere he could get the man on his own for a time.

Once he was in court, Gill could breathe easy; Marshall would never let Gill or, more importantly, his client down once he had sight of him in the dock and breathed the familiar aspect of the place. He would fight then, and fight harder than ever, his own desperation giving edge to his arguments.

When Gill sensed a real suicidal blackness falling on his friend he would stay with him, sitting by the hour in their club, pouring brandy when brandy was needed, keeping silent when that was what Hall wanted, and talking when talking would help.

The clerk to Hall's Chambers knew something of what was going on, of course. But the solicitors seemed to be happy enough so, as far as he was concerned, things were right enough. Briefs kept coming, that was the main thing.

Then one day when Gill called at Chambers, ostensibly on a social call but truly to pick up one of Marshall's briefs, he saw, to his intense relief, that Hall had been working on it; it was covered in pencil notes. He put it back on the pile on Hall's desk and closed his eyes in a quick but heartfelt prayer of thanksgiving. Tonight he could dine out with an easy mind.

He was about to leave, his work done, when Hall came into the room. There was a bit of colour back in his cheeks, Gill noticed.

Hall came over to him, took his hand and held it, putting his other hand on his shoulder. 'Charlie —' he said, then shook his head, his eyes closed.

'What the devil's the matter with you now?' Gill asked.

'Dear God in heaven,' Hall sighed.

'What is it?'

Hall moved away and sat at his desk, looking up to him. 'Man never had a truer friend. Never.'

Gill shook his head. 'You've been a bit of a confounded nuisance, but that's all.'

'Damn it, man! That's not all!' Hall cried, banging a fist on the desk. 'What you've done — what you've done for me — all these weeks. How can I —'

'Will you shut your clattering mouth, now?'

'How can I repay you? Ever?'

Gill had his head on one side, as usual with him when considering some knotty point of law. 'If I were to say dinner, with a magnum of the very best bubbly tonight?'

'On!'

'That's that, then,' Gill said, going towards the door. He turned to face Hall once more. 'Oh, and by the way, those pleadings you've presented on that brief, there: you're wrong, my boy. Fight it that way, and they'll take the hide off you.'

Hall threw his head back and laughed. 'Get out, Gill!'

'Don't worry. I'm going.'

He ducked out of the doorway, just avoiding the brief as it was thrown at his head.

Ethel gave up her social life for weeks, and she was happy enough without it. As winter gave way to summer she would take the walks in the park that she had taken of old, but now she hadn't got the cold thought of facing Eddie at the end of the day. Her time was her own to spend as she wished and, as she walked slowly home in the golden twilight, she would think of the evening to come, the maid fetching up a nice light meal, with a glass of wine to it. That was something to look forward to and, really, the food here was far nicer than the plain cooking that had been dished up night after night in her previous existence. After supper she could sit on the rug by the fire and practise her cigarette smoking. Eddie didn't approve of women smoking, so it must be a good thing to do.

Sometimes she hankered for her friends and their supper parties, but she was still worried about money. Not that it would have cost her anything to be with them; they were endlessly kind to her, but her dresses had been seen too often and then there would be the cab fares home. No. She was quite cosy enough here, in her own little kingdom.

As she sat, she would wonder about the gentlemen who came for their music lessons at such late hours, but she supposed that they were busy in the City during the day and that these were the only times they could fit in. She would hear Hermione playing the piano and singing, then there would be a time of silence before the gentlemen left. They must, she though, be studying theory.

As for the other three ladies in the house, she saw little of them. They didn't seem to get about much during the day. And they too had their callers at strange hours. It was none of her business, she decided, what they did. And, anyway, it must be all right, for Hermione made such a fetish of respectability. The word was seldom off her lips.

The days and weeks passed very agreeably indeed. Then, at the end of the quarter, when she went to her bank for her allowance from Eddie, she got a shock. She could feel her heart pounding as she looked at the slip of paper which the teller had pushed over the mahogany counter.

'Are you sure that there's no mistake?' she asked him.

He had a ledger to hand and flipped it open, running a finger down the column of figures, then comparing it with the paper. He shook his heard. 'No mistake at all, Mrs Marshall Hall. It's quite correct.'

'Thank you,' she said, signed a cheque, crammed the money into her reticule and walked, in a daze, from the bank.

In the street she stopped to get her breath and looked again at the paper in her hand.

It was three times more than she'd ever had for all their housekeeping in the old days. 'My goodness me,' she sighed. 'He *must* be doing well.'

She thought about him, drudging away, and all for her. Oh, what a wonderful man he is, she thought. If only ... She shook her head. It couldn't be, and that was the tragedy of it all. Then she wondered how he would want her to spend all this money and, straight away, she knew. She could just see him laughing.

She lifted a hand to a passing cab and, by some miracle, it was empty. Keeping her skirts out of the dust, she crossed the pavement and got in.

The cabbie leant down. 'Where to, Missus?'

She smiled up at him. 'Bond Street, please. I've some shopping to do. And you may wait for me while I do it.'

Hermione saw the cab draw up at her door, then the cabbie helping that silly little goose of a lodger down and carting God knows how many hat boxes and dress parcels up to the door. Hallo, the good Mrs Grandt thought, we must be in funds.

She sipped her tea, glanced at the clock and decided that, in a minute or two, she'd go up and see what was what. Maybe at last she'd found a fancy-man to look after her. Not before time, either. No point paying rent here for nothing. It wasn't a convent.

Ethel stood before the cheval-mirror and looked at herself in the cherry red dress. She wondered if, perhaps, it wasn't a little too *décolleté*, but the manageress of that very exclusive shop had assured her that it was the very latest thing from Paris. Captain Worth himself was designing just such dresses, she said.

And it was lovely, she thought, with its flaring half sleeves, the waist so attractively pulled in, holding the line of her body, and the pleated train circling her feet.

She looked at the neckline again, though, and wondered. No, she thought, it was too much. She got a lace handkerchief from the dressing table and tucked it into the cleavage of her breasts. That was better. Much better. It still most certainly wouldn't do for Ada – but who cared about her?

There was a discreet tap on the door and Mrs Grandt came into the room. Ethel smiled at her in the glass.

'Oh my goodness me,' Hermione gasped, a hand on her breast.

'Do you like it?' Ethel asked.

Hermione bustled over. 'Like it! Oh, I should say I like it!'

'It is nice, isn't it!'

'Oh! It's the very last word! The *dernier cri*!' Hermione said, tugging at the front hem. She stood back, hands clasped, then whipped the lace from the corsage. 'Better without that, I think, my dear.'

Ethel looked down. 'It's not too . . .?'

Hermione laughed. 'Not a bit of it! Let the gentlemen have a little glimpse of paradise, I say! After all, we always hold the key to the gate!'

Ethel blushed, but she laughed, and Hermione laughed with her. She hadn't realized that the girl was quite such a looker; knock any man with blood in his veins sideways, she would. Now to find out where the money's come from. She sat, holding her skirts in the approximate position of her knee.

'Sorry,' she groaned, 'little touch of the rheumatics.'

'Oh, dear. Is it painful?' Ethel was already at her side.

Hermione gave a stoical smile. 'Mustn't grumble. But if I could just sit for a minute.'

'Of course you can.'

Hermione closed her eyes with relief. 'Buy anything else nice, did we?'

'Oh, lots of things. It's my allowance day today.'

Hermione's eyes were open now and she was giving her a steady look, though keeping a smile on her lips. 'From your husband, will that be?'

'Yes. And it was a lot more than I expected.'

'That's nice.' The man's as big a fool as she is, she thought.

'He must be doing very well. My income depends, you see, on how much he earns.'

Mrs Grandt levered herself to her feet. 'Then let's hope he goes on doing well. Eh?'

'I'm sure he will. He's very clever.'

If you call that clever, Mrs Grandt thought, to pay to keep your wife in a house like this. One born every minute, there is really. Thank God. She gave Ethel a motherly smile, as best she could remember one. 'Why don't you go out tonight? See a bit of life?'

'I hadn't thought of it.'

'Oh, go on! I would! It's a shame to waste such a nice frock.'

'I could wear this?'

'Course you could! Tell you what – I'll settle it for you. There'll be no dinner here tonight. I'm giving cook the night off. So there!'

'Then it doesn't seem as though I've much choice,' Ethel laughed.

'No more you have. Enjoy yourself, my girl! You're only young once.'

'That's right!'

Hermione gave her a quick kiss on the cheek. 'I know what I'll do – I'll send the girl round to see that friend of ours – Florrie Green. She'll get you a comp. for a good seat in the stalls, then you can go on with 'em after the show, wherever they're off to. How about that?'

'Hermione – you're so kind!'

'Like I say – we girls have to stick together.'

CHAPTER
FIFTEEN

Lieutenant Raoul de Ponthieu would never rise to any great height in Her Majesty's Indian Army. His colonel thought he gave himself too many airs and graces, the adjutant didn't like the way he sprinkled scent on his hands and the rest of the mess couldn't fathom the fellow at all: there was always that damned supercilious smile on his lips. They all detested his looks: handsome enough, they'd grant you that, but in the wrong sort of way. There was no manliness about him, with his delicate hands and soft, dark eyes. More like a blasted woman, they felt. Not that any scandal was attached to him in that sort of way; the subalterns were safe enough. In fact, just the reverse seemed to be true: memsahibs in the hills went over like ninepins for him, or so it was said. Well, there was no accounting for women's tastes. But they all kept a damn close eye on wives and sweethearts when he was around.

There was one thing in his favour, and it was no small thing, either: when it came to hunting big game, he was your chap, there was no doubt about that. Walking wonder, the fellow was. Go with him, and you could always be sure of a decent bag. Patient, you see; he'd sit on his arse up some tree for days, if need be. Sooner or later buffalo, buck or tiger would come into his sights, and he'd only take the one shot. Nor was he bothered about bagging horns or skin for himself. Once the killing was over, he'd give that little smile of his and walk away. Funny fellow, all round.

He'd used his hunting skills tonight, choosing his seat in the circle for its clear view of where he'd been told she'd be sitting, as if selecting a hide, taking care to arrive after the lights in the theatre had dimmed. He could see her perfectly below him in the orchestra stalls, focused in his opera glasses as the soft light from the stage spilled over her. His tongue darted to his lips at the sight of the perfect slope of her shoulders and the soft creaminess of her skin. For a moment he let his mind speculate on the rest of her body, but he immediately dismissed the thought. His mind had to be kept very clear. Such thoughts were as dangerous as thinking of the grace of the tiger before the beast was shot. All the same, he crossed one leg over the other and thought that the £5 he'd given to that fat tart of an actress was money well spent. She'd promised information and by George she'd delivered.

Romano's did she say they were going on to? Well – that was all right. All the same, it was pushing the boat out a bit for that crew, he'd have thought. One of them must have come into some money.

The musical comedy dragged on its tedious way. He was almost entirely tone deaf, so the shrieking, scraping and banging was agony enough, without the fatuity of the plot. But it gave him time to think, and to wonder if he should make his move tonight. He'd excited an interest there, he was sure of that, but then she'd disappeared from the scene. Supposing she did that again? There was only so much time to spend on this quest; leave could be extended by old Northesk pulling a few strings, but sooner rather than later he'd have to rejoin the regiment. Then again, he thought, as he watched her laughing at some silly joke from the stage, living at Ma Grandt's had to be taken into the reckoning. It was one thing to be some dull attorney's flighty wife, but quite another to be a Grandt girl.

All things were possible. He'd go to Romano's, set out his stall and wait and see what happened.

She was aware of his being there, of course, as soon as he came in, looking round the supper room as if trying to find some missing companion. She saw him call over the head waiter and exchange anxious words with him. He sat alone at a table in the corner, occasionally looking at the entrance, then at his watch. Someone, she thought, must have been unable to join him.

She leant across the table to Florrie. 'He's here again,' she whispered.

'Who is, dear?' Florrie asked, one hand keeping her bosom out of the soufflé.

'That man! The one I told you about before!'

Ethel nodded to the corner table and Florrie turned to take a look. 'Are you sure it's him?'

'Yes!'

'Well, dear, take no notice.'

Ethel frowned, biting her lip. Florrie patted her hand. 'Come on, love, eat your supper! You're paying for it, so you might as well enjoy it.'

Actors are funny people, Ethel thought. She had never known anyone able to eat so much, so quickly, whilst at the same time continuing to talk – mostly about themselves. Terribly amusing, though. At last they had done, and swore that they couldn't eat another crumb. She was relieved to hear it; generous though Eddie's allowance was, she had a horrid fear that the bill for tonight was going to call for economies for the rest of the quarter. Still, they had paid for her supper often enough in the past, so she'd just have to grin and bear it. When it came, it wasn't quite as bad as she thought, and she counted the sovereigns out on to the plate with a grand air.

'My goodness me,' the young actor next to her said, admiringly, 'I've heard of the bally New Woman, but aren't you just it!'

Ethel, leaning into him to catch his words, didn't notice Florrie, who was standing at her side, flick her reticule from the cloth and kick it under the table.

Then Florrie was crying, 'Now, come everyone! The night's yet young! I know where there's a drop or two in, all ready for us!'

The actors rose with alacrity at this, and Florrie swept them all into the foyer. They had all got their capes, cloaks, hats, sticks and boas from the cloakroom and were ready to go when Florrie turned smilingly to Ethel.

'I've not had chance to say this before, dearie, but you look lovely.'

'Do I? Do I really?'

'I should say so!' Then Florrie frowned. 'But where's your reticule gone? Not put it down somewhere, have you?'

Ethel looked round. 'How stupid of me – I must have left it on the table.' She expected the men to help, but they were all busy gossiping in the doorway.

'Want me to come with you?' Florrie asked, but she can't have meant it, since she was already on her way towards the rest of the party.

'No, no, it's all right, I'll get it.' And she went back into the supper room. Out of the corner of her eye she saw that the army man had gone and the waiter was clearing his table.

When she got back to her own place, she could see no sign of the missing bag. The headwaiter came over and she explained her predicament to him, but he couldn't find it either. It was only when the table was pulled away that they saw it. She murmured her apologies and thanks as he escorted her to the door, bowing as she went out.

When she got into the foyer, she was surprised to see that her friends had gone. The cloakroom lady was of no help: they had all been laughing, making such a racket, that she hadn't heard any of 'em say where they were going. She felt angry and humiliated; to pay all that money for the food and drink, and for them to waltz off, leaving her here, stranded. It was too bad, it was really, and no amount of theatre eccentricity could excuse or pardon it. She'd give them a piece of her mind next time she saw them. But who knows when that would be, for now the evening was in ruins and the only thing left for her, out of all the laughter and talk, was to get the doorman to call her a cab and go home. Eddie would never have treated her like that, she thought with a pang of loss and, blinking back the tears, she went towards the doors.

Before she got there she heard a voice behind her, deep and concerned.

'It seems as if we have both been deserted.'

She turned to see who it was. And there was de Ponthieu, frowning in sympathy.

'They must have forgotten – my friends, I mean – I went back into the supper room –'

'Did you?'

'My bag, you see; I'd foolishly forgotten it.'

'Not foolish at all. It could happen to anyone.'

'Now they've –'

He bowed his head. 'So I see.' He paused, looking at her, and his jaw tightened in anger. 'I think their behaviour is simply appalling.'

'They were talking amongst themselves. I'm sure they didn't mean it.'

He shook his head. 'I know that they are friends of yours, Mrs Marshall Hall –'

'Oh! You remembered my name! You remembered –'

'Paris,' he smiled. 'How could I forget such a night?'

'And you are in the army. I remember that.'

'That's more thought than I deserve. I'm not a very memorable man.' He took her hand and bowed over it. 'My name is Raoul de Ponthieu.'

'Of course it is,' she smiled. 'You were a lieutenant.'

'And, I fear, I still am.' He gave a rueful shrug. 'And will ever be.'

'Oh dear.'

He moved closer to her. 'There are other things in my life more important than soldiering.'

Something in his voice stirred her. She caught her breath. 'Are there?'

He looked round. 'But this isn't solving our problem.'

'Problem?'

'Getting you safely home to your husband.'

'No,' she blurted, 'he and I –' She let the words die. 'The doorman can get me a cab. I'll be perfectly all right.'

He took her elbow in his gloved hand and led her towards the doors. 'I could never permit it. It's a question that simply doesn't arise. With your permission, I will escort you to your rooms and see you safely inside.'

They were in the cold of the street before she had a chance to make any objection, and a cab was already coming towards them in response to his raised stick. He handed her up and followed her in.

The cabbie looked down at them through his little roof light. She gave de Ponthieu her address and he passed it on to the cabbie. The roof light snapped down and they were on their way. 'I'm putting you to an awful lot of trouble,' she said.

He didn't reply, but smiled at her from his corner. His small, even teeth gleamed white in the darkness. Nor did he make any further attempt at conversation as the cab rattled through the brilliantly lit and crowded streets. Ethel, remembering his aristocratic connections, felt that it was incumbent on her to make small talk, so she prattled on, growing increasingly desperate for something to say in the face of his still and watchful silence.

At last, as they left the crowded thoroughfares of the West End and bowled down a deserted side road, invention ran dry and she, too, sat in awkward silence.

Then, in a low voice, which she could only just hear, he spoke. 'All these weeks, I have been where I thought you would go.'

Startled, she turned to him. 'I know,' she said, before she had time to think whether or not it was the proper thing to say.

'Did you notice me?'

'Yes. I saw you.'

'Has my presence been – embarrassing to you?'

'No, not embarrassing.' She shook her head. 'Not at all.'

He looked away, at the passing street lamps. 'I could do no other. I have to be near you.'

'You mustn't say these things.'

He sighed. 'How can I not?'

Despite the chill of the night, she felt breathless. There was something about this man, something she couldn't find words for, a sort of power that upset and disturbed her. She must not see him again. There was a great danger in him. She shivered and pulled her cloak closer.

'You're cold,' he said, and slipped his scarlet lined opera cloak off and laid it carefully over her knees.

'Thank you,' she said in a small voice.

He had one hand on her knee, holding his cloak in place. 'I have loved you from that moment I first saw you, by candle-light, in Paris.'

'I want you to stop this cab, please. I want to get out.'

He took her hand and held it. 'I can't allow that.'

She pulled her hand away. 'Please, please!'

'No.' He leant back. 'You could stop it yourself, if you wanted to. Just call to the driver.'

'I don't know where we are,' she whispered.

'No more you do. But I do.' He smiled at her. 'And we are near to the Island of Cythera.' She shook her head. 'A place of endless happiness.'

'Oh, there is no such place!' she said. But her voice showed that she longed for it.

He thought about this for a moment, his face close to hers. 'There is no harm in me, there is no danger,' he whispered.

She shook her head, turning away from him.

'Only great peace and happiness. For both of us.'

She turned to him. 'Happiness?'

'Oh, yes. If we are brave enough to face the truth within us and take it.'

The hansom stopped and the cabbie lifted the flap in the roof. 'Here we are then, guv.'

De Ponthieu nodded, but still looked at Ethel. 'Your key, please,' he whispered.

Almost as if against her will, she opened her bag and passed it to him.

Head bowed, as though in a dream, she went into the house, along the hallway and up the stairs, never looking back to see if he was following her or not, nor listening for the sound of the front door closing.

In her sitting-room she stood, not lighting the lamp, moonlight flooding through the windows.

The door closed quietly, and she could feel his warm breath on her neck as he stood behind her. Calmly, almost as if he were putting a child to bed, he slipped off her cloak, folded it neatly and put it on a chair. He waited for a moment, letting her sense him there and then, when she was about to turn to him, slipped his hands down the front of her dress, gently holding her breasts, making no demands, but circling, warm and tender. She closed her eyes and leant her head on his shoulder.

Slowly he turned her to him. She opened her lips for his kiss, but he put a finger on her lips and whispered in her ear, 'I promised happiness. And I know how to give it. Quietly, easily.'

'There's always hurt, though.'

'No. There will be no hurt. Only a pleasure such as you have never known.'

She nodded and, without looking back, walked towards her bedroom.

Mrs Grandt, who had seen all through her window and then, when they were in the hall, through a crack in the partly opened door, turned to her client and smiled. 'Little love-birds! Bit of billing and cooing will be going on there tonight. Oh, my word, won't there just be.'

She sat on the bed, opened her negligé and patted a place beside her. 'Now, dear. Let's get a bit of practice in on your arpeggios.'

*

What he had promised he had delivered. There had been no moaning, groaning, fumbling and thrusting as there had been with Eddie. He had been so gentle, so loving, so patient and, when he had come into her, it was as if, at last, her life was complete. Never, ever had she dreamt that it could be as wonderful a thing as this.

He was lying on his back now, his eyes closed, breathing easily, his arm under her head. She cuddled closer to him, letting a leg slide over his. He kissed her hair.

'Raoul,' she whispered.

His arm held her closer.

'I love you,' she said.

He kissed her again, tenderly.

'I think that perhaps I wanted this. All the times you were there,' she said.

'And I.'

Her hand was moving over his chest, feeling the soft hairs, marvelling at the beauty of him. 'Could we – please –'

He turned to her again, kissing her, deeply.

Indeed and indeed, he thought. An extension of leave is very much on the cards.

She slept soundly, a great, peaceful sleep, and when she woke it was with a sense of wonder and surprise at the feeling of fulfilment and joy that flooded through her whole body. Then she remembered what had brought this feeling and turned, lazily, in the bed.

But he wasn't there.

And his clothes were gone.

It was like being a child again, having a marvellous dream of Christmas or holidays, and waking to a rainy morning in Brighton.

But the sweet ache in her body told her that last night had been no dream.

She got out of bed slowly, and she knew no fear as she

looked round the room. Happiness came quickly back. He would be with her again. She knew that. They were complete.

Her lover had bestirred himself for good reason. Arrangements would need to be made and he was busy making them, facing Mrs Grandt across her chenille-covered table. 'I know you,' he said. 'Ma Grandt. That's what they call you.'

She smiled easily. He wasn't half a dasher, she thought. So far as she could like any man, she liked a man of his sort. No pretence with 'em. Straight at their fences, over and away and devil take the hindmost.

'And I know you – Captain.'

'Don't promote me,' he laughed.

'Seems to me like you've been promoting yourself, my boy.'

He shrugged his shoulders, still smiling, took out his pocketbook and laid it on the table. 'Business?'

Mrs Grandt could see that it was well stuffed with bank notes. 'Business,' she agreed.

De Ponthieu looked round the room. 'You keep a very pleasant house here.'

She nodded graciously. 'I try to please.'

'I think that it would suit me very well.' He took a couple of bank notes from his pocketbook and threw them on the table, like a negligent gambler.

She looked at the notes, then at him. 'Afraid we're full, dear.'

He accepted this without demur, but took another note out and threw it on top of the others. 'Not even a little corner?'

Mrs Grandt cast her eyes upwards, towards Ethel's room. 'In . . .?'

'That's right. A certain lady needs – protection.'

Mrs Grandt laughed. 'And no mistake!' But, as she looked again at the money on the table, her laugh died. 'Now, Captain, talk sense. What sort of a reputation would I get once word got round that –'

'It won't, I promise you,' he interrupted. He shoved the bank notes towards her. 'Every month, the same.'

She shook her head. 'Every three weeks, Captain. On the dot.'

He nodded. 'Done.'

She inwardly cursed herself for not asking more. 'Only hope the merchandise is worth the money.'

De Ponthieu smiled as he got up. 'Where does the lady usually take her breakfast?'

'The girl carries it up, same as all her meals.'

'How very – convenient. Today, she can save her legs. I'll take it, for two. And I like my coffee strong and black.'

'Fussy, are we?'

'Very. And I have crisp rolls, the freshest of butter and a decent pot of jam.'

'Well! You're going to be quite a handful, I can see.'

He waited by the back stairs for the maid to get the tray ready. Then when he had it he took a mouthful of coffee, put the cup back and went up the stairs, whistling tunelessly.

He tapped on the bedroom door with his foot. Ethel opened it and the expression of relief on her face at seeing him almost touched his heart. She wasn't dressed yet, her peignoir over her nightdress. He kicked the door shut behind him and put the tray on the table.

'I was so frightened,' she said. 'I thought you'd gone.'

Unsmiling, he shook his head. 'I'm not leaving you. Ever.'

'Oh, my darling, my own darling,' she sighed.

He nodded, and came towards her. Slipping the peignoir off, he lifted her nightdress over her head and carried her into the bedroom.

Of one thing de Ponthieu was sure, and that was that the world of the middle classes and his world were far apart and could never meet. It was the business of his class to spend money and set an example of style; it was the business of those beneath them to make money and gawp in fascinated wonder at their betters. So it had always been, and so it always would be.

So he was quite sure that however publicly he flaunted his relationship with Ethel, it would be a confined scandal; indeed, it would scarcely be even that, for she wore the cloak of protection, woven from a modicum of discretion and the possession of a married name. For a woman living her sort of life it was an essential garment.

The Prince of Wales set the tone: all his mistresses were complaisantly married; Mrs Langtry, the Countess of Warwick and so on and so forth throughout the upper reaches of the social register. There was great safety in a wedding ring. De Ponthieu's mistress would always be 'Mrs Marshall Hall', and no hostess would inquire further than that.

The London season was in full swing and now, for the first time in her life, she was a part of it. She was Cinderella without a boring clock chiming at midnight. Whatever dreams she had dreamt as she lay before the fire on those endless foggy afternoons in Seymour Street now, in the full golden glory of spring and summer, he made come true.

She wanted to ride in the park? So she should . . . and a gleaming carriage, drawn by perfectly matched chestnut horses, with a liveried coachman on the box, waited at her door. And, in the green and sun-dappled park they would go their stately way, with her all pink and white in the shade of her parasol, her lover lounging at her side, top hat pulled fashionably down almost over his eyes. And the women of her age would smile and nod in greeting from their carriages as they passed.

A drive up the river for tea at Skindle's, and de Ponthieu expertly punting her through the shade of the overhanging trees? What could be more pleasant. Then home, slowly, and dressing for the evening delights; a box at the theatre and supper in some quiet restaurant, where he had only to lift an eyebrow in command and the waiter came running. It was bliss to be alive.

On some evenings they would go, as of right, to a ball in one of the great houses; Portman Square, Grosvenor Square and Park Lane were open citadels to them. And she would thrill to the sight of the house, brilliant with light, music floating down to the street from the open windows of the ballroom. And, most gratifying of all, there would be a respectful knot of gawpers at either side of the red carpet that stretched from steps to pavement, watching as she walked, so elegantly, a hand lightly resting on his arm. To them she would give a small smile and a gracious nod. They deserved no less, she thought.

Best of all would be the nights when he would wear his full-dress uniform; the silver and blue of his hussar regiment set off his olive skin and dark eyes to perfection. And the elegance of his narrow waist and tight-fitting trousers! She could have fainted at the sight of his perfection. Then to be led by him into the languorous turns of the waltz, with his hand so firm on her back, his dear face so close, eyes always looking deep into hers, promising, oh so certainly, the sweet joys of the bedroom to come.

On such a night, their dance ended, he led her back to their seat and she, aware of the glow of her cheeks in the heat of the June evening, excused herself and went to the small drawing room off the ballroom, which had been set aside as a dressing room for the ladies.

She sat before a looking glass, applying a discreet touch of powder, and was aware, as she touched and dabbed, of an older woman smiling at her in the glass. She knew her to be a friend of Raoul's: the Countess of Northesk. Nellie, he called her, which seemed a common name to go with such a grand title. But the aristocracy were above such things.

'Charming, my dear, quite charming,' the Countess said. 'You make the rest of us seem dull and dowdy.'

'I don't think so, Countess,' Ethel modestly demurred.

Lady Northesk leant over her, touching the diamond clip that Ethel wore, at the corner of her décolletage. 'And such a pretty brooch! May I see?'

Ethel handed it to her.

'But it's beautiful! And so – unusual!'

'My husband had a great knowledge of such things,' Ethel murmured, looking down.

Lady Northesk handed the jewel back to her. 'I am sure that he still has.'

'Oh, yes, I'm sure he has.'

The older woman sat at her side, adjusting her own glittering tiara in the looking glass. 'Something like this,' she said, giving it a look of extreme distaste, 'does me no credit whatsoever. It's a whimsy of inheritance, whereas your jewellery is the result of intelligence and discretion.'

That, thought Ethel, is me put in my place – though in the nicest possible way.

'Your husband,' the countess went on, 'must be a rare man.'

'Very,' Ethel agreed, rising to go.

But Lady Northesk detained her with a hand on her arm. 'He's doing quite well, I hear. At the Bar.'

'I believe he is.'

Lady Northesk gave her a smile. 'Not one of the front men, yet. But well spoken of, all the same.'

Ethel bit her lip, frowning. All this talk of Eddie was ruining her evening. 'I wonder if you'd excuse me, Lady Northesk? I'm sure I've promised the next dance.'

'Dancing partners will always wait for a woman as beautiful as you, my dear. Sit with me for a little while, would you?'

Ethel had no choice. She sat.

'Your escort . . . that young scamp, de Ponthieu . . .'

'Yes? What of him?'

Lady Northesk shook her head. 'Nothing, nothing at all. Handsome boy, wouldn't you say?'

Ethel nodded. 'Very.'

'Though God knows what sort of future he's got. There's no money there, not a penny piece.'

'Does that matter?'

'It will do, if or when he chooses to marry. It will matter a great deal. Until then – no, of course it doesn't matter a jot. Friends will always support his high jinks.'

Ethel felt herself colouring under the Countess's shrewd gaze. 'High jinks?' she murmured.

'Well – whatever one calls them.' She turned away from Ethel and looked at herself again in the glass. 'I seem to remember that you and he are dining with us – on the 28th, isn't it?'

'I believe so,' Ethel said, stiffly. 'We are looking forward to it.'

'Oh, so are we.' Her scrutiny of herself complete, she turned again to Ethel. 'My dear, will you always remember something – if I were to tell you that thing now, in friendship?'

'Of course.'

'It is simply this. Society will overlook – forgive even – a great deal. A very great deal indeed,' she paused for a moment, 'so long as it isn't compelled to . . .'

Ethel rose. Her hands, as she pulled her long white gloves on, were trembling. 'I do know what you mean, Lady Northesk. And you need have no worries on that score.'

'Bless the girl!' Lady Northesk laughed. 'I am not in the slightest bit worried! Whatever gave you that idea?'

'I must go,' Ethel said.

Lady Northesk was holding a piece of jewellery from the table. 'Not without this charming clip, I hope. Your husband would be so upset if you were to lose it.'

Mentally cursing the woman, Ethel took it and slipped it on. 'Not in the least,' she smiled. 'He would welcome the opportunity of buying me another one.'

The Countess sat for a moment, thinking about the girl and wondering if, perhaps, she'd gone too far when she had talked so freely that morning with her man of business about the de Ponthieu affair. She dismissed the thought: these attorneys were, after all, discreet by profession.

*

Charlie Gill was not in the best of moods that same night as he strode through the moonlit Temple gardens. In fact he was swearing freely and volubly under his breath. He needed to talk to Marshall and had hoped to take him back to his club, after dinner, where some quiet corner would be found, and the business broached. But Hall had not turned up. As he expected, a solitary light was burning in the chambers at number three. With a grim nod he went in at the door and ran up the stairs.

Throwing open the door he saw Hall slumped over his desk. For a moment, he knew a stab of fear; then he saw him move slightly, seeking comfort as he slept.

Gill stood for a moment, taking in the mass of papers on the desk, the wig and gown thrown carelessly on a chair, then went over to his sleeping friend, shaking him by the shoulder. 'Marshall! Will you wake up, for God's sake!'

Hall stirred himself, lifted his head, saw Gill and blinked in the light. 'What are you doing here, Charlie?' he asked.

'I was supposed to be eating my dinner in Lincoln's Inn. And you were *supposed* to be of our company.'

Hall buried his head in his hands. 'Was it tonight?'

'It was.'

'Sorry.' He leant back in the chair, trying to get the ache out of his neck. He waved a hand at the piles of papers. 'But you can see how things are.'

'That's devilling work,' Gill said. 'Half of it, anyway. There are enough hungry young fellows in these chambers. Let one of them do it.'

Hall shook his head, picking up a brief. 'No! I can't do that.' He threw the brief down again. 'I'm that poor devil's only hope. Without me he goes down.'

'That's not true, Marshall, and you know it. Or you should do. The law is his only chance. And you're only part of that.'

Hall looked away. 'I can do no more tonight, anyway.'

To his surprise, Gill sat down, looking at him and frowning. 'What's the matter, Charlie? Is there something else you want to badger me about?'

Gill looked hard at him. 'I wouldn't say "no" if you offered me a drink,' he said.

'Help yourself. You know where it's kept.'

Gill went over to the cupboard, and got out the brandy decanter and a couple of glasses.

'I don't want one, thanks,' Hall said, as he saw him pouring for both of them.

'I don't drink alone, so take it and shut up.' He passed him the glass, then sat, pulling his chair nearer to him.

Hall felt uneasy. All this was very unlike Charlie. 'There's something you want. Something serious. What is it?'

Gill took a mouthful of brandy and swallowed it, grimacing. He put the glass down and looked again at Hall. 'First thing is –'

'What?'

'You're to keep your temper during all that I've got to say.'

Hall looked at his watch. 'Look, it's very late. Can't this wait? Whatever it is?'

'No. I don't think it can. Have a drink.'

'No, thanks,' Hall said, shortly. 'Get on with it.'

Gill leant back. 'All right. Firm of solicitors. Name of Simpkins, Simpkins and Thompson.'

'What of them?'

'They fetch a good deal of business my way.'

Hall got up. 'Charlie: it's very late and I'm very tired. I do not want to know about your instructing bloody solicitors! *Some other time!*'

Gill was quiet, then he spoke. 'Will you please sit down, Marshall. This concerns you. Deeply.'

Hall looked at him, and something in the older man's expression silenced him. He sat, leaning forward. 'Then say it.'

'Old man Thompson does a very great deal of work, family business, that sort of thing, for a certain titled lady.'

'And?'

'She spoke with him today. And, without breaking confidentiality, but knowing of our friendship, he indicated that, on your behalf, I might make certain – inquiries.'

'What sort of inquiries?'

Gill was silent a moment. 'Marshall,' he said, 'a deed of separation was drawn up, between you and your wife.'

'Do you need to tell me this?' Hall asked, bitterly.

'Yes, I do. Because, Marshall, the inquiries I have made lead me to believe that she is in breach of it.'

Hall leant back, the colour drained from his face.

'You must know this. The generous allowance you give her is only to be paid if she lives a chaste and virtuous life.'

'*Which she does,*' Hall hissed.

Gill shook his head. 'I have ordered that all payments to her should cease, forthwith.'

The skin was stretched tight on Hall's face and his lips were a narrow line. 'You have done *what?*' he asked, his voice shaking with rage.

'It must be faced!'

Hall's hands were clasped tightly under his chin. 'By what right, Gill, have you done this unspeakable thing?'

'By right of law!'

'No!' Hall shouted.

He got up to go, but Gill held him. The two men were face to face and Gill could feel the trembling of Hall's muscles under his hand. 'She is living openly in adultery in a house kept by a notorious whore!'

Hall broke away from him and leant on the desk, his shoulders bowed. 'If you were any other man,' he said, 'I would kill you for that!'

Never, in all his life, had Gill hated a task as much as he hated this one. But it had to be done. 'There are witnesses, Marshall.'

'Liars!' Hall cried. 'Creeping, slime-bellied, filthy *liars*!'

'No!' Gill shouted.

Hall ran at him, and instinctively Gill raised a hand to protect himself, but Hall knocked it away with a sweeping blow. 'My wife is pure! She is a goddess amongst women! God in heaven! *Don't I know that of her?*'

Gill wearily shrugged his shoulders and picked up his hat and stick. 'Do you wish me to resume payments?'

'If you don't, then my business will be given to some other lawyer, and I shall never speak to you again, so long as I live.'

Gill nodded, expressionlessly. 'I will so instruct.' He went out of the door. 'Good night,' he called from the outer office.

Hall, alone, swept the papers from his desk on to the floor. Then, after a moment, he picked them up and, turning the lamp higher, began to work feverishly.

The goddess herself knelt astride her naked lover, feeling him inside her body, swaying backwards and forwards, gasping with pleasure.

'Easy, take it easy,' he whispered.

'Oh, teach me, teach me,' she cried.

'I'll teach you all right,' he smiled, lifting himself.

But she was past obeying her tutor's commands.

·CHAPTER
SIXTEEN

The season drew towards its end in a blaze of glory. The sun shone, day after day, and she was in Elysium. Surely, the heavens themselves were with them that it should be such a perfect summer. Perhaps, though, she thought as they drove in the golden park, it was too perfect. Today really was very hot, and the parasol gave too little protection. She felt quite faint.

A glass of iced lemonade, as soon as they got home, would be very pleasant. And then, this evening, she would ask for something really spicy and sharp-tasting to eat. That would revive her; Raoul would know the sort of thing she fancied. She smiled at him at the thought, but he was frowning, looking away. He too must be finding the day uncomfortable.

Tonight, in bed, she'd talk to him about their going away for a holiday. Lake Como would be lovely; so cool. Maybe they could get a room at the hotel where she and . . . She shook her head, blotting out the thought.

If the park was hot, the Old Bailey was an oven. The windows were open, but the air was too heavy to move.

Hall was on his feet. This case was a hard one to fight, and it had dragged on for four days now. For three of the nights that separated those days he had worked all night, using, for once, Gill's method of patiently writing down every question to be asked and every possible answer that could be given. The nights had been almost as hot as the days, and he had sipped iced coffee by the window as he worked, his lamp gradually dimming as dawn put it to shame.

He was desperate for a way forward for his client, some sweeping stroke of the sword that would end the case and set him free. But no way could be found, and the city clerk who, it was alleged, had been too free with his master's money via double-entry bookkeeping, must sit on in the dock, awaiting his fate.

Hall's shirt was clinging to his back and the sweat ran down his cheeks. For the first time he cursed his archaic costume of wig and stuff gown. The words on his brief danced and blurred before his eyes. With an apologetic glance at the jury, he took his handkerchief and wiped his brow, but no sooner had the sweat been cleared than it began to flow again. He took a sip of the tepid water before him, cleared his throat and tried again to make sense of the papers in his hand.

'The evidence, then,' he said . . . and there really must be something wrong with his blasted handwriting, for he couldn't make it out at all. He peered closely at the brief, then threw it down. He would have to manage, as best he could, with whatever thoughts he could dredge from memory, but his brain felt as dry and bereft of inspiration as the room he stood in. 'The evidence that has been offered must be regarded as doubtful at best . . . and ludicrously unconvincing – as ludicrously unconvincing as . . .' He was trying to focus his eyes on the jury, but they kept on disappearing into a sort of fog.

He clasped the bench and stooped over it, shaking his head, trying to clear the mists from his eyes. A barrister next to him was holding him, saying something to him, but he couldn't make out what it was. He turned on him, pulling himself up, trying to get a breath of air into his lungs. 'Thank you, but I'm quite capable of standing on my own two feet in court,' he gasped.

He looked at the floor, and it was coming nearer to him, then going away. From a great distance he could hear the voice of the judge.

'This case, Mr Marshall Hall, like his late majesty King Charles II . . .'

What the devil's Charles II got to do with the business, Hall thought, and he racked his brain for any relevant Act from the late king's reign.

'. . . has been an unconscionable time a-dying.'

Ah. That was it. A judicial joke. Very bloody funny.

'So would you either proceed with your speech, or pass on the responsibility to counsel more capable.'

The old bastard! He'd have to be shown something, he would.

Hall drew himself up to his full height, head back. 'Capable, my Lord?' he cried.

'Oh, get on with it, Mr Marshall Hall! You are trying my patience.'

Right, then. If it's a scrap you want, you stupid old woman, a scrap you shall have.

'And you, my Lord,' he flung back, the title sounding like the most foul of insults, 'are *supposed* to be trying this case! But I see scant sign of it in your Lordship's impertinent interruptions!'

'Impertinent, sir?' the judge croaked, his face as red as his robe. 'I will not have such things said in my court!'

'You will have whatever said to you, my Lord, that I deem to be in my client's interest!'

'This is intolerable!' the judge roared. 'Mr Marshall Hall, your remarks display all your customary insolence to the judiciary! I shall report them to the senior Benchers of your Inn!'

Breathing was getting harder for Hall. He made a huge effort and, holding on to the bench, swung to face the jury; but they had gone again from his sight, back into their mist. 'Gentlemen,' he said, 'I came into this place to defend my client. But it seems now that I must also defend myself.'

He lurched forward, knocking the papers from his bench onto the floor. He stooped to collect them, but the room was now too dark to see them. His hand was scrabbling on the stained planking and then, with a great roaring in his ears, he fell. Someone was trying to release his bands and collar stud, and the judge was saying something . . .

It all faded into silence and darkness.

Husband and wife were, for once, acting in perfect unity. As he was carried from the Old Bailey and into a cab, she was trying to dress. They had tickets for a play, and Raoul had arranged for them to meet friends for supper first. She had told him that the heat of the day had made her feel unwell, hoping that he would suggest that they spent the evening quietly at home. She would have given anything to have sat by an open window, wearing her loosest, coolest dress, but he had looked so disappointed at the thought of a ruined evening that she had summoned up a smile and told him to wait for her in the hall.

But getting ready did seem to be taking her much longer than usual; her limbs felt heavy, the room kept turning around her and there was a bilious sickliness in her throat. She could hear him shouting up to her, asking if she was ready yet. She tried to make her voice sound as if she was smiling when she called back, telling him that she wouldn't be a minute. She could see him standing by the open door, the golden sunshine of the street beyond him, and a cab waiting. He sat talking with Mrs Grandt; they were both smiling and turned to look up at her as she came down the stairs.

She did her best to smile back, but really, she did feel terribly sick. Holding on to the bannister, she was mentally counting the steps as she came down and, by doing this, she got as far as the bottom step. Then the hallway seemed to spin round her very fast: she closed her eyes for a second to stop it. But she couldn't seem to get them open again.

When she did, it was in Mrs Grandt's sitting room. A window was open, and the lace curtain stirred a little in the slight breeze that was beginning to blow. Thank goodness for that, Ethel thought. She would feel better now. To her surprise she found that she was lying down. This would never do; she must get up, they were going to be late and Raoul would be furious.

But as she put an arm on the back of the sofa to pull herself upright, Mrs Grandt leant over her, pushing her firmly back.

'No, please, Hermione, I really do have to go,' Ethel said.

Mrs Grandt held a glass towards her. 'Drink this and be quiet,' she said.

'What is it?'

'Drop of my best brandy, so don't waste it.'

'You don't understand! We're late already.'

Mr Grandt looked down at her. 'I think I understand only too well, my girl. Now drink up and shut up.'

Ethel took a sip of brandy, but it immediately rose again in her throat. She looked round, desperately, but Mrs Grandt was already holding a bowl.

'Come on, then, if that's the way it is. Better out than in.'

Trying to be as ladylike as she could, Ethel accepted the bowl.

'Finished?'

Ethel nodded, and Mrs Grandt passed her a handkerchief. 'Wipe round your mouth with that,' she ordered.

Ethel did as she was told. She was feeling cold now, and her brow was clammy.

Mrs Grandt sat beside her and began to dab her face with the stopper from an Eau de Cologne bottle. 'That better?' she asked.

Ethel nodded and Mrs Grandt sat back, looking at her.

Ethel wondered why the woman was frowning: she couldn't help being unwell. And after a day like today – so very hot – it wasn't surprising, was it? She wondered if she'd had a touch of sunstroke. She'd ask Raoul about that; he'd know about such things, having been in India.

'I think I got a touch of the sun,' she murmured.

Mrs Grandt laughed. 'You've had a touch of something, all right. But it comes out at night, not in daytime.'

Ethel shook her head, not understanding. 'What else could it be?'

Mrs Grandt gave a sigh and stood up, putting the scent bottle on the mantel. She turned to face Ethel. 'Come on, then, out with it,' she said. 'When was your last show?'

'I'm sorry,' Ethel stammered, 'I don't know what you mean.'

'Period! Monthly sickness! The curse!'

Ethel could feel herself blushing. 'I honestly don't think that it's any of your –'

'As long as you're in this house, it's my bloody business all right, my girl, and don't you go forgetting it,' Mrs Grandt interrupted. 'So *when*?'

Ethel looked away. 'Two months ago,' she whispered.

'Are you usually regular?'

Ethel nodded. 'But I thought – with our being so busy –'

'I know. I've heard you, every night, being busy.'

This was too much for Ethel. She certainly wasn't going to lie there and listen to this dreadful person talking about her like this. She swung her legs to the floor.

'Just stay where you are!' Mrs Grandt shouted.

'No! I will not! I think you're being, you're being –' But she couldn't find the word she wanted.

'You do know what's happened, don't you?' Mrs Grandt said, and it was more a statement than a question.

'No.'

'You're up the spout, that's what you are, my dear. Pregnant.'

Ethel was shivering in the cool air from the window. 'That's not possible,' she said, longing for this dreadful meeting to finish.

'Why isn't it?' Mrs Grandt asked. 'Did you take any precautions to stop it?'

'No.' Ethel looked longingly towards the door. 'I didn't know how,' she murmured.

'You could have asked me!'

The thought of doing anything that dreadful was so appalling that she could only stare at Mrs Grandt, wide-eyed.

'What you going to do about it, then?'

'I don't know,' Ethel said. 'But Raoul mustn't know.' A fear seized her as she saw the expression on the older woman's face. 'Please!'

'Finish off that brandy,' Mrs Grandt said.

'I don't like it,' Ethel whispered.

'Like it?' Mrs Grandt laughed. 'Oh, my girl! When you've finished that there's a bottle of gin you've to drink. And a bath hotter than you've ever imagined.'

Whether de Ponthieu guessed what was going on or not, Mrs Grandt neither knew nor cared. He'd certainly done what she had told him to, which was to scarper for the rest of the day, while his fancy bit got over a woman's problem, without asking any questions.

Ethel, very frightened now, had drunk as much as she could of the gin and endured the almost scalding waters of the tin bath. It had made her feel very ill, and Mrs Grandt and one of the other women had put her to bed, but it hadn't produced the effect that the women looked for.

She felt violated by them and deeply humiliated. Why should such a beautiful day have such a nightmare of an ending?

At last, drunk and despairing, she slept, her mouth sagging open, snoring.

De Ponthieu wasn't too sorry to have the evening to himself. Whatever ailed Ethel, he trusted Ma Grandt to put right. He knew that she was probably a bit overdue with a period; that was something that he'd had every opportunity of realizing, but women like Grandt could always sort a thing like that out. They knew how: it was their business.

And, to tell the truth, to always have Ethel clinging to him was, on occasions, proving to be a little irksome. She was a pretty little thing and he was very fond of her and all that, and there was no doubt that she was fun in bed but, all the same, a man needed a bit of time to himself.

He sent round a note apologizing to their dinner companions

and set out to enjoy himself with some fellows he knew in the Lancers. They always had bright ideas for passing an evening, and they hadn't let him down. A hand or two of cards, a few bottles of wine and then off in cabs to this fantastic house that some of them knew, where the booze flowed free and the women did the most amazing things; things that you simply wouldn't believe. He was assured that he'd seen nothing like it since Port Said. They were right.

So it was late when he got back to Ma Grandt's. He'd almost forgotten how it was that he'd had this night of freedom. Something to do with Ethel having a woman's problem he remembered, as he lurched along the hall. What those women had got up to had excited him, so he hoped that she was over her problem.

Mrs Grandt had been waiting for him. The door of her room opened, letting a light fall upon him. He turned to face it, blinking.

'She better? Better now?' he asked, trying to stand upright.

'God! Just look at you!' Mrs Grandt said.

He shook his head. 'Quiet supper with one or two army friends,' he replied with dignity.

'Oh, yes?'

'I asked how the lady was,' he said, mouthing the words carefully.

'Pregnant. That's how she is,' Mrs Grandt snapped.

He slowly sank down onto the bottom step of the stairs. 'Pregnant?' he echoed.

'You heard.'

He shook his head, slowly.

'So what are you going to do about it?' she asked.

He thought about this, trying to get his mind straight, looking for a way out.

'Isn't it something that you can . . . sort out?' he asked.

'We've tried. Nothing doing. So – it's up to you, Captain.'

The horror of the situation dawned on him at last. His mind was clear enough now. 'If this were to get out . . .' he muttered.

'Which it will, in seven months,' Mrs Grandt said.

'Oh God,' he murmured, leaning against the wall, his eyes closed. Why hadn't the silly little bitch done something against this, he wondered. He'd asked her, God knows he had, if she was 'all right'. And she'd said she was. Now this. It really was too much, and he couldn't see how he was to blame for it.

'You do realize,' he said, beginning to feel angry, 'that if anyone knew of it, I'd have to send in my papers.'

'What's that supposed to mean?'

'Resign my commission.'

'God! England trembles!' she spat at him. 'Then what would you live on, the pair of you? Money that fool of a husband sends her? Oh, that's nice, that is! Very gentlemanly that is.'

He looked up the stairs. This was no place to discuss his private life. 'I think we ought to talk somewhere a little bit more –'

She jerked her head towards her room. 'If you think there's anything to talk about, then you'd best come in.'

She put a mug of coffee in front of him. 'I've had this keeping hot on the hob,' she said. 'I know what you buggers are like once you get off the leash.'

He sipped it slowly.

'What's to be done, then?' he asked.

'Don't ask me,' she replied, sitting at the table, her hands folded in her lap.

'Surely there's something.'

'Like what?'

'How should I know? I know nothing of such things.'

She looked at him, her head on one side. 'No. Why should you? Don't need to, do you? Just enough to get her into bed, that's all you need to know. And you know that only too well!'

He got to his feet. He wasn't to be spoken to like this by some raddled old whore! 'Now just look here . . .' he began.

'No!' she interrupted, and she was stronger than he was, so he let her be. 'You look here! If you want any help from me, you'll keep a civil tongue in your head!'

He sat down again.

What airs and graces men like him gave themselves, twiddled their stupid little moustaches, always taking a peep at themselves in the mirror, grinning at their own silly faces, thinking that a big whatsit and a few muscles made them God almighty. 'You and that husband of hers have made a right bloody mess of her, and no mistake.'

He leant forward, trying to force a smile. She was his only hope, he knew that. 'Come on Ma, you'll think of something.'

'Like what?'

'Like – fixing it.'

'You want shot of this baby of yours? Is that what you want?'

'Well . . . it's not really a baby yet, is it now?'

She contented herself with letting her expression show what she thought of him.

'I can get money,' he said. 'However much is needed.'

She nodded. 'Oh, yes? And that finishes it, doesn't it? Easy when you know how.'

He pulled out his pocketbook. 'I've not much about me at present.'

She shook her head. It was late and she felt sick of the whole business. 'Put it away,' she said. 'You'll get a bill, don't worry.' She got to her feet. 'I don't care where you doss down tonight,' she said, 'so long as it's not in her bed.'

'I'll sleep on the sofa.'

'Come on, then,' she ordered, holding the door open. 'I want you on parade bright and early, Captain. There's a telegram you'll have to send.'

Hall woke and looked for a moment in puzzlement at the flower-sprigged wallpaper of the bedroom. There was a scent of lavender from his cool sheets. He'd never slept in this room at the club. Then he remembered something of the day before; the judge being foul, the case wearisome, the dreadful heat, then darkness. Then people getting him into a cab and Charlie

Gill's wife coming into it somewhere, talking to him, saying something.

That was where he must be, at the Gills'. But wherever he was, he had to get up, or he'd be late for court and that would give his Lordship an unfair advantage.

Small rest first, though, to get his strength back for the fray. His eyes closed, he stretched his legs and slept.

The rattling of the brass rings woke him. He opened his eyes as Charlie's wife pulled the curtains open, letting sunlight flood into the room.

'Good morning, Marshall,' she smiled. 'How are we feeling now?'

'Fine,' he said. 'Much, much better.' He shook his head, trying to fetch memory back. 'I must have fainted in court. It was so hot.' He tried to sit up, but his limbs were like lead. 'I'd better be getting back.'

'Back?'

'Is it too late? I mean, how long have I been asleep?'

'About fourteen hours – give or take a minute.'

'Oh Lord.'

'And it wasn't a faint that you had there. Collapsing more like. From what Charlie tells me, it's no wonder, the way you've been working.'

'I'm sorry,' he said. 'I must have put you to a good deal of trouble.'

'Away with the man!' she said. 'Haven't Charlie and me been trying to get you to stay here for months now, and you always too busy? So hush, and I'll fetch up a bite of breakfast.'

'No, really,' he said, sitting up. 'I must get back to court. I must.'

She turned to him in the doorway. 'Then you'll be wasting your time. Charlie's got old Atkinson to finish that case for you. He says the miserable skinflint owes you a favour or two.' She looked at her fob-watch. 'And since it's half-past eleven in the morning, I'd think he was pretty well on with it by now, wouldn't you?'

'I can get up though.'

'What! And me telling the doctor to call to see you! Fine thing that would be, if the man came round and you were skipping about like a spring lamb. You'd put me to shame with the entire medical profession, truly. And you a doctor's son! Your pa would have you across his knee, no doubting it, slippering the hide off you.'

He lay back. There was no arguing with either of these two, he knew that. And it was good, really good, to have all decisions taken away from him. Just to rest. Sleep. His eyes were closing; from downstairs, he could hear the sounds of the household. A happy family makes its own music, he thought, as he drifted away. He dreamt of living in such a house with Ethel. It was a sweet dream.

De Ponthieu wrote the telegram to this doctor friend of Ma Grandt's. She dictated it; there was a certain form of words that had to be used, she said, and he was more than willing to be guided by her.

'Will he be able to – fix things?' he asked her.

She tucked the paper into her handbag. 'If Bertie Laermann can't, Captain,' she said, 'then you're in a right fix, and no mistake.'

She went off on her errand. He wondered, dully, why it had to be a telegram to request a consultation, but dismissed the thought. He had to trust her in everything. He was in her country now, and he had no maps.

Straightening his shoulders, he ran up the stairs to their rooms.

Eddie hadn't often talked about their having a child – he knew that the topic distressed her – but when he had she had seen his longing. And she had turned from him, telling him that such a thing could never be, and that he'd have to make up his mind to accept a childless marriage. He'd taken on a loveless match, so why should he baulk at that?

And now, here she was, carrying a baby. But it wasn't his. She rubbed her hand over her stomach; only thin skin separated her from a life within. He would get to know of it, there was no helping that, and she knew that, of all the hurts she had done him, this would be the most terrible.

At least now he would have to divorce her. There would be that to be gone through too. But then, out of all this shame, she would be able to marry Raoul. Yesterday the thought would have elated her, but today she merely accepted it as something that would be.

She thought for a moment of things being different, of this being Eddie's baby. She could imagine how he'd have fussed round, making her put her feet up, dashing off to buy things, talking about names, planning a whole life for their son or their daughter. He wouldn't have minded which, so long as there was a child in the nursery.

Raoul came into the room. He was looking well, she noticed: freshly shaved, hair macassared and brushed and his clothes, as always, immaculate, whilst she was feeling like death, her head aching intolerably from the gin of the night before and a horrible taste in her mouth.

He was smiling, and she did her best to smile back. She held out a hand to him and he, after a moment's pause, came across the room and took it, kneeling by the side of her chair.

'My poor darling,' he whispered, gently stroking her brow, 'so pale.'

'I feel terrible,' she said.

'Of course you do,' he murmured. 'But it will be better soon.'

'Will it?'

'Oh, yes. Of course it will.'

She clung tightly to his hand, looking into his eyes. 'Mrs Grandt should never have told you. I begged her not to.'

'I'd never have forgiven her if she hadn't.'

'So much worry for you.'

He shook his head, smiling. 'No, no. My only worry is for you; getting you well again.'

She leant her head against the chair back, closing her eyes. 'Yes. I know.'

'I've sent a telegram to this doctor friend of Ma Grandt's.'

'Is he good?'

'She says so.' He was silent for a moment. 'He's willing to – arrange things.'

She opened her eyes and looked at him. 'What does that mean?'

'Make things as they were before.'

He was still mechanically stroking her forehead. She pulled away from his hand. 'Kill the baby?'

'It would only be a baby if it were born!'

'No. It's a baby now.' She put her hand on her stomach. 'It's here. It's here. It's in me.' Her eyes were wide as she looked at him. 'I'm not having it killed. *I'm not!*'

He got up and walked to the window. 'Mrs Grandt says that that was what you wanted – last night. She says you did your best to get rid of it.'

'I didn't know what I was doing!' she cried.

He turned to face her, his hands in his pockets, frowning. 'Have you thought this over?'

'I don't have to think,' she said. 'I *know.*'

'What about me?'

'What about you? I'm the one who'll be having it!'

'My career?'

'Career?' she said, frowning.

'I would have to leave the army. This, my darling, is one thing that couldn't be accepted.'

She thought about this for a moment. 'Unless you left me,' she murmured.

'That question doesn't arise,' he said, lifting his head. 'Lots of things can be said against me – and they are, God knows. But no one will ever say that I spurned my duty.'

'Ah. Duty.'

'That's right.'

She spoke slowly, thinking through her words. 'If it came to that – and you had to give up . . . being a soldier . . . then we could still be together, couldn't we?'

'How? How could we be together? I've no money apart from my army pay. Can't live on air, old thing.'

'But we could work! We could both of us do something!'

'Anything in mind?' he asked.

'We'll think of something! And we'd get a little house, somewhere in the country, something really cheap! We could manage – other people do!'

'I don't quite see it,' he said, smiling at her.

'Eddie will divorce me – he's got to now! Then we can marry.'

He came to her side, pulling a chair close to her and sitting down. 'You are such a little innocent,' he said, still smiling. 'Doors that have been open to us would slam in our faces. We'd know no one – for no one would wish to know us. Think of that life: no money, no friends. It would be hell on earth for both of us.'

Her heart was pounding so hard she thought he would hear it. 'You don't want him to divorce me?'

He shook his head. 'Divorce would be as bad as an illegitimate baby. Just as bad. It simply isn't done.'

She was beginning to weep. 'Then what's to become of us?'

He took her hands and held them. 'We shall be as we were. This doctor will put everything right. *You must trust me in this.*'

Charlie had run over to Hall's club to fetch him a change of clothes; Hall was longing to be out of bed and threatened to come downstairs naked if Charlie refused to help him.

He'd not been able to eat much of a dinner, but at least he'd got some food down him. The three of them sat, sipping their wine in the candlelight, the long windows open to the garden and the birds' nightsong; old friends, at ease in each others' company.

Charlie put his glass down and looked across the table at Hall. God, he thought, how the flesh has fallen from the man.

His cheeks were shadowed by their high bones and his eyes were dark circled. He shook his head.

Hall smiled at him. 'Penny for 'em, Charlie.'

'Whoever got a lawyer's thoughts for less than a guinea?' Charlie replied.

'Are they worth so much?'

'I think so.' He filled Hall's glass. 'As a matter of fact, I was thinking of something Elaine and I were talking about before you came down.'

'Which was – if I can intrude between husband and wife?'

'You tell him, my love,' Gill said, looking at her.

'Just a question, really,' she said, 'of where we pack you off for this holiday.'

'I can't afford a holiday!'

'And you can't afford not to,' she said. 'It's what the doctor ordered.'

'He said a change of surroundings,' Hall said. 'That could mean taking rooms in Hampstead.'

'Oh! God forbid!' Gill cried. 'Very strange class of customer lives up there! You'd be a nervous wreck inside the week. No, it's foreign parts for you, Marshall old friend. And that right soon.'

'Not Brighton? I could stay with my people.'

Gill shook his head. 'And you'd be on the first train up to town and into the Bailey like a rabbit to its burrow. Abroad, Marshall, abroad.'

'I've briefs waiting, piles of 'em!'

'Already seen to. All sorted out. And your head of chambers and I did it in no time. So, it looks as though you've no excuse whatsoever.'

Hall drummed his fingers on the table, looking from one to the other of them. 'Or choice?'

'Just listen to the man, will you,' Elaine smiled. 'No choice at all . . . other than which fleshpot of sin you pick for your jaunting.'

Hall leant back. 'To tell you the truth – I think I could do with a bit of a breather.'

'Of course you could,' Elaine said, squeezing his hand. 'And you'll come back brown as a berry and right as rain. Now, to bed with you. Come on!'

'I was thinking that Marshall and I might have a cigar and a brandy,' Gill murmured.

'Then you can just think again!'

Hall shrugged his shoulders and pushed his chair back. 'Just one thing – before I go up –'

'And what might that be?'

'There's a letter I need to write. So if I could have pen and paper.'

'No law business,' Elaine said.

'I do promise you that. This is a personal matter.'

'Make it a very short letter, then,' she warned.

'A mere note,' he smiled.

My dearest,

The doctor has told me that I have to go abroad for a while. There is nothing to worry about, nothing at all, but I have been going at things rather strongly and a rest is called for.

These last few days I have been thinking of you more than ever, and several things have come to me. I know now that what was wrong between us was no fault of yours, but of mine. I thought of myself (and you must forgive my clumsiness here, my darling, for I've no gift with words when it comes to writing), I thought of me in a certain way, and it wasn't a true way and then it made me see you all wrong. You couldn't be expected to play the part I had written for you. You are too honest for that. You rejected it and, naturally, its author. I drove you out with my stupidity. Forgive me.

I wanted to be a knight in golden armour kneeling at the feet of his lady. But I'm not that, am I? Just a dull lawyer stuck in the nineteenth century, not the fourteenth. A dry stick who had the good fortune to live, for a time, with the most beautiful woman in London. And who, like a fool, threw it away.

I love you more than ever, and I always will.

Your,

Eddie.

PS If ever you felt that you could forgive me and let me begin again, I would be the happiest man in the world.

*

An office lad tipped his cap and handed her an envelope as she was getting into the carriage. A glance at the handwriting told her who it was from and she slipped it into her pocket.

'Anyone we know?' de Ponthieu asked, as he sat opposite her.

'No one you've met, no,' she said.

'Always nice to get a letter, so long as it's not a bill,' Mrs Grandt smiled, sitting beside her.

The rest of the journey to Dr Laermann's consulting rooms passed in silence.

They each had plenty to think about.

The waiting room was like no doctor's place that Ethel had ever seen. The carpet was deep and soft, the walls silk-lined and the furnishings elegant. There was even – and what that had to do with medical practice she couldn't imagine – a grand piano, its lid open and a book of music ready on the stand. There was a strong smell of perfume in the air.

The place reeked of more than scent; it smelled of wealth, and so it should, for it was from here that 'Dr' Albert Laermann, also known to the forces of law on both sides of the Channel as the Vicomte de Larma, practised his highly lucrative trade of supplying drugs and abortions to the highest of society. Not that birth mattered to him. All could call on his ministrations, as long as they could pay his exorbitant fees, and, at some later stage of the business, if he found himself pressed, give a satisfactory reply to his crested and elegantly worded blackmail notes. The police slavered for his arrest, but he was too clever, his clientele were too powerful and all concerned too discreet for there ever to be a shred of evidence that would stand up in court.

The three of them waited in this opulence. De Ponthieu was restless, walking about, peering at the paintings, looking at the view from the window. Ethel, white-faced, sat in a corner of a huge sofa and Mrs Grandt kept a careful watch on her, fearing that, at the last, the fool of a girl might bolt.

From an inner room they could hear a woman talking excitedly and sobbing. Then a deep masculine voice would interrupt her, soothing, mollifying. There was a silence and, at last, the door to this room opened and a tall, gaunt, but very well-dressed woman came out, heavily veiled. She clutched a small package to her breast.

The man who followed her was fluttering attentively around his patient. If he had been an actor playing the role of a distinguished Harley Street physician, he would have been perfectly cast; tall, his face ascetically boned, with wings of greying hair swept back from a high and noble brow. Only his heavy hands, perfectly framed though they were by his starched white cuffs and gold links, were at odds with the rest of him. They were the hands of a butcher.

He held the outer door open for the woman and leant close to her. 'When you require some further – medicine – my dear Countess, do not hesitate to call upon me,' he said in his deep, melodious voice, with just the slightest trace of an accent. She looked at him for a moment, then hurried out. 'Until then – *au revoir*,' he murmured, as he closed the door.

He turned to Ethel and her companions, smiling, easily. 'Poor dear lady. She suffers so terribly with her nerves.'

'And you reckon morphine's good for 'em, do you, Bertie?' Mrs Grandt asked. Both her voice and the question seemed unbelievably coarse in these elegant surroundings.

Laermann gave her a smile. 'Dear Mrs Grandt,' he murmured, 'I prescribe whatever my diagnosis indicates.' He turned to Ethel and gave her a slight bow. 'I fear we have not yet been introduced, Madame.'

Mrs Grandt was standing, at his side. 'Do you need names?' she asked.

'But of course. How else can we conduct our business?'

'I am Mrs Marshall Hall,' Ethel said.

Laermann's smile disappeared as if it had been switched off, and he shot a sharp look at Mrs Grandt. 'The lawyer?' he asked. It was his business to know such things, and he did.

She shook her head. 'Separated. Never see each other.' She

nodded in the direction of de Ponthieu. 'This is the fellow that sent the telegram, and I'm sure you don't want to know who *he* is.'

'No, that will not be necessary.' He turned again to Ethel, his reassuring smile in place again. 'I understand that you need some medical assistance.'

Ethel nodded.

'Then I am at your disposal,' he bowed. 'Won't you come through to my consulting room?'

He led the way and held open the door. With a last look at de Ponthieu, who nodded bravely, she went in.

Laermann, a hand on the door, looked at Mrs Grandt. 'Before we begin the consultation, there is, alas, the slight question of my fee.'

'Half now, and the rest when you've brought it off. As usual,' she said.

He nodded agreeably at this and she turned to de Ponthieu. 'Time to pay up, Captain,' she said.

'Oh, yes – I'm sorry,' de Ponthieu muttered, getting an envelope from his inner pocket and handing it to him.

Laermann flicked the envelope open and took a quick glance at the bank notes. 'That seems to be satisfactory,' he said, and went into the room, quietly closing the door.

For a long time there was silence from the inner room: then a shrill cry of pain was heard. De Ponthieu's eyes widened, and he looked at Mrs Grandt; but she, her lips pursed, shook her head.

He sat, shoulders bowed, hands clasped in his lap.

Laermann came back into the room, wiping his wet hands on a towel. De Ponthieu saw that it was blood-stained and looked away.

'Well, Bertie?' Mrs Grandt asked.

Laermann shrugged his shoulders, threw the towel down and went to a Louis Quinze escritoire by the window. He pulled down the flap, took out a large ledger, dipped a pen neatly in the inkwell and wrote. 'Removal of polypus,' he murmured. 'Operation successfully concluded.'

'That what you call it?' Mrs Grandt laughed.

He replaced the book and closed the desk. 'That is what I have done,' he said. 'But I think that the lady's health will now be considerably improved.'

'That's all right, then,' she nodded.

'I think so.'

Ethel could scarcely walk when she came out of the consulting room. She clung to the door-post, breathing heavily. De Ponthieu sprang to help her, but Mrs Grandt was there before him. 'This is women's business, Captain,' she said. 'You get yourself a cab and bugger off. I'll see to her.'

'No, I must –' he began.

'I've given you a job to do. Go and do it. Go on!' she ordered.

Ethel nodded. 'Do as she says. Please!' she gasped.

He shook his head but, with a shrug of his shoulders, he went.

'How are you, then?' Mrs Grandt asked, as she got into the carriage.

'Bleeding,' Ethel whispered.

'Bad?'

Ethel shook her head.

'It will be, if things go right. There's a po in your room. Use it. But don't throw it away when you've done. I'll be wanting to have a look at it.'

Ethel, her eyes closed, could only think of her pain. But she remembered something that Mrs Grandt had said. 'What's this job Raoul's got to do?' she gasped.

'Find you rooms.'

'But we –'

'No,' Mrs Grandt said decisively. 'You can stay with me tonight, but then I want you out till you're better. Then you can come back, if you like.'

A wave of pain swept over Ethel. She was past caring where she went.

*

Raoul, presumably on Mrs Grandt's orders, stayed away all that night. From time to time Mrs Grandt came in to see her. It must have been early in the morning when she came with a cup of tea. 'Still losing?' she asked.

Ethel shook her head. 'It seems to have stopped,' she whispered.

Mrs Grandt looked at her, frowning. 'Drink your tea,' she said, and left her alone.

Ethel pushed herself up in the bed and picked up the cup. It rattled against the saucer as she held it.

She noticed that Mrs Grandt, as she undressed her, had put her bag and the contents of her coat pocket on the bedside table.

The letter from Eddie was there. She turned her head away; it was almost as if he were present in the room, seeing her in her shame.

What had he once called her? 'His blessed damozel'? He was so romantic, so foolish, treating her like a plaster saint. She never had been, that was the trouble and, God knows, the statue he'd made of her was now smashed and lying in pieces on the floor of this horrible room.

Silently she began to weep; not at the thought of him and their marriage, but at the memory of them both as children. So innocent they had been, so happy: playing on the beach in the long summer days; gardener's bonfires in the autumn; the smell of wood smoke and the two of them raking and piling leaves. Then frosts and parties at Christmas. She could hear some grown-up playing the piano for their games. Hide and seek – was that what it was? When the music stops . . . A dark cupboard with long clothes hanging, and her snuggled into a corner. The door opening, letting light in and Eddie there. He always found her, keeping looking when all the other children had given up. And claiming a dry, quick kiss on her cheek as her forfeit.

She picked up the envelope, tore it open and, through the blur of her tears, began to read.

*

The writer of the letter stood at the rail of the cross-Channel steamer looking at the castle – its flag proudly flying in the early morning sunlight – and the white cliffs behind the town. The engines pounded, the wheels churned and England grew smaller and smaller.

He shivered and pulled his overcoat close. He would go below and see if he could get some coffee, he thought. By this afternoon he would be in Paris, where the coffee was worth drinking. Charlie had sent the telegram booking his rooms, though he didn't know the significance of the name of the hotel. It was the Domenice. Above all else, Hall needed to be in a place where she had been, touch the chair she had sat in and lie in the bed where she had slept.

If she had longed for a good address, she had got one now. 'Duke Street, Mayfair', she would have been able to say to their friends, with a modest smile. But the rooms weren't particularly large, or terribly clean, and the furnishings were mean. It looked, in fact, what it was; a place where men like de Ponthieu kept women like her.

Mrs Grandt had taken her there and, after making sure that the slut of a servant girl would take her up some food, she had left.

Ethel collapsed in weariness on the bed, but the pillows smelled of the sweat of the previous sleepers and, with rising nausea, she got up and sat in a high-backed chair by the table.

The day went by, and still she sat. She had thought that Raoul would come to her, sit with her, but the only step on the stair was the girl fetching up a tray of greasy food. She shook her head and sent her away again.

She heard the lamplighter in the street whistling as he flicked open the glass panes and touched the mantles with the tiny flame at the end of his pole. In their cold light she sat on, not moving or wanting to move.

Her eyes closed and her head nodded forward on her breast.

The door opened and she woke with a start. He was there, fiddling with a table lamp, cursing under his breath as he burned his fingers on the match. She turned to him and he came over to her, kissing her, holding her hand. His breath smelled of wine.

'I thought you would have been here long since,' she said.

'I know. I'm sorry, my darling, but I've had a lot to do.'

He wasn't lying. His bank manager had grimly refused to allow his overdraft to be increased by so much as a penny, and he had been on a wearisome round of such friends as could be touched for a loan. They had all either been out of town or unable to assist until, at last, he'd found that old pansy Temple-Smith in his club. He had said that he wouldn't lift a finger to help until he knew the whole story of the dear boy's indigence. And that had meant dinner and the telling of all that was creditable in his affair with the attorney's silly young bride.

Temple-Smith had enjoyed the tale; there was, he said, a rather delicious irony in it, worthy, almost, of the pen of Maupassant. Then he had looked again at his companion. 'On second thoughts,' he said, 'perhaps Ouida would get the flavour of it better.'

De Ponthieu had to endure this nonsense to the dregs of the port and cigars before the fellow coughed up. And then it was only on the condition that he received regular reports of the development of the business.

'How are you, anyway?' he asked Ethel.

'The same.'

'No . . .?'

'No.'

'That blasted doctor! And the money he cost!'

He must be very concerned, she thought; he was usually far too much the gentleman to swear before a woman. Not like Eddie who, if he caught his hand in a door, would let fly with a string of oaths. Always apologizing straight away, of course. She put her hand under the shawl on her lap and felt his letter to her.

'I'm sorry,' she said.

'It's not your fault! I'm sure you've done your best. It's him I blame. Well, he's going to have to put it right, that's all.'

She sighed and turned away. 'I'm tired,' she said. 'I think that perhaps you'd better go now.'

'Go? I thought I'd be staying here.'

'I'd rather you didn't. Not tonight.'

'I can't leave you here on your own!'

'Truly,' she said, 'I'd rather.'

'If you're sure . . .'

She nodded. 'Quite sure.'

She turned her cheek to him and he kissed her. 'Sleep well, then.'

'I shall, don't worry. Put the lamp out as you go, please.'

'And I'll come round first thing in the morning.'

She waited until she heard the front door slam behind him, then dragged herself from the chair. As soon as she got up, a knife-thrust of pain shot through her abdomen. She bent double, biting her lip. After a moment the pain eased enough for her to get to the bed, throw the pillows on the floor, spread her shawl on the counterpane and lie down. She lay on her back, looking at the shadow of the square-paned window on the ceiling, and listening to the cabs and carriages in the street. Some people in the street were laughing as they passed. What, in this hellish world, was there to laugh at?

It was Mrs Grandt who came first, quite early in the morning. 'Still no sign?' she asked.

'No. Just the pain.'

Mrs Grandt looked at her. 'What a mess you are,' she said. 'Have you slept in these clothes?'

'Yes. Why shouldn't I?'

'Because it's not the end of the world what you're going through, that's why! Lying about like bloody Ellen Terry!'

Ethel closed her eyes, praying that she'd go away.

'Up with you!' Mrs Grandt ordered. 'Let's get you washed and changed before smart-arse gets here.'

Once she had dressed her, Mrs Grandt put her in the chair where she'd sat the day before and went downstairs, to chivvy the girl into making a pot of tea.

As soon as she'd gone, Ethel took Eddie's letter from under the counterpane where she'd kept it and went back to her chair, holding tightly onto the sheet of paper. It was like a talisman; so long as she had that in her grasp, she would be all right.

She heard Mrs Grandt coming up, talking with someone on the stairs. Then she heard him reply. It was Raoul. It was a little time before they came into the bedroom, however. Ethel, her throat dry with thirst, was longing for the tea that had been promised, but had to sit, hearing them still talking in low voices. He raised his voice once, but she couldn't make out what he said. She supposed that it all had to do with her, but she had no particular interest in what they were saying. They'd tell her what they wanted her to do when they were ready.

Mrs Grandt came in at last. 'Cold as charity, and stewed to hell and back, but it's wet,' she said, handing Ethel a cup of tea. She drank it greedily.

Raoul was in the doorway, smiling at her. 'Are we ready, then?' he asked.

'Ready?' Ethel repeated wearily, giving the cup back to Mrs Grandt.

'We're off to see Bertie Laermann again,' Mrs Grandt told her.

'No! Please! I couldn't face it!' Ethel cried, pressing herself back in the chair.

'I promise you he won't hurt you,' Mrs Grandt said. 'I'll get him to give you something to take the pain away.'

'We only want him to look at you, to make sure you're all right,' de Ponthieu added.

Ethel shook her head, but she had no strength to fight them.

Mrs Grandt looked over her head to de Ponthieu. 'You take one arm, I'll take the other.'

Limp as a rag doll, they carried her down the stairs and into the waiting cab.

Laermann held the hypodermic syringe up to the light and expelled a little of the liquid. 'Just a tiny pinprick,' he murmured, 'then you'll have a nice, warm sleep.' That was an understatement; there was enough morphia in the syringe to pole-axe a navvy.

He pushed the needle home and stood by to await results. They weren't long in coming. Before he could count to ten, her lips began to flutter and her eyelids closed. As she went under, she seemed to be murmuring someone's name. Presumably her lover's, he thought as he pulled her skirts up and lifted her legs into the stirrups that hung high at the end of the bed. God knows what dreams she'd have of him, given the work he was about to undertake.

But she wasn't thinking of her lover at all. She was in a dark cupboard that smelled of mothballs, waiting for Eddie to come and find her.

The manager and the servants at the Domenice knew Hall immediately. Of course, they assured him, the rooms that he and his wife had occupied before would be his. He was more than welcome. 'And how is Madame?' the manager asked.

'Still very poorly, I'm afraid,' Hall told him. 'She wanted to come with me, but the doctors would not permit.'

'Alas,' the manager sympathized, bowing his head in commiseration.

A click of his fingers produced a porter who, giving Hall a friendly smile, took his bags and carried them up to their room.

Once alone, Hall looked round, remembering. To his annoyance, some of the furniture had been shifted to new positions. Before taking his coat off he pulled it back to where it had been before. Then he sat, closed his eyes and tried to conjure up a ghost.

Ethel was past thinking of anything. Laermann had been no more successful in killing the life within her at his second attempt than at his first, and they had brought her back, looking more dead than alive (that, Laermann had assured them, was merely the after-effects of the 'anaesthetic'), and put her to bed in the narrow room at the good address in Mayfair, where she lay as they had placed her, slipping in and out of consciousness. She longed for those times of sleep; when she was awake, the pain was unendurable.

Sometimes, through her agony, she could see dark shapes against the window: de Ponthieu and Mrs Grandt. They were standing at the foot of the bed, looking at her. She wished they would go away; what was happening to her was bad enough without the humiliation of being watched. It was such a waste of time; they couldn't touch her now, whatever they planned. Days, nights went by, broken only by one or other lifting her head, spooning drinks and soups into her mouth and asking her questions to which she had neither strength nor interest to reply.

On a bright morning, the sunshine hurting her eyes, Mrs Grandt lifted her onto the edge of the bed and dressed her, then wiped her face with a wet cloth that had a bad smell to it. Raoul was there too; she could hear him somewhere behind her. Then she felt his hands on her arm as he and Mrs Grandt lifted her and carried her down the steps to the waiting carriage.

She was slipping again into her deep sleep as they went towards the door. Perhaps, she thought, they were taking her home at last.

Laermann was not pleased to see them; God knows, he'd earned his money with this case already, and he could see no end to it. He nodded to them curtly and opened the door to his consulting room, where they laid her on the bed.

He gave a glance at de Ponthieu who, reading it aright, went out and left them. Laermann and Mrs Grandt lifted the girl's skirts and examined the damage.

He shrugged and put the dress back. 'As you see,' he said, 'the vaginal area is far too swollen for me to attempt any further intervention. No instruments could possibly be inserted.'

Mrs Grandt nodded. There was no disputing what he had said. 'We need a drink, Bertie,' she said, going towards the door, 'while we think what's best to do.'

More expense, he thought, following her. Would to God he'd never clapped eyes on any of them.

De Ponthieu was sitting by the window and turned to face them as they came in. 'Well?' he asked.

'I've only champagne,' Laermann said, opening the doors of an elegant cabinet.

'That'll do,' Mrs Grandt nodded.

'It isn't iced.'

'Who cares?'

'I don't think that this is a time to sit drinking wine!' de Ponthieu cried.

Mrs Grandt turned to him. 'You'll change your mind in a minute, believe me.' She looked back at Laermann. 'Go on, pour him one. He'll need it.'

Laermann mournfully shrugged. 'I already have.'

Mrs Grandt took her glass and sat on the sofa. 'Now,' she said, 'the way I see it's this. Leave things be, and we're going to lose that girl.'

'Oh God,' de Ponthieu murmured, 'this can't be!'

She ignored him and kept her eyes on Laermann. 'That's right, isn't it?'

He took a sip of wine and wiped his lips with a silk handkerchief. 'The patient is very ill, certainly.'

'And if we do, Bertie . . .' She let the thought sink home. 'I don't like to think about what happens then, I don't really. Who likes post mortems?'

He sat, head back, legs elegantly crossed. 'I have merely given medical attention for the removal of a polypus.'

'Oh, yes? Try that one in court and see how it sounds.'

He gave her a humourless smile. 'I wasn't aware that you were a medical practitioner.'

'As much as you bloody well are, any day in the week.'

His smile faded. 'So, then, Mrs Grandt? From the heights of your knowledge, what do you suggest?'

She sat back comfortably. 'Not up to me to suggest anything. That's your midden. Fetch this baby off or face the law.'

Laermann moved a Meissen figurine from the table at his elbow and put his glass down. He sat for a moment, finger tips together. 'There is one way,' he murmured. 'But it is action *in extremis.*'

'Yes?'

'An injection of corrosive spirits of mercury. Directly into the womb.'

De Ponthieu was sitting, shoulders bowed, head in his hands.

'Would it work?' she asked.

'Undoubtedly. But it would cause her intense agony.'

'You could give her something for that. Like last time.'

He shook his head. 'No. In addition to what I've to do, the shock would kill her.'

Mrs Grandt stood and took the champagne bottle. 'Then see she drinks the rest of this. Drop of bubbly never did anyone any harm. And it might just knock her out.'

Laermann pushed himself out of his chair. 'I do this at your request. Remember that.'

She shoved the bottle at him. 'Get on with it, for God's sake.'

Hall had slept badly. He could have sworn that the scent of Ethel was still there, in the bed, and several times in the night it seemed to be so overpowering that he had reached out to hold her. But she was never there; only a cold emptiness in her place.

As dawn broke he lay still, thinking of her. He thought, as he had so often and so agonizingly, of what Gill had told him, of these liars alleging that she was living in some adulterous liaison. That wasn't possible, he knew that. But the thought would not be resisted. Charlie Gill knew a liar when he met one. It could be true. What then? What if she had lain in some other man's arms, turning to him, groaning with ecstasy in their lovemaking? Perhaps even now she was waking to the sight of this man, sleeping at her side.

With a gesture of contempt for his own lack of faith, he threw the coverlet back and sat on the edge of the bed. It was impossible. But, then again . . .

He went to the window and looked down on to the court-yard. The hotel was beginning to come to life. A porter from the market had a barrow full of vegetables, and he and the chef were deep in discussion of a cabbage, which they passed, from one to another.

Poor they might be, those men, and no hope in them for a rich, a famous future. But they had come from homes, from families. Kissed as they left the house, however perfunctorily. And, at the end of the day, it would all be waiting for them again. He would have given anything to have been that porter and to have gone home, weary, to the most wretched *arrondissement* in Paris, finding heaven in a garret.

He turned away from the sight and stood, deep in thought. Whatever she had done, even the unthinkable, it would make no difference. His folly had driven her to it. Why shouldn't she go to some man who saw her clearly and loved what he saw, when she had spent those dead years living with a blind and pompous prig? He hadn't wanted a wife, he thought, bitterly: he'd wanted a mirror in which his own virtues would shine back at him.

He and he alone was the cause, no one else. Very well, then: his stupidity and arrogance had sent her away; his new-found sight and his love must fetch her back. Whatever had happened between them there was no hope and no happiness for either of them if they lived apart. This he knew, more surely than he knew anything. As soon as he got back to London, he swore it, he would find her, beg her forgiveness and bring her home.

He breathed deeply. It would be a good day. A great surge of hope and happiness rose within him. Already he was feeling strong, refreshed, ready for all that lay before him. Life was never finished! The brave, the strong could fight any battle, however fearful the odds. Could fight and could win. And he would; he felt it within him.

He rang for hot water for his shave. Today he would enjoy Paris, he would enjoy life. And enjoy it he did, swinging his silver-headed cane along the boulevards, smiling back at the ladies who glanced approvingly at him. He found a restaurant where once, as a young and poor man, he had spent the whole profit from a jewellery transaction on a meal that the gods might have eaten. It was as it had been; a place far from the haunts of the English and Americans, where serious Parisians, napkins tucked in their collars, gave food its due consideration. He ate, he drank, and he was content.

De Ponthieu gazed moodily down on the rain-washed street. It wasn't serious rain that hisses and splashes on the pavements, but slow veils of drizzle that the few passers-by endured, their collars pulled up and heads bowed.

There had been silence for some time from Laermann's den, and he began to hope that, at last, things were going easily and well. Then she screamed; and it was a cry such as he had never heard in all his life, not even when a tiger he had been stalking sprang from cover and took his bearer. It was high, constant on its note and unwavering.

He felt the colour drain from his face and stood, unable to move, transfixed by horror.

Mrs Grandt, tight-lipped and as white as he, looked across at him.

Power returned to his limbs and he stumbled towards the door of the inner room. Mrs Grandt was there before him. 'Leave it!' she cried.

He lifted a hand to shove her out of his way. 'I told you to leave it!' she shouted in his face.

He stopped, irresolute.

'What did you think it would be like?' she hissed. 'Take this powder, dearie, and you'll be as right as rain by morning? Is that what you thought? *Is it, Captain?*'

The screaming started again.

'I can't let this happen to her! I can't!' he sobbed.

Mrs Grandt still blocked the way to the door; her strength was greater than his and she was unmovable. 'Can't? Can't let it happen?' she echoed. 'Oh, my man! You put her on the road that ends up in that room. You and no one else. And there's no getting her off it now.'

He sat. 'I never knew, never knew it was like this.'

She nodded. 'You know now, but you'll forget it soon enough. You all do. Only women remember.' Ethel was still sobbing and screaming, shouting for help.

'I can't bear it!' he cried, standing.

'Then don't.' She looked at him, this doll soldier with all the stuffing kicked out of him. 'Get out! Go on! Shift!'

'I feel so sick,' he gasped.

'Then go and throw up – in the gutter.'

He ran for the door. 'I'll be there – if I'm wanted –'

The screams seemed to be getting louder, and Bertie Laermann was shouting at her, but it was in some foreign language, so she couldn't tell what he was saying.

Bloody hell, she thought. We'll have all London on the doorstep before we know where we are. She went quickly to the window and looked out. There was no sign of de Ponthieu but, sure enough, a passer-by had stopped, and he was looking up at the house, rain dripping from the brim of his hat.

She was frightened; any minute now that nosey bugger would be running for a bobby. Then they were all up the spout.

Looking round in desperation, she saw the open piano. She ran to it, sat down and began to play as loudly as she could. Nothing fancy, like the Mozart on the stand, but songs from shows. She hoped to God that the fellow in the street would be fooled by it. She played on, never letting a second pass between pieces. She couldn't hear the shrieking now, so perhaps no one else could.

The woman had been much further on than she had led him to believe, and the bloody mess that he was burning was, quite clearly, a boy. His mother lay on the bed, unconscious at last, her breathing fast and shallow. They'd have to get her out of here, and that damn quick.

He turned away from the incinerator and took a clean shirt from a drawer, stripping off the blood-spattered one he had been wearing, throwing it into the flames. Nothing, not a scrap of evidence, must be left.

Someone, Hermione Grandt almost certainly, was playing the piano next door. It was the first time he'd noticed it. Yes, it would be her, he thought, as he realized why she was doing it. 'You can stop that now!' he shouted. And she did, mid chord.

She opened the door and looked in. 'Finished?' she asked.

He nodded. 'You didn't tell me she was so far gone.'

'I only knew what she told me. How far?'

'Four months. Five maybe.'

'Oh, the silly little bitch!' she gasped. 'Then it wasn't her fancy man's!'

He shook his head as he scrubbed his hands at the sink. 'I don't know about that, nor do I want to.'

'Nor does she want to,' Mrs Grandt murmured. 'It'd just about finish her, that would. It's all been for nothing.'

De Ponthieu, frightened and in despair, ran from their rooms in Mayfair, looking for a doctor. At last, in Hanover Square, he saw a brass plate on a door: 'Dr Vintras, MD'. He rang the bell. On the surface of things, he'd struck lucky; Dr Vintras had a fashionable practice and was very well thought of.

He came at once, of course, in reply to this well-spoken young man's pleadings, trying to assure him, as they walked briskly through the Georgian streets, that his wife was in good hands now, and would soon be well.

'A miscarriage, you say?'

De Ponthieu nodded.

'Unfortunate, most unfortunate. Better luck next time, eh?'

'Hurry, Doctor, please hurry!'

'You young fathers!' the good doctor smiled. But he quickened his pace.

He came from the bedroom, folding his stethoscope and dropping it in his top hat. He looked from the woman to the husband.

'Well?' the young man asked.

Vintras gave him the coldest of stares. 'The immediate concern is that the woman is suffering from peritonitis, and I must warn you that the outcome of that is invariably death. Prepare yourselves for that, if you have not already done so.' De Ponthieu collapsed onto a chair. 'But I must also tell you,' the doctor went on, his voice that of a hanging judge, 'that the cause of that peritonitis is, undoubtedly, a botched and criminal abortion.'

The woman said nothing, but looked at him as coldly as he looked at her.

'Who performed this illegal operation is none of my business,' the doctor said. 'It is a matter for the law, not me.'

'Cut the cackle,' the woman said. 'What are you doing for her?'

He looked at her, frowning. 'Doing, Madam? I?'

'You're a doctor!'

He was already making for the door. 'There is simply no question of my intervening in this case,' he said. 'It is not my responsibility, nor will I shoulder it.' He paused in the doorway. 'Under the circumstances, however, I will waive my fee.'

It had to be Laermann again. There was no one else, but it took all Mrs Grandt's strength and a few not very hidden threats, before he would come.

He saw at once that it was hopeless. 'You need a doctor – her family doctor. Someone close enough to agree with my diagnosis.'

'Which is?' Mrs Grandt asked.

'Dysentery. Get him to sign the certificate to that effect.' He was already putting his coat back on. 'And remember,' he said, 'that the treatment I have given was within the law, and at your urgent request.'

Mrs Grandt turned to de Ponthieu. 'I reckon it'll pay all of us to remember that. We none of us knew she was pregnant till Bertie saw her. And he did an ordinary female operation. What happened after that was God's doing, not ours.'

De Ponthieu looked at her, dull-eyed.

'Remember, Captain! Get it into your skull!'

He shook his head. 'You're all talking nonsense,' he said. 'She'll get better, I know she will. I've friends. I'll take her away, and we can stay with them, in the country.'

Mrs Grandt gave a sharp laugh. 'Dartmoor's the only country you'll be seeing, my lad. And, believe me, you'll have plenty of time to enjoy it. *Unless you get the story straight.*'

Laermann pulled her to one side. 'For God's sake, watch that one.'

'Don't worry. I won't take my eyes off him.'

Laermann nodded, then, as an afterthought as he was going, turned to her again. 'She was calling for someone,' he said.

Mrs Grandt jerked her head in the direction of de Ponthieu. 'Him?'

'No. Someone called "Eddie".'

Mrs Grandt thought for a moment, biting her lower lip. 'Hang on, Bertie,' she said, 'while I get my bonnet. We can share the cab. I've a call to make.'

*

He toyed with the idea of buying her a very nice bracelet that he saw in a shop window. It was underpriced, and he reckoned that he might be able to get the man to knock a few francs off even that: the clasp was a later addition to the piece and that had to affect its value.

But, as his hand was on the door, he thought again. She wasn't a child, to be brought presents to cheer her up. That had been his mistake last time. He turned away and walked slowly back to the hotel, enjoying the late afternoon sunshine. An aperitif, he thought, sipped slowly, then a pleasant dinner. Tonight, he knew, he would sleep, with easy dreams.

He was going up the stairs, his mind full of thoughts of a bath and dressing for dinner, when he heard his name being called. He turned and saw the manager, at the foot of the stairs, holding a small envelope in his hand.

'Telegram, m'sieu,' the manager said.

This was surprising; only Charlie knew he was here. He came down the stairs, smiling, to take the envelope. Maybe Charlie was telling him how a case had gone, or of some fat brief waiting his return.

'Thank you,' he nodded, tearing the envelope open.

The manager was still hovering, solicitously. 'Not some bad news, m'sieu? The Madame Hall?'

Hall was shaking his head, trying to make sense of the words.

SORRY TO INFORM STOP WIFE ILL
CALLING FOR YOU STOP RETURN AT ONCE
STOP GILL

In a daze, he turned to the manager, whose question had been answered by the stricken look on the Englishman's face.

'Have someone pack my bags quickly. And find out the time of the next boat train.'

The manager scurried away, but all his efforts could not produce a railway train when none was due. He tried to persuade Hall to wait, eat a little food, but he refused. Nor would he go up into his room. Bags had to be packed for him and brought down.

He paced up and down the station platform, looking constantly at the huge and pitiless clock, willing its creeping hands forward, then looking down the track for the first sight of the lights of the engine. Never, in all his life, had time so tortured him.

His mind was in a turmoil. Ill? How ill? Why the devil hadn't Charlie told him? She was a young girl. It couldn't be anything serious, it couldn't. Not at her time of life. Then his mind ran to accidents in the street – some bolting cab-horse, people shouting, her crossing a street, the horse rearing, falling, plunging, trampling, hooves and wheels crushing her.

Oh God! Where was this train?

There were illnesses though, that no one was proof against. Cholera, diphtheria, typhoid. These came without warning in a hot summer like this, and struck down the strongest.

Move, time! *Move!*

She was calling for him, needing him, whilst he stood among chattering English tourists, impotent, failing her.

Her cries rang in his head. He had to be there, he had to be with her. She was still alive, or Charlie would have told him. He would never be so cruel as not to. Once with her, holding her hands, he could pour all his strength, all his will into her. Let her be on the very brink of the grave, and he would pull her back.

He blundered through the crowds on the platform, scattering them, not hearing their shouted complaints, until he found an empty bench under a bridge that spanned the tracks. It was dark there. He sat, leaning forward, hands clasped, his eyes tight closed and he prayed desperately to the God who he knew was always near him.

The porter who had been watching his bags tapped him on the shoulder. 'Your train, m'sieu.'

Blindly, Hall followed him and climbed into his carriage. An Englishman, his wife and their two daughters got in after him. They were full of gossip about their holiday and grumbles about how dirty the French were compared to the people back home. He gave them a stare of such despairing hatred for their vacuous, empty chatter that the man looked at his wife in warning, and they all trooped out to find saner company for the journey home.

At last, in the grey light of early morning, he was at Victoria. He ran from the platform, shoving his ticket at the collector, carrying his bags himself. He couldn't waste a moment of time finding a porter.

Charlie Gill was there, waiting for him. He grabbed some of Hall's baggage and walked towards the forecourt. 'I knew that was the train you'd be on,' he was saying. 'It was the first you could get.'

'How ill is she?'

'I've a cab waiting,' Gill said. He looked at Hall's ravaged face. He should tell him, but he hadn't the courage for it. 'I don't know. Some woman went to your chambers, and they sent a message to me.'

'Not seriously ill, then?'

'I don't know.' He put the bags down. 'Here's your cab. I'll come with you.'

Hall turned to him and shook his head. 'Charlie . . . no. I want to be on my own with her.'

'If that's what you want.'

'Yes.'

Gill nodded. It would be best. And, God knows, there'd be work enough for him and Elaine in the days to come. 'Here's the address, then.' He shoved a piece of paper into Hall's hand, then looked up at the cabbie. 'Quick as you can,' he shouted.

The streets were still empty and only the occasional house-maid was about, scrubbing the steps of the pillared houses.

Hall was leaning forward, looking at the street names until the one on the paper came into view. At the end of it, before one of these houses, a policeman stood, at the top of the steps. Hall wondered, his heart pounding, what he was there for.

The cab stopped by that house. Hall fumbled in his pocket for the fare, but the cabbie told him that the other gentleman had already seen to all of that.

He got out and the cab rattled away. The policeman came down the steps to meet him. 'Have you business in this house, sir?'

'Yes. I have.'

'Might I ask your name?'

This was a nightmare from hell. What business of this policeman's was it that his wife was ill? 'Look. Would you please get out of my way,' Hall said, his voice shaking. 'I'm told that my wife is very ill in there.'

'Would you be Mr Edward Marshall Hall, then?'

'What bloody business is it of yours?' Hall cried, pushing the man aside.

All right, then, the policeman thought. If that's the way you want to play it, suit yourself.

As soon as he came into the musty hallway, he saw another man come from a room at the top of the stairs.

'I know you, sir,' the man said. 'Seen you in court.' His voice echoed in the empty space.

'Where's my wife?'

The superintendent thought that the constable on duty on the door had told him the news, so he merely gave a sorrowful bow of the head. 'She's in here, sir,' he said.

Hall was running up the stairs, two at a time.

'Doubtless you'll want to be alone with her for a time . . .'

Hall pushed past him and threw the door open.

The room was in half-light, the holland blinds pulled down. There was no one there. A door opposite him was open.

He stood for a moment, looking at it. It must be the bedroom. That was where she would be.

He called her name, softly, not wanting to wake her if she slept, and went into the other room.

The blind was flapping slightly in the morning air, letting light come in and out of the barely furnished room.

She was lying in the bed, her eyes closed, a slight smile on her lips.

He tiptoed to her. 'I came as quickly as I could,' he whispered, and kissed her cheek.

It was cold, so cold to his lips. He pulled away, his eyes wide. Sinking to his knees he saw, at last, the stillness of death.

The superintendent heard his cry of desolation and closed his eyes at the pain of it. He walked down the stairs towards the basement. He'd get that daft young girl to make them all a pot of tea. He put his hand on the brandy flask in his pocket. Well laced with this, he thought.

Hall knelt, his fist in his mouth, biting on it. He mustn't shout, not like that.

Her hands were together on top of the coverlet. He saw that she was holding something in one of them. In that warm season, her body had not yet stiffened and the hand opened easily in his. The letter he had written to her, creased and torn, fell between them. Holding her hand in his, he bent his head and sobbed helplessly.

CHAPTER
SEVENTEEN

The room was darkening and a sea mist was drifting into the garden. One by one, as he watched, the trees disappeared from view, as if they were slipping away from him into a grey cloud. From far out at sea there was the melancholy wail of a ship's siren.

The door behind him opened, but he didn't hear it. It was only when he felt the hand on his shoulder that he looked up to see his sister. She kissed him lightly on the head.

He picked up a newspaper and let it fall over the objects before him. The headline shouted its news: 'HORRIFY-ING MURDER. GERMAN WOMAN TO FACE TRIAL'.

'The woman is worthless, Eddie,' she whispered, her hand still on his shoulder.

'No one is worthless,' he said. 'No one.'

She was surprised at the feeling in his voice. It was almost as if he was about to cry. 'This case means so much to you?'

'Yes. It does.'

'More than your career?'

'Much more.'

She sat on the edge of his desk, looking at him. 'I think you're mad to take it on. You know that.'

'I've no choice. I must fight it.'

She nodded and looked out of the window. 'Sea fret again. It reminds me, more than anything else, of being a child here.'

'And me,' he said. 'I used to quite like it, being tucked up snug in bed, with a night light burning, and the mist all round the house.'

'I hate it,' she said, as she stood up. 'It means I won't be able to go home tonight. I've sent a telegram, telling them. You should stay too.'

He rose to face her. 'I have to get back.'

'You can get the early train in the morning. It will have cleared by then.'

He turned away from her and picked up the newspaper. 'She's been tried already, you see. And found guilty.'

Ada shivered. 'It's cold here. Let's go down. We'll get them to make us some tea.'

She saw the dance card and the other things on his desk. 'You should burn those. It's not good for you.'

He put a hand on them. 'No!'

'The past is dead. Finished.'

'I was thinking of a ball. That's all I was doing.'

'Why?'

He turned to her. 'Because this case begins with one.'

'I'm going down,' she said. She opened the door and a shaft of light from the stairwell flooded into the room.

There was a ball, certainly, but the plight of Marie Hermann, the German prostitute for whose blood every newspaper in the land was baying, did not truly begin on that night. It would be difficult, in fact, to say when it did start. Perhaps her whole life had moved, like a train on its tracks, inexorably towards the cell in which she sat. But that would be to accept the rule of fate in our lives, and to take away our only freedom. Good or ill; we have the freedom of choice.

It is certain that Marie moved a step or two nearer to her fatal choice on the day that she had a client in the middle of the afternoon; and they were rare enough; these days, she got more custom when it was either too dark to see her or the clients were too drunk to care. A businessman, he said he was, from Yorkshire. She didn't know any more of him than that, apart from the fact that he made so much noise in his rutting that she was afraid that her five-year-old daughter, Ilse, might hear, and come running in from the next room.

But the good thing about men like him was that they'd soon done. He was no exception, heaving himself off her, wiping himself dry on the sheet, then pulling up his long underpants and trousers.

'I've a bloody train to catch, you know,' he grumbled.

'I've not kept you,' she said, fastening her bodice.

He squinted at his watch. 'Just look at the bloody time!' Then he was dancing about, trying to pull his boots on.

She went into the other room, to make sure that the child was all right. She was just as she had left her, sitting on the table, ankles crossed, swinging her legs.

She had been crying again, though, and Marie gave her a quick kiss and wiped her cheek with her hankie.

'There's a cab rank at the end of the street,' she called to her customer.

'Cab?' he shouted back. 'Do you think I'm made of money?'

He came in, fastening his waistcoat.

'My present, please,' she said.

He cursed under his breath and slapped five shillings on the mantel.

'That's not much of a present,' she said as she put it in her purse.

'All you're getting, and a damn sight more than you're worth.' He looked at Ilse as he struggled into his top coat. 'And another thing – do you have to have that kid sitting there? Puts a fellow right off, she does.'

'Don't worry about her. She can't speak English and she can't see you.'

'What's that mean?'

'She's blind, that's what that means.'

He opened the door and took a last look round, to make sure that he hadn't been robbed, or left anything. 'That's all right then. But I've a position to keep up. Chapel, and that. And I don't want anyone blabbing.'

'Don't worry.'

He was gone, clattering down the stairs without so much as an *au revoir*.

Marie put her arms round Ilse and held her close. 'No need to cry, *liebchen*,' she murmured. 'It will be just like a holiday.'

Ilse wasn't to be comforted and clung tightly to her mother.

The doorbell rang, downstairs. Marie listened as someone opened it. This couldn't be the woman, she thought; not so soon. She glanced at the cheap alarm clock on the shelf. No, it couldn't be her, she'd said four o'clock, and it was only half-past three.

But there was a tap on the door; it was her. Marie went to let her in, thanking God that she hadn't come even earlier.

The woman was large, filling the doorway, dressed from bonnet to shoes in grey. It looked like some sort of uniform. 'Mrs Hermann?' she asked.

'That's right.'

'I'm Mrs Forrest. From the Home.'

Marie nodded. 'Please. Come in.'

Mrs Forrest swept past her, taking a quick and appraising glance round the room. The child looked quiet enough sitting there, that was one good thing, she thought.

'You are early,' Marie said.

'Best to be, I always say. Saves a lot of tears and tantrums.' She looked at Ilse. 'Is she ready, then?'

'I've just got to get her coat.' She went into the bedroom.

Mrs Forrest took a closer look at the few cheap furnishings. She couldn't see someone from a place like this affording the money. 'You know our terms?' she called to Marie.

Marie came back into the room, carrying the child's coat and bonnet. 'Yes. They told me.'

'Payment in advance, first of every quarter.'

Marie was lifting Ilse's arm into the sleeve of the coat. 'I've already paid the first one.'

'That's right. But it's the others I'm worried about.'

'You needn't be.'

'Any failure . . .' Mrs Forrest began.

'I know all about that.'

'. . . and the child would be returned,' Mrs Forrest finished.

Marie was putting the bonnet on, touching the girl's curls under the brim of it. 'You will get your money.'

'So long as you're sure.' She saw the carpet-bag on the floor. 'Those her things?'

'They are all clean and packed.'

'Right, then,' Mrs Forrest said, her hands folded under her breasts. 'We'd better be on our way. Wouldn't like her to start off by missing her dinner.' She lifted Ilse from the table and swung her to the ground, then tried to take her hand; but she pulled away and clung to her mother's skirts.

'*Ich kenne Sie nicht!*' she cried.

This was a lot more than Mrs Forrest had bargained for. 'She speaks English – doesn't she?'

Marie was bending over the child, kissing her. 'Oh, yes,' she said, 'but with me . . .'

'Blind *and* a foreigner – we couldn't take that on.'

'*Ich bleibe hier,*' Ilse was sobbing.

'*Nein, nein, liebchen,*' Marie murmured. She looked at Mrs Forrest, still holding on to Ilse. 'This is the kind lady I told you about. She is going to look after you for a little while. You'll live in a big house in the country, with lots of other children to play with.'

'*Wann werde ich Sie wiedersehen?*'

'Soon,' Marie told her, 'very soon.'

She had tried to keep control, not cry before Ilse, making it seem like some glorious treat, but at the last she couldn't keep it up. The tears welled up in her eyes and she pulled away from her daughter. 'Take her, please, take her!'

Mrs Forrest bent over Ilse, smiling. 'Ilse, is it?'

'Ilse,' Marie whispered, wiping the tears away.

'I think we'll call you Lucy! Something nice, like that.' She tried taking her hand again, but the child still pulled away. This would never do. She grasped her again, this time holding her fast. 'Now, let's see if we can find you a nice sweetie downstairs. Then we'll be going for a lovely ride on an omnibus. Come along, Lucy.'

She was brooking no argument, but dragged her towards the door.

'Mama! *Mama!*' Ilse cried, trying her best to get back to her.

Marie couldn't trust herself to speak, but shook her head, her hand covering her mouth.

The door closed behind them, but she could still hear her daughter's cries as she was bundled down the stairs.

It was better so, she had to keep telling herself that. It was the only thing to do; she couldn't go on leaving her, night after night whilst she got about her work.

She went to the window and pulled the greying lace curtains back. The woman and her child were walking down the street, but Ilse was still crying and pulling away.

At least the Home looked to be clean and well run. God knows, it was the best she could afford. But that was the other thing; four times a year the money would have to be found. Could it be?

Men would pay. Oh, they would pay! Every farthing she could screw out of them. And, as she suffered their bad breath in her face, their animal fumblings, it would be Ilse she would think of. Ilse. And the quarterly bill.

It grew harder. Trade was going through a bad patch, factories were shutting and women, thrown onto the streets, had a straight choice: stand on their feet and starve, or lie on their backs and make a sort of living.

Of course, there were the sweatshops, in the East End, they were keeping going; there were plenty of folk rich enough to want the suits and frocks that these women, crowded into ill-lit, unventilated rooms, would turn out, hunched over the endless whir of their sewing machines. Fourteen hours of it every day brought in fifteen shillings a week. The match factory paid a little bit better, but phosphorous poisoning saw you off before you had time to enjoy it.

So Marie was facing stiff competition, and the iron rules of the market reigned as supreme in the oldest profession as in the newest. Her beat in the Haymarket and the Dilly was crowded with younger, more flashily dressed rivals, and she could give herself all the airs and graces she liked, but she had been priced out of the market. Who wanted the favours of a wrinkled Duchess when they could dally with a debutante on the game? She was driven off those bright pavements and into the back streets and low pubs. There she sat in state, sipping a port and lemon.

On this night, this memorable night, she looked round the noisy and crowded bar-parlour, seeing if she could spot a punter. She'd had no luck all night, her feet were aching and it would be chucking-out time soon. This place offered no prospects; all the men there were in company – sweethearts, wives and friends.

A fat man at the opposite side of the room was giving her an interested look, but he was with a younger couple; his son and daughter-in-law, like as not, she thought. With a ladylike lift of her head she looked away. There'd be no doing anything with him, anyway, whilst he was with that pair.

She took another sip of her drink. There was always the chance that some lone man might come in at the last for a quick half, and she might just strike lucky. But customers were going out, not coming in.

She took a lace handkerchief from her bag and dabbed her lips. The fat man's son and daughter-in-law were in the doorway, shouting good night to all and sundry. They'd had a drop in she thought by the look of them, her clinging to his arm like that. And if they'd had a drop too much, then –

She stole a sideways glance at the fat man. He was still there, looking fixedly at his glass of rum and hot. Getting on a bit, by the look of him. Big fellow, not just fat but tall wth it. Red-faced, sweating, well gone in booze. That wouldn't be so bad; what with the age of him, and the state of him, brewer's droop would take its toll and she'd only have to show him a bit and then make him think he'd done what he couldn't. First to last, half an hour should be all it would take. And that would be another five bob under the mattress.

As he looked up, bleary-eyed, she gave him a genteel smile. He didn't smile back but gawped at her, his mouth wet and slack. She sat upright, pulling down her tight-fitting jacket, the better to show off the bosom within. (A pair of stockings, carefully placed, gave the right shape.) He still wasn't smiling. He drained his rum and hot, staring at her, then jerked his head in the direction of the door.

Hooked, she thought. Now let's play you.

Frowning slightly, as if annoyed at being accosted in this ungentlemanly way, she slowly finished her drink. Then a quick glance at the fob-watch on her breast (which had long given up trying to follow the hurry of time) and, as if late for an appointment with her husband the Duke, she rose, straightened her hat and, with great dignity, parasol in hand, walked to the door.

As she expected, he was there before her, leaning close. 'How much, then?' he said. The fumes of rum from him would have knocked out a drayman.

'I'm sure I don't know what you mean,' she replied.

He was swaying back and forth, one hand clutching the door post. 'Bit o' fun. You know what I bloody well mean. How much?'

Maybe he was too drunk to know what he was at. 'A pound,' she murmured.

He gave her a broad leer, showing a set of dead white false teeth and black gutta-percha gums. 'Five bob. How about it, then?' He wasn't, after all, drunk enough.

She looked him up and down. 'You're in no state to walk home, and that's a fact. I'd better look after you.'

'That's what I mean,' he grinned.

She took hold of his arm. 'Come on, then,' she said. 'Sooner you're in bed, the better.'

Getting him up the stairs at her Grafton Street lodgings was going to be the difficult part, she knew that. He stood at the foot of them, a hand on the newel post and belched. He grinned at her. 'Better out than in, eh?'

'Upstairs, come on,' she urged, knowing what her neighbours were like.

'Ooh, in a hurry for it, are you?' he grinned, swaying. 'Don't you worry. Going to give you a good time. Time like you've never 'ad.'

'Quiet, can't you!' she hissed.

He went a step or two, her hand in the middle of his back, then turned to her, blinking. 'You foreign, or something?' He leant against the wall, laughing. 'Frenchy, eh? Oh, bloody hell!'

'If you like,' she said, keeping an eye on the doors that gave on to the stairwell.

He leant down to her. 'I bet you know some tricks, eh? I bet you do!'

Marie gave him another push. 'A trick or two. You'll see. First we must –'

He slipped down a step and began to sink on to his bottom. She grabbed his arm and held him up. The weight of him was terrible. Dear God, she thought, let it not come to this bulk lying on top of her.

He put an arm round her and pulled her closer, kissing her neck and then, finding her mouth, sticking his fat tongue under hers. She gagged on it, but he persisted. Some sailor had once told him that Frenchies liked that.

She pulled away from him. 'Not here! Upstairs! Come on,' she whispered.

He looked at her, frowning. 'I've money!' he cried. 'I can bloody well pay!'

'Good, that is good. Now . . .'

And, pushing, shoving and heaving, somehow Marie Hermann got Charles Stephens into her room.

*

Now was the night of the ball and Louise, Mrs Hutchins's daughter, was nearly ready for it. They lived on the top floor front in the Grafton Street house, and Mrs Hutchins (who was respectable, she made sure everyone knew that – well, you had to if a Marie Hermann lived in the flat straight under yours) closed the door quietly and looked at her daughter, who stood, pretty as a picture, in front of the big looking-glass. That German woman had just got some disgusting man into her room, and Mrs Hutchins had seen enough.

Louise looked at her mother. 'Was that . . .?'

Mrs Hutchins went to her and tugged at the bodice of her ballgown, pulling it up a little. 'Never you mind about that,' she said. 'Just look at you! Never be ready. I don't know what you do with your time, really I don't.'

'It was that German woman, wasn't it?' Louise whispered.

Mrs Hutchins made no reply, but dashed off to their bedroom. 'Oh, Lord! I nearly forgot,' she was saying, as she rooted about in her chest of drawers, 'and after me going out special for it, too!'

Louise took her chance and went to the door to the stairs. Opening it a crack she looked out and down the stairwell. There was nothing to be seen; all the excitement there seemed to be over, but she could hear groans and sighs from the room. She wet her lips. What they could mean, she didn't dare think. Her mother was coming out of the bedroom, so Louise quickly shut the door and turned to her.

She was holding out a piece of ribbon with a brooch in the middle of it, and smiling. If she had seen what her daughter had been up to, she was ignoring it.

'Come on, Louise, let's put this on, love,' she said.

Louise obediently went to her. Her mother turned her round and started to fasten the ribbon round her throat. 'Oh, that's a nice bit of ribbon!' she cried. 'Real silk, you know! And your poor grandma's best brooch – so you just take care of it. Finishes things off nicely, that does.'

'Too tight!' Louise complained. 'You're pulling it too tight! *Mother!*'

Mrs Hutchins patted the pretty knot she'd made in the ribbon. 'Meant to be! Not called a choker for nothing, my girl! You ought to see the way the Princess of Wales wears hers!'

She stepped back to admire her. 'Now, you just take a look at that!'

Louise peered at herself in the glass.

'Aren't you the pretty one! Like a princess!' Mother and daughter smiled at each other in the mirror. Louise saw her mother's smile fade. 'I don't like you going out this late, though. I don't really.' She gave a glance at the floor and, by extension, at Marie's room beneath their feet. 'Such people about, these days. *Horrible* people.'

'That German woman,' Louise whispered, round-eyed.

Mrs Hutchins shook her head. 'Young girls like you shouldn't be talking about folk such as her.'

'There's a man in there with her again, isn't there?'

Mrs Hutchins tightened her lips. 'You got your cab fare?' she asked.

Louise lifted up her fancy reticule with the nice bead fringing, and shook it. There was a reassuring rattle of coins.

Her mother nodded. 'And don't you go coming home late now. Do you hear? You'll have me worried to death.'

'It's all right. Johnny'll fetch me back.'

Mrs Hutchins took the cloak from the chair back and slipped it over Louise's shoulders, gave her a kiss and opened the door.

All was quiet, below. Louise stood by her mother as both looked down the stairwell. 'Do they give her *money*?' she asked. That Hermann was practically an old woman; old as her mother, anyway. It was a disgusting thought. Fancy! Money for *her*.

Mrs Hutchins pulled the cloak round her daughter's shoulders. 'Just you watch out for yourself with that young man, now. Nice he may be, for all I know, and I'm sure he is. But all the same, they're all alike, under the skin, and I want you —'

The words died in her throat. They both heard a crash from the room below, as if someone had fallen heavily.

Louise had got a few steps down from their landing. She stopped, a hand on the bannister, and looked up at her mother.

Mrs Hutchins shook her head. 'Back here,' she went on, 'I want you back here by . . .'

It was a man's voice now, saying something and groaning.

Louise was frightened, looking at her mother. 'Did you hear that?' she whispered. 'He said –'

'It's nothing. Nothing at all. It'll be the old woman in the basement back, scrapping with her husband. You know what they're like.'

'It wasn't the basement! It came from –'

'Then least said, soonest mended,' Mrs Hutchins said, sensibly. She went down the steps to her daughter and gave her another kiss, for luck. 'Now come on, love. You're late enough, already – you'll never get a cab, not this time of night.'

Louise went on her way, but she took a last glance up at her. 'You take care now, Mother. Keep the door locked.'

'It's you that wants to take care,' her mother replied.

Mrs Hutchins watched her down the stairs and into the hall. 'Night, Mrs Bricknell,' she said, to someone Mrs Hutchins couldn't see.

'Off out, dear?' Mrs Bricknell asked.

Glad she's still up, Mrs Hutchins thought. I'd like a word or two with her about what's going on. The landlord would have to do something about it, he would really. This house was no place to bring a girl like our Louise up, and she wouldn't have it a week longer.

The front door closed behind Louise, and Mrs Hutchins tiptoed down the stairs. She stopped for a moment by the Hermann woman's door and listened. She could hear the man's voice again. He was still moaning. Something about £5, best as she could make out. Then she heard the woman.

'I give you account of that £5 presently,' she said, clear as a bell. Then: 'I'll get you brandy – you'll soon be better. I'll make you better.'

Dirty old devil must have been taken ill, Mrs Hutchins thought. Not surprised, either, man of his years. Should be ashamed of himself.

Before she could hear any more there was the sound of footsteps coming towards the door. Fast as she could she scampered down the rest of the stairs and into the hallway. As she'd hoped, Mrs Bricknell was at her door, looking up and listening. Not much got past *her*.

Mrs Bricknell put a finger to her lips. Mrs Hutchins nodded. Then, as they heard footsteps coming down the stairs, they darted into the room; but they took care to leave the door open an inch or two, so that they could see what was going on.

Marie walked past without seeing them, pulling a shawl round her shoulders. She slammed the front door, not caring whom she woke.

'Gone to get some brandy, I heard her say,' Mrs Hutchins told her friend, who tutted at the shame of it. 'For the fellow she's got up there.'

Mrs Bricknell pursed her lips. 'Best thing we can do, Mrs Hutchins, is to have a nice cup of tea. The kettle's on the hob and near boiling.'

'Not to put you to any trouble –'

'No trouble at all. I was going to have one meself.'

'Oh, it would be nice. Honestly, I don't mind telling you, my nerves are that bad, what with one thing and another in this house.'

'You sit yourself there by the fire, dear, and we can have a little chat.'

Chat they did, stopping only to have a peep at Marie as she came back in, with something hidden under her shawl.

'That'll be the brandy,' Mrs Hutchins whispered.

'She'll have been to the jug and bottle,' Mrs Bricknell agreed.

They heard no more sounds from above, and settled themselves down to talk about what might best be done to get shot of their scandalous neighbour.

It must have been nigh on two o'clock by the time that Mrs Hutchins went back upstairs. Time flies when the fire's burning bright, the kettle's on the hob and there's something terrible to talk about.

As she passed Hermann's door she bent an ear to it, but all was silent. Must have fallen asleep, the pair of 'em, she thought.

She undressed quickly and got into bed. Louise had a key, so she would be all right. She said her prayers, closed her eyes and, in no time at all, she was asleep. But her dreams were broken by another crashing sound from below. She sat up in bed, quick as a flash, and fumbled for the matches on the table. The candle lit, she peered at the clock. It was half-past three. Then she heard the woman shrieking, bold as brass, at the top of her lungs.

'Speak! Speak!' Then, more loudly, '*Speak!*'

Good God! What could be happening? She lay down again, pulling the covers over her ears, only lifting her head from the pillow to blow the candle out.

An hour later, Louise let herself in. Mother had been right; he had tried to make advances in the cab on the way home, of all blessed places, with the world and his wife looking in. She'd soon put him in his place, though. Wedding ring first, then a little bit of hanky-panky, as and when she felt like it, was her motto, and she was sticking to it. Take more than a glass of wine, three waltzes and a polka to get her to change her mind.

The other girls had told her what men got up to. Dirty beasts. Don't know how they could, for shame. With these resolute thoughts in her mind, she made her way upstairs. The gas light had been turned out, so she had to go carefully. On the landing below theirs she remembered the woman and what had been going on when she went out. She stopped for a moment to listen, but all was quiet. The fellow must have gone home.

Then as she went up their stairs, she could have sworn she

heard something being dragged over the floor. Something heavy, like furniture shifting. No making out what that could be, but it was a funny time of night or, rather, morning, to be doing it.

Louise had got the day off work, and her mother wasn't too keen on that, nice jobs like hers not growing on trees these days. But, never mind, a young girl needed a bit of pleasure now and then, else, before you knew where you were, they were kicking over the traces and gone. So she let her lie in, just giving her a shake and telling her that there was a pot of tea brewed and under the cosy.

She couldn't take the day off work, oh dear no, she could not. Today was washing day, come what may, and she bundled their smalls into a basket, covered them with a clean cloth for decency's sake and went down to the front basement wash room. Someone had already lit a fire under the copper and she shovelled in a bit more coal. That was a blessing; she hated lighting that blooming thing. All that was to do now was to get the lading can off the shelf and fill the copper with water. Then she could have a nice gossip with Mrs Bricknell while the thing boiled.

She got the can, tutting as she always did at the cobwebs on the shelf. It wasn't her job to clean them up; once start doing that and you'd finish up scrubbing the front step for everyone to walk over. She went to the sink and turned the tap on. The lading can dropped from her hand and rattled over the flagstones and Mrs Hutchins only just managed to stop herself from screaming out loud.

The sink was stained with blood, and there was a pool of it in the plughole.

Backing away, wiping her hands on her apron, she could only think of one thing; she'd have to get to Mrs Bricknell. They really had something to talk about now.

She ran up the steps and into the hall, going straight to Mrs

Bricknell's door. Then whom should she see, coming down the stairs, coat and bonnet on, but that Mrs Hermann herself, brazen as you like, looking at her.

'Going out, Mrs Hermann?' she asked, not thinking of anything else to say.

Mrs Hermann didn't answer, but looked up to her room. There were two workmen, heaving and sweating between the pair of them, with a great big trunk.

'Take care of that box,' she told them. 'It contains treasures of mine.'

Then she started coming down the stairs, slowly, one at a time.

'Not leaving, are you, Mrs Hermann?'

Marie waited until she was level with her before answering. Even then she made her wait while she pulled her gloves on, ladylike as can be. 'A better house than this,' she said, her nose in the air. 'This place is not *suitable.*'

As if that wasn't enough for one morning, whom should she see next but her friend Mrs Bricknell coming out of the German woman's room. And she had a face on her like an undertaker's plate.

None of them, not the struggling men, nor Mrs Hermann nor, oddest of all, Mrs Bricknell, said another word to her as they passed. When the front door was opened, she saw that there was a handcart waiting in the street. It was the sort of thing that costers had at Covent Garden.

Oh, something was going to have to be done about this. Running so fast she was out of breath when she got there, she went upstairs to her rooms.

Louise had got up and was sitting at table, sipping her tea. Mrs Hutchins gave her a nod and went straight to the window. Taking care not to be seen, she pulled the lace back a bit and took a good look down into the street. They'd started off, now: one workman pushing the cart, the other alongside, his hand on the trunk to steady it, and the two women walking, not saying much, on the pavement.

'Whatever's the matter?' Louise said, seeing the expression on her mother's face.

'Just be quiet a minute, Louise, will you,' she replied, taking another look at this strange procession in the sunshine. Then a horse and cart got in the way and she'd lost them. She bit her lip in vexation, then came to a decision, going to the hook behind the door and getting her everyday coat and hat down. They weren't going to shake her off that easy.

'Is there something going on in the street?' Louise asked.

Mrs Hutchins skewered her hat with a pin. 'You get on with drinking your tea. Then you'd best go down and see to the washing; copper'll be boiling by now.'

'It's my day off!' Louise moaned.

'There's other things than days off, my girl,' her mother said darkly, as she went out.

It had been six years since the Jack the Ripper killings, but the police still had women like Mrs Hutchins who saw murder in every doorway and killers on every corner. They'd learned to take it with a hefty pinch of salt. All this talk about a neighbour, supposed to be on the game. That was a bit of spiteful gossip, like as not, covering up one poor fellow who stayed after half-past nine at night. As for all this nonsense about a trunk – the woman had the right to flit if she wanted to.

But this one was insistent, demanding to see the inspector if Sergeant Kane didn't stir himself. So the sergeant, with a weary nod to his constable, took his helmet from under the counter and said that they'd walk past the address she'd given and note anything suspicious. She wanted to come with them, but the sergeant wasn't having that.

'We'll be in touch, madam, if there's anything further to report.'

It being a nice day, and the station being quiet, he and the constable set off through the bustling streets.

Number 56 Upper Marylebone Street, she'd said. The policemen stood on the pavement, looking up at it.

'Respectable enough, given where it's at,' the sergeant said.

'Should I give a knock?' the constable asked, already going up the steps. Keen, that lad was.

'It's all women's talk,' the sergeant said, but his constable was already hammering on the door.

'Steady on, lad!' the sergeant called. 'You're not arresting the Ripper!'

The door opened a little, and a thin-faced woman looked out, frowning at them, as well she might, since she'd nearly had her door knocked in.

'Mrs Marie Hermann?' the constable asked.

The sergeant sighed and walked slowly up the steps. This was going a lot farther than he'd ever intended. What the hell could they do, anyway? They hadn't even got a search warrant.

'I am Mrs Hermann,' the woman was saying.

'We'd like to ask one or two –' the constable began, but his sergeant put a hand on his arm, stopping him.

He gave a flick of a salute and smiled agreeably, but there was no smile back. That was no wonder, either. 'Just routine inquiries, really.'

'Yes?'

'I understand that you recently vacated premises at 51 Grafton Street.'

'This morning.'

'And were your personal effects packed in a large black trunk?'

'So?'

He shook his head, still smiling. 'So nothing, really, Madam.'

To his surprise, she opened the door wider. 'It is here. You may see it if you wish.'

The sergeant hesitated. 'You're not obliged to do this, you know.'

She shrugged her shoulders. 'I have nothing to hide.'

He slipped his helmet off and went inside. For the first time there was a faint buzz of suspicion in his mind, like a wasp in a room. She hadn't asked them what all this was about, and she should have done, at the very least. He'd have been more impressed if she'd told him to go to hell and slammed the door in his face.

The hallway was narrow and dark now that the front door was shut. She opened a door on the left and, with an indication of her head, beckoned them in. Funny folk, foreigners.

The room was as dark and gloomy as the hall; curtains half pulled and the blinds down. In the middle of the thin carpet was the trunk.

'I have not yet had time to unpack,' she said, standing at the side of it. 'When I have, of course I will move this to the attic. They tell me there's room there.'

'Do you wish to open that trunk, Mrs Hermann?'

She shrugged her shoulders, took keys from her pocket, selected one and put the rest on the shelf.

The constable came up to him. 'If you'd excuse me, sergeant, I'll just . . .'

He nodded. 'Go on, lad, get a breath of air.' That's a fine start, he thought, feeling sick before the damn thing was even opened.

The constable went quickly out of the room, closing the door after him.

Mrs Hermann gave a tight-lipped smile to the sergeant, put a key in the lock, turned it and threw the lid open.

What a mess, Kane thought as he looked at the jumble of clothes, ornaments and papers.

'I packed in rather a hurry,' she said, seeing his expression.

'Why, Madam? What was the hurry?'

'The people in that house hated me.'

'I see.'

'I couldn't wait to get away from there. I heard that this room was available, and I had to jump while the irons were hot.'

He put the lid back. 'That makes sense.' He looked round

the room for a last time. 'I'm sorry to have troubled you, Mrs Hermann.'

'Was it that Mrs Hutchins who sent you here?'

He put his helmet back on. 'That's neither here or there, is it, really?' He went to the door. 'I'll bid you good day, then.'

Before he could open it, the constable came in. 'All right, now?' Kane asked.

The constable nodded. He had a look about him of the cat that's just lapped a saucer of cream. He pulled the sergeant to one side. 'She has another room, sergeant,' he whispered.

'What's that?'

The constable held out three keys on a ring. 'I saw that there were three. And I reckoned that one must be the front door, the other to here,' he held up a key, 'and this one to somewhere else.'

'Are those my keys?' Mrs Hermann cried.

Kane took them from him. 'You had no right to touch those, lad!'

He was turning to hand them back to her.

'And there's a trunk in there.'

Kane's hand snapped shut on the keys. 'You didn't tell us of this, Madam.'

'You didn't ask me.'

Kane took a risk. 'I'd be obliged if you'd show us this room, and the trunk.'

'I do not have to!'

Kane considered this, his head on one side. 'No, Madam, you do not. But if you refuse I shall leave my constable on duty outside the house and return to my station to obtain a search warrant. Shouldn't take long.'

'Look, then, if you want to,' she said.

He noticed that such colour as there had been in her cheeks had drained away. 'I'd be glad if you would accompany us.'

'I will not do that!'

He put a firm hand on her shoulder and pressed her towards the door. 'Very glad indeed.'

This room was in total darkness. The constable went to the window and pulled the curtains back. He was about to loose the blind, but the sergeant stopped him. 'Enough's enough, lad. We'd have every gawper in London looking in.' He looked at the well-corded trunk. 'Is this your property, Mrs Hermann?'

She made no reply, but stood, her hands folded.

'I must ask you if you would untie those cords.'

'No.'

He sighed. 'Very well, then.'

He took his clasp knife from his trouser pocket, released the blade, looked at it, touched the edge to make sure that it was sharp and cut the first cord. The lid of the trunk lifted a little and Kane's nostrils twitched. He knew that smell, knew it of old.

The rest of the cords were cut. He took a deep breath and swung the lid back.

There was a rug, tucked neatly in at the sides. With a glance at the constable, then at her, he took a corner of the rug and slowly pulled it back. There he saw, battered and bloody, the face of Charles Stephens.

CHAPTER EIGHTEEN

A solicitor may well be a dry old gentleman who sits in his room overlooking a leafy square in some quiet town, japanned metal deed boxes all around him, quietly ordering the uneventful affairs of his clients.

Or he may not be.

Mr Arthur Newton certainly was not. No comfortable family friend he, ever ready with a glass of tawny port and comforting advice about wills, trusts and probate.

If he drew up your will, like as not it would be before you went down for a long stretch of penal servitude on the Moor. His living (and it was a good one) came from haunting the police courts, picking up unrepresented prisoners, matching them to the right barristers and making sure that his name appeared prominently when the case was reported.

A sharp man in his well-cut suits, with a keen eye and a quick manner, he sat before the fire in his comfortable office, toasting his toes and going speedily through a pile of that day's newspapers.

His managing clerk, Harry Bishop, was beside him, back to the flames, his coat tails lifted up the better to enjoy the warmth.

Newton ringed an article in a paper with his pencil. 'Oh, what a thing,' he murmured, 'what a thing this is. German murderess indeed. Disgraceful, quite disgraceful, shouldn't be allowed at all.'

Bishop looked at the newspaper. 'Marie Hermann?' he asked.

Newton nodded and went on reading. 'Black for her, all the

same. Silly woman, oh, very silly.' He smiled up at his clerk. 'She's offered no defence.'

'No?'

'No. She's undefended. *Unrepresented.*'

Bishop thought about this for a moment. 'Given the facts, sir, I'm not altogether surprised.'

Newton shook his head. 'Can't have that.'

'Are we interested?' Bishop asked.

Newton picked up the heap of newspapers and threw them on the desk. 'Just look at this lot; everyone's interested!'

He leant back, hands behind his head and gave Bishop one of his shrewd looks. 'Well?'

Bishop sucked in a breath between pursed lips. 'Whatever – and whoever – she'll hang.'

Newton got to his feet. 'Of course she'll hang! Be a damned disgrace if she didn't!' He tapped the side of his nose and smiled. 'All the same –'

'In the meantime?'

'In the meantime.'

'Much attention would be paid –'

'Oh, yes, Bishop. A lot of attention would be paid –' He pulled his scarf from the hatstand and wrapped it round his neck, tucking the ends into his coat. '– to whoever set up the defence. And the thought will have occurred to more than one solicitor, mark my word.'

'Then there's no time to be lost, Mr Newton,' Bishop said, sitting at the desk and pulling a battered cardboard box towards him. 'Any thoughts as to a barrister, sir?'

Newton was quickly buttoning up his top coat. 'One step at a time.'

Bishop shook his head. The box was open and his fingers were moving amongst the upright cards within. 'With respect, sir – two steps at the same time.' He lifted a card out and looked at it, thoughtfully. 'Eldon Banks, QC?'

Newton was pulling on his gloves. 'He's too clever. Wouldn't touch it.'

Another card was in Bishop's hand. 'Percival Clarke?'

'Too dear. There'll be no money in this one.'

That card went back, but another was in its place, quick as a conjuror.

'Eustace Fulton?'

Newton wiped the nap of his silk hat with his sleeve. 'No. Sees himself in scarlet and ermine, and that right soon. He won't risk blotting his copybook.'

'Mr Edward Marshall Hall?'

Newton put his hat on and gave the crown of it a tap. 'Unpredictable; nervy type of chap, that one. And if the going gets heavy – as it will, newspapers and so on – then I don't think he'd stay the course. Never handled a big case, you see.'

'Will it be big?'

Newton nodded and smiled as he went to the door. 'When I've finished with it.'

Bishop sat back, tapping the card on the desk.

'Throw out a line or two, Bishop,' Newton called, from the passageway. 'And see if any fish nibbles.'

Bishop did his rounds of the Inns of Court, but the big fish weren't feeding. Cases that had the whole country thirsting for the client's execution weren't the meat and drink of the made men, especially when there wasn't a penny piece to be made.

His pile of cards had moved from his left pocket to his right, until there was only one left. Mr Newton would be back in the office by now, and the fur was going to fly, that was for sure, if he came back empty-handed.

He was up against the last hope, and there wasn't much prospect there, he thought, as he looked at the wavy-haired young lad on the opposite side of the pub table.

'New to the chambers, aren't you, Mr Bowker?' he said as he sipped his half pint of mild.

'Just joined.'

Bishop nodded. 'Thought I hadn't seen you around.'

'Nor I you.'

Bishop took another sip. 'If you don't mind my saying so –

you've done well. Young chap like you clerk to chambers already. Very well.'

Bowker grinned. 'I did it all by cheek.'

'Oh?'

'I heard the clerk was leaving, and I just sat there till he gave me the job.' He looked down, turning his glass round. 'It had always been my ambition to work for him, and I wasn't going to give up.'

'Ambition?' Bishop asked, lifting an eyebrow.

Bowker looked at him. His cheeks were pink, as if he was embarrassed. 'Oh, yes. He's the greatest man I've ever met.'

Bishop leant against the high wooden back to his seat that effectively isolated them from the rest of the bar. 'Well, then,' he murmured, 'I'm offering him a chance to prove that, aren't I?'

Bowker frowned. 'Not with this case, Mr Bishop.'

Bishop sucked in a breath. 'I don't believe my principal's ever briefed your gentleman, Bowker.'

'No more he has.'

Bishop leant forward, speaking in a quiet voice. 'Then let me tell you this. If he once gives a mark of his favour to any barrister – then that man's made his fortune. We're a very busy practice, with a lot to offer.'

Bowker gave him a thin smile. 'We're doing well enough, without any favours from Mr Newton.'

Bishop waved this away. 'Middling well – I'll grant you that.'

'Middling's where the money is.'

Bishop took his last card from his pocket, laid it between them and put on his spectacles. 'Let me see, now. This last two years he's done three firm frauds –'

'*Very* big sums of money involved.'

'Four burglaries and receiving stolen goods in Sussex –'

'All well reported.'

'In the Mugthorpe *Bugler*,' Bishop shrugged.

Bowker took a long drink of beer and put the glass down.

'And every brief handsomely marked. Nothing less than 100 guineas every time. Most more.'

Bishop shook his head, more in sorrow than in anger. 'This case isn't about *money*,' he said, like a monk taking a vow of poverty. 'It's about *fame*.'

This impudent young imp had the cheek to laugh in his face. 'Oh, is it now?' he said. 'And how much coal does that put in the scuttle?'

Bishop shrugged his shoulders and looked away.

'How much is the brief marked at?' Bowker said, leaning across the table.

'Won't go more than ten guineas.'

'And no refreshers?' (These additional fees for each day that the advocate was in court could often redeem an unpromising brief – if the proceedings could be drawn out. Which, with a little bit of effort, they usually could be.)

Bishop shook his head. 'No question of refreshers.'

Bowker got to his feet, fastening his coat. 'I'm taking up your valuable time, Mr Bishop. I've no doubt you've other clerks to see.' He drank up the last of his beer and slammed the glass down.

Bishop played his last card. 'On the other hand – we might well get up a defence fund.'

Bowker wasn't taken in. 'For *her*? With respect, pull the other one, Mr Bishop.'

Bishop smiled at him. 'Sit yourself down, Mr Bowker.'

Bowker shook his head and gave him a knowing smile back. 'I've got to be off, actually.'

'When you've heard what I've got to say.'

Bowker leant, arms folded, against the high back of his seat.

'Now you know and I know,' Bishop said, leaning forward, 'that this is the case of the century. Open any newspaper you like, and you'll see that's true. What I'm saying to you is – forget the ready money. For what I'm doing now, Mr Bowker, is offering you – on a plate – fame, fortune and the eyes of the world – all, all on your gentleman. Are you walking away from that?'

'She'll hang.'

'We know that!' Bishop cried. He looked round, anxious in case he had been overheard. 'Of course she will!' he said, in a low voice. 'But a good steady defence – bit of dignity to it, you know the sort of thing, I'm sure – and all reported, in every newspaper in the land, word for word –' He spread his hands.. 'Oh, *what* a chance!'

Bowker looked at him, frowning. He picked up his empty glass, tapping the rim of it with a fingernail. He straightened his shoulders. 'The other half, Mr Bishop?'

'I don't see why not, Mr Bowker.'

He was not in a good mood; that was quite clear from the moment he stalked through the outer office. Like Hamlet's father's bloody ghost, as one unemployed young barrister remarked. And, now that he was head of chambers and the lessee of these splendid rooms, his moods mattered. Everyone else in chambers did everything but tap him like a barometer at the beginning of the day.

Even Bowker, who usually had his ear, if not an invariable smile, only got a cursory nod of greeting, and he cleared his throat, warningly, to the others. His name was bellowed from the inner room, and he straightened his tie, smoothed his hair, pulled his waistcoat down and went in. Within seconds the bellow had given way to a roar, and the three barristers found urgent business elsewhere in chambers.

The door was thrown open and Bowker came out, faster than he'd gone in, a sheaf of papers flying round him. 'How dare you!' was the cry from within. '*How dare you*!' More papers flew out, all, luckily, missing the target. '*Get out of my bloody sight!*'

The man himself emerged, white-faced with rage. 'All over the Inns of Court! *All over!* Every piddling barrister who can stand on his hind legs and bray like a donkey has turned that brief down! And you have the sheer bloody temerity to fetch it to *me*!'

Bowker was on all fours, trying to collect the papers. 'This is not proper, sir!' he shouted.

'*Proper?* I'll give you *proper!*'

'Mr Bishop said that Mr Newton −'

'Bugger Bishop! Bugger Newton! *Bugger the lot of you!*'

He disappeared back into his room, slamming the door so hard that a picture on the wall crashed to the floor.

Bowker, still on his knees, was cursing his folly in ever putting his neck into this yoke when he saw, in front of him, a pair of highly polished boots. He sat up and saw, to his acute embarrassment, who their owner was. When did he come in, he wondered? And how much had he seen − and, even worse − heard? 'I apologize for this, sir,' he mumbled. What else was there to say?

Before any reply could be given, the door was thrown open again. He swivelled to face it, prepared for another onslaught. But, as always happened, the sun had come out from behind the clouds.

'Edgar! *Edgar* . . . I'm so sorry. So *damnably* sorry.'

The visitor spoke. 'Mr Marshall Hall − if you decline this brief, you'll be the sorriest man in England. My name is Arthur Newton.'

'Ah. I see . . .' Hall's thoughts were running on as fast as his clerk's.

'And I don't really think that I fancy being buggered this morning.'

Hall cleared his throat and shifted from foot to foot. 'Sorry about that. Form of words, don't you know.'

'Quite.'

Hall looked down at Bowker. 'Edgar, what on earth are you doing? Take Mr Newton's coat and see if you can find us a pot of coffee, there's a good chap.'

With one of his most charming smiles, he held his door open and gestured Newton in.

'Fine chambers,' Newton said, as he looked round the spacious room, with its splendid views.

Hall pulled out a chair for him. 'I'm happy here.'

'I should think you are,' Newton said, sitting. He looked at Hall shrewdly. An immediate attack was called for, while he was still embarrassed. 'That Marie Hermann killed Stephens is beyond dispute.'

Hall sat and fiddled with a paperknife on his desk. 'Mr Newton, this is a case I am unable to accept.'

Newton pressed on as though he hadn't been interrupted. 'And she will hang for it. We all know that.'

Hall nodded. 'Precisely. The case is open and shut.'

'But the man who defends her –'

'Will make a laughing-stock of himself.'

Newton leant back, as if giving the matter thought. 'Not necessarily,' he murmured.

Hall spread his hands. 'What advantage? What possible advantage? There's not a single extenuating circumstance that can be brought forward for the woman.'

'You've obviously given the case serious thought,' Newton said.

'So has everyone else in the country. It's on everyone's lips.'

Newton nodded. 'Which is why you must take it.'

Hall leant back. 'I'm under no such compulsion, Mr Newton. The bigger the audience, the greater the shame.'

Newton shrugged this aside. 'We've a pretty healthy defence fund; I've tapped every legal charity in the country. It's marked at ten guineas, but refreshers will build it up nicely.'

Hall smiled. 'You don't tempt me with that. My fee book's healthy enough.'

Newton made what seemed to be his last effort. 'Fame, Mr Marshall Hall, *fame*!'

Hall shook his head. 'Of the wrong sort.'

Newton got to his feet. 'There's nothing I can say?'

'Nothing. I'm sorry to have wasted your time.'

'Very well, then.' He smiled at Hall. 'I tried, at least.'

Hall smiled back at him. 'You did indeed.'

Newton nodded and opened the door. He'd studied his man

before coming to this meeting, and he had one parting shot. He aimed and prepared to fire, turning slowly to him.

'Of course,' he said, very quietly, 'you are absolutely right. The life of a woman such as this is of no consequence. None whatsoever. If she lives – or if she dies – what matter?'

'I never said that,' Hall said, stung by the inference.

'A whore?' Newton went on, still in a quiet voice. 'Hard-bitten, avaricious, desperate. Oh yes. She is all of those things, and worse.' He shook his head. 'No – a woman such as that is no more than the mud in the gutter.'

Hall's anger was rising again. 'I find that to be a deeply offensive remark, Newton.'

Newton looked at him, as if surprised. 'Really?'

'Deeply offensive.' He picked up a sheaf of papers from his desk. 'I'm sure that my clerk will show you out.'

Newton was pleased to see that his hands were shaking with rage.

'Offensive or not, you will not lift a finger to help her.'

'I cannot,' Hall said, coldly.

Newton closed the door quietly, and walked over to the desk, putting both hands on it and leaning forward. 'Then who can? *Or will?* Whatever she may have done, she is a woman who stands alone and forsaken.'

Hall's eyes widened as he looked at him.

Newton nodded, wearily. 'And, yes, of course, you are perfectly right. I *have* scoured the Inns of Court. End to end, up and down so many stairways. And there is not one man who will speak for her, however little there may be for him to say. Not one.' He straightened. 'It is, one might say, no more than she deserves.'

At that moment, whilst the two men faced each other in silence, the door opened and Bowker came in with a tray of coffee.

Hall gave him a glance. 'Put it down there, would you, Edgar, and be prepared to work late tonight. Mr Newton and I have much to discuss. And you must be part of it.'

*

314

Interview rooms were a luxury unknown in Newgate Gaol. It was to Marie's cell that the wardress led them, a sort of milking stool under her arm.

She unlocked the door and let them in, seating herself in the corner on her stool.

From the bed where she sat, her back against the wall, Marie gave them an uninterested glance, then looked away.

'Mrs Hermann,' Newton said brightly, 'I want you to meet your defending counsel, Mr Edward Marshall Hall.'

'I thought you were defending me,' she said, still not looking at them.

'I am a solicitor, not a barrister.'

'So?'

'I may not appear in a higher court. But Mr Marshall Hall is a –'

'Waste!' she snapped. 'All of this, all – a waste.'

'I do hope not, Mrs Hermann,' Hall murmured. He looked at the chair. 'May I sit?'

'Can I stop you?' He sat, taking papers from his case.

She turned to Newton, who was leaning against the table. 'You said you'd raise money for me.'

'Your defence – yes,' he said.

'How much did you get?' she asked.

'Let's not wory too much about the money,' Hall said.

'We've raised enough,' Newton told her.

Hall leant forward. 'Now I want you, if you please – and take all the time you need – to tell me exactly what happened from the first moment when you met the man Stephens until his death.'

Marie sat up, pulling herself forward from the bed so that her feet were on the flagged floor. She ignored Hall but leant towards Newton. 'I will want an account of all that money.'

'Mrs Hermann, please!' Hall said, firmly. 'In your own words –'

Marie waved him aside, like a troublesome bluebottle. 'A true account! I don't want any stealing from me!'

Hall's nose straightened in temper. 'From the moment that you first saw him –'

'What does it matter!' she cried. 'You will hang me! *All of you!*' Her voice had risen to a shriek. 'I am the German whore, the murderess! Doesn't everyone say so?' She jabbed a finger into Newton's chest. 'Now listen, you! I want that money used, and I want it used properly, for my children. There must be made a fund in some bank. Somewhere you can put my money when I am dead. And they will have it.'

Hall had bent forward, his eyes closed. 'Oh, dear God,' he whispered.

Ellen was tired. The performance hadn't gone well; three times she had fluffed her lines and Henry, back to the audience, eyes blazing, had had to prompt her. After the play he had gone from the theatre without a word of thanks or good night.

But the young man had been waiting on her doorstep, needing her, and she was incapable of turning anyone away. So she brought him in from the cold, let him sit on the hearthrug at her feet, listened and poured him coffee.

'It's hopeless, you see, Nell. Hopeless.'

'I've thought that about many a play – at the first reading – not seeing what I could possibly make of the part. But I've always found a way.'

'Not for me,' Hall said. 'Not this time.'

'Tell me, tell me all about it,' she murmured, covering her glance at the clock with a natural movement of her head.

From the hearth he picked up the book she'd been reading. 'Let this stand for Crown evidence against her. Yes?'

She nodded.

He had a single slip of paper in his other hand. 'And this is what I've got. Not a single witness can I call.' He balanced them: book and paper. 'The scales tip somewhat.'

'You must have known this, Edward, when you took the case on.'

He shook his head. 'I thought that she would bring something forward, something I could use. But she will give me *nothing*.' He let the book fall.

Ellen looked at him, frowning. 'Why should she? She expects nothing.'

He shook his head. 'That isn't the point –'

'Of course it is! She's caught in a trap! And then you come in, trying to find out – oh, I know you're desperate to help, but you must see – she's never met anyone like you, or your Mr Newton. And, when she gets into court, who'll be there? Judge, jury, more men in white wigs. And she knows nothing of any of you! Lost amongst strangers, talking in a foreign language! Of course she won't trust you, won't tell you. Neither would I, in her shoes. It's like going on and finding you're in the wrong play, and a cast you've never met are saying lines you've never heard. It's a nightmare! I'd freeze, dry up, and just want the whole thing over and done with.'

He listened intently, leaning forward, hands clasped over his knees. 'Then what do I do?' he asked.

'What I've always told you. You get inside her mind, inside her soul. You live her life. Then you'll know.'

'Can that be done with a woman such as her?'

She shook her head impatiently. 'Not as long as you look at her like that – from above. "Woman such as her" indeed! You should be ashamed of yourself! She's a woman! Not a type, not a class: a *woman*!' She paused. 'Start from there – and you might finish up somewhere near the truth.'

'And these witnesses the Crown will bring forward?'

'Yes, the same with them! Find out why they're doing what they are!'

He leant his back against a fireside chair. 'Newton could make a few inquiries.'

She got to her feet, looking down at him. 'All that is something I know nothing about.'

'But you know about so many other things, Nell.'

She smiled at him. 'I know that I'm tired, my dear.'

He scrambled to his feet. 'I'm sorry, so sorry.'

She put a finger to his lips. 'No, you mustn't be.' She turned away. 'There's a bed made up in the guest room. Sleep well, Edward.'

CHAPTER NINETEEN

The crowd outside the Old Bailey had been building up since dawn, and everyone there hoped for a place in the public gallery. But since that held only thirty odd, and nervous policemen on the door thought that there must have been over 6,000 in the crowd, there were going to be a lot of disappointed people in London that day.

Hall and Bowker got the first sight of the mob as they turned out of Fleet Street. 'Strewth,' Bowker murmured, 'We're never going to get through.'

Hall, white-faced, looked at his clerk. 'Brute force, Edgar. Brute force. Though rugger, I must confess, was never really my game.'

They advanced on the crowd unrecognized and, shoulders down, heaved and shoved their way through, taking plenty of pushes and curses themselves as they struggled. At last they got to the barristers' entrance but even there the policeman on duty was disinclined to let them pass. 'This is Mr Marshall Hall,' Bowker told him.

The policeman cast a cold eye on them; their dishevelled appearance – collars like limp rags, cravats somewhere under their ears – certainly didn't give them the look of lawyers.

'He's for the defence – in Crown and Hermann.'

'Oh yes?'

'Look at your list, man!' Hall snapped.

Still giving them a watchful glance, the constable ran a stubby finger down the piece of paper pinned to the board.

'Edward Marshall Hall?' he asked.

'Yes!'

The constable gave a sigh. 'All right, then,' and, after a moment's pause, 'sir.'

Hall gave him a fierce look, then strode quickly towards the robing room. 'I'll need fresh linen, Bowker,' he said.

'Two shirts and four collars here, sir,' Bowker assured him, patting the bag he carried.

Once in the robing room he took the shirt and collar Bowker held out and, without a word, strode past the lawyers lounging round the big table, and went straight into the washroom.

Bowker stationed himself at the door. As he expected, he heard the sounds of Hall being violently sick. One of the barristers looked as if he was about to make a joke of it, but a steely glance from Bowker killed the thought before it was spoken.

Hall came out, looking paler than ever. Bowker helped him into his wig and gown and the two of them went to the door and stood by it in silence, Bowker keeping a careful eye on the watch in his hand.

'All right, Marshall?' a barrister said, walking up to them. Neither man made any reply. Hall was staring ahead, his face taut.

The barrister tried again. 'Hell of a bloody case you've got on there.' Hall was still silent, unmoving.

'Ask my opinion, I think you were mad to take it on.'

Bowker turned to him. 'Not now, if you please, sir.'

The lawyer gave up. 'Oh well,' he said, sauntering away. 'Suit yourself. We all know how it'll end.'

The police on the doors exchanged looks. The older of them nodded and the other officer unlocked the doors. He had no need to open them; the weight of the pressing crowd did that. They flooded in, knocking the policeman aside, racing for the stairs, each determined to get a good view.

'Like running for the gallery at a bloody theatre,' one policeman shouted to the other, as they struggled to get the doors shut again.

*

Marie had been moved to a cell under the dock and through the open door she could see the stairs and, beyond them, the smoke-darkened ceiling of the court. A wardress leant against the wall at the foot of the stairs, waiting for the word of command. They both heard the thunder of the crowd as they fought their way towards the gallery, and then the cries and shouts of them as they came in.

'Don't worry, Mrs Hermann,' the wardress said. 'There's a big space between them and you, and plenty of police to keep 'em off.'

Marie made no reply, but sat on her chair, wondering why she couldn't have been hanged without having to endure this torture first.

Ellen Terry and Irving had, of course, been recognized by all the officers, and deferentially led to the places in the body of the court which Hall had reserved for them.

Irving, his pince-nez perched on his nose, looked round the shabby and cramped room, wrinkling his nose at the stench of it. 'Damn poor set, Nell,' he murmured.

'A foul place,' she said. 'Horrible.'

He leant closer to her. 'Is it possible to buy a programme?'

Mr Justice Wills was robed and ready and stood by the door of his room that gave on to the bench.

Jackson, his clerk, silently handed him his white gloves, the traditional small posy of flowers and then, almost apologetically, the black cloth that would be donned as the judge passed sentence of death.

Wills looked down at it and nodded. 'Yes,' he murmured, 'yes . . .'

Jackson held the big doorhandle and kept an eye on the clock as it ticked the seconds away.

*

It was the moment, and Bowker nodded to Hall and went through the robing-room doors, bearing in his arms all the things that would be needed; the papers in the brief, a shagreen-leather case that held a magnifying glass, tape measure, bottle of antacid medicine and other strange properties and, atop it all, the air-cushion which old Atkinson had so wisely recommended.

Hall counted to ten slowly, took a deep breath, straightened his shoulders and followed his clerk.

Newton was waiting for him in the long corridor and, seeing him approach, gown billowing, ran towards him.

'Don't forget, Marshall,' he urged, 'stay on the lines we agreed! Straightforward, no fuss, no fireworks.'

Hall marched on, not even giving him a glance.

With a frown of annoyance he trotted after him. As he'd said to Bishop in the first place, this chap was a damn sight too nervy and unpredictable for comfort. He'd be glad when the race was run and the woman was safely back in her cell.

Not even the looks of awed admiration that the bystanders gave Hall as he went on his magnificent way could mollify him. Anyone could look like a bloody matinée idol. Soundness and sticking to the brief were what counted in this business.

As ill-luck would have it Charles Mathews, who was leading the prosecution, came to the doors of Court Number One at the same time as Hall. They stopped, each giving the other a frigid bow; at this stage etiquette forbade anything else. The two men couldn't have been more sharply contrasted: Mathews was a small man, sharp featured and with quick, nervous movements, and his tattered black robes hung on him like the wings of a scabby crow. But he was a deadly prosecutor, and Hall knew it.

Newton stepped forward to break the deadlock. 'You're senior, Mathews,' he said. 'You go first.'

With a quick bow of the head, Mathews acknowledged the sense of this and went into court. Newton held the door open for Hall to follow, but he shook his head and stood, waiting.

Newton let the door close. 'What's the matter?' he asked, but got no reply. The damn fool was counting, for some reason. When he got to fifteen he nodded and, feeling like a flunkey, Newton opened the door for him.

Hall stepped into the arena and halted once he had come to a spot where all could see him. He looked round, his head held proudly high, taking the gaze of everyone in court. So spectacular was this entrance that the gallery fell silent and even the barristers at the table and on the benches looked at him in wonder.

'I taught him to do that,' Ellen whispered to Irving.

'Very effective,' he conceded.

'Glad you think so. I borrowed it from you.'

The minute finger of the clock clicked into place. It was eleven o'clock precisely.

'Now, my Lord,' Jackson whispered and held the great door open.

Mr Justice Wills swept into court, all the majesty of law in his bearing.

'All be upstanding!' the usher bellowed.

With a murmuring rustle the court rose to honour the Queen's justice.

All of these sounds came down to Marie in her cell, but they seemed separate, remote. What was this to do with a dark room in Grafton Street? Or a blind girl in a Home?

'Fetch up the prisoner!' was shouted by someone a long way off.

The wardress nodded to her. Marie got to her feet and began to walk up the steps, but the wardress put a hand on her arm, halting her. 'Not yet,' she said.

'Fetch up the prisoner!' was shouted again, this time nearer.

'Now,' the wardress nodded, making way for Marie as she went up the stairs. When she got to the top she looked round. The place was smaller than she had expected, apart from the railed space where she found herself. That was as big as a room, but empty, apart from a couple of high-backed wooden chairs.

Someone in the gallery started hissing, and they all joined in. She looked up at them expressionlessly. This pack of animals was no surprise; what else could you expect from the English?

A man was calling for silence and, after they had shouted a few obscenities at her, they obeyed.

She took her eyes from them and looked round the rest of the court. There was no one there she knew, apart from this lawyer who was using up all her money. He was leaning forward, staring at her. God, he looked ill, she thought. Anyone would think that it was he who would hang at the end of this farce.

The judge was saying something to her, though she couldn't hear him. The wardress tapped her on the shoulder and pointed to one of the chairs. With a disdainful shrug, Marie sat. The most important thing to do was to behave like a lady. So she had lived, and so she would die.

The ritual droned on its way, but she paid no attention to it. Twelve men shuffled into a high-backed box under the dirty windows, read out gabbled promises from a dog-eared card, then sat down. She noticed that after they'd all had a quick glance when they came in none of them would look in her direction.

A little man was speaking now in a high voice. She wondered who he was in all of this. She looked round at the wardress, lifting an eyebrow and pointing at him. The wardress put a finger to her lips but whispered to her that he was Mr Mathews, for the Crown. Marie wondered why, if her life was so important to the Crown, the old Queen herself couldn't come down and do the business.

'The facts in this sordid, distasteful and repellent case are straightforward enough,' Mathews began, his arms behind his back, gown tucked up in them. 'Prisoner at the Bar is an

Austrian by birth, though, following her marriage to a man of English nationality, she has been resident in this country for some years.

'Charles Anthony Stephens, of whose murder she is charged, was a retired hansom-cab proprietor. There is no evidence that, up to 15 March last, he and the prisoner had ever met.

'But that they met on that fateful night, there can be no question.

'On 16 March, in a room taken by the prisoner, in a tightly corded trunk, which was the property of the prisoner, the dead body of the said Charles Anthony Stephens was discovered. After this discovery by officers of the constabulary, a doctor was quickly summoned and, the body being examined by him, there were found, on the right side of the deceased's head, many and terrible injuries.

'On the left forearm, two further injuries were noted.

'Gentlemen of the jury, I shall be suggesting to you that the deceased's left forearm was raised in front of the right side of his head to ward off a most violent assault – in this manner –' He raised his left arm, cowering, and covered the right-hand side of his face with it.

Satisfied that the jury had all seen this demonstration, he lowered his arm and glanced at the papers before him. 'In addition to those injuries, there were three bruises – one on the right eye, one on the nose and one under the lower jaw.

'It was unquestionable, according to the doctor at the scene of discovery and other eminent medical men who later examined the corpse, that death was due to a massive haemorrhage resulting from the six wounds to the head.

'These wounds were consistent with those which would have been inflicted by some heavy and blunt instrument – such as, for example, a poker.'

He gave a meaningful glance at the tagged and labelled row of objects that lay on the table below the judge's high bench. The jury obediently looked at the ornate brass poker.

He waited until they had looked their fill and then, in a quiet voice, recalled them to their duty. 'The scene will, I am sure, be vivid enough in your minds. The deceased, an old man of seventy years of age, is seated in a room leased by the prisoner, number fifty-one, Grafton Street. Then, from behind his back, without a cry or warning, vicious, savage and terrible blows rain down upon him. He lifts his arms against them, but still they fall!' Once more, he cowered in his bench, an arm raised to cover his head.

'He shouts for mercy!' He paused, looking at the jurymen one by one. 'But mercy there is none!' he whispered. He lifted his hands, helplessly, then let them fall to his sides. 'Why, we must ask? Why were these savage, incessant and deadly blows rained on this poor, defenceless old man?' He shook his head. 'What motive for this malign execution?' He paused again, giving a sigh of deep regret. 'I fear that we need seek motive at no great distance. For there are *facts* to guide us in this case, gentlemen. *Facts*.'

He swept the tails of his gown behind him and rattled off his facts. 'On 15 March last, prisoner was in such desperate want of money that she was reduced to pawning the very coat off her back. *But*, by 17 March last, she was in possession of such sums of money that were far, far in excess of what may have been gained by that desperate transaction.' He nodded. 'Oh, yes. Far in excess.'

He picked up a sheet of paper and read from it. 'Item: money was paid by her in lieu of notice when she so suddenly abandoned her lease on her rooms in Grafton Street. Item: money was laid out by her for the purchase of furniture for her new abode.'

He threw the paper down and let his gaze sweep over the jury. 'Now where, you must ask yourselves, did these moneys come from?'

The expression on their faces told him that they knew the answer to that as well as he did. But he hammered the point home. '*Where?*' He spread his hands towards them. 'Abject poverty, profound need before the death of Charles Anthony Stephens, comparative riches after it.'

He shook his head in wonder at human wickedness. 'And a witness will be brought before you who will swear that Stephens was in the habit of carrying large sums of money about his person. Though I must point out to you that his pockets were empty when his poor battered body was discovered. So – unless you resolve that the prisoner's affluence came from her looting of that body, there can be no answer to your proper question.'

He pulled his gown round his thin shoulders. 'The prisoner made certain statements at the time of her arrest.' He flicked through the stack of papers before him and picked one out – though he held it as if it were contaminated by some deadly disease.

'She said that the deceased tried to strangle her and that she hit him with a poker to defend herself, and afterwards fetched some brandy in an attempt to revive him. She also claimed that he had struck her with that same poker and indicated a contusion at the side of her head as evidence of that assault.' He looked up from the paper and shrugged his shoulders. 'It is true that there was some such bump on her forehead, but medical evidence will be brought before you to prove that it was not caused by any such violent assault.

'There were, however, some marks on the prisoner's throat – and these might, *might* only, mark you, have been caused by the grasp of hands around it. The grasp, perhaps, made by a dying, driven old man, trying, at the last, to save himself from a hideous death.

'I shall call witnesses who will prove to you, beyond any doubt whatsoever, that the woman Marie Hermann, the prisoner at the bar, did, on the night of 15 March last, wilfully and wantonly, motivated by her insensate greed for moneys known by her to have been in Charles Anthony Stephen's possession, by a series of murderous blows –'

Hall, who had been leaning back on his bench, his eyes closed and his face impassive during Mathews' opening speech suddenly sat upright at this. But, before he could get to his feet, the prosecutor amended his speech.

'Very well, then,' he said, with an impatient shake of his head, '*lethal* blows –'

Hall, with a nod, sank back on the bench, once more closing his eyes.

Marie, looking down on him, was more sure than ever that her money was being wasted.

'Lethal blows,' Mathews repeated. 'And, with them, she brought about his death.

'And I shall further prove to you that, in a most foul and unnaturally cold-blooded way, she ransacked the battered and bloody corpse, bundled it into an old trunk and had it carted away to some new abode, some new resort, along with the rest of her traps. Her purpose here, coldly planned, coldly executed, was concealment.

'My learned friend who appears for the prisoner can offer no argument against that whatsoever.'

Hall's eyes were still shut, but he lifted an eloquent eyebrow.

Mathews ignored him and turned all the force of his personality on the jury. 'And, gentlemen, hold fast, in the days that follow, hold fast, I say, to this sure and certain rock of truth. That the very act of concealment howls her guilt to the skies, to the very steps of the throne of the everlasting judge.'

His arms raised, he cried, as if to God Almighty: 'There can be only one verdict in this case!'

He let his arms slowly fall and then sat.

He had done all that he had intended; if the court was against Marie Hermann before the proceedings began, it was now wildly inflamed. The public gallery erupted in a storm of booing and hissing, men and women on their feet, pointing at her, shaking their fists, spitting down into the dock. Wherever one looked in the place one would search in vain for an expression of pity or kindness for the prisoner.

The jurymen shifted in their seats, impatient to have the business done with and their verdict spoken.

Hall still sat, impassively, his only movement being a turn of his head to exchange a look with Newton.

The usher was roaring for silence and the judge banging his gavel furiously, but the uproar continued until the first force of passion had been spent.

'If there are further demonstrations of this nature,' the judge warned, 'I shall have this court cleared!'

Irving leant towards Ellen. 'That,' he murmured, 'would be to ruin the drama of the thing utterly.'

'Animals,' she frowned.

He nodded. 'Nell – need we stay for the Second Act?'

She had her eyes on Hall, noting his white and drawn face. She could enter into his soul, too, easier than any, and she trembled at the thought of his agony. 'We stay, Henry,' she whispered back.

Mathews had called Stephens' son, and was examining him. A tall young man, with sleeked-back hair and an easy, confident manner. A man well able, one would be right in thinking, to deal with whatever these lawyers threw at him.

'You are Charles Anthony Stephens?' Mathews asked.

'S'right,' Stephens nodded, affably.

Mathews cleared his throat. He had his most important witness here, and he would make sure that nothing clouded his testimony. 'Answer "yes" or "no", please, to my questions and those of my learned friend.'

'Yes, then.'

'Thank you. And you are the son of the late Charles Anthony Stephens?'

Stephens found difficulty in speaking, swallowing his manly tears. 'He was my dad. Yes.'

'And what was your father's profession?'

'Used to run hansom cabs, didn't he. Retired from it, though –' he sucked in a breath, '– best part of seven years gone.'

'And what was your father's age at the time of his death?'

'Seventy-one, he would ha' been.'

Mathews nodded. 'And did your father enjoy good health?'

'Fit as a lop.' He looked round the court, enjoying the

329

sympathy of all there. 'Yes,' he added, a sob in his voice, 'very good health.' He shot a look of murderous hatred at Marie. 'Till she —'

'Thank you, Mr Stephens,' Mathews hastily cut in. 'He was an active man, would you say?'

'Oh, yes. Very.'

'And could you tell the court of the tragic event that overtook your father in January last?'

Stephens gave him a puzzled frown. 'What?'

'Your father's sad loss.'

'Oh, yes! That's right! Me mum died.'

'Your mother died,' Mathews emphasized. 'And your father was now a very lonely man, was he not?'

Hall, who had been leaning forward, his head on his clenched hands, gave Mathews a warning shake of the head, but didn't rise to make any complaint.

'Terrible lonely. All on his own, really, poor old man, apart from his ever-loving family.'

'Quite so,' Mathews sympathized. 'And tell me — was your father in the habit of carrying large sums of money about his person?'

Hall pushed himself to his feet. 'My Lord, I must object. I have given my learned friend all the latitude in the world, but he is leading the witness.'

The judge looked at him and shook his head. 'Mr Marshall Hall, I cannot see that. The question is perfectly proper in examination.'

'No, my Lord! It is not!' Hall flung at him.

'I have given my opinion here, sir. Sit down!'

With a glance at the jury, and a shrug of his shoulders, Hall sat.

Not much to worry about from that one, young Stephens thought. Proper pricked balloon, he is. He looked forward to any questions that might come from him. Have some rare sport there.

Mathews gave a look of pity at Hall. To handle the defence in this case was onerous enough, without the judge being against the poor young fellow. 'In consideration of my learned friend, I will, of course, re-phrase my question.' He turned once more to Stephens, who was leaning now on the bar of the witness stand. 'What, Mr Stephens, would your reaction have been if your father had left the house without any money in his pockets?'

'Oh, I'd have been very surprised, my Lord. Warned him, time and again, I did; we all did. Never left the house without £50 in his purse. Sometimes more. And all in gold and silver, too.'

Mathews nodded. 'A witness will swear that, as your father entered the house at number fifty-one, Grafton Street, on the night of his death, he was under the influence of strong drink. Tell me – was he often in that state?'

Stephens blew his nose. 'No, sir,' he gulped. 'Only since me mum was took. Trying to forget, he was, poor old man.'

'And, when in drink, was his behaviour in any way different from his customary behaviour?'

Stephens gave him a puzzled look.

'Did his mood change?'

'Oh, yes! I should say so!'

'In what way?' Mathews asked.

'Jolly, like, he'd be. Hail fellow well met. Drinks all round, that sort of thing. Know what I mean?'

'Not precisely, but I follow your gist. He was not *quarrelsome*?'

Stephens gave an incredulous laugh. 'Him? No! Never a cross word. Reg'lar Santa Claus, he was.'

The judge leant forward. 'Santa *who*, Mr Mathews?'

'Claus, my Lord,' Mathews explained. But, seeing his Lordship's evident puzzlement, he elaborated. 'A mythical character of extreme joviality believed by children to bring them gifts on the eve of Christmas. It is, I believe, an importation from the Americas.'

'I see,' the judge growled disapprovingly. 'Pray continue.'

'Thank you, my Lord.' And then, to Stephens, 'And when did you see your father for the last time – alive?'

'That very afternoon.'

'And he was in his usual state of health?'

Stephens couldn't restrain his sobs any longer. Through them he brokenly cried, 'Last time I ever see him – he was – he was – healthy as you or me!'

Mathews shook his head in shared grief. 'Thank you, Mr Mathews.' He sat down, murmuring, 'No further questions of this witness, my Lord.'

The judge looked across at Hall, who seemed to be in some confusion, desperately flicking through his papers. 'Mr Marshall Hall?'

Hall half rose, but continued to look first at this paper, then at that. 'Thank you, my Lord,' he murmured. He gave an apologetic smile to Stephens. 'I am sorry, Mr Stephens, but I seem to have got my notes into a most awful muddle.'

Some of the jurymen looked away, embarrassed at his discomfiture. Irving kept his eyes on him, leaning back, a quiet smile playing about his lips, ignoring the dig in the ribs from Ellen. Stephens gave him a grin. This was going to be even easier than he'd thought.

'So, I wonder if you could assist me,' Hall mumbled, 'by telling the court of your profession?'

Stephens gave him a look of withering contempt. 'Horse trainer, aren't I?'

Hall spread his hands in wonderment. 'I don't know. Are you? Is that what you do?'

Stephens nodded. 'Yes, that's what I do.'

'Thank you,' Hall murmured, as if his mind weren't on the witness, or his replies, but lost somewhere in the chaos of papers on his bench. 'Now,' he said, not looking at him, 'about – about – your father. How tall was he?'

''Bout five foot ten.'

'Quite tall, quite tall,' Hall murmured, as if musing to himself. 'And – as near as you can tell us, of course – what was his weight?'

'Give or take –' he shrugged, '– about sixteen stone.'

Hall looked at him, and gave him a gentle, rather nervous smile. 'And in good health? He was in good health?'

Stephens cast his eyes to heaven in exasperation. 'Already said so, haven't I?'

Hall, evidently having found the paper he was seeking, gave a smile of satisfaction. 'Oh, indeed you have. I had forgotten. Please forgive me. And I recall that you told us that he was of an active disposition. So –' As if glad to be shot of them, he threw the papers down. 'You have given us a picture of your father. A clear picture: of an active man, a large man, a strong man. Would you say that was a true likeness?'

'True enough. Yes.'

'I am – we all are – so grateful to you. And, tell me, Mr Stephens, merely so that the picture may be complete, is it not true that your father, a man, as we know, of abnormal strength for his years – had a most violent temper?'

'No.'

Hall gave him a long look, the smile slowly fading from his lips. 'Ah,' he murmured. 'I can, if you wish me to, summon witnesses – who will swear –'

'Summon who you like!' Stephens shouted. 'It's a lie!'

'Who will swear that your father, when in drink, when in rage, would abuse, beat, throw about anyone who dared cross him – *women in particular*! He had done this, time and again! He has been seen to do this!' He was leaning towards Stephens now, his whole body tense, his eyes cold as ice.

'Must I call these witnesses, Mr Stephens? Who will swear that you are lying upon oath! Must I call them?'

He swung towards the doors of the court, his arm raised, as if they would come at his call. 'They wait!' he cried.

Newton held his breath. Marshall was out on the high wire now, and if this young man had an atom of sense, he'd let him tumble.

Stephens licked his lips. 'He wasn't always like that,' he muttered.

'Thank God,' Newton breathed.

'Only when in drink?' Hall thundered.

Stephens looked round for help, but there was none to be had. 'Sometimes,' he said.

'Sometimes, then, when drunk, he would beat and abuse any woman who dared disagree with him?'

Stephens shrugged his shoulders and looked away.

'Would he or would he not, when in drink —'

There was no escape from those piercing eyes, that hammering voice. 'Yes!' Stephens cried. And then, desperate for a way out, 'It was loss of my poor mum.'

'Never mind the cause. He would do it. *Yes?*'

'Yes.'

Hall paused, but his eyes never left Stephens. 'Thank you. Now, this money that you allege your father carried about with him. Where did these large sums of money come from?'

'His business.'

'The cab business?'

'That's right. Yes.'

Hall frowned. 'But he had retired from that business. You have told us so.'

'Money in the bank, then!' Stephens shouted. 'He had money there, hadn't he? And he drew it out, I tell you! Fifty pounds, in sovs! I was with him! I saw!'

The words had scarely left Stephens' mouth before Hall pounced. 'When? When were you with him when he drew £50 in sovereigns from a bank?'

'Many a time!'

'A particular time, if you please! *When?*'

'Two days before that bitch killed him!' Stephens shouted.

The judge leant forward. 'Mr Stephens, I must warn you that —'

Hall was not to be stopped; he had his man on the run and he must not be given breathing space. Cutting across the judge, his eyes blazing, he insisted: 'Two days? *Two days?*'

'Mr Marshall Hall, I was addressing witness,' the judge said, hammering the bench with his knuckles.

The most he got from Hall was a lifted hand, restraining him. '*Two days?*' he repeated.

'*Yes!*'

Hall nodded quickly, as he spoke. 'And, in those two days, he could well have spent the lot. Yes?'

'Not him!'

Hall leant back, a thin smile on his lips. 'Come, sir! This hail fellow well met character you have drawn for us, accustomed to buying drinks for a full public house? This *Santa Claus?*'

'Not fifty quid worth.'

'But you can't know that! You cannot possibly know that! The money may well have been disbursed during those two days! *Might it not?*'

Stephens had his handkerchief out again, but now he was wiping his sweating palms with it. 'Might have been. But it's not like him.'

Hall considered this, his head on one side. 'I see,' he drawled. 'Not like him to be – generous? Open-handed?'

'No.'

Hall folded his arms and looked down, silent for at least a minute. Then he slowly lifted his head again. 'What a very different picture of your father is beginning to emerge, Mr Stephens.' He let his gaze travel along the rows of jurymen, taking each eye. 'However, let us pass from the spending of the money to the getting of it. Drawn from the bank, you say? These £50?'

'Yes.'

'I must repeat my question to you. Where did these funds of your father's, in that bank, come from?'

'How do I know?'

Hall shook his head, impatiently. 'Oh, but you do know! You know very well indeed! They came, did they not, from a house of prostitution, a disorderly house – your very parental home! And this infamous den was managed by your mother until the day of her death! *Is that not true?*'

Stephens, white faced and sweating, was leaning against the back of the witness stand. His lips opened and then closed.

Newton scribbled something on a scrap of paper and handed it to Bowker, at his side, who glanced at it and leant forward to place it before Hall who, without looking at it, picked it up and stood, his eyes still on Stephens, tapping the paper against the fingertips of his other hand.

Stephens was still silent.

When he spoke again, Hall's voice was quiet, slow and measured. 'Your father grew rich on the profits of a house of ill fame managed by his wife, your mother. *Is that not the truth?*'

'Might have been – might not of been,' Stephens whispered.

'Don't you yourself live with one of these poor women, at Albany Street?'

'No!' Stephens shouted.

'Don't you live with –' he glanced down at the paper in his hand, '– Amy Chase?'

'*No!*'

'Will you swear to that? In the face of the testimony I have here from one who should, above all others, know?' He was lifting another piece of paper, holding it high.

Oh, the stupid little cow, Stephens thought. He'd kill her for this when he got home. He gave a grin round the court, thinking to make them like him again. But the smile was a mere pulling back of muscles, and they looked away from it. 'What's that to do with anything?' he said, his voice dry.

'You must answer the question,' the judge told him.

'Then – no. I don't.'

Hall looked down at the paper, pointing a finger at a line of writing and cleared his throat, ready to speak.

'I wasn't living with her!'

Hall raised an eyebrow and leant forward.

'She was living with me!'

Someone in the gallery laughed and Hall wheeled on him.

'Do not laugh!' he cried. 'I most earnestly beg you not to laugh! A woman's life is at stake here!'

He quickly looked back at Stephens. 'How many times have you been convicted of being drunk and disorderly?'

Stephens fidgeted, his shoulders twitching. 'Two or three . . .'

'*Seven* times, I put it to you, in the last two years!'

'I couldn't say. I've a bad memory.'

Hall nodded, throwing the papers down with a gesture of contempt and disgust. 'Then I am glad to have refreshed it for you – to the point where you now recall that your father was a large man, a hugely strong man, a drunkard, living off the immoral earnings of hapless women who had fallen into his clutches. A man who would, if a drunken fit so took him, inflict grievous bodily harm on any poor woman who was unfortunate enough to cross his path. And that you yourself are no stranger to these courts of justice.'

He sat. 'Thank you, Mr Stephens.'

An officer of the court, seeing the witness's eyes turn up and his shoulders sag, took his arm before he could faint.

The judge lifted his watch from the bench and gave the time due consideration. He looked across at Mathews. 'Have you any further questions of this witness, Mr Mathews?'

Mathews half stood. 'I have not, my Lord. And, even if I had, the bullying tactics of my learned friend have rendered the witness incapable of answering them.'

'Very well,' the judge nodded. 'The day is well advanced. I shall therefore adjourn until half-past nine in the forenoon of tomorrow.'

Even as the usher was calling on the court to be upstanding, Hall was moving quickly from his bench and out of the foetid room.

Truth to tell, he was as near collapse as the witness.

The day began with a routine procession of witnesses who swore that they had seen Marie Hermann and Stephens leave the public house together. Beyond establishing that she made no attempt to solicit him, but that he approached her, Hall let them pass without much ado.

Then Mrs Hutchins came into the witness box. Mathews handled her well and her evidence was clear. She had heard what was evidently an argument about money between Mrs Hermann and a man, she had heard bangs and crashes, as if some desperate struggle was taking place in the room below and, most telling of all, she had heard the foreign woman shouting 'Speak! Speak! *Speak!*'

The final word, she said, had been uttered in a shriek.

Well content, Mathews sat down. Let this young fellow, he thought, make what he could out of *that* one. There was no possibility of discrediting the respectability of Mrs Hutchins. It was as a religion to her.

Hall rose. He leant forward on to his bench, his fingers spread. 'Mrs Hutchins,' he said, 'is it difficult to bring up a daughter in such a house as the one in which you live – at fifty-one, Grafton Street?'

'I don't understand what you mean,' she replied.

'Then let me put it more clearly. What problems have you faced, in that house, so far as the moral welfare of your daughter has been concerned?'

'There never used to be any,' she answered, grimly.

'That answer leads me to suppose that you have encountered some problems more recently, though. Is that so?'

'Yes.'

'And what is the nature of these problems?'

'Until she came –'

'She?'

'Mrs Hermann – the house was as nice and quiet and respectable as a body could wish. But after her –'

'After her – then what?'

'Men. Coming in all hours. Drunk, like as not.'

'Did you feel that the presence of Mrs Hermann in that house was a threat to your daughter?'

'She should have been got rid of long since! I said so, time and again, I did!'

Hall paused. 'Got rid of?' he repeated, quietly.

'Shifted!' The hatred in her voice was there for all to hear.

Hall nodded. 'Did you dislike Mrs Hermann?'

'Women like that!' she said, spitting the words out.

'You have not answered my question. Did you have a strong dislike of Mrs Hermann?'

Mathews was on his feet. 'My Lord – my learned friend is leading witness quite blatantly.'

The judge nodded, but Hall got in before him. 'Then I will re-phrase my question. What were your feelings towards the woman here before us?'

'What could they be?'

'Don't fence with me, Madam!' he shouted. 'What were your feelings towards –'

'I hated her! Women like that should be swept off the streets!'

'Thank you, Mrs Hutchins,' he said, quietly. 'You hate Mrs Hermann, you feel that she should be got rid of and, with all the other unfortunates like her, swept from the streets – like so much rubbish.'

'It's the only way a right-minded woman can think! Who wants to be lumped with people like her?'

'Not you, evidently,' Hall murmured. He paused for a moment, deep in thought. Then, briskly, 'However, let us leave your feelings of hatred and revulsion for my client.' He turned to the jury. 'I am sure, though, that members of the jury will bear your strong sentiments in mind when they consider the objectivity of your evidence. Let us consider the events of that terrible night. I do not intend to drag you through the whole of your evidence, so clearly given to my learned friend appearing in this case for the Crown. Sounds were heard by you, which you interpreted as being those of a struggle between my client and a man in her room.'

'They were!'

He gave her a smile. 'Mrs Hutchins, you must not interrupt me. I was about to say, that I do not dispute your reading of these things. A struggle was indeed taking place. What I would like you to recall once more for us, are the words which you claim that my client uttered. In particular, the phrase: "Speak! Speak! Speak!" Would you repeat that, please, as you heard it?'

She took a breath. 'It was someone very angry. Shouting. Like this: "Speak! Speak!" And then, with all the fury that she was capable of, she shrieked, "*Speak*".'

Hall thought about this, nodding. 'You cannot be mistaken?'

'No, I can't. I'll remember it to my dying day.'

'Will you, indeed? As you said it?'

'Of course.'

'You will not remember something like this –' His shoulders went down, he bowed his head. When he spoke his voice was quiet, pleading. 'Speak, speak –' and then, in a voice of desperation '– oh – *speak!*'

She looked at him, her eyes wide.

'Well, Mrs Hutchins?'

'They were as I said.'

He gave her a long look, a slight frown on his brow. 'Why should such words be spoken in fury and shrieked in rage? They can only be pleas, can they not?'

'What I remembered – I remembered,' she said. But the certainty had gone from her voice.

'Mrs Hutchins, we all know – oh, how deeply we know – that memory is fallible. We are apt to load present feelings on to past recollection. I lay no blame on you for that. Just answer me this: is it *possible* that you remembered the words spoken, but not the tone of voice in which they were said? Is it, Mrs Hutchins?'

'It's – possible.'

Hall sat. 'Thank you, Mrs Hutchins. I have no further questions of this witness, my Lord.'

*

With Louise, he was even more gentle – like a loving father to his daughter, as one of those who saw him said.

'This has all been a most terrible experience for one so young as you,' he began. 'I would to God that you had not had to endure it – or this present ordeal. But go through it we must. Together. Are you ready, Miss Hutchins?'

She nodded, her lower lip trembling.

'I'll see that you come to no harm, my dear. Now – on the night of 15 March last, you have told my learned friend –' he smiled at her, '– forgive the pompous language – it is the way in which we lawyers must always speak of each other.'

'Do get on with it, Mr Hall,' the judge growled.

'I shall proceed as rapidly as courtesy permits, my Lord,' he said, turning again to Louise. 'You have told the other gentleman, on the night of 15 March, you heard the sound of a man's voice coming from some other room in your house. That is what you said. Yes?'

'Yes.'

'Where were you, Louise, when you heard this?'

'On the landing – looking down.'

'To the floor below?'

'Yes.'

He nodded. 'And the sounds were coming from the other side of a closed door, a heavy door – a solid door?'

'Yes.'

'And would you tell us, once more, what you thought this man was saying, at that considerable distance?'

'Murder,' Louise whispered.

'Was that all that he said?'

She shook her head. 'No. Three times. "Murder – murder – murder." Like that.'

'But now, Louise – and I really do not wish to add to your distress, you must believe that – would you tell us what you did after hearing this cry?'

'I –' She faltered, her eyes downcast.

'Yes –?'

'I went out.'

'Out of the house?'

'Yes.'

'And where did you go?'

She looked at him, her eyes clouding with tears. 'To a ball.'

'To a ball,' he repeated. 'And – did you enjoy yourself there?'

'Yes. Very much.'

He smiled at her. 'I'm glad that you did. But – did it not occur to you that such a cry as you thought that you may have heard should have been reported to the police – without a moment's delay? A uniformed constable was at the corner of your street –' He picked up a piece of paper. 'I have the times of his beat here. So why, Louise, did you not seek him out and tell him what you thought you had heard?'

'Thinking about it,' she said, 'I wasn't *that* sure that the word was "murder". I thought it was, but once I was in the street –'

'Like the good and honest girl that we all see you to be – did it occur to you that perhaps you were mistaken?'

'It was so very faint.' She looked up at him. 'Yes, I did think that I might have been mistaken.'

'The man might well have been saying something completely different?'

'It was very indistinct.'

'Had it not been, you, of course would not have dreamt of going to a ball, leaving your mother alone in a house where murder was being committed. You wouldn't have done that, Louise – would you?'

'No. I wouldn't.'

'Of course not.' He paused. 'But tell me, how is it that in the other court where this case was first heard, and just now when you were replying to that gentleman's questions, you were so very sure of what you had heard?'

'They kept on saying the words, over and over at me, till I thought I was certain.'

'The word "murder"?'

'Yes.'

'And tell me who "they" are, Louise.'

'My mother, then the policemen – then, today – your clever friend.'

'"Learned" was the word you were looking for, Louise. But, no matter. You have given your evidence well, and truthfully. And I hope my learned friend will indeed be clever enough, and merciful enough, to release you from this torture. You should never have been submitted to it.' He sat, with a final grateful smile to the girl, who was now weeping into a scrap of a handkerchief. 'I have no further questions, my Lord.'

'Mr Mathews?'

Mathews, with a baleful look at Hall, had the choice between appearing in the eyes of the court as an inhuman monster, or letting the witness go. Through gritted teeth he told his Lordship that he had no further questions.

The judge was adjourning the case until the next day, but Hall seemed to be deaf and blind to what was happening around him. He sat, leaning forward, his chin resting upon his hand, his eyes unblinking.

Newton tapped him on the shoulder, not once but several times, until at last he rose. With a nod to Newton he left the court.

He was watched in a deep silence.

Newton wanted to get in touch with him that night, but he was nowhere to be found; not in chambers, nor in his club. He seemed to have disappeared from the face of the earth. And if Bowker knew his whereabouts, he wasn't saying.

He had peace and he had quiet in his room in the small private hotel in Kensington. There he sat on the edge of his bed, the events of the day going round and round in his mind. He knew, though the mood of the court was changing, that the little that he had done could soon be undone by Mathews.

Though the whole Stephens clan had been shown to be

lying, whoremongering drunkards, and the Hutchinses to be hopelessly unreliable witnesses, the salient facts still remained: Marie Hermann had taken this man to her room, and had there bludgeoned him to death and then done all that she could to conceal the deed.

Mathews would hold on to those facts and hammer them until he forced a verdict. And Marie Hermann would hang.

He sat on, his watch chain in his hands, letting the links slip through his fingers until, with a snap, he pulled them back again. Eyes unseeing, over and over, the same action.

A way forward must be found. But where?

Mrs Bricknell was rock-like in the witness box, as Mathews had hoped she would be, for it suited him perfectly. The woman resolutely denied that she had helped Marie Hermann to lift the body into the trunk. She knew nothing of any such thing, she swore. The first she knew of Mrs Hermann flitting was when she came, early that morning, and asked her help in moving her bits and pieces to her new diggings.

Mathews left the thought with the jury, and it was a damning one. If Mrs Bricknell hadn't helped her, then how could the frail woman of no more than nine stone in weight lift a man of sixteen stone unaided? Clearly she could not. Someone must have helped her. There was an accomplice somewhere and, that being so, the enticement of Stephens to the house, and his murder there were, beyond any doubt, a premeditated plot, hatched by Marie Hermann and this other person.

'At what time in the morning,' Hall began, 'did Mrs Hermann call upon you?'

'My clock's not working so good, sir, so I don't really know.'

'Was it daylight?'

'No.'

'Were you in bed when she called?'

'Yes.'

'Would you kindly address your remarks to me, Mrs Brick-nell,' the judge intervened, 'as I'm having great difficulty in hearing you.' Which was a lie: the woman had a voice that would have done useful duty as a foghorn.

'I'm sorry, your Lordship,' she bellowed.

'Do carry on, Mr Marshall Hall,' the judge nodded.

'Thank you, my Lord.' He turned again to her. 'It could well have been the middle of the night when she came to you, then?'

'I've no way of telling, have I?'

'And what did the prisoner at the bar say to you, on this nocturnal visit?'

'That she was flitting come morning and wondered if I'd give her a hand.'

'And how did you reply to this request?'

'Said I'd be glad to.'

'That was most generous of you, Mrs Bricknell. Not many would have been so accommodating at such an hour. And, tell me, did she stay long after she had made this request?'

'A fair time, yes.'

'How did you pass that time?'

'Chatting, you know. About this and that.'

'And enjoying your drink?'

'Such a raw morning as that, it was welcome.'

'Where did this drink come from?' he said, quickly.

She drew in a breath. She'd walked right into that one. 'She – Mrs Hermann – brought it down. Drop o' brandy.'

'What else did she bring?'

'Nothing.'

He drew himself up to his full height. 'Come now, Mrs Bricknell! I will ask the question again. And I should warn you that I know what your answer must be – and of the punishment that awaits perjury. *What else did she bring?*'

She looked uneasily round the court. 'One or two things.'

'What sort of things?'

'A brooch. And a hat.'

'These were gifts that she was making to you?'

'She said so.'

He put his hands on his hips and looked down. 'Does it not seem to you to be an extraordinary tale that you are telling, Mrs Bricknell? That my client should descend upon you, bearing gifts and refreshments, in the middle of the night to solicit your assistance at a task that could well have been requested of you at any moment before she left? *Does not that seem very odd?*'

'She's an odd woman.'

'Is she now? Is that what you think of her?'

'So does everyone.'

'So odd that, out of her straitened means, she makes over things to you that she could ill-afford, for assistance of a trivial nature – that you might have been expected to offer as a mere act of neighbourliness?'

'Like I say, my Lord – she was always peculiar.'

'Peculiar indeed, to have had the strength to lift this huge man without help.'

'I know nothing of that,' she said guardedly.

'And do you know nothing of the thimble found in the trunk, which my client maintains that you for some superstitious reason placed there?'

'It wasn't mine!'

'No? *Was it not?*' He produced a silver thimble from the bench and held it towards her. 'This belongs to you, Madam! Take it!'

An usher took the thimble from Hall and laid it on the ledge of the witness box. She looked down at it, shaking her head.

'Anyone can see it's not mine.' She put it on her sewing finger. 'It doesn't fit!'

'I own a ring that doesn't fit me. But it is still my possession.' He paused, looking at her. 'It is very easy to say that it doesn't fit.' He leant forward. 'Do you apprehend the reasons why I ask these questions? It is not to suggest that you knew anything of the way in which this man met his death, but for the purpose of establishing the truth of what this woman has said. You

346

stand there in the box as a witness of truth. Now, on your oath before God, *did you not help put that body in the box?*'

'No! I did not!'

He turned towards the jury. 'I find it strange, Mrs Bricknell, that you put on with such unconcern an object which you know to have lain in the blood and gore of that trunk. So strange that I can only explain it by thinking that you knew well the state of the body, having helped to put it there, and that there are no imagined fears associated with it – or its attendant trappings.'

'My Lord!' Mathews protested.

But Hall was already sitting, saying, 'I have no further questions of this witness, my Lord.'

The court rose for lunch, but Hall had no appetite. He fled to the robing room and there he sat, apart, looking out at the gloomy scene. Other barristers there glanced at him from time to time, but he was as unmoving as a statue, and they knew better now than to risk speaking to him.

Bowker brought him a glass of brandy and seltzer and he sipped at this occasionally. Ten minutes before the court was to sit again he went into the washroom, stripped to the waist and sponged himself down like a prize-fighter between rounds. Bowker had his clean linen ready and he slipped into it, making sure that his appearance was cool and immaculate once more.

He stood by the doors, wigged and gowned. Bowker gave him the signal and he went back to the fray, knowing that he was to face the climax of the whole case. If he should fail during the next three hours, then all was lost. If he succeeded – then, indeed, his client would not yet be safe; Mathews was too skilled and tenacious for that, but she would, at least, have a glimpse of hope.

Hall may have credited Marie with such emotions, but he would have been wide of the mark. At the end of the day, she knew that the might and majesty of England would trample her into the dust. What right had she, a foreigner and a whore, to expect anything better? She was accused by the Crown of the greatest empire that the world had ever known, whose reach held the world in awe. Would the engines of that empire miss so much as a beat on her behalf? These mumblings and rituals were mere glorifications of power; the prelude to the act; the moment when, as the wardress had delighted in telling her, she was led from her cell, a chaplain mumbling prayers, and the canvas hood was pulled over her head. Then the rope, the crashing fall and darkness.

It was there, it was waiting, and all this fool of a man could do only delayed the inevitable.

They brought her up from her cell and he was there, looking at her, his eyes wide. She turned away. Let it be done with soon, she prayed. Over and finished. When she dragged her mind back to the court in which she sat a doctor, a man she knew, was in the witness box. He had examined her in prison, saying nothing, but by the way in which he handled her and looked at her telling her everything. He might as well have been examining a corpse.

'Tell me, Dr Taylor,' Hall was saying, in his most agreeable manner, 'these bruises found on the neck of my client when she was committed on this charge – how, in your opinion, were they sustained?'

Taylor was a fussy little man, constantly adjusting his cuffs, straightening his cravat, making sure that what he showed to the world demonstrated the neatness and clarity of his mind. He gave a prim smile at Hall. 'Following the example of my colleague, Dr Walker, the prison physician, I placed my fingers on those bruises on the woman's throat –'

'By "the woman", you mean my client, Mrs Hermann?'

'Yes,' Taylor told him, testily.

'I do not want there to be any misapprehensions in your evidence,' Hall said, smiling.

'I shall endeavour to ensure that there are none whatsoever,' Taylor said, icily.

'I am most obliged to you, Doctor. Pray continue. You put your fingers on the bruises. And?'

'I found that my thumbs exactly covered those bruises.'

'My client had been held, then, most violently, by the throat?'

Taylor thought about this for a moment, turning his wedding ring. 'She had been held, certainly,' he allowed.

'As if an attempt at strangulation had been made?'

He shook his head. 'I cannot know that.'

'But you *can* know that sufficient force had been exercised against her to have produced death by strangulation had it been maintained. Yes? Can you know that?'

'No, my Lord, I cannot. The pressure required to produce bruising varies from person to person. Light force may produce considerable bruising on one, but would leave another unmarked.'

'But in this case,' Hall persisted, 'what were your own conclusions?'

Taylor had taken his spectacles off and was polishing them vigorously with the handkerchief he had whipped from his top pocket. 'I would say that there had been considerable force.' He thought for a moment. 'Yes, I would be prepared to say that.'

Hall sighed. 'Thank you, Doctor. And now, I must ask you as a highly skilled and well qualified medical man if you can believe that an old man of seventy years of age – after he had been struck six times with some heavy instrument and had suffered, in consequence, wounds sufficient to have brought about his death – would have had the strength left to have inflicted those bruises on my client's neck?'

Taylor put his spectacles back on and, head back, looked at the prisoner in the dock. He pursed his lips. 'No. I do not believe that.'

Hall too turned to look at Marie and then, slowly, at the doctor. 'So,' he murmured, as if musing on some abstract speculation, 'she must then, it follows, have been seized by the throat, from in front, *before* the blows were delivered?'

'It would seem so.'

The next doctor in court was Dr Lloyd, a thin and gloomy Welshman. Mathews took him carefully through the evidence that he had already given in the lower court, and Lloyd still maintained that Stephens had been struck, from behind, whilst standing.

Hall immediately attacked this. 'Doctor, you have suggested to my learned friend that the fatal blows, over the right ear, were struck from behind. Is that still your opinion?'

'I have no doubt whatsoever about it.'

'And the man Stephens was standing at the time?'

'I have said so.'

Hall gave the matter deep and troubled thought, his chin cupped in his hand. 'But I have a difficulty here, Doctor, and it is this: how, when my client was held by this powerful and heavy man by her throat, did she contrive to get behind him, find the lethal instrument and deliver the blows?'

Lloyd gave a shrug of his shoulders. 'I cannot answer that without delving into the realms of supposition.'

'Come come, Dr Lloyd! You and your colleagues have not shied from supposition until now!'

'I repeat, I cannot answer your question. It is not within my competence. The woman had bruises on her neck. I do not know when they were inflicted, nor by whom.'

Hall seemed to accept this. 'Very well, Doctor, I respect your professional reticence. No, more than that, Doctor, I glorify it! For we must proceed on no other grounds than those of scientific objectivity. We shall never leave those solid grounds, lest we sink into the mire of speculation.'

Dr Lloyd had never been known to smile, but he now elongated his lips slightly. 'I am relieved to hear it.'

Hall gave him a bow of his head. 'I am equally relieved to say it.' He glanced at his notes, turning a page. 'The deceased had a contusion on his left elbow. Did he not?'

'Yes.'

'Yes. And is it not possible that this left arm of his was so hurt when he used it to ward off a blow directed at the right

350

side of his head – like this?' Hall lifted his left forearm, covering his face with it, the wrist almost touching his right shoulder.

Lloyd's lips turned down. This fellow was a charlatan, an actor, merely. But, all the same . . . 'Well, of course, it would have been *possible*.'

'Thank you. What would then be *impossible* though, is that the blow then came from *behind*. The only arm to have used then would have been the *right* one. Like this –' He went through his demonstration again, this time using his other arm. 'Isn't that true?'

Lloyd gave a grudging nod. 'Yes. That would seem to be so.'

Hall turned away from him for a moment and looked at the jury. Some of them were leaning forward, engrossed by these events. So far so good. He came back to the doctor.

'You are right, sir, to be reluctant to put before this jury matters which can only be supposition. But I am going to ask you now to give me room to put certain suppositions of my own before you. And I would beg you to bring to these *suppositions* of mine all the scientific rigour of your mind.

'And if there be any fact, however trivial, that you cannot *scientifically* accept, I entreat you to make your objection plain. Lift but a hand, and I shall desist. Will you do this, so that truth and justice may be served?'

Lloyd wrinkled his nose in disgust at these histrionics, but there was only one answer that he could give: 'Yes.'

'Thank you.' Once more, Hall turned so that it was the jury, not the witness, who got the full force of his performance. 'There is a struggle between this small woman, this frail woman. See – there she stands – and this strong, violent, drunken man. And you have heard it said that it was not uncommon for him to viciously assault anyone weaker than he who was unfortunate enough to excite his easily inflamed rage. Of women, especially, this was true.

'There is, then, a quarrel between them. He, true to his nature, seizes her by the throat. He holds her fast, his hands gripping, choking. All her puny strength is draining from her as she tries, desperately tries, to pull away from him.

'*But she cannot.*

'Only moments of life are left now. Moments. Then, at the very last, a final effort takes him off balance. They fall to the ground, the man on top of her; but his hands, those great crushing hands –' he was holding papers as he spoke, twisting, grasping them, '– are still at her throat!

'As he fell, his left elbow struck the ground, and it is bruised in the fall – but it is his elbow only that is bruised – for his fore-arm is lying on the woman's right arm, pinning it to the ground!' He paused, still clutching the papers in his own strong hands, his left arm pressing down. The court was completely silent, spellbound, seeing the scene as clearly as he.

'She reaches out with her left arm, stretching, grabbing for some means of defence. Her hand finds and holds something – she finds that object before you!' he shouted, suddenly pointing at the heavy poker on the bench below the judge. Every eye immediately went to it – but he pulled them back. 'She takes it, and holding it *in her left hand*, she beats in pitiful self-defence at her drunken, bloated, panting assailant. Those blows to the right side of his head fall upon him!'

He opened his hands, letting the papers fall to the floor, then swung to the jury, leaning in to them, as if he would touch them.

'Would anyone in this court, have their wife, their daughter, their loved one, do less in her place?

'She could, you might say, have called for help, for assistance. *How?* With the very breath being squeezed from her body?'

His shoulders drooped and his head went down. 'Six times, she strikes,' he said, quietly. 'Six blows. Six desperate, life-gaining, random blows.' He lifted his head, looking at Lloyd. 'For you know, Doctor, that forensic evidence has been given to my learned friend for the Crown that the wounds he suffered were not "clean" wounds, such as would have occurred if the blows struck had been direct, decisive and offensive. *No!* Those wild blows were such as would have been struck with the imperfect power and directive force of the *left* hand.'

He looked round the court, his eyes full of the terror he had seen. He seemed to make an enormous effort to pull himself back to that crowded and dark courtroom where he stood as, slowly, he turned to the doctor.

'Well?' he asked, his voice quiet, 'what, in my account, is impossible?'

Lloyd shook his head. 'Nothing,' he whispered.

Hall closed his eyes for a moment. 'Thank you,' he murmured. 'Thank you for that.' He paused for a moment. 'You must now answer this question: is it *possible* that the fatal blows were struck by my client's *left* hand?'

'Yes. It is possible.'

The answer gave Hall new life. He straightened his shoulders, pulling himself up to his full height. 'Just as possible, in fact, as the previous supposition that they were struck from behind with her right hand?'

'Yes.'

He collapsed more than sat on his bench. 'I have no more questions of this witness, my Lord.'

The judge had been making notes throughout the examinations and cross-examinations. He leant back in his chair, threw down the pencil and sat, his chin on one hand, frowning, looking at Hall. He roused himself from these thoughts and glanced at Mathews, lifting an eyebrow, ready to speak. But a quick shake of Mathews' head told him that there were no more questions from him of this witness.

'You may stand down, Dr Lloyd,' he said.

'Thank you, my Lord,' the Welshman said in sepulchral tones, and went about his business.

'Have you further medical evidence to put before us, Mr Mathews?'

Mathews bobbed up. 'I have a Mr Pepper whom I wish to call, my Lord.'

Wills nodded, but looked at his watch. 'It is now very late. I think that we should defer hearing your witness. I shall, therefore, adjourn. Today being Saturday, court will take up this heavy burden once more on Monday next in the forenoon, at ten in the morning of that day.' He rose to his feet, and the court shuffled up with him.

'All those who have business before this court do now depart,' his clerk intoned, 'and give their attendance again at ten o'clock in the forenoon of Monday next. God save the Queen!'

CHAPTER TWENTY

The city on a Sunday in 1894 was a hushed place; no business was done, and the rattle of the thousands of carts, drays and omnibuses was silenced. Even the hansom cabs had only desultory trade: the middle classes walked to church, since churches were so thick on the ground, and the rich drove in their own carriages to the fashionable places of worship – St George's, Hanover Square for the Anglicans and the Jesuit church in Farm Street for the Mayfair Papists – who could have the peculiar pleasure of hearing themselves being castigated for their wealth and indolence, with the comforting reassurance that it was but for an hour, and that then the dear father would come home to luncheon, when he would tell them, at leisure, of the progress of the son and heir at Stonyhurst.

As for the lower middle classes, they were provided for by endless chapels, where there was a certainty of loud singing, impassioned preaching and a solid contract with the Almighty, in which due provision was made for prosperity flowing like a river on those of sober and industrious habits. God was held to be very much in favour of double-entry bookkeeping; indeed, he had such a system of his own, totting up profit and loss every week, and sacking idle workers.

The poor were often mentioned in prayer, hymn and sermon, in which they could be sorted quite quickly into the deserving, the idle and the shiftless, or even, the very lowest of them, into the black box of "the criminal classes". God was implored to make them quiet in their place, be it Whitechapel, Wapping or the Old Kent Road; He must make them safe in their appointed station in life, give them humility enough to prevent envious eyes or, even worse, thieving hands, being laid upon the heavy burden of wealth their neighbours bore so manfully, in Grosvenor Square and Blackheath.

They were much prayed for, but rarely seen on Sundays. In the ragged flesh, the huge and dreadful armies of the poor found little welcome and less sustenance in these temples. It was left to some bold and saintly adventurers from the churches, who encamped like missionaries in the fearful jungle of the slums, and to General Booth with his bands and banners, to offer them soup and salvation, bread and hope.

Above all, on this sabbath day, there was one thing that these bowed heads and bended knees agreed upon, and that was – sin. Sin existed, sin was abroad in the world, it was seen every day, in every walk of life. And the blackest sins were those of the flesh, which was born of woman, and brought in its train foul and unspeakable diseases. The men stood in the pulpits in spotless white and proclaimed the message: women must beware of temptation. Not in themselves, for a sane, good woman could scarcely know it, but of being themselves objects of temptation to men, causing their downfall. Womankind, in holiness, would take away temptation, be vessels of purity, angels of the hearth and home, obedient to their husbands as a slave is to his master. Anything less than this was to bring hell into the house, damnation to herself and ruin to the social order.

As for the "fallen" women, the "unfortunate" women, the "sisterhood" of whores who crowded the streets of the city, they were walking sties of iniquity and sinks of corruption. They could, of course, be redeemed. There was always hope, and many a collection plate rattled with the offerings of the faithful for the establishment of Houses of Correction, where prostitutes could relish the sweet delights of being taken from the streets, locked indoors, given, of charity, plain grey habits to wear, simple food to eat, water to drink and homilies to read by way of entertainment.

What then, on this Sunday in 1894, did respectable London

make of the ugly and bitter whore who had killed a lecherous customer? Where did she figure in their prayers and pleadings? Was God asked for mercy on her behalf? Or for divine justice and immediate retribution?

Hall had found a small church off the High Street and gone to the first service of the day. There were few worshippers, but even amongst them one or two recognized him. Heads were turned and whispers exchanged. He had wanted fame, and now he had it. For the week. But, after that . . .?

As soon as the last prayer was said, he hurried away, back to the quiet of his hotel room, like an animal to its burrow.

He stood by the window hearing the bells of London. The sunlight was bright in his eyes, and he pulled the blind down, but still stood, twisting the cord in his fingers.

'You must come and eat something, sir,' Bowker said, from his chair by the dressing table.

Hall turned to him. 'Must I, Edgar?'

'Indeed you must.'

Hall shrugged his shoulders and looked away. 'Who will they believe, when it comes to it? Mathews, with solid fact at his call and respectability at his back – or me, with flights of speculation and a foreign prostitute in the dock? Who, Edgar? *Who*?'

'We've done much. There's no booing and hissing now.'

Hall gave a bitter laugh. 'Oh, now! No, there isn't. I can hold them, for a small while. But book yourself a place at the prison gates on the day they hang her. They'll have their fill of hate then.'

'My wife's doing our usual Sunday lunch. Nothing special – nice piece of topside, gravy and veg. She's set a place for you. You're not going to disappoint her, I hope.'

Hall gave a small smile. 'Will there be a pudding?'

Bowker nodded. 'I'm partial to treacle tart, myself.'

'You tempt me.'

'Then give in to it. Though I should warn you – she won't have any law talk at table. She says it gives her indigestion.'

Hall threw his head back and laughed.

'I have your coat here, sir, and a cab waiting.'

Marie, in her cell, heard those same bells and remembered a morning, long since, in a small town near Innsbruck. It was a day of hot sunshine, and the murmur of the priest saying Mass was one with the hum of bees in the churchyard, heard through the open windows.

The little Englishman in his heavy cloth suit was sweating, wiping the inside of his high collar with a red handkerchief. After Mass, as her mother talked with her friends, he had smiled at her.

In the days that followed, he had smiled again, often, as they had passed in the street; she, music-case in hand, on her way to give a piano lesson to some tone-deaf and clumsy-fingered child and he, Baedeker under his arm, searching out the places in the neighbourhood worthy of interest. She had marvelled that there were so many in that small and dusty town.

One day, because she had never met an Englishman before, she had nervously smiled back. Then he had stopped, lifted his hat and talked to her in his atrocious German.

Those smiles had taken her from that sunshine and into this cold darkness.

Mr Justice Wills sat by the open french window of his drawing room, listening to little Flo, his granddaughter, struggle through a ballad on the grand piano. Poor soul, her toes could barely touch the pedals. Yet there was a talent there, that couldn't be gainsaid.

And she did her very best to please, always. They were bringing her up well, despite their dangerously odd and modern views. Fabian Society, indeed! Lot of useless chatterers, if you asked him. And it hadn't gone unnoticed that the pair of 'em had pleaded to be excused church that morning.

What sort of example was that to set the village? Be knitted ties and homespun next.

However, time and a bit of money in his pocket would soon knock all that nonsense out of them, he thought, comfortingly.

He gave an encouraging smile and a beat of his hand to Flo, who shone him one of her winning little grins back, missing a note or two as she did, but pushing on like the best of them.

Ah, yes, she'd be a real little lady, she would.

And Charles Mathews sat in chambers, whistling quietly as he put the last touches to his plan of campaign.

This young fellow was flashy, there was no doubt about that, but he'd have him in the end. By God, he would. Bringing juries to their senses and their duties was his forte, and he rarely failed. At the finish, justice would be done, and a stern warning posted to any who might be of the same inclinations as her. If the law failed to deter whores of a murderous inclination and a greedy hand, then what was the use of it?

Thank God those bells had finished; a man could scarcely think with that tuneless racket going on.

CHAPTER
TWENTY-ONE

Mathews had kept Mr Pepper as the last of his medical witnesses, knowing that he would be steady under fire and would
leave the jury on this last day with an impression of mastery of
his facts and certainty of their necessary implications. The two
of them had worked together so often in the past that each
knew the other's mind; the questions that Mathews would ask
and the answers that Pepper would give ran like well-oiled
machinery.

Pepper did not fail him. There was no doubt whatsoever, he
said, that the facts in the case were that the deceased had been
struck, from behind, by a series of savage and well-aimed
blows. As for the bruises on her neck, he shrugged those aside.
A woman living the life of Mrs Hermann was likely to meet
violence at any time. There was no possibility, at this date, of
saying when, or from whom, she received those marks.

Well satisfied, Mathews sat down. Whatever impression Hall
had managed to make with his treatment of the other doctors
had been more than set aside by this man. And, after all, hadn't
he got more letters after his name than any two men put together?

He saw some members of the jury exchange significant nods
and glances, and he gave a tight-lipped smile. He looked at the
clock. The horse that can canter longest wins in this race, he
thought, and they were too near the finishing post now for any
last minute turns of speed. He permitted himself the treat of
taking a discreet look at the papers for his next case.

Hall got to his feet slowly, rubbing his nose between thumb
and finger. No wonder, Mathews thought, the poor fellow

doesn't know where to begin. He wouldn't wish himself in his shoes. Well, he'd fought the ground well enough; the decent thing to do now would be to get the case over, with as much dignity and decorum as possible, and make a hopeless plea for mercy.

'I must say, Mr Pepper,' Hall began, 'that it is a wonder to all of us that you are so certain of the events in this case. A great wonder.'

Pepper couldn't make out whether this was a compliment or an insult; he was not a man of irony.

Since he was frequently complimented and seldom insulted, he decided that he was being praised for his exactitude and nodded, agreeably.

'You have no doubt at all that Stephens was struck from above and behind?' Hall said in a monotone, as if the question were a mere prelude to what would come later.

'None at all.'

'I repeat my question, so that we may all be sure of your answer. Was Stephens, in your experienced view, struck from above and behind?'

'He was.'

Hall went for him like a terrier after a rat. 'How could a woman of the height of my client − look at her, Mr Pepper − how could she possibly strike a blow from *above*, against a man a foot taller than she?'

Pepper frowned. He hadn't listened carefully enough to what the damned man was saying. It wasn't a problem, though. 'He may well have been sitting at the time.'

'*May?*'

'That is what I said.'

'I see, Mr Pepper. We have now left the safe shores of certainty and launched our frail craft on the seas of "may" and "possibly"!'

'The blows were struck from behind, that is the important thing!'

'Is it? Is it, now? Well, so you say.' He took a sheet of paper from his notes and glanced at it. 'You are aware, are you not, Mr Pepper, that in your "he may well have been sitting at the time", you part company with the evidence of your medical colleagues? Do you know that?'

'I am not responsible for what they may say!'

'Answer my question, sir, with a straight "yes" or "no"! Are you aware –'

'Yes! I am well aware!'

Hall paused, letting this disagreement between the expert witnesses sink into the jurymen's minds.

'We must carefully pick and choose between you, then, mustn't we?' He put the paper down. 'I do not condemn you, Mr Pepper, far from it, for fetching the humility of "may" into your evidence.'

He stopped for a moment, then took a deep breath. 'Truly, sir, in this case, it is all that we have before us. There is only one person in this court who knows what happened on 15 March last in that room in Grafton Street. She is there, in the dock, and the laws of this land forbid her coming into the witness box to tell us! She may not give evidence on her own behalf and is gagged and bound before us!

'Imperfect as I am, I must be her tongue and voice in this court. I have done what I can to fulfil those functions. For her – and for justice.' For a moment, he bit anxiously on the forefinger of his clenched hand, then shook his head and clasped his hands behind his back, under his gown. 'In so doing, I have laid before the court a supposition of mine – as you have laid before us one of yours, Mr Pepper. Do you know of that supposition? That my client was attacked and that in the struggle she fell and, still under the force of strangulation, struck her assailant six blows with her left hand? Do you know of that?'

'Yes, I know of that.'

'And I know, sir, that you have a quite different supposition. I respect it, as I respect you. But tell me this, with a straight "yes" or "no". Is it impossible that my supposition is true?'

Pepper thought about this, and glanced at Mathews. But he was sitting, shoulders hunched, hands clasped in his lap, looking down.

'Is my supposition impossible?' Hall pressed.

'No.'

'Thank you, Mr Pepper,' he said, and sat.

Mr Justice Wills adjourned his court for luncheon, and Hall fled the place, still in wig and gown, escorted by Bowker into the waiting cab which, watched by a flabbergasted Newton, rattled away at a great pace.

But it did not rattle far, turning off Ludgate Hill into a side street and stopping by a book shop. Wig and gown were stuffed into a bag and the two men ran into the shop and up the stairs to the stock room.

'Won't be disturbed there, gentlemen, I promise you that!' the shopkeeper cried after them, but the door was closed in his face before he had the words out of his mouth.

'Well done, Edgar,' Hall said, as he sat at the table.

Bowker gave him a brief smile and laid a pile of papers before him. 'I got a lady typewriter to do this,' he said, 'knowing your handwriting.'

'Nothing wrong with my writing. Perfectly clear.'

'So you say.'

Hall flicked through the pages. 'This is our last throw. All hangs on this.' He leant back in the chair. 'If only I knew what line Mathews would take in his speech.'

'He'll play to his strengths. That's for sure.'

'The witnesses?'

'Absolutely,' Bowker nodded. 'You've done a lot to discredit them, so he'll bring them back into the picture and pit their word against yours. Now the jury will have to take that – he'll think.'

'They probably will, too,' Hall murmured.

'It's very likely.'

Hall took a couple of coloured pencils from his pocket, and skimmed through the papers. 'Do you think I've covered it?'

'As best as possible.' He pulled his chair nearer to Hall's. 'But, if I may say so, we could do a little bit more with this section here. Page two –'

Their heads together, they went line by line, through the final speech for the defence.

The sad and sombre courtroom was packed as never before for this, the last act in the drama. There was not a bench that wasn't crowded, not a wall that wasn't lined with spectators, craning forward, desperate for a good view.

Two people were lifted above the crowd: Mr Justice Wills, tapping a pencil in time to a ballad played by an innocent child who would, one day, be a great lady, a credit to her class and an ornament to her husband; and Mrs Marie Hermann, who had decided, on this, her last appearance before men, to make the best of herself, rouging her thin cheeks and draping a fine shawl round her shoulders, given her long ago by a man who said he loved her.

But the audience had little regard for them. They would walk into the limelight when sentence was passed. But the battle must first be concluded, and the gladiators held all eyes as they sat, ready for the fray: Charles Mathews, Queen's Counsel, practised, skilful, and hoping, through this case, to stake his claim to the appointment of Public Prosecutor. Edward Marshall Hall, raw, unpredictable and filled with a passion, that even he could not explain, to save the life of his client.

The physical contrast between the two men was stark. Mathews had eaten a good lunch in a chop-house, and the crumbs of his bread lay in the folds of his waistcoat to prove it. His gown had been slipped on absent-mindedly, and hung off one shoulder. With his bright eyes and sharp nose, he was more crow-like than ever, looking round the court with sudden twists of his neck. Hall had eaten nothing, but his linen had been freshly changed, starched and gleaming. Bowker had laid out his best gown and a new wig. He was motionless, gazing sightlessly ahead as Mathews rose.

'My Lord, gentlemen of the jury,' Mathews began, 'justice is not served, nor truth brought to light, by idle suppositions, nor airy fancies, such as those that the counsel for the defendant has laid before you. 'The facts in the case, gentlemen, *facts*, are all that may guide you. And those facts are damning.

'In pursuit of her loathsome profession, the prisoner met the deceased in a low public house, notorious as a haunt of women of her kind. He was, it must be admitted, already in an inebriated and enfeebled state.

'She induced him to accompany her to her lodgings, for a purpose which I need not dwell upon. Once lured to that house and in her rooms, there was an argument between them, which had to do with money – a matter of some £5 which, evidently, she had, by some means or other, taken from him.

'The argument becomes heated, but it is resolved by the prisoner as she grasps an instrument of death, stands behind him, and then, with all the vicious animal power in her body –' his right arm was raised, his hand clenched, '– rains blow after blow on the head of this foolish old man.' His fist crashed down on the bench.

'My learned friend has induced medical witnesses to give their reluctant and doubting assent to the possibility – and I emphasize the word, gentlemen – the *possibility* of some fantastic flight of fancy. But, really!' He shook his head. 'This is no more than to say that the tale in some cheap and trashy novelette, pored over by candlelight by one's parlourmaid, *could* have occurred, *might* have happened, *may* have taken place! "Oh, yes!" they *dubiously* agreed, events, in a fiction, may have so fallen out. But not once, gentlemen, not once, did they leave their own true accounts behind! They did not depart from them!'

His arms fell to his side and he stood, motionless, deep in thought. Then his head came up, quickly, and his eyes flicked from juryman to juryman, challenging their judgement. 'There are matters of great moment here,' he said, his voice rasping, 'and they are not to be decided by the hazards of fiction, nor cast with the dice of speculation!

'*Facts!*' he screamed, his voice ringing round the room. '*Facts* that rest upon scientific observation and deduction! Hold fast to those facts as to life itself! The doctors have, despite all the efforts of counsel for the defence to throw dust in their eyes, and in yours!'

He gave a dry and bitter laugh. 'I marvel, I do really, that counsel's whimsical meanderings could have been put forward, much less seriously entertained. For, oh, gentlemen – and I do not want to insult your intelligence to remind you of this, but I am compelled to do it – *if* prisoner at the bar did strike in self-defence, the victim of some motiveless and gross assault, why, then, did she endeavour, by devious, sinister and heartless means, to conceal the body?'

He let the question rest for a moment, his head on one side, a slight smile on his lips. 'Would not an immediate, truthful and contrite account of her doings in that room – to her neighbours, to the police, to the whole wide world – have shrieked her innocence from the very roof-tops? Would it not?' he whispered.

He shook his head. 'No such account was given. On the contrary! Every effort that she could make to hide the events of that night, *she made*! And what final ghastly disposition of the mangled body she had in mind, only God, the omnipotent arbiter, alone knows.

'But to us mortals one thing is open and beyond any reasonable doubt whatsoever: and that is that Marie Hermann did wilfully, cruelly, bludgeon Charles Anthony Stephens to death, ransack his corpse of all moneys and valuables, and then endeavour, by all means in her power, to conceal the terrible proof of her crime.

'Has one tittle of evidence been entered to refute this? *One?*' He spread his hands, as if inviting a reply. 'I read your answers in your eyes,' he said. He pulled his gown on to his thin shoulders and held it there, hand on each lapel, as if otherwise it might take wing. 'Much has been made of the character of the victim in this case – he was a drunkard, he lived off the income of a house of shame, he was violent. Well! He may have been all of those things! He may well have been! One does not expect a man who resorts to the hired favours of a woman such as the prisoner to be other than an immoral wretch! His deep and foul immorality does not, however, put the sword of justice into her hands! Where, gentlemen, would we be if women such as her arrogated to themselves the right to destroy men? Chaos would be upon us, the order of society undermined and an everlasting night would fall upon the streets.

'If prisoner at the bar walks free from the gallows, then I say to you, the dusk of that night would be in this place. Be resolute. Stand against it! Hold fast to fact!' He leant forward, his bony hands clasping the edge of the bench. 'The duty before you is awesome, but you must do it. You must find her guilty!' He took a final breath. 'Of murder!' he cried.

A ripple of excitement flowed through the court as Mathews flung himself back in his bench. Mr Justice Wills gave a slow nod and the jurymen shuffled in their seats, some clearing their throats, as if they, not Mathews, had spoken. None of them looked at the prisoner.

Wills turned towards Hall, his eyes cold. 'Mr Marshall Hall?' he intoned.

Hall rose slowly and then stood, immobile, only his eyes moving, as he looked round the crowded court. He took from his pocket some small object on a fine gold chain and laid it carefully on the bench. Bowker, seated behind him, thought that it must be some sort of watch, though he had never seen him use it before.

He held out the typed pages of the speech, but Hall ignored him. 'Your speech, sir!' Bowker whispered, pushing the sheets forward.

Hall gave him a glance and, almost absent-mindedly, took

the papers. 'Yes . . . yes,' he murmured. He turned to face the jury, lifted the speech and then, with a savage gesture, threw it down.

'Facts, gentlemen,' he began. 'My learned friend sets great store by *facts*. Well, so do we all. But what are these *facts*? A procession of medical men has trooped before us. And each of them saw these facts in some crucially different light. One doctor says this, the other that. And the third says something else again. The doctors differ. There is no certainty amongst them, no exactitude, no holding fast to facts! They cannot agree! Save on one thing, one thing only, that ran like a thread through their testimony.'

His voice had been quiet, but now it fell to a whisper. 'And that is that they conceded, whatever my learned friend may say, to the *fact* that my truth is every bit as likely as theirs! Every bit! Gentlemen, gentlemen, I implore you to remember this: that one may look over the scene of a crime and that there one may come upon pieces of evidence. – marks that indicate the probability of events that occurred. But you view these marks with an open, with an unprejudiced mind. And that, I suggest to you, the Crown has most lamentably failed to do. They looked upon my client and saw only a fallen woman, a woman of the streets. And, seeing that, they were blind to all else! Blind to the marks of attempted strangulation on her throat. Blind to the bruises on the deceased's left elbow, blind to the fact that a woman of her height could not possibly have struck a man of his height from above, blind to the fact that the first blow, if struck from behind, must have resulted in his immediately turning to face his assailant. And then, of course, even if, in the face of him, the blows continued to fall, *they would have been on the other side of his head*!

'What, gentlemen,' he cried, lifting his arms, 'are we seriously to believe that he stood, or sat – and the Crown cannot decide whether it was one or the other – and made no move whilst the life was beaten out of him?

'And if the Crown had considered that salient point, and

ventured an explanation, it would certainly have been on the lines of a suggestion that the first blow was delivered with such huge force that he immediately fell to the ground, as one pole-axed. Look at my client, gentlemen,' he said, pointing at her. 'Can you believe that she is possessed of that vast strength? *Can you?* And, even if she were, once the man is on the ground, at her feet, how then can she go on striking the side of his head? And why should she? The mission which the Crown has attributed to her is achieved. If robbery is her motive, she may rob now at her leisure. If that first blow had been of such force as to render him unconscious, he would have fallen to the ground. And the side of his head which took the blows would have been concealed.

'Prejudice blinds, prejudice deafens, prejudice stills the very processes of thought and reflection that alone may lead us to the truth.' He looked down at his hands, as if surprised to see that they were trembling; he impulsively brought them together in a gesture of prayer, and held them so against his lips, but his eyes never left the jury. Slowly, his hands came down.

'I do not defend my client's way of life. I am not called upon to do so. She does not stand on trial for it. But I say to you, with all the force of my being, that it is for that, above all else, that she stands before you.

'Prejudice. Prejudice in the mind of Mrs Hutchins, when she thought that she heard a woman shriek "Speak! Speak! *Speak!*" in tones of violence, of passion, when in fact she heard the entreaties of a woman attempting to succour the life of a man who, only moments before, had been attempting to strangle her!'

He leant towards them. 'And it is a fact, gentlemen, that the most immediate symptoms of attempted strangulation is that the voice becomes hoarse, becomes harsh. That is what Mrs Hutchins heard, but her prejudice came between her and the truth.

'The truth.

'This drunken, lecherous, treacherous brute had made so violent an assault upon her that she had been dragged by his animal strength to the very gates of death and alone, *in extremis*, she had defended herself. And now, even now, she ministered to him.

'And, when tearful entreaty was in vain, this hapless woman, represented by the Crown as being avaricious to the point of mania, ran from the house to buy him brandy and sought, by its means, to revive him. It was not to be.

'And she has been brought, at last, to this place of judgement.

'By *prejudice*. Prejudice in the newspapers, in their shrieking placards. Prejudice in the gossip of the streets. What need these people of you, gentlemen? Or of his Lordship on the bench of judgement? Let the penny press be judge! Let their deluded readers be jury! Are they not enough? For God's sake, let us pack our bags, gentlemen, and go from this place, leaving justice in the hands of purveyors of falsehood and traders in malice.'

He stood, white-faced. 'Prejudice such as we have witnessed, before this case came before you, and during it, is a foul tide that rises from a sea of corruption, staining the very hem of the white robes of justice. Cleanse it! From your minds, from your hearts and from all that is true and noble in this place! I beg you to do this!

'Look upon my client afresh, clear-eyed. And remember this – that women such as she are what we men make them. Even this woman was once a beautiful and innocent child. But beauty is a flower that withers, purity may be trampled into the dust and innocence blasted by an evil wind.'

He was holding the object from the bench in his clasped right hand, the gold chain hanging through his fingers. His pale cheeks shone with tears.

'She was once a woman of respect in her small world. She taught little children and was mother – a loving, devoted mother, to three children of her own. But that sweet world was broken and smashed for ever when the man to whom she had given her love and her trust abandoned her. She was left, weeping, on an alien shore. Alone to feed and care for her children.' He was swaying as he spoke, his eyes closed against his tears. 'And, gentlemen, one of those children is blind.'

His voice rose to a cry as, arm outstretched, hand shaking, he led every eye to Marie, who was huddled in a corner of the dock, sobbing. 'Do you now point the finger of *respectability* at her? *Dare you?*'

The mascara had run from her lashes; lines of black ran down her thin cheeks. The cheap and gaudy shawl had fallen from one shoulder and she was vainly trying to pull it back.

Hall's arm fell to his side. 'She was driven to the streets by the bitter need to put bread into the mouths of her children and to buy shelter for a blind girl. And, at the end of those dusty, broken-hearted streets there is a room – a darkening room in a common lodging house where a man, keeper of such a house as had encompassed her ruin, a violent man, a murderous man, is choking the very life from her body.'

He looked at the jurymen, taking each eye in turn. Three of them were openly weeping, and all were hunched forward, scarcely able to breathe.

'Some of you may have children,' he whispered, 'and you give those children all love, all protection. But see now, one of those children – a daughter, dearer to you than life itself, grow. Into beauty, into the glory of womanhood! And that beloved spirit falls into the hands of some man, a man who will seize, ruin and discard her.' His voice was dry as leaves in an autumn wind. 'God forbid it happen to any of you. You will be taken into hell and left there at the sight of it. But it happens. It happens.

'And this glory of your heart is now –' A sob racked him, and his voice rose to a shout, 'as she was, facing her death at the hands of a loathsome lecher! What would you that she should do? *What?*'

The court was silent. Hall, his shoulders bowed, his head down, clung to the bench. Only that saved him from collapse. He lifted his head, and all could see his ravaged eyes.

'Gentlemen – on the evidence before you,' he gasped. 'I almost dare you to find a verdict of murder.'

He blindly reached for the back of the bench, lowering himself into his seat. And then he looked again at Marie. Holding himself in that position, the very last of his strength in the effort, he pointed at her.

'Look at her, gentlemen of the jury!' he cried. *'Look at her!'*

He was fighting for breath. The jury, aghast, turned to Marie. 'God never gave her a chance! Won't you?' he whispered as, at last, he sat.

The court was utterly silent, save for the choking sobs of Marie.

Mr Justice Wills was leaning forward, a hand covering his eyes. Mathews leant back, eyes closed, all colour drained from his cheeks. The feeling in the dark room was that of a house before a thunderstorm: heavy, down-pressing, when the clap of thunder and the drenching rain are prayed for. It was unbearable and had to be broken, and a woman at the back of the gallery did it, rising to her feet, giving a hoarse and vibrant shout of praise.

It was seized upon by all of them; the cheers, the sobs, the shouts rang out, and the usher's voice was lost in it.

Bowker, weeping, lowered his head and saw that the object Hall had held had fallen from his hand and lay, at his side, on the bench. He reached for it, picked it up and saw that it was a miniature of a girl, a young and beautiful girl, facing life in hope and joy. He held it towards his master, who turned, wide-eyed, to take it. For a moment it was held by both of them and, at the sight of Hall's face, a chill like death itself ran through the clerk.

Still looking at him, Hall took the chain and picture, kissed them and put them back into his pocket.

The cheers and shouts rolled round them. They stood and, Hall leading, left the court.

His summing up done, and the jury sent out to consider their verdict, Mr Justice Wills sat in his room, an untasted glass of wine before him and his clerk at his side. He lifted his head, wearily, and looked at him.

'Never, never in all my life at law,' he whispered, 'have I seen such a thing.'

'Powerful pleading, my Lord. Fine words,' Jackson murmured.

Will shook his head. 'Words? Oh, we all have words. They are our stock in trade.' He leant back in his chair. 'No, Jackson, we have heard more than words. And seen –' he closed his eyes, as if he would remove the sight that haunted him, '– I have no words for what I have seen.'

In a corner of the robing room Hall sat. Bowker had pulled a chair into the space before him and, one leg crossed over the other, there he sat, keeping guard lest any speak or approach. He need not have taken such precautions. On that day, no one in the room would have dared come near.

Most of the barristers who had not been in other courts had made sure of a place in Court Number One for this last day, and the rest had rushed in as soon as their cases were cleared, settling them in haste so as not to miss a moment. They had been there, and the memory of it would never leave them. In years far off, old men in an honoured place in chambers would smile at the stories of young thrusters and say, 'Ah, but then – you never saw Marshall Hall in Crown and Hermann . . .' And, best as they could, they would repeat such words, such actions as they could remember of that final speech. They were the generous spirits, who saw the face of genius, and knew it.

And there were the meaner men who saw only their own failure in his success. It was bitter to them. With the passing years, their envy grew and festered. 'Old Marshall – complete charlatan! As full of tricks as a puppy dog, don't you know. And unsound. Very, very unsound,' they would laugh. But today they were silent.

*

The wardress had got Marie a bowl and cloth, so that she could wash, and a looking glass in which she could comb her hair.

Both women had been silent until the wardress handed these things to an assistant, to be taken away. Then the wardress said, 'Feeling better now, dear?'

Marie nodded and she sat on her chair, bolt upright, her hands folded in her lap.

'I'll say this much,' the wardress went on, 'no matter what happens now, with the jury, an' that – this fellow's fought for you. No one could have done it better.'

Marie didn't look at her or speak.

'I reckon, all ways round – you're a very lucky girl.'

Marie turned to her. 'Lucky?' she said.

'I should say so! Heart and soul he put into it!'

'Why not?' Marie asked flatly. 'He's been paid.'

An usher came into the robing room, looked round, saw Bowker and went quickly to him, bending low to whisper in his ear. Bowker nodded expressionlessly and turned to Hall, touching his sleeve.

Hall took a breath, straightened his white wig and stood, pulling his gown into its proper folds.

Bowker was at the door, holding it open for him. Looking neither to right or left, Hall went through.

Ellen, Irving and Charlie Gill sat on a side bench in the long corridor. Seeing Hall approach, Charlie leant forward, a hand outstretched and a greeting on his lips, but Irving laid a hand on his arm.

'I think not, my dear Gill,' he murmured. 'There is only one response to what we have seen.' He got to his feet and stood, tall hat held at his side.

Hall passed them, not seeing.

They bowed.

The door was opened for Marie and she began to climb the

long steps back into court, straightening her shawl and biting her thin lips to get a bit of colour into them.

The question had been put, and the foreman of the jury stood to give his answer.

'Of the charge of murder, my Lord,' he said, hoping that he got the words right, 'we find the prisoner – not guilty.' There was a sound as if all in the crowd had drawn breath.

He cleared his throat. 'We wish to enter a verdict of manslaughter. And we beg your Lordship, most strongly, for clemency in your sentence.'

The cheers and shouts rang out again and those in the gallery were shaking hands with each other, slapping each other's backs, as if they had won a victory. The clerk was demanding silence, but it was a long time before he got it.

The judge looked down at the scrap of paper before him. He had written the lines of his speech of condemnation before passing sentence of death and, with relief, he drew a pencil stroke through them. He was a humane man, and never, unlike one or two of his colleagues, got any pleasure from intoning those words, with the black cap atop his wig.

He looked at the other lines of writing, and at the end of them, three figures: a two, a three and a six. The jury had urged him to be clement, and he himself could be merciful.

But, he thought, the woman was, after all, a whore. There was no getting away from that, and some sort of example must be set, and society protected. Two years would scarcely suffice. A figure was crossed from the list.

And she had chosen this ghastly method of attempting to dispose of the body. Only three years for that? One figure was left. He put his pencil down and sentenced her to six years' penal servitude.

The quality of mercy was strained to breaking point.

The crowd outside the Old Bailey was even more dense than

at the opening of the trial. They had had one satisfaction when a prison van came from the courts. They assumed that Marie Hermann must be inside, and they cheered and shouted as if she had been a princess on the way to her wedding, instead of a convict passing to Holloway.

But they hadn't stood all those hours for a glimpse of her. At last the signs seemed promising: twenty policemen came through the doors, forced a way through the throng and, arms linked, pushed the crowd back and made a pathway from the doors to the road's edge. A hansom cab managed to make its way, slowly, to the end of police lines. A pale-faced young man took a look round the doors, saw that the cab was waiting and disappeared back inside.

The crowd was shouting his name now, raggedly at first, just a few voices, but soon they had all taken it up, and beat it out in a rhythmic chant. The doors were opened once more and Hall was there, looking down at them expressionlessly as they burst into a frenzy of cheering.

He briefly lifted his shining top hat, gave an unsmiling nod of thanks and walked, quickly, down the steps and along the policed pathway, ignoring the outstretched hands and imploring cries. The young man followed, looking nervously to left and right, and climbed into the cab after him.

'Quick as you can, cabbie!' Bowker shouted through the trap door in the roof.

The cabbie peered down at them. 'Through this lot? Be like driving a hearse.' He gave a flick of his long whip and they began to force a way, foot by foot.

Faces were pressed against the windows, each one with mouth agape, shouting something, but it was impossible to tell what in the deafening clamour.

At last they were clear of them, and the cab picked up pace.

Hall leaned into his corner, his eyes closed. 'Well, Edgar,' he sighed.

'Well, indeed, sir.'

He was silent for a moment. Then, 'Thank God that's over.'

Bowker nodded.

'I couldn't do it again. Not for the life of me.'

'No, sir?'

'No.'

'I think that's a great pity, sir.'

'Pity or not, it's true.'

Bowker nodded. 'Then you'll be wanting me to turn the brief down?'

Hall's eyes opened and he looked at him, frowning. 'What brief's that?'

'One that Mr Newton's brought in. He says it's the most sensational case he's ever handled.'

'A capital case?'

Bowker drew in a breath. 'Oh, it's a hanging matter all right. And the defence is nigh on impossible. But one thing's for sure – the man's innocent.'

'Is he, now?' Hall murmured.

'I think so, and so does Mr Newton. And he says you're the only man in England who can get him off.'

'Well, now . . .'

'Yes, sir?'

Hall thought for a moment. 'I think we might just take a glance at it.'

'I think we might, sir.'

At long last he was home again and, with a sigh of relief, Hall closed the door behind him and leant against it, glad to breathe once more the old familiar smells: of the maids' special floor-polish, made from a recipe of his mother's; of carbolic and cigar smoke from his father's surgery; and warm cooking smells from the kitchen.

But even here, where he longed for peace, he wasn't to get it. Ada had lined up their few servants in the hall, instructing them to shout, 'Welcome Home Master Eddie,' as he came through the door. They hadn't been pleased at this; they needed no telling in how to make him welcome and, as things turned out, the plan misfired: they were all too overcome by tears of pride to say a word, much less shout, and stood instead, in a weeping huddle.

His father was at the foot of the stairs, smiling, hand out-stretched. He went straight to him, took his hand, held it for a moment, then flung his arms round him.

'Did I do well, Father?' he whispered.

'Very well. You did very well,' the old man murmured.

Ada touched his arm. 'I told them to give you a cheer when you came in,' she said.

'You didn't!' he laughed.

'And just look at them!' she said, giving them an icy look.

He went over to them, shaking hands with the butler and coachman, and giving a quick kiss to cook and the maids. Ada gave them a brief smile, and a nod of dismissal. They bowed or bobbed and withdrew to their own land, on the other side of the green baize door.

'There's champagne cooling – in the drawing room,' she said, opening the door.

He looked at her, then at his father. 'That's kind. Very kind. But first – I need to have some time on my own. You mustn't think I'm being rude – or ungrateful. But I do need that.'

Ada was about to speak, but their father laid a hand upon her arm. 'Of course you do,' he said. 'Come down when you're ready.'

Hall nodded his thanks and went quickly up the stairs.

He didn't need to light the lamp; pale moonlight flooded through the window but even without it he could have found his way round that room.

He sat, looking out on the silver garden, letting silence flow into his heart. He thought of the crowds, the cheers and shout-ing, of the lawyers; some of them old men, great figures of whom he'd stood in awe, reaching out to him, wanting to shake his hand. It had come to him now, all that he'd dreamt of, all that he had offered.

Fame was his, for as long as he wanted to hold it. Wealth was his, to spend as he wished. Any one of the briefs that would fall on his desk like leaves in autumn would buy that house, that small house looking out over the lake, that she had wanted.

But he had walked away from it, promising her more, far more. And he had been as good as his word. The gift was in his hands, but where was she, to take it?

He turned away from the window and knelt by the trunk. He remembered Marie Hermann, standing at the foot of a stairway and calling up, 'Take care of that box. It contains treasures of mine.'

Treasures? An old man, dead at her hands?

He turned the key in the lock and swung the trunk's lid back. The scent of her was there, scent that she had worn on a golden day in June.

Treasure? A life that his arrogance, his pride, his folly, had ended.

He laid his hands on the soft folds of her silken wedding dress and closed his eyes, longing for her to be there, to touch her soft hands, to hear her voice again, to be able to beg her forgiveness.

So he knelt, not moving. Far away he could hear the ceaseless murmur of the waves on the shingled beach. Softly, quietly, a great peace and happiness came to him and though his eyes were closed he knew that there was a light in the room, a light softer than moonlight and gentler than the fire of the sun. And there was music; a waltz, played sweetly.

'I love you,' he murmured. 'Oh, my heart's own darling, how much I love you . . .'

He had offered his gift, and this time it had been taken.

It was the gift of life.

FOR THE BEST IN PAPERBACKS, LOOK FOR THE

In every corner of the world, on every subject under the sun, Penguin represents quality and variety – the very best in publishing today.

For complete information about books available from Penguin – including Pelicans, Puffins, Peregrines and Penguin Classics – and how to order them, write to us at the appropriate address below. Please note that for copyright reasons the selection of books varies from country to country.

In the United Kingdom: Please write to *Dept E.P., Penguin Books Ltd, Harmondsworth, Middlesex, UB7 0DA*

In the United States: Please write to *Dept BA, Penguin, 299 Murray Hill Parkway, East Rutherford, New Jersey 07073*

In Canada: Please write to *Penguin Books Canada Ltd, 2801 John Street, Markham, Ontario L3R 1B4*

In Australia: Please write to the *Marketing Department, Penguin Books Australia Ltd, P.O. Box 257, Ringwood, Victoria 3134*

In New Zealand: Please write to the *Marketing Department, Penguin Books (NZ) Ltd, Private Bag, Takapuna, Auckland 9*

In India: Please write to *Penguin Overseas Ltd, 706 Eros Apartments, 56 Nehru Place, New Delhi, 110019*

In Holland: Please write to *Penguin Books Nederland B.V., Postbus 195, NL–1380AD Weesp, Netherlands*

In Germany: Please write to *Penguin Books Ltd, Friedrichstrasse 10–12, D–6000 Frankfurt Main 1, Federal Republic of Germany*

In Spain: Please write to *Longman Penguin España, Calle San Nicolas 15, E–28013 Madrid, Spain*

In France: Please write to *Penguin Books Ltd, 39 Rue de Montmorency, F-75003, Paris, France*

In Japan: Please write to *Longman Penguin Japan Co Ltd, Yamaguchi Building, 2–12–9 Kanda Jimbocho, Chiyoda-Ku, Tokyo 101, Japan*

Titles published and forthcoming:

Who Killed Hanratty? Paul Foot

An investigation into the notorious A6 murder.

Norman Birkett H. Montgomery Hyde

The biography of one of Britain's most humane and respected judges.

The Complete Jack the Ripper Donald Rumbelow

An investigation into the identity of the most elusive murderer of all time

The Riddle of Birdhurst Rise R. Whittington-Egan

The Croydon Poisoning Mystery of 1928–9.

Suddenly at the Priory John Williams

Who poisoned the Victorian barrister Charles Bravo?

Stinie: Murder on the Common Andrew Rose

The truth behind the Clapham Common murder.

The Poisoned Life of Mrs Maybrick Bernard Ryan

Mr Maybrick died of arsenic poisoning – how?

The Gatton Mystery J. and D. Gibney

The great unsolved Australian triple murder.

Earth to Earth John Cornwell

Who killed the Luxtons in their remote mid-Devon farmhouse?

The Ordeal of Philip Yale Drew R. Whittington-Egan

A real life murder melodrama in three acts.

BIOGRAPHY AND AUTOBIOGRAPHY IN PENGUIN

Jackdaw Cake   Norman Lewis

From Carmarthen to Cuba, from Enfield to Algeria, Norman Lewis brilliantly recounts his transformation from stammering schoolboy to the man Auberon Waugh called 'the greatest travel writer alive, if not the greatest since Marco Polo'.

Catherine   Maureen Dunbar

Catherine is the tragic story of a young woman who died of anorexia nervosa. Told by her mother, it includes extracts from Catherine's diary and conveys both the physical and psychological traumas suffered by anorexics.

Isak Dinesen, the Life of Karen Blixen   Judith Thurman

Myth-spinner and storyteller famous far beyond her native Denmark, Karen Blixen lived much of the Gothic strangeness of her tales. This remarkable biography paints Karen Blixen in all her sybiline beauty and magnetism, conveying the delight and terror she inspired, and the pain she suffered.

The Silent Twins   Marjorie Wallace

June and Jennifer Gibbons are twenty-three year old identical twins, who from childhood have been locked together in a strange secret bondage which made them reject the outside world. *The Silent Twins* is a real-life psychological thriller about the most fundamental question – what makes a separate, individual human being?

Backcloth   Dirk Bogarde

The final volume of Dirk Bogarde's autobiography is not about his acting years but about Dirk Bogarde the man and the people and events that have shaped his life and character. All are remembered with affection, nostalgia and characteristic perception and eloquence.